THE THISTLE AND THE GRAIL

Robin Jenkins (1912–2005) studied at Glasgow University and worked for the Forestry Commission and in the teaching profession. He travelled widely and worked in Spain, Afghanistan and Borneo before settling in his beloved Argyll. His first novel, *So Gaily Sings the Lark*, was published in 1951 and its publication was followed by more than thirty works of fiction, including the acclaimed *The Cone-gatherers* (1955), *Fergus Lamont* (1979) and *Childish Things* (2001). In 2002 he received the Saltire Society's prestigious Andrew Fletcher of Saltoun Award for his outstanding contribution to Scottish life.

ROBIN JENKINS

The Thistle and the Grail

Polygon

This edition published in Great Britain in 2006
by Polygon, an imprint of Birlinn Ltd
West Newington House, 10 Newington Road
Edinburgh EH9 1QS

www.birlinn.co.uk

First published in 1954

ISBN 10: 1 904598 76 5
ISBN 13: 978-1-904598-76-3

British Library Cataloguing-in-Publication Data
A catalogue record is available on request
from the British Library

The publisher acknowledges subsidy from

 Scottish
Arts Council
towards the publication of this volume

Printed and bound by CPD (Wales) Ltd

Introduction

The Thistle and the Grail by Robin Jenkins was first published in 1954, just over half a century after the great anti-kailyard novel *The House with the Green Shutters*, by George Douglas Brown. There is a key link between the two novels, which undoubtedly rank among the five or six finest to be written about Scotland in the course of the twentieth century. Both deal with a big man in a small Scottish community who is constantly pulled down by lesser, petty men, pygmies who indulge in spite, gossip and malice. Both these big men are superficially successful, yet at heart lonely and isolated. John Gourlay in *The House with the Green Shutters* is essentially a brutish figure, although Brown does suggest an unlikely sensitivity from time to time.

Andrew Rutherford, the protagonist in *The Thistle and the Grail*, is an altogether more complex and sympathetic figure. He, too, is ostracised by his small town, a town that he genuinely loves, whereas Gourlay has contempt for his community.

Like Gourlay, Rutherford is wealthier than most of those he lives amongst. He is a businessman, an employer of many, but he is uneasy with his material success; indeed, he resents it. He certainly does not glory in it, as Gourlay does.

For all that, Jenkins presents Rutherford as a man whom it is not particularly easy to respect, let alone like. He has a sanctimonious streak, a tendency to moralise, and constantly flirts with self-pity. He is trapped in a bleak, sterile marriage; while his wife Hannah may be a shallow, snobbish social climber she is viciously clear-sighted about her husband's failings. At a key point in the novel she concedes that he has done his best to live according to his principles, but she goes on to taunt him that when he fails to achieve the standards he has set for himself, his town shows him neither respect nor pity. Instead he is mocked. Foul calumnies are spread about him, and believed.

Worse, Rutherford can find no succour from those who might

help him sustain his burdens. His brother is a drunken waster who despises him; his father is a bitter, spent, socialist idealist who also despises him; his son Gerald, whom he loves dearly, always sides with his materialistic mother; and even his minister has doubts about him and asks him to stand down as the superintendent of the Sunday school.

Rutherford is thus a man of apparent standing and substance whose foundations are fragile; his relatives are hostile rather than supportive; he has no real friends; he needs a prop, a release, a sustenance. This, it rapidly emerges, is to be found not in drink, nor sex, nor even religion.

Thus far I have managed not to mention what for many is the true theme of *The Thistle and the Grail*: football. Yet this is not a football novel as such. Jenkins is far too clever a novelist to tackle Scotland's obsession with football head on. Instead he treats the great game in the context of Rutherford's broken life. For Rutherford, football provides beauty, excitement and release. Jenkins writes about the game as a sustaining counterpoint to Rutherford's quiet despair.

He also suggests, frequently, that football has become in Scotland a surrogate for religion. Thus we are told that Rutherford's pride and pleasure in skilful football 'sustained him' and gave him a 'keener and clearer joy than religion'. Rutherford is physically big and he is a big figure in the meagre town of Drumsagart, not just because he is a major employer but also because he is president of the local Junior football club, Drumsagart Thistle.

As Rutherford's domestic tensions build up ominously, he is forced to make a difficult choice. He can choose either utter capitulation to his scheming, socially ambitious wife, which involves leaving Drumsagart for a suburban life on the Clyde littoral, or a life of barren and lonely isolation in his home town. As he confronts this dilemma, football represents some kind of meaningful escape; it also encapsulates the pull of Drumsagart, where, despite everything, he belongs. Football gives him the benison of identity. If religion will not serve, football will.

The treatment of football by Robin Jenkins is masterly in its subtlety and literary cunning. For a start, Thistle, as we have noted, is a Junior club. The novel would have carried too much baggage if Jenkins had described a real Senior club or even a fictitious one – some readers would have been furiously trying to work out which one it was.

Secondly, there is remarkably little in the novel about the actual Thistle team and their play. The best player, the prolific goal-scorer Alec Elrigmuir, is presented not as a hero but rather as a vacuous figure, almost a simpleton. His brains are most certainly in his feet rather than his head. A celebrity on the pitch, he is a naïve nonentity off it. The only other member of the team who looms at all largely in the narrative, Turk McCabe, is very much a type. He is a boozy veteran defender, newly returned to Drumsagart after failure in the south, a player who just about makes up in craft and cunning and determination for what he has lost, if he ever had, in athleticism.

Jenkins shows swiftly that he is not particularly engaged by the players, or the action on the pitch. It is rather the spectators who fascinate him. He handles with finesse and assurance a large cast of supporters. *The Thistle and the Grail* is not a long novel, but it has a vast array of minor characters, most of whom are delineated with precision and care.

Take, for instance, Rab Nuneaton, a pathetic, defeated and altogether reprehensible human being who nonetheless clings to football to prevent himself from going mad. In a brilliant central passage in the novel Jenkins describes how Nuneaton buries his daughter at lunch-time and within minutes is off to watch the Thistle in a crucial Cup-tie. He opens this brilliant chapter with the deftly ironic sentence: 'Saturday was a fine day for football match and funeral.'

Towards the end of this chapter, Rutherford is driven over the moors to the same Cup-tie, an away game, and is close to despair. Even the beautiful scenery and the anticipation of the exciting match to come offer him little consolation. Instead, he broods: 'Scotland was a country where faith lay rotted like neglected roses, and the secret of resurrection was lost. We are a dreich, miserable, backbiting, self-tormenting, haunted, self-pitying crew, he thought. This sunshine is as bright as any on earth, these moors are splendid: why are not the splendour and brightness in our lives? Seeking them, here we are speeding at fifty miles and hour to see what – a football match, a game invented for exercise and recreation, but now our only substitute for a faith and a purpose.'

This is great writing, among the best writing about Scotland there has been in modern times, and anyone who knows Scotland and its obsession with football will understand just how pertinent it is. Yet Jenkins himself, with an almost religious compassion and insight, can cut through the dreichness, the misery and the self-pity and find something life-enhancing and almost redemptive amid the rottenness.

Jenkins understands the football crowd. He understands its changing moods, its impotence, its defiant vitality, its ardent quest for glory yet its contradictory fear of victory and its perverse, very Scottish delight in defeat, and above all its sheer necessity to the game: all of which anticipate Jock Stein's famous remark that a game without a crowd is meaningless.

As the Thistle progress towards unlikely Cup glory, Rutherford moves in the opposite direction, towards personal defeat. He succumbs to his wife and moves to Helensburgh. He returns to Drumsagart almost as an exile. And when the Thistle triumph, he cannot indulge for very long in the boisterous celebrations. He moves off to be alone.

The moving passage that describes this momentary detachment reminded me uncannily of something I once read, not in a novel, but in a factual account of the aftermath of the greatest victory of the greatest football team there has ever been – the Brazil team that won the World Cup in 1970, playing football of a sublime quality that we shall probably never see the like of again. During the frenetic victory celebrations in Mexico City, one of the team's best and most sensitive players, the celestially gifted forward Tostao, suddenly needed to be absolutely apart. He slipped away and went back to his hotel room, alone and overwhelmed.

Rutherford moves away from the boozy mayhem to the town graveyard. He goes to the grave, the pauper's grave, of a recently buried old supporter, Tinto Brown. He then realises he is not alone: another supporter, a crippled man called Crutch Brodie, is also there. Even now, in their quiet conversation, Rutherford feels himself rejected. But this time the rejection is without contempt or animosity; it simply marks, as Jenkins notes, the ultimate, irremediable loneliness of every human being.

This is a bleak ending yet one that is not with out a kind of austere hope.

*

Robin Jenkins was a prolific novelist, but despite his fecundity he always seemed to be a reluctant one. Towards the end of his long career, in the 1980s, he took to writing various novels that he could not be bothered to send to publishers. (His relations with his various publishers – there were nine altogether – were at times problematic). The typescripts lay, literally, in a bottom drawer in his house near Toward, above his beloved Clyde Estuary.

When the journalist Jack Webster wrote, in 1984, a sympathetic and insightful profile of the novelist in the *Glasgow Herald*, he revealed the existence of these typescripts. The revelation prompted a minor outcry. There was indignation in Scotland's literary community. Why was the man whom many regarded as Scotland's greatest living novelist writing for himself rather than a wider public?

I was then deputy editor of *The Herald*, and, perhaps presumptuously, I thought that the paper should play a role in bringing at least one of the unpublished novels to the light of day. So I decided to intervene. Through the good offices and patient persuasion of Jack Webster, Jenkins agreed to release one of the novels. The one he chose was *The Awakening of George Darroch*, a historical and religious novel about the aftermath of the Great Disruption of 1843.

The following year, it was published by Paul Harris in association with *The Herald*. The launch was held at The George Hotel, Edinburgh, chosen not because it was one of the capital's more posh hotels, but because it was situated next to the Kirk of St Andrew and St George, the scene of the mass walk-out of clerics that had started the Disruption.

The launch party was a convivial occasion, attended by a variety of media and literary folk. The one person present who seemed slightly ill at ease was the guest of honour, the author. It was the only time I met Jenkins. He was courteous and gracious, but it was obvious that he was slightly embarrassed. He was clearly an exceptionally private man, and not one for whom any kind of projection or promotion came easily. He patently did not regard himself as any kind of celebrity. I almost formed the impression that we had done him a disfavour, and that he would have been happier if the novel had remained unpublished. It was as if he was performing, with reluctance, but with as much grace as he could muster, a professional duty.

Something of that unease, that diffidence and ambivalence, informs much of his best fiction. It certainly lurks constantly in the pages of *The Thistle and the Grail*. He writes with enormous empathy and understanding about football, yet he remains apart, the ultimate spectator, watchful and perhaps just a little disdainful. Like most of his novels – and *The Thistle and the Grail* is one of the very best he wrote – it achieves that rare combination of extreme readability and profundity. But it is also distant. He loves Scotland, but my goodness his love is not blind. It is all too clear-sighted.

Jenkins was an artist, a man apart, a man patiently and persistently at odds with his times and his country, yet very much of them and of it. In Andrew Rutherford, he created a good but weak and flawed man, a man who would win a few skirmishes but always lose life's bigger battles. Jenkins understood him and blessed him, in an almost beatific way, through the understated and gentle, ironic reverence of his writing.

It is the subtle and complex portrait of Andrew Rutherford, rather than the treatment of football, excellent though that is, that ultimately makes *The Thistle and the Grail* an outstanding piece of modern fiction.

Harry Reid
2006

THE THISTLE AND THE GRAIL

1

A thousand martyrs were being persecuted. Their howls of anguish mingled in one enormous snarl of lamentation that fluttered even the hardened sparrows on roofs around and made the women shoppers in the adjacent main street pause a smiling moment in their gossip. Drumsagart Thistle Junior Football Club was again being defeated at home, for the ninth time in succession; and its devotees were on the rack.

Defeat can be accidental, unlucky, honourable—even, against impossible odds, ennobling; but in football seven goals to nil, at home, can never be anything but amaranthine humiliation.

This week, too, the conquerors were their traditional rivals, the Violet from the neighbouring village of Lettrickhill. The modest name was, of course, even at the christening a misnomer. Lettrickhill men bawled their pride, roared their triumph, and oathed their joy as arrogantly as any other men in Scotland. But that afternoon they merely guffawed and sniggered and patted their Drumsagart foes pityingly. There was no satisfaction in rejoicing over the pulverisation of such a team as that afternoon, bow-legged and bald, fushionless and floundering, cowed and costive, disgraced the light-blue jerseys with the red thistle on the breast.

"Fegs," piped old Tamas Dougary, frail and saintlike with his wispy white beard and mild, purblind eyes, "it would provoke a saint to swear." And he did swear—not the terrible heaven-shaking curse necessary to the occasion, but a wee furtive 'damn' into his blue muffler, carefully inaudible to his nineteen-year-old granddaughter, who often took him to the football matches, and who now stood beside him gnawing at her hand-knitted gloves, blue in the Thistle shade, and wearing her blue red-tooried tammy flat on her head in dejection. Tamas and Mysie were kenspeckle at Thistle games, she cleeking him tenderly and he droolingly proud of her rosy-cheeked bonniness.

5

"Right enough, Grandpa, they're not very good," she admitted, shaking her head; and then she added what no-one heard: "My Sandy's better than the lot of them."

"I'm eighty-two," squealed Tamas again, "and I could still play better than some of them, see, wi' my boots on backward."

Those round about nodded reverently in the midst of their sorrow. In his heyday Tamas had been a celebrated footballer. From Drumsagart he'd ascended in glory to the great Glasgow Rangers, and thence still upwards to Scotland's team: six times had he fought against the auld enemy England. Already canonised, he was the burgh's most famous citizen, and even his senile boasts were potent.

One jaundiced man could feel no reverence then for anything. "Maybe that's whit's wrang wi them," he bellowed. "They've got their boots on backward and are too damned glaikit to notice it."

Tinto Brown, over seventy himself, and famed more for his past debaucheries than his present buoyant brags, lifted up his stick as if it was a bishop's crozier and sent forth a stream of profanity with ripples of merriment in it. "Boots on backwards, is it? Worse than that, Christ help us. Their backsides are where their heids should be; aye, and backwards at that."

"Wheehst, Tinto," warned someone. "Young Mysie'll hear you."

Instantly and craftily contrite, Tinto reached forward through the crowd with his stick, jabbed one man in the neck, knocked another's fag out of his mouth, nearly poked off another's ear, ignored all protests, and finally succeeded in tapping Mysie gently on the shoulder.

She turned and gave him a smile of reproof.

Again like a bishop he lifted his ragged greasy bonnet.

"Begging your pardon, Mysie," he cackled, with philanderish wink.

"Aren't they awful, Tinto?"

"That lot?" he cried, wiping drivels of humour away with his hand. "When I was young, two or three years ago, I could hae put eleven spits on the pavement wi mair spunk and dance in them than's in that shower of dreeps."

His fat one-legged crony, sixty-eight-year-old chronic smiler Crutch Brodie, whispered into his ear: "That's coarse talk to use to a young lassie that goes to kirk."

6

Tinto was indignant. "How often hae I told you, Crutch, I'll take ony kind of advice frae you except aboot women. D'you think, because you got married, into the abyss, and I stayed single in the sunshine, you had mair experience? Everybody kens I had mair women in my day than there's violets on Drumsagart Hill."

"Nobody's ever coonted the violets, Tinto," chuckled Crutch.

"Hae you ever," asked Tinto urgently, "in the lang braw licht of summer, wi the licht and sweetness of manhood in your bluid, laid a woman on the wavering grass up yonder, and violets all round her, till you couldnae be sure what were violets and what were her een?"

Crutch's reply was never heard. All private conversation had to be suspended for a communal bellow of abuse against the Drumsagart centre-forward, who, with only the goalkeeper to beat, had kicked the ground instead of the ball. His sin was heinous: in the desert, he'd punctured the last water-bottle; in bitterest retreat he'd thrown away a chance to regain at least one lost flag. No pity was shown towards his stubbed toe. He limped out there on the field more vociferously reviled than Judas or Menteith or any traitor in history; and he suddenly showed his resentment by putting his fingers to his nose.

He had committed the ultimate, nameless, inexplicable sin: he had returned the insults of those who had paid for the privilege of insulting him. Theirs was the ferocity of virtue outraged. They threatened to leap the barrier and emasculate him or at least kick his buck teeth down his throat. They slandered his parents. They promised to toss him into the nearby river, which, they fervently assured him, like Christ's mercy rejected nothing. They reminded him of other peculiarities in his appearance, such as his spiky hair and mushroom ears. His ears especially were maligned: perhaps they suggested, subconsciously but poignantly, the Junior Cup whose handles similarly protruded.

In two minutes he had his simple but ample revenge by again failing to score from an easy position. This time he struck the goalkeeper on the nose with the ball; but as it bounced back out into play and no goal resulted the blood it had drawn was no propitiation. As the Lettrickhill trainer scooted on to the field with therapeutic sponge soaked in water and dabbed his goal-keeper's bloody snout the Drumsagart supporters redoubled their denunciation of their centre-forward.

7

It was apparent there was a unanimous opinion he would not do, he was not skilful enough, he could not score goals, he must be got rid of.

He, arms folded, stood out on the field, teeth jutting in a rather imbecilic satisfaction. Displeased himself with his display, he felt nevertheless this censure was excessive. Thus his ineptitude was a kind of vengeance. Moreover he knew, and knew that his censurers knew, every centre-forward previously tried had been, despite these calumniators on the terracing, worse even than he.

His ten colleagues, maimed in their souls by similar vituperations, walked about the field praying for the release of the final whistle. Their opponents laughed and plucked daisies.

It was thus every Saturday. All last season only three home games had been won, and those flukily. The team had been at the bottom of the League for three seasons in succession, a record in shamefulness. It had also been knocked out of the Scottish Junior Cup in the first round. Glory, without a fragment of which no faith can survive, was become as scarce as whisky at a poorhouse Ne'erday. Former glory, such as being runners-up in the League in 19— and reaching the final round of the Cup in 18—, was now quite used up: there was no substance in it any longer; faith could gnaw on that dry bone no more.

Yet at the start of every season hope springs up. Maybe a miracle will happen, maybe each flat-footed fumbler will burst out of his chrysalis and become a swift, gorgeous goal-scorer; maybe the League will be topped, or, more gloriously, the glittering Cup won. Well, that season, as usual, hope had sprung up in Drumsagart, but a grimacing jack-in-the-box caricature of hope; and now here it was so terribly soon crushed back down into the broken heart again.

It was well known that during the past two or three years more than one Drumsagart man who formerly had hurried straight home from the match to take his wife to the pictures now returned circuitously via Sam Malarkin's and other pubs, and gave her a swollen neb if she as much as sniffed.

"What we need," snarled Archie Birkwood, who drove the hearse for Sowlas the undertaker, "is a new committee."

"What we need," said a bystander, "is a loan of your hearse, Archie, and aboot a dozen coffins."

8

There was macabre laughter, but Archie didn't join in. He was a big fat man with a face fashioned for jolliness; but long ago his plump cheeks, extra chins, and cherry nose had betrayed their purpose. He was never heard laughing and seldom smiled: he saw no fun in his trade. Some said it was the necessity of keeping his black Rolls-Royce so gleaming; and of course when polished it became, like the coffins themselves, a mirror.

"I mean it," he cried, hard lumps of bitterness forming under his eyes. "We need an entirely new committee. We need men wi' imagination. There's Andrew Rutherford, president. What does he ken aboot football? He never was a judge of a football player in his life."

"Nor of a woman," murmured wee Rab Nuneaton.

Others in that group nodded; some to flatter Rab, whose maliciousness they feared like a disease, and all because Mrs. Rutherford, the president's wife, was admitted to be snobbish, unbraw, icy-hearted, and stupid. But, all the same, she was an irrelevancy there.

One man did not nod. Like Nuneaton he was undersized, but in body only. His smooth ruddy face was always smiling. Tom Kennox kept no secrets; he said what he thought, and it was always charitable. He drove one of the burgh's scavenger lorries, which disconcerted any stranger meeting him over a pint of beer in Malarkin's pub. Tom's job ought to have been tending the roses and pansies in Drumsagart Public Park.

"Andrew Rutherford's a good man," he said, calmly, but making sure he was heard.

"A blackleg though, Tom," reminded Nuneaton.

Kennox was known to be a staunch trade unionist, treasurer of his branch. "That was a long time ago, twelve years and mair. A man can live doon a mistake."

"But are you sure he's lived it doon, Tom?" Nuneaton fingered his long nose, cold even in June; slowly his fingers slid from base to point and lingered there, as if there was nowhere else to go, the rest was oblivion. "Ask his brither Robbie."

"Ask his faither," added one of Nuneaton's cronies. "Ask the auld cooncillor."

Kennox smiled undauntedly. "Say whit you like. I ken I'm in a minority. I like Andrew Rutherford. I think he's misjudged."

9

"Are you so simple then, Tom, to be taken in by his handing oot scraps of broken biscuits to the weans in the street? That costs him nothing, and forby a man that's been lifted by a swindler over the heids of better men to be made manager of the factory can surely spare a crumb or two to buy favour. In a toon that's rotting Rutherford's one of the few men flourishing; and we're the dung that makes him flourish."

Some grunted agreement.

"As you said, Tom," murmured Nuneaton, "you're in a minority."

"Why was he made president then?"

"Christ kens," said one.

Birkwood scowled at the blasphemy. He was not religious although he attended church occasionally in the interests of his job; but, considering his cargoes, he took no chances. "I ken why they made him president," he said. "Because there was apathy, because nobody else wanted the position. Who would want to be president of a team like that?"

"Rutherford wanted it," sniggered Nuneaton. "Onything for ambition. Is he not superintendent of the Sunday school? And a member of the bowling club committee? He's got his finger in every pie."

"There's hardly a pie made," said Kennox, "withoot Andrew Rutherford helping to pay for it."

"That's maybe true," agreed Birkwood.

"It's true," admitted Nuneaton. "But his generosity's got a purpose. He buys favour wi' it. Can you blame him? Wha in Drumsagart would gie it to him gratis, for nothing but love?"

"Me," said Kennox.

"I was never aware, Tom, you and he were such bosom friends. I'd hae thought your social status would hae kept you apart."

"I ken him only to nod to."

"See?" murmured Nuneaton.

"Let's stick to the point," said Birkwood. "It was his money got Rutherford his position, and the same goes for Sam Malarkin. Does Sam think his scented whiskers and his fancy waistcoats gie him the right to dictate in football matters?"

The question was not answered. Everybody then united in a groan of torment. Lettrickhill Violet had scored again, making the score eight-nil. It was, that goal, the revolutionary spark.

"Sack the committee!" began to be bellowed round the terracing, right up to the pavilion enclosure.

"Aye, sack them," wheezed Archie Birkwood. "Aren't they ruining our lives for us? Are we to work all week and then on Saturdays, instead of some pleasure and relaxation, suffer this? I'm one, too, that needs a cheering up more than maist folk."

"Whit aboot us, Archie," whispered Nuneaton, "that hae no work? That every day rot by the Cross? That listen to wives greeting and weans girning because of hunger and need? After the game, whatever the result, Rutherford goes hame to steak pie and chicken."

Slogans were roared all round the field. "Kick the committee oot! Into the river wi' them! Burn the pavilion!"

Birkwood squealed into the tempest. "We should go in a deputation to the pavilion at the finish of this farce. Eight-nothing! Worse than Flodden ever was. If right was right, we should find them all hanging frae the ceiling in yonder."

"Work for you, Archie," whispered Rab Nuneaton, with a far-away malice.

This idea of a deputation quickly spread. Roars of resign kept reverberating. The footballers thought at first they were intended, and were indignant at thus being treated like Cabinet Ministers who earned more in a day than they did in a year, and who, though guilty of calamities like war and unemployment, were always secluded from public abuse like this. No footballer, in any case, resigned: either he was given away for nothing or was sold for a handful of silver or was just handed his boots.

One man did not approve of all those rebellious threats. Tamas Dougary conceded the team was terrible and had been terrible for years: maybe the committee had been a bit inefficient. But he could not forget that the pavilion was a sacred place. Photographs of famous Drumsagart men hung on its walls; and those walls had been built by Drumsagart men, not for pay or praise, or even duty, but for love of their native place and its team. To burn them down, as the hotheads bawled, would be sacrilege. They might as well burn him too, white beard and all.

"No, no, no," he kept whimpering. "They shouldn't even talk aboot burning. It's wicked, it's sinful, it's against nature and God."

Mysie, angry herself, had to soothe him and explain that the men were just angry and didn't really mean what they were shouting.

In one case at least she seemed mistaken. Little Geordie Bonnyton's maledictions seemed as genuine as they were impassioned. "Burn the pavilion," he screamed, "but shut the doors first, lock them, let nobody escape. Let Rutherford's fat reek, let his moustache stink."

Those who heard couldn't help laughing in spite of their larger exasperation. Geordie's timidity was a joke in the town. An insurance agent, he saw his children's starvation in one sticky payer; men's drawers on a backcourt line jigged like ghosts in the dusk for him; cows were monsters; boys yelled "Tom Mix" after him because of his great wide-brimmed hat; and any housewife, not willing or able to meet that week's instalment, could scare him off by banging a teaspoon on the table.

He took the laughter for encouragement. "Burn them all, the whole damned lot. And let them try to put oot the fire wi' Malarkin's bad beer." He saw the pavilion then, and all reality with it, transmuted into magnificent cathartic flames. Not only the committee men shrivelled in them, but also hundreds of greasy insurance-books, dozens of thrawn payers, and many private persecutors, among them a taciturn superintendent from Glasgow with a mole on his chin, and a small terrier called Rags that every Tuesday afternoon raced out of its gate and snapped at his ankles.

Then the referee at last blew his whistle for time-up. There were really forty-seven seconds to go, but he calculated no-one would notice, and even if anybody did he'd hardly think it worth while protesting with the score eight-nil.

Nevertheless the referee, a married man with two small children and breakable bones, sprinted towards the pavilion. He grinned as if his running was out of zest for his job: he'd been running all during the game, and here he was still keen. But his reason was otherwise. He knew a colleague who had had to ford a stream in his shorts to escape from a berserk crowd. Of course that game had been a Cup-tie, and in the last two minutes, with the score one-nil against the home team, he'd been so foolish, heroic, and just as to deny them a penalty kick though it had been vociferated for with cannibalistic fury.

The pavilion was shut off from the field by a breast-high wall like a fortification. There was a gate open, and the referee darted through to safety, so grateful that when one desperate Drumsagartite called him a 'knock-knee'd bastard' he merely nodded, as if every man was entitled to his opinion.

On the pavilion steps he had a moment of terror. His way was barred by a burly man in thick tan tweed plus-fours, with a brawny fist upraised; but it was to pat the referee's shoulder and give him a friendly push into the sanctuary of the pavilion.

This was Andrew Rutherford, the president.

"Don't be frightened, lad," he said, laughing. "Our bark in Drumsagart's aye worse than our bite. You did your job well."

Sergeant Elvan, aloof and imperturbable, as if he didn't even know the score though he'd been circumambulating the field throughout the game, arrived at the pavilion with young Constable Dunsmore behind him.

"There's a mob on its way, Mr. Rutherford," he said calmly, "to demand your heid on a plate."

Rutherford nodded. "Like John the Baptist, eh?"

"Just so; if it's proper to mix religion wi' football."

Rutherford smiled. "Oh, why not, sergeant? Surely whatever's happy is religious?"

Without descending from his aloofness, the sergeant indicated that Rutherford's definition struck him as false, sentimental, and weak-brained: he had seen men happy half-murdering their own wives.

"There's not much happiness here," he said.

"I'm forgetting," murmured Rutherford. "You're like my faither; you think football's a waste of time."

"Like him in that respect, aye."

The gibe went home. Rutherford's smile faltered, and the policeman, observing closely through his mask of remoteness, almost smiled himself. He knew, as all the town did, how Rutherford the successful capitalist pretended to revere his father the Socialist councillor. In Elvan's opinion the latter was an old windbag and impostor, as anyone claiming his ideals must be, who spoke great words of clearing away the mountainous midden-heaps of poverty and injustice, but had to be content with such piddling triumphs as squeezing an extra half-crown from the parish for some widow or winning a campaign to have the latrine in the main street open all night.

Rutherford glanced away towards the approaching crowd. "Wha can blame them?" he asked. "Defeat's a gey thin gruel to feed on for weeks; something like your own jail bread and water."

Elvan wondered if that was a gibe in retaliation. "When I jail a man," he said grimly, "he gets what the regulations say he should get."

As always, Rutherford, having tried to prick even so invulnerable a man as the sergeant, felt penitent and ashamed. "That's so," he muttered. "Me now, I'd make a fool of the business. I'd be feeding them on chocolate biscuits."

Elvan narrowed his eyes. Showing no pity and allowing no involvement, he found most men easy to read; but in Rutherford, apparently so shallow and naïve, there were some pages that puzzled him. Simple in many ways the president was, stupid too, selfish, bullied by his unpleasant wife, and over-anxious to placate those who hated and slandered him; but now and then he gave a sign, vague and equivocal, which seemed to suggest that deep under the simplicity and humility lurked a powerful dangerous pride.

"The trouble is," said the president, with a laugh, "good players are so scarce."

"Like good men."

"Surely not that." Smiling, Rutherford was now greeting his team slinking into the pavilion. "Hard lines, Lachie," he said to the captain, with genuine commiseration.

Lachie was a bald man, but dirt from the ball had given him a wild freakish hair. Sweat glistened on his face and made patches of black over his jersey; his left knee was dirty and bloody; his eyes were inflamed. In front of the president he summoned up what breath he had left. "You'd think," he gasped, "we'd raped their wives to hear them. They can go and——" What he added was a filthy if commonplace obscenity.

Rutherford frowned in regret. He wanted to sympathise with Lachie and the rest of the team, but was alienated by that foul vicious talk; especially as he saw his own thirteen-year-old son Gerald, kilted, innocent, and attentive, had come within hearing.

The Thistle centre-forward swaggered past. His ears were

fiery, but it was the exertions of the game which had caused that, not the derision of the crowd, who had not forgiven him his fingers-at-nose defiance.

"You were in the wrong, Tommy," murmured the president.

Tommy buck-toothed an obscenity.

The president had to continue smiling, for the Lettrickhill team were now coming in.

"Well played, lads," he said. "Keep that up and you'll go far in the Cup this season. Good luck."

One of the visiting players muttered something at which his team-mates laughed. Rutherford heard it but kept on smiling. It had been to the effect that if all the teams they were picked to play were as poor as the Thistle they'd win the Cup all right, even with their legs tied together. Perhaps the taunt was permissible, but not the vileness with which it was bespattered. Gerald must have heard again, must have had this second lump of filth flung into his innocence. Yet Rutherford went on smiling. To rebuke, to protest, to frown would have been inhospitable, unsporting, perhaps unmanly.

He stood then on the steps alone, smiling, and fingering the gold watch in his waistcoat pocket. The crowd yelled insults from outside the enclosure.

He recognised most of them: old Tinto Brown, for instance, enjoying himself amid the riot and hilarity, and old Tamas Dougary frightened and unhappy; wee Geordie Bonnyton with cowboy's hat, and poor Rab Nuneaton embittered as any Redskin driven from his ancestral lands.

The president laughed down at the sergeant guarding the gate. "Surely not, Sergeant," he cried.

Elvan had forgotten. Under his helmet he frowned, unwilling to admit even the failing of forgetfulness.

"I mean," said the president cheerfully, "surely it's not true good men are scarce? Surely that's never been true, in Drumsagart especially."

Elvan was not a native. "Listen to them," he said.

"Och, that's just noise. They're disappointed, and rightly so. The team's rank bad; there's no denying it. I could greet myself. But wha is there to greet to?"

"A man wouldn't greet for his wife dead, Mr. Rutherford. Would he for a rotten team? I'd get the boy in."

"You think so?" Rutherford turned sharply towards his son.

"Is that language for a boy to listen to? And one of them might get so bold as to throw a stane."

The president was instantly and frankly worried. He ignored the scorn in the sergeant's tone. In the smallest stone hid hurt, infection, irretrievable loss. He remembered the dirty mad violence of men.

"Gerald," he shouted, "get into the pavilion. Go on, son, get in quick."

The boy resented the order and was slow to obey. He was amused by the sallies and antics of the crowd, and indeed felt on their side. All during the game he had hooted mockery of the team.

"Get in, didn't I say?" shouted his father.

"But why, Dad?"

In the insolence of the question and the wink towards the crowd that accompanied it Rutherford saw again what for years he had been forcing himself to accept: the physical resemblance in his son to Hannah's brother, the unscrupulous Harry, who'd gone into the war poor and come out of it well-to-do, who'd been foremost in organising the memorial in the public park and had insisted that the bronze kiltie on top should be in the likeness of Gavin Rutherford, first man from Drumsagart to be killed. Harry would give a tramp a lift in his flashy car but would refuse him a penny. He would laugh his gold-toothed contempt of poverty, and could prove, with purple-lidded winks and jewelled manipulations and golden spittles, how no man of enterprise needed to be poor. It was natural enough in the complexities of human kinship that Gerald should inherit some features from his uncle; but might not the inheritance go deeper still, invading the sacred soul itself, without even God Himself being able to prevent it?

"Why?" he shouted. "Because I said so, that's why."

Gerald shrugged his shoulders and went into the pavilion. At the door he lifted his kilt in a gesture intended to impress the crowd and slight his father.

Rutherford saw only that first purpose, and thought his son had been trying in some obscure boyish way to help him. Encouraged by that loyalty, he faced his hecklers.

As he held up his hand for attention he realised how defenceless he was there on the pavilion steps, with all those hundreds of

16

Drumsagart eyes and memories concentrated on him. From his cradle to this very moment his history was known to them, and there had been episodes of shame. He was at their mercy. If they were preponderantly bad and cruel, as the sergeant suggested, they could savage him and tear from him not only his self-respect—often so flimsy—but also his brightest and strongest armour, his love of them as his fellows in his native town.

The sergeant was speaking. "I ought to be lifting half a dozen of you as examples. Are you not aware it's an offence to assemble in angry mobs?"

"We're not angry," cried somebody; but someone else, far louder, bawled that they damned well were angry and with good reason.

"In my opinion," said the sergeant, "you should be sent straight back to your wives. But it seems Mr. Rutherford, as president of the club, is willing to hear what you've got to say, provided it's said decently and calmly."

"What we've got to say," wailed someone, "cannae be said decently or calmly."

There was laughter in which the president eagerly joined. At the windows of the pavilion appeared other smiling faces—of committee men, of players, of Gerald, of the referee.

The spokesmen turned out to be a miner called Nathaniel Stewart, a tall, gaunt, stooped, dark-faced moribund man who in chain-mail would have resembled the Ruthven that rose from his death-bed to plunge his sword into Mary's Rizzio; and a fiery-faced smelter called Ned Nicholson, chubby and keen, but handicapped as negotiator by his perpetual need to laugh, for he by nature saw fun in everything—even, it was rumoured, in his wife's long slow dying of cancer.

Stewart sagged forward and gripped the wall with black hairy fists. His face grew darker with bitterness, and his voice ached in a passion that electrified them all and embarrassed many.

"For God's sake," he cried, "resign. Resign and go away. You, Rutherford, and all your damned committee. Resign. I tell you, none of you could run a Sunday school for weans, let alone a football team for grown men."

That sarcasm, by no means delivered as a witticism, earned loud laughter and handclaps. Stewart thought at first he was being derided by his own side and twisted round to spill some of his inexhaustible spleen on them; but one or two stroked him appeasingly and reminded him that Rutherford did run a Sunday school, being boss of the parish kirk's.

Even the sergeant grinned.

Rutherford, too, smiled, but felt excluded. He half turned to look at Gerald, in whom always shone reassurance; but he had sent him away in anger.

"That man should be in his bed," he muttered. "He's dying on his feet."

The sergeant nodded, but said: "He's better out of it. How many weans is it? Eight or nine. I've lost count."

Rutherford, too, wasn't sure, but he knew that Stewart's wife, tormented in poverty's familiar hell of children to love and deny, nevertheless still smiled in the street and still was proud of the roses in her cheeks.

He held up his hand again.

"I ken you're all dissatisfied with the play of the team," he said reasonably.

Reasonableness is provocation to incensed men. They yelled abuse: amidst it was the snarl 'scab!' That word frightened the president, although on hearing it he set his feet further apart and held his head higher, so that Rab Nuneaton amid the hubbub screamed privately Tom Kennox was wrong, himself right: Rutherford the creashy hypocrite, the festering scab, far from being ashamed of his past gloried in it.

"You and your committee Rutherford," cried Ned Nicholson, with chuckles like a hysteria of merriment, "would make a man pay for admission to his ain execution? Is it no true you charge the weans a penny every Sunday to ram doon their throats your propaganda aboot sweet Jesus Christ?"

Again they laughed. The sergeant shrugged his shoulders as if he'd decided, as umpire, that the scoff was justified.

"Laugh away," shouted Rutherford, "for it's better to listen to honest laughter than foul or blasphemous talk, which never got anybody anywhere. Do you think it wouldn't be the happiest day of my life if the Thistle won the Cup during my term as president? Do you think I'm not disappointed like the rest of you? But it's one thing being disappointed, it's another being mean and spiteful and unfair. Some criticism's to be expected, but let it be helpful and fair-minded. Don't try to crush a young player's spirit. I'm putting it to you: is it loyal, is it honourable, is it decent to miscall your own team? Or any team for that matter? Football's a great game, and I owe to it some of the happiest moments of my life; but I'd give it up gladly if it was to turn us all biased and vindictive."

"Don't preach, for God's sake," they yelled.

"Do you think this is your Sunday school?"

"Hypocrite!"

"Scab!"

"You mind the rhyme we had as weans?" roared Rutherford, laughing. "Sticks and stanes will break my banes, names will never hurt me."

"Your hide's as thick as your heid."

"I'll not deny in many ways I'm a bit thick in the head. But alang with Wattie Cleugh, our secretary, I've not been thick-headed in the matter of trying oot new players. Do you ken how many we've tried already, wi' the season just started? Nineteen. I think we'd better face the hard truth; there just happens to be a scarcity of good players these days."

"Why is it then, for God's sake," cried Stewart, his hands twitching on the wall like gigantic spiders, "other teams can get good players? Tell me that. How is it the Violet has a good team?"

Rutherford was baffled. "They've been lucky," he said.

"Lucky? I'm one that's not been lucky. Everybody in this toon kens I'm deeing." Furiously he thumped his chest and coughed. "God in heaven, am I to get no comfort before I dee? Am I never again going to see a good team come oot of that pavilion wearing the blue jerseys wi' the red thistles? Is that too much to ask?"

"No, no, that's not too much to ask."

"Hell roast you all then, for that's what I'm asking, and it's what I'll not get."

"The trouble is," screamed Archie Birkwood, "not one of you in there would recognise a good player if you saw one. Are you all Eskimos or Fijis?"

Rutherford, like Archie himself, couldn't laugh with the others: he was too hurt. Next to his son's company, his pride and pleasure in skilful wholesome football sustained him most; certainly it gave him a keener and clearer joy than religion.

"It's maybe not for me to say it," he cried, "but I think I'm as good a judge of a football player as the next man."

"Aye, if the next man's Harry Lynn," screeched Nicholson.

Again Rutherford couldn't laugh: for him Lynn the blind moocher was a symbol of disaster, not of humour. Last Ne'erday, sober enough himself, he'd come across the blind man drunk and scurrilous in the gutter and had shoved into his claws a ten-shilling note instead of the sixpence they begged. Lynn had burst into an astonishing slobbering gratitude and, as if taking Andrew for a priest, had tried to confess to him sins he'd committed long ago. It had been a hideous experience, and Rutherford had been haunted by it for months. Now as the crowd brayed its laughter he remembered afresh, and felt, there at the very heart of his beloved Drumsagart, a sense of blight and withering.

Stewart was punching the stone wall. "Where's the rest of the committee? Where's Wattie Cleugh? Are they skulking in there like the rats they are?"

The sergeant considered 'rats' impermissible. He warned Stewart.

"Mice then," giggled Nicholson. "Will you let us call them mice?"

"Where's Sam Malarkin?" yelled a voice. "Give us jaunty Sam."

They hurrahed. There were shouts of "Good old Sam! Give's a sniff of your whiskers! Show us your waistcoat! Old pansy Sam! If we cannae get goals, give us beer!"

Like an astute actor, Sam Malarkin, the vice-president and burgh bailie, came jouking out of the pavilion at that cue of mostly good-natured acclamation. His part in public was to be the jester: he was always to supply the comedy and win the applause; the hero's role, with its chance of doom, was never for him. He made every comic feature tell, his slightly rouged cheeks, scented pin-sharp moustache, curled kiss-me-quick, bow-tie, foppish clothes, and especially his waistcoat, bright blue that afternoon.

He had an enthusiastic liquid lisp, irresistibly fetching to his drouthy customers.

"I've got a complaint to make, so I have. You should have advised me you were for holding an indignation meeting. I'd have arranged it in the Lucky Sporran. Indignation's a thirsty thing, so it is."

"Aye, for bluid," shouted someone not altogether conciliated.

"Is Scots blood," asked Sam, surprised, "not another name for whisky? There's old Tinto: scratch him and see."

As he'd calculated, he quickly won their indulgence. Even the implacable Stewart tried to grin, for he was one of the many who in the dry middle of the week were pleading in Sam's ear for a pint or a nip on the slate.

But tolerance was rationed. What Malarkin was granted was deducted from the other officials.

"Wha's got a mouse-trap?" cried Nicholson, and even the committee men themselves had to snigger, for at least three of them, especially Wattie Cleugh, the secretary, had almost visibly long tails of timidity between their legs as they sheltered behind their president.

Rutherford crashed his great hands together. "It's your team as much as ours. It's your duty, then, to help us to build it up."

"It would be as easy to build up Logan's chimney-stack," shrieked Nicholson.

That was a good joke. The stack had collapsed during a storm in the middle of the night, and folk had rushed out in their shirt tails thinking the end of the world had come.

Rutherford laughed heartily with the rest: the tall chimney had been in the sky every morning when he had gone to school with his two brothers, Gavin and Robbie.

"True enough," he cried. "But there's no getting away from it, lads; if we were to resign en bloc as the saying goes, would you be able to find anybody better, anybody that's willing to take on the responsibility?"

Tamas Dougary for some minutes had been trying to make himself heard above the uproar. He persevered with senile petulance, tears dribbling down his cheeks. At last, with the help of some considerate leather-lunged neighbours, he was given his chance.

"You're all Drumsagart men," he piped, "and I'm a Drumsagart man, born and bred; and my forebears before me were Drumsagart men. I've heard it said there was a Dougary waving his bonnet in the toon the day Robert Bruce rode through. Are you all remembering where you are? This is Drumsagart toon, and that's the pavilion. That's a holy place, I'm telling you. Famous men hae their photos on the walls in there, famous men of Drumsagart, wha in their day, lang-syne in some cases, played for the Thistle, aye, and played weel. There was Hamish Kerr, deid now, killed in the war, as fine a right back as ever kicked a ball; and there was Dougie Leish went to the Hearts in Edinburgh; and there was——"

"Tamas Dougary!" roared at least a hundred voices.

There was tremendous cheering, with much kindly irony in it. The old man took it as his simple due.

"Aye, and me as weel."

There was even louder cheering. One hand, coarse in its congratulation, thumped the old man's back and nearly choked him. Mysie had to wipe his mouth and eyes with her handkerchief. Her indignation against the remorseful thumper she suddenly diverted against the president.

Her face was as red as the toorie on her tammy, and her voice, usually so friendly if cool, was sharp with a strange aggressiveness.

"You never gave Alec Elrigmuir a trial," she cried.

"Wha?" asked Rutherford.

"Alec Elrigmuir."

"And wha's he, Mysie?"

"He's the best centre-forward in Scotland, that's who he is."

After a moment's breathlessness nearly everybody applauded that prodigious boast. Some, however, like Nathaniel Stewart, thought the business much too serious to be interrupted by a silly lassie's brag about some sweetheart better at kissing than kicking. Stewart coughed at her to go home and make her grandfather's tea.

Rutherford's delight in the general humour was mitigated by Mysie's distress. She obviously felt she was making a fool of herself but couldn't keep quiet. Despite the ridicule, galling though good-natured, she was under some compulsion to go on speaking about this Alec Elrigmuir, praising him, proclaiming his fitness to be the saviour of the Thistle.

"You got a letter asking for a trial for him," she cried, "and you never even answered it."

"That's likely enough, Mysie, for we get letters from all sorts of queer characters making out they're better than Alan Morton."

"He *is* better than Alan Morton."

Again they cheered, but not all: some thought that claim too impious.

"He *is*," she screamed, shaking her fist.

Rutherford was in a quandary. He was anxious to keep the crowd laughing and at the same time not to tease the girl unfairly.

"That's a big claim, Mysie," he said. "What team does this Alec fellow play for?"

"Dechmont Colliery."

"A pit team?"

"Aye, but he's no bandy-legged collier, mind."

There were some humorously indignant protests from colliers in the crowd, some of them as bandy-legged as her scorn pictured.

"We have no doubt he's a braw young chap, Mysie, but——"

"I never said that. Please watch what you're saying, Mr. Rutherford. Don't put words into my mouth I never said."

"I thought you hinted at it, Mysie."

"I did not. All I said was he's a good centre-forward. He's nothing to me, so you neednae laugh, nane of you. Your team's a disgrace to Drumsagart as everybody kens, and I'm trying to help you to improve it."

"We recognise that, Mysie, and we're grateful. You'll have seen this Elrigmuir play?"

"Of course."

"How often?"

She hesitated.

"Come on, Mysie, how often?"

"Twice."

"Twice just? Good heavens. And yet you say he's better than Alan Morton?"

Stewart yelled: "Send her hame, I said, to make the tea. This is a matter for men to decide. Women should never be allowed inside a football park."

But the crowd was interested in the mysterious Elrigmuir.

"Give the boy a trial," bellowed one. "Even if he's a damned chimpanzee out of the zoo, give him a trial. He cannae be worse than what we hae."

"He's not a chipanzee," screamed Mysie.

The president had stolen a glance at his watch. Already he was late: Hannah would be furious.

"All right," he cried, holding up his hand. "Just to prove to you I meant what I said about being willing to experiment, we'll send an invitation to this lad. We'll take Mysie's word for it. Her judgment's likely to be as sound as any man's, even if she might happen in this case to be a wee sight partial."

"I told you, I am not."

"We'll invite him here to play in our next home game, which happens to be against Fernbank United, wha, as you all ken, are top of the League. If that's not being bold and experimental, I'd like to ken what is."

"Would you?" cried Ned Nicholson. "Then I'll tell you. Go and take a loup from the Sodger's Brig. That's what I call being bold and experimental."

A soldier on leave had committed suicide by jumping from that bridge.

Then the sergeant decided it was time the proceedings ended. His tea would be waiting, and, besides, he had humoured this childishness long enough.

"All right," he shouted, with authority. "I think that about concludes it. You can get away hame now. Your wives will be wondering what's happened to you."

They growled, for they thought he'd gone beyond what his uniform sanctioned. Yet the price of revolt might be a Saturday night in jail, with bread and water for supper and a Bible for entertainment.

Ned Nicholson, whose wife would be in bed moaning bravely, hinneyed as if the sergeant had cracked the best joke of the afternoon.

Rab Nuneaton grinned bleakly; his wife would start her grumbles as soon as she heard the outer door opening, while he was in the dark lobby, before she had set eyes on him. More than once he'd turned and gone straight back out to stand hunched and hungry at the Cross till the stars shone.

Nathaniel Stewart was afraid of neither wife, cell, nor grave. "Wha the hell do you think you are, Elvan? Away and do your duty. Go and lift the weans for firing squibs in the street."

The sergeant deliberated. That slur about the squibs was derogatory to the law. Last week he'd got two boys fined five shillings each for setting off crackers to the public danger. Still, if he arrested Stewart there would be the coughing all night in the cell.

"There's another thing," he cried. "Lavatories are provided at this football ground, according to sanitary regulations, and I'd advise you all to get into the habit of using them."

The abrupt change of attack confounded them for a minute; then they howled their annoyance, with much self-pity in it. True, there were two lavatories, but each held about half a dozen at a time, and if a man was to wait in a patient queue outside the game'd be finished and his bladder burst before his turn came.

"That's your own look-out," he shouted. "See you're empty before you come here. Leave the beer till after."

Some then pointed out he was being coarse in bringing up such a subject with a young lassie present. Others called on Sam Malarkin as a publican and a bailie to reprimand this policeman in uniform advocating abstention from beer; while others again, more metaphysical, wanted to know who in hell had given the sergeant the right to instruct them in the morality of relieving themselves or partaking of drink.

Malarkin had been simpering in a disgust that the crowd thought assumed for comedy's sake, but which one or two percipient committee-men near him suspected was inexplicably genuine. Maybe Sam, who rouged his cheeks, was a male conundrum of some kind, a prude, or eunuch, or worse. Anyway, he suddenly began a frantic caper on the steps and flagged with his hands.

They listened to him, for among the faithful attending his pub persisted a prophecy, renewed again and again, that one fine night, a Saturday for preference, Sam would stand a free round. Armageddon was not awaited with greater hope and relish by the Jehovah's Witnesses in their brick tent behind the main street.

"There's something I must say," he cried.

"Good old Sam! How about that free dram to help us forget our sorrows?"

"You all heard the president make a serious decision without consulting the rest of the committee. I mean, about this champion Mysie seems to have dug up. I see she's gone now, like a sensible girl. Now the president, no doubt at all in good part, has acted a shade ultra vires."

"What's that, Sam? A fancy French drink?"

25

"But we'll hold a meeting and make the decision democratic. That's the correct procedure, and I'm the boy that likes to stick to the correct procedure."

"That's you, Sam: booze for money, that's the correct procedure."

"I've always been particular about the rules. When we used to play at rounders long ago, I was the wee narky chap saw to it the big fellows just got their one shot with the bat. Well, Andrew Rutherford's a big fellow all right." He laughed and patted Rutherford's arm, but everybody noticed how the president scowled. "Now," went on Sam, "somebody said something about a free dram."

They gasped. Was the prophecy to be fulfilled? Agnostics gaped; sceptics shook their heads; unbelievers swore. Then the faithful cheered.

"There's a free dram," cried Sam, "of the choicest stuff in the shop for every man able and willing to drink it."

It was apocalypse. Smiting one another in an access of faith proved and rewarded, they made to surge off towards the Lucky Sporran, where the consummating miracle was to take place.

Sam was appalled. He shrieked: "I meant the day the Thistle wins the Cup."

A few heard, were shocked, tried to communicate it to those still enraptured, failed, doubted, and listened again.

No man drowning could have been shriller than Sam. "Are you all turned crazy? Can't you take a joke? There must be a reason for such a bonus. I meant the day the Thistle wins the Cup at Hampden Park."

More heard, disillusionment spread, faith expired in a long exasperated groan. Some booed.

"My God, Sam, you're generous!"

"A miracle for a miracle, is that all?"

"Just the Cup is it, not the League as well?"

One was unchivalrous. "While you're at it, Sam, couldn't you throw in a kiss from Margot?"

At all the other pleasantries he'd smiled as if with a beetle in his mouth; but at this one, concerning his sister, the beetle ejected acid. Those near him heard him making queer little moans as if indeed his tongue, or his soul, was burnt.

Margot was his sister; they lived alone in a detached villa in a

26

quiet avenue on the hill above the main street. Some said reck-lessly she was over fifty, but careful research had established her age as forty-one. More jokes were manufactured about her than about her brother. She had spent much time, money, and courage in achieving a formidable synthetic beauty. How she kept so slim no-one knew—whether it was by unrelenting exercises or pills or starvation or witchcraft—but the recipe was marvel-lously successful: below the neck she was as trim and shapely as any debutante. Above the neck artifice struggled with age: her hair was various tints of blonde; her eyelashes were as deciduous as the elm leaves in the main street and sometimes drifted down into the perfumed dust of her cheeks; her teeth were expensively and ostentatiously false, claiming with every confident snap to be superior to real. She did no work, not even in the house, and often was seen being driven home after midnight in a big car by someone as beefy as a bookie; it wasn't always the same car or the same driver. Her status was conjectured to be that of a tart—an amateur, though—of about the second class: amateur in the sense she got no pay, only experience and expenses. Mascu-line Drumsagart liked Margot, who, after all, had been born in the burgh and had grown up in it, a black-haired rotten-toothed skinny lass called Maggie Malarkin. That the swanky name she'd adopted rhymed with the Scottish bedroom receptacle was a godsend to dozens of would-be Burnses. But to feminine Drumsagart she was anathema. At the town generally, male and female, Margot put her vermilion-tipped thumb to her powdered nose and released her celebrated laughter, which, though not melodious, somehow reminded her hearers of swans in stormy rivers or wild geese overhead.

It was not known for certain what Sam's attitude to her was. Many believed he disapproved, while there were, of course, the bad-minded who hinted at incest. Few suspected he on his knees, almost weeping, begged her to give up her sexual adventures.

He stood on the steps, in the limelight, in all his clown's array, but he seemed close to tears.

The bawdy cries proliferated.

"Why stop at a kiss? She's weel practised."

"A go at Margot!" That became the favourite slogan.

As they shouted they moved away towards the big gate, shoved by the sergeant and his assistant.

Wattie Cleugh, the secretary, now that the danger was past twirled his tail; he became daring and jocose, but still in a mousy fashion. He was a small quick man with pointed ears, and the real leader of the committee.

"Man, Sam," he chuckled, "you'll be on your knees from now on praying we don't win the Cup. It's a good job for your peace of mind we get Carrick Celtic in the first round, at Carrick too. A free dram for everybody would cost you hundreds of pounds. They's come flocking in from miles around. There'd be organised charabanc trips. And how'd you keep a check on them in the crush? Some would get a dozen free drams, not just one. Sam, if we win the Cup you're ruined."

Malarkin did not respond to those squeaking jests but seemed to be trying to spit out fragments of the beetle in his mouth.

Angus Tennant, another committee-man, the dunce, low-browed and skelly-eyed, thrust in his sycophantic face. "It was mean of them," he muttered, "to drag in Margot." At the same time, in a melancholy lust, he thought of her at the winning of the Cup serving every man in Drumsagart, with a turn for him-self. His own wife Nell was jovial and obliging, but she was so fat three of her could block the space between the goalposts.

"I'm sorry," said Rutherford abruptly and harshly, "I'm sorry if I seemed to act out of turn."

They fell silent, outwardly respectful towards a man contrite. Donald Lowther's respect was sincere; his sympathy towards any creature in trouble belied his yellowed lugubrious face.

"That's all right, Andrew," he said. "Nobody's blaming you. They had to be pacified somehow. I thought they were going to be nasty. There's no anger more terrible than football anger."

"Bunch of cowards," grunted big Henry Neilson, the plumber.

"I didn't hear you confront them, Henry. Like the rest of us, you were glad to leave it to Andrew."

"He's president."

"Sam spoke up," said Tennant. "It was him got them away in a good temper."

"Here's my boy," said Rutherford, again harshly.

They knew he meant they must now guard their speech. One or two of them, snubbed in the past, had entertained the hope that some day he'd find worse to preserve the boy from than a stray swear or randy laugh. Nor were they assuaged by the knowledge, common to everybody but Rutherford himself, that the boy, thick-headed enough at the Academy he paid fees to attend, was as gleg as any thirteen-year-old ought to be in his understanding of the facts of life.

Rutherford saw none of the winks exchanged. He put his arm round Gerald's neck in affectionate apology for the roughness with which he had ordered him away. This public display of love, so rare in Drumsagart as indeed in all Scotland, he had always been capable of. If it was a softness of nature, more suitable for the gushing English, he never regretted it or tried to restrain it. As a boy he'd often embarrassed his two brothers by hugging them or taking their hands in sight of strangers.

"We'll have to hurry home now, Son," he said. "Your mother will be getting anxious."

Anxious was not the honest word, but he was resolved to be loyal to Hannah and shelter her from her own faults. Some day Gerald must grow up and judge with adult perception. Rutherford shrank from that day; he could not bear to think of his son striding bravely and eagerly out of the sunlight into the shadows and dubiety of manhood; but of course there was nothing he could do to stop it.

By this time most of the crowd had gone. It was safe now even for the referee to appear, dressed in mufti, with his kit in a small suitcase that during the week was used for his daughter's school books. He murmured an apologetic farewell and then hurried away, with his fee jingling happily in his pocket.

As the officials themselves were about to disperse there was hurled in their direction a solitary shout, hoarse, malevolent, yet with a kind of humour in it.

"Scab!"

They saw the shouter. Though he was about seventy yards away, near the gates, he stood on the highest part of the terracing there, outlined against the grey sky. He seemed to have his hands in his trouser pockets and was bent forward, as if peering at something on the ground or contemplating a pain in his belly.

He did not repeat the shout, but after a minute, during which his slouch seemed by simple necromancy to convey a virulence of amused hatred, he suddenly straightened and, still with hands in pockets, vanished behind the terracing.

All on the pavilion steps, including the boy, glanced cautiously at the president. He stood gazing towards where his brother had been. There was no anger on his heavy face, only sorrow, suffering, and bewilderment. One hand remained on his son's shoulder, the other made an abortive gesture, of waving, of summoning his brother to come back to him; not just across the seventy yards of ash terracing and grassy field, but across the barrenness of ten years' estrangement and grudge.

"Aye, aye," muttered Tennant, with a twisted smile; then he went into the pavilion to take the kink out of his amusement.

The rest followed, leaving Lowther.

"Never mind, Andrew," he murmured.

"But I do mind, Donald," said Rutherford, "and I don't care who kens it. You ken if it was left to me it would be different."

"I ken, Andrew. But human affairs aye get into a fankle."

"When we were his age," said Rutherford, indicating his son, "you couldn't hae found better pals than we were. You ken that, Donald. Many a time I'm sure we wouldn't play wi' you because we had one another."

Lowther nodded.

"Gavin was there as weel, of course. We were three inseparables. You saw old Tinto Brown? I mind once, behind Caughey's pigsty, we found him helpless, paralytic drunk he was, wi' his nose streaming blood. We wrestled him hame, the three of us, for fear the police would get him. We liked Tinto."

"It's not everybody likes him," said Lowther gloomily.

"That's so, and right enough he's been an old reprobate in his days, but he's part of the history of the town."

"There's many in Drumsagart would feel cheated if he escaped the lowes of hell."

Rutherford had turned to go, but suddenly he swung back and stared into his friend's sad face. "Where are those lowes, Donald, if not in here?" and he tapped his chest once, twice, in blows that by their very gentleness suggested great affliction.

Then he was gone.

They were watching from the pavilion window.

"Some day," said Wattie Cleugh, "it'll come to blows."

"If it does," grinned Tennant, "it'll not be the first time."

"Can you keep a secret?" smirked Malarkin.

They nodded and crowded round him so close they could smell the scent off him amidst the stench of sweat and liniment.

"I was hearing," whispered Malarkin, "that our noble-hearted and forgiving president's been paying Robbie's rent for years past."

Cleugh twittered but frowned. "How can that be, Sam? Surely Robbie would never accept such charity."

"Pride stops short at money," muttered Neilson; it was his profoundest belief.

"Robbie doesn't ken," said Malarkin. "It's an arrangement between Isa and our president and the man wha told me."

"Was that Jordan the factor?"

"Secret, Angus."

"D'you think," whispered Tennant, "there's onything in what they say aboot Andrew and Isa?"

"You're forgetting Andrew's superintendent of the Sunday school."

"I'm forgetting nothing, Sam. Isa's a soft-hearted soul. Maybe there's more in the arrangement than you think."

"It could be."

"There he goes," whispered Tennant.

They watched Rutherford move off with his arm round his son.

"That boy's a Gemmell," said Neilson, "not a Rutherford at all. We'll live to see him laughing at his faither."

"As it tells us in the good book," said Cleugh, "it's not for us to judge a man or say what his fate should be. That's in other hands than ours, and, I'm thinking, in far more skilful hands. I mean, could we, d'you think, have invented Hannah Rutherford?"

They all shook their heads and softly laughed.

2

Walking towards the main street, Rutherford and his son passed some posters; one showing a gigantic young housewife in ecstasy over a tin of scrubbing-powder in her hand, and another with a huge box containing pills that claimed, by moving the bowels regularly, to make the eyes bright and the soul joyful. Rutherford, as he glanced at them, thought of Hannah unhappy in her well-scrubbed well-furnished home, and of his brother Robbie, once so cheerful and convivial, who now, out of unforgiveness and malignancy, made a game without meaning or end.

He swerved into a soliloquy on young Elrigmuir.

"I hope for Mysie's sake the boy's not an awful dud. Next week they'll howl like wolves at him if he doesn't satisfy them; and to satisfy them he'll have to play as if he'd wings as well as feet. It'll break Mysie's heart, especially if she's fond of the lad, as I'm sure she is, though she denied it. It's always like that wi' young folk in love: accused of it, they deny it with passion and temper; but they're guilty all the same, thank God."

Smiling, he pretended to notice suddenly his son walking and chattering by his side, one of the young, for whom, with a little luck, the benediction of love lay ahead. For a minute or two he kept apart from Gerald in mind and tried to foresee the girl he would marry. Let her be bonny, he thought, but as an extra: first, she must be loyal, then generous, then sympathetic; if these, she would be happy and her children fortunate. As he came close to his son again, Rutherford felt confident that embodied in this boy, as in all children, was a great store of human wealth, returning a far more valuable interest than any amount of money in the bank.

Gerald was talking about the films showing that night in the town's two picture-houses.

One was a cowboy, the other a tearful, kissing love-story. Gerald grumbled his mother would be sure to prefer the latter. Rutherford, amazed and humbled, agreed: Hannah, so mercenary in her ambitions, nevertheless had a weakness for films where all was lost for love; though while others wept she criticised. Obscurely he realised there must be deep in her a green sunny meadow shut off by thick stunted trees and rocky deserts. Surely if he was unable to penetrate to it, even to look on it for an instant, the fault must be his? Glancing down at his son, he wondered why he could not follow him through the trees and across the sands. But Hannah was as vigilant and hostile as any redskin; she would lie in wait and prevent him.

"All the same," he said, "it's up to us, as men, to leave the choice to your mother."

"But I hate love-pictures."

"No, don't say you hate them, Son. They're maybe a bit simpler in their outlook than they should be, but they're often truer to life than the stories about cowboys and Indians. The Indians weren't always the villains, you know, though the films make them oot to be."

Suddenly Gerald turned and looked back.

"What is it?" asked his father.

"I thought that man was Uncle Robbie."

His father, taken in, stared anxiously at the stranger.

"It's not him," muttered Gerald.

"No. No, that's not him." Rutherford smiled, and then, in a confusion of boyhood memories, expected an arrow in his back. Robbie's voice could be heard uttering war-cries and claiming a victim. The president almost sank down on to his knees, coughing up blood.

They entered the famed main street. It was said to be the widest in Scotland, with its pavements broad enough to contain many flowerbeds and more than fifty trees. From its lamp standards hung wire baskets filled with flowers; now, at this summer's end, red geraniums. Snapdragons crowded the plots, lemon, yellow, pink. Bees and wasps buzzed in from surrounding fields, and butterflies flitted in and out of shops, chased by children.

The great tower of the Town Hall with its four clocks dominated the street. It was high, with several turrets all out of symmetry; architecturally odd perhaps, but to a Drumsagart man's heart beautiful and exalting. Exiles in America and Australia were known to close their eyes and see that tower constant against the shifting sky.

Beside it stood the parish kirk with its ancient graveyard. Of the original building founded in John Knox's time only a square tower remained, roofless, with rowan trees growing in it. Nobody was sure who lay buried there; not a name was to be made out on the smooth slabs; but most people supposed they had ancestors under that hallowed grass. Daffodils grew there in the spring, and there were several rowans now in crimson berry, which in olden times had been credited with the power to ward off evil spirits that menaced both living and dead.

The old gateway survived. After angry dispute it had been preserved as an historical relic; some had demanded its demolition as an eyesore. On its archway was carved the date 1565, and

33

within it stood, like a lidless stone coffin on end, a sentry-box whose purpose the antiquaries still debated. The popular opinion was that it had been installed in Covenanting times when church services were held in defiance of the law and armed sentries had to be posted.

Rutherford liked to linger at that gateway, as he did that evening. Gazing through the rusty bars, he saw again in that cold stone, mossy box himself as Covenanter, faithfully sentinel, standing there in loneliness, while the dead slept and inside the kirk the living prayed, safe under his surveillance.

"Come on, Dad," urged Gerald. "Look, it's twenty past five."

Slowly, from his son representing the impatient present, Rutherford left the sad, resolved past to gaze up at the great white clock in the tower. Clouds tinged by the pink of evening were higher still. He remembered how many times from all over Drumsagart, from hundreds of loved, unforgettable places, with Gavin and Robbie he had looked towards these clocks to see if it was time to go home; to their father grumpy over the salvation of the world, and to their mother placid and uncomplaining over their own particular salvation. Now she was dead, and Gavin lay buried in France, and Robbie was estranged. Smiling, in tears almost, with one hand on his son's fidgeting shoulder and the other clasping the corroded bar of the gate, Rutherford for a minute felt in his imagination all those personal memories flow like a tributary into the wider calmer past, that itself flowed serenely towards an unknown sea.

The boy tugged his father's jacket.

"You know my mother'll be angry if we're late, and we're late already."

Rutherford returned. He looked down at his son's fretful face. The bar became cold and dirty in his grip. The stone box was seen to have in it, drifted in from the street, discarded bus-tickets, fag-ends, spent matches, bits of orange peel, and scraps of sweetie paper. Things were as Hannah saw them.

"Well, should we be moving on?" he asked.

His son gasped at the fatuousness of that question; he looked then very like his mother.

"There's one thing," he said, "we'll not have time to look in at Grandfather."

"You think not?"

"How could we, Dad? Look at the time. There'll be queues at the picture-houses, and we've still to get our tea."

"Your mother's got influence."

They moved on, Gerald hurrying and trying to make his father hurry.

"Surely we've got a minute to spare?" asked Rutherford, with a strange smile.

"No, no."

"To peep in at the window just?"

"No, Dad. You'll look in too long. You know you will. Remember what my mother said."

"I remember that your grandfather's a fine old man, and he's lonely."

"Yes, but we've got to hurry, Dad."

"Sergeant Elvan said good men are scarce. I said it wasn't true. I like to take the optimistic side of an argument, even against myself. But is it true? Surely to God it canna be." Then he laughed, in such a way as to cause not only Gerald to glance at him with sharp disapproval, but one or two passers-by as well: it was laughter with private anguish in it, not fit for the open street. "Funny thing is my faither, your grandfaither, is always condemning folk: lazy-minded he calls them, selfish, lunatics that waste their time on films and football. Yet he's sure the day will come when the brotherhood of man will be set up on earth, and all his life he's been working to bring that day nearer. Now take me, on the other hand: I just can't believe this brotherhood will ever come to pass. It's not in me to see it, maybe because I'm one of the dull and selfish and lazy-minded. Yet I like folk. There's nothing I like better than to be among them when they're all laughing and friendly. That's why I became a football man; well, it's one of the reasons. I admire the skill and excitement of the game too. But is that not queer now? Your grandfaither despising folk and yet seeing them some day in glory; me liking them, but seeing them get no better and no worse. Is it that I'm really religious, as he says? Am I for leaving the glory till after daith?"

They came to the corner of the side-street down which lay the dingy little ex-barber's shop, now the I.L.P. headquarters, where his father this Saturday evening would be busy among the faded placards and the dusty pamphlets.

"There's no time," insisted Gerald shrilly.

"There would be time for sweeties, though," muttered his father, who immediately repented. "All right, son, we'll just push on home." As he resumed his introspections he no longer spoke aloud lest he should corrupt the boy. Superintendent of the Sunday school though he was, he could not swear, with hand on Bible, he was convinced there was an after-life where he would meet Gavin again and their mother. That Hannah seemed to find such a belief easy astonished him, especially as she had no scruple about maligning or even threatening the dead, including his mother.

I'm a fraud all the same, he thought, and Robbie's accusation —scab, which meant sordid traitor—began to reverberate in his mind. Worse, though, than betraying your fellow-workers was, as church-goer, as elder, as superintendent, to renounce heaven and so abandon his mother to the clay for ever and make all children transitory as roses. A fraud, he kept thinking, but how in Christ's name can any man avoid it?

When they turned into the quiet avenue of semi-detached cottages where they lived they noticed a car outside their gate. Gerald was instantly interested.

"Whose is it?" he asked. "It's a Morris. It's not Uncle Harry's; his is a Bentley."

"I couldn't say," said Rutherford shortly. Years ago he'd bought a car himself, after much bullying by Hannah, but he'd proved to be an unconfident driver. Dourly, despite Hannah's almost hysterical sarcasms and the boy's disappointment and outspoken loss of faith, he'd given it up, pretending he found no pleasure in it.

"I know whose it is," cried Gerald, as they came nearer. "It's the new minister's. Do you think he's here to stop us going to the pictures?"

"Don't be silly." Yet as he spoke Rutherford was thinking it might well be. The young minister had arrived from the wilds of Dumfriesshire just three months ago, and he'd been behaving circumspectly, as any wise man does in his new job. But there had been hints, a frantic flash of big pale freckled hands, a hugging of the Bible, a sudden discordance in the decorous voice. It could be the young man was evangelical. Well, it would be odd in these days of idleness to cavil at a man doing his work too

36

enthusiastically, especially where there was no chance at all of his working a mate out of a job. All the same, if he tried it he'd soon find there were many odd people in his douce-seeming flock.

Gerald inspected the car and sneered at several signs of decrepitude. His father ignored it, but paused inside the gate to gaze at his own cherished roses, and even to stoop and lift from the dark soil some shed petals. He crouched with them in his hands, smelling their fragrance, feeling their silkiness, admiring their colour, and pitying their transience.

"It's an old model," said Gerald. "I bet if it did over thirty it'd fall to bits."

His father let the petals drop, one by one, ritually, as if in a kind of measurement.

Gerald had been right. The minister was in the sitting-room, with one of Hannah's best cups, all roses itself, in his hand; on the arm of his chair, on a fragile plate to match, were crumbs of cake of her own excellent baking. Fewer crumbs were scattered down the front of his dark-grey jacket, but enough to indict him of untidiness—in that house next to ungodliness—and Andrew noticed immediately his wife's eyes pecking at her Persian carpet, where more crumbs lay.

The Reverend Mr. Lockhart was lanky, with uncouth elbows and knees. He had sandy hair and many freckles. His mouth was small and his lips had a habit of still further diminishing for moments at a time till they formed a tight ball, expressing some indeterminate judgment upon either what was being discussed or what he was privately cogitating. More than Rutherford had already noted the idiosyncrasy—ascribed by some to diffidence, by others to an unfortunate tic, and by a few to lack of breeding. These last had discovered his father was a farm labourer. Certainly if the ladies of the guild were considering, say, the arrangements for whist drives to augment church funds, it was rude of the minister to be pondering in his mind the worth of Christ's sacrifice or the prerogatives of God. He was twenty-nine, and his wife was pregnant for the first time.

Hannah was seated on the one uncomfortable chair in the room, an elegant article with thin curved legs and no padding. It had been given to her as a birthday present by her brother Harry, who had asserted, with no one contradicting, that it was a genuine antique out of a nobleman's mansion and guaranteed to be worth at least a hundred pounds. Hannah sat up in it appropriately, like a countess, except for her irredeemably plebeian face, upon which, as usual, the wrinkles kept coming and going round the eyes and mouth, causing the minister to smile too and yet wonder what all the humour was. He was not the first to be deceived by those involuntary twitchings. Her hair was still black and was imprisoned within a wall of high pearled combs. Her erectness, and dozens of little black buttons, made her purple dress like a uniform.

The minister had been perched on the edge of his armchair, uncomfortable out of courtesy to his hostess. Now when Andrew came in he flung to his feet with a whirl of elbows and heave of knees.

"The cup," said his hostess sharply, with no alleviating smile.

As he apologised and set it down with stuttering caution on a table, she remarked, grimly sensible, "As you can see, it's a rare piece of china. Twenty pounds wouldn't buy the set."

"I'm sure it wouldn't," he murmured. At the same time his lips congealed: materialism he hated and he was under a suspended vow to attack it wherever it showed.

"They're seldom used," she added.

"I'm honoured then."

"I hope the day will never come when a minister of the gospel is not honoured in this house."

Andrew nodded towards the minister's chair. "Sit down, Mr. Lockhart." He sat down himself with a pech of relief. "I've been on my feet all afternoon."

"For your own pleasure," said his wife. "For nobody's good."

"That's true enough, Hannah. I'm sorry we're a shade late. The game finished a bit later than usual."

"Are you daring to lie to me, Andrew Rutherford, in the minister's presence?"

Andrew frowned. The minister found a lucky itch on his hand and scratched it.

"Gerald," said his mother, "there's no need for you to be here. Go and take your tea."

The boy hesitated. "What about the pictures?" he mumbled.

"Go when I tell you."

He went, obviously displeased. His mother smiled briefly after him.

38

"I know why you were late, Andrew," she said. "Mr. Lockhart has just been telling me."

Andrew turned to the minister, who met him with frankness.

"It's true, Mr. Rutherford," he cried. "I'm sorry to say I'm the clypeclash. You see, I was there myself this afternoon."

"You mean . . .?"

"Yes, at the game. I witnessed, I'm afraid, the wilting of the Thistle."

Andrew grinned; he felt one of his moods of irresponsible humour coming on. For propriety's sake he tried to resist it. He spoke solemnly. "Then you would hear all the cafuffle at the finish, in front of the pavilion?"

"I did."

"Well, I don't suppose you'd find it very edifying."

"Could anybody?" cried Hannah. "The blasphemous rubbish of scum and rogues and idlers."

"No," murmured Mr. Lockhart. "We must not judge too harshly."

Andrew nodded. "Mind you, to be candid, I doubt if any of them would worry much about our judgment, be it harsh or mild. But I never noticed you."

"I was disguised."

"Disguised?" Again that humour simmered.

"It's not meant to be funny, Andrew," said Hannah.

"Well, perhaps it is a little odd," admitted the minister. "I suppose ministers are uncommon kye to be seen at football matches."

"Not altogether," said Andrew. "There's a Churches' League, you ken, and ministers whiles turn out to watch their team playing. I've heard it said there's some pretty wild stuff at such games, and the language is scarcely Christian."

"The language is scarcely Christian anywhere, Mr. Rutherford."

"Maybe not. But you haven't said what your disguise was. Maybe I'll be borrowing it next Saturday. If Mysie's young man's a flop they'll be after me with hatchets."

"Disguise was hyperbole," said the minister, somewhat stiffly. "I merely meant I was there as a civilian, without any outward sign of my calling."

Andrew laughed. "Would one of your old collars, d'you think, disguise me? If it didn't, it might at least protect me."

"Andrew!" Hannah's brows darkened.

Mr. Lockhart's grew paler. "I'm afraid I'm keeping you from your tea."

"Well, I am a bit peckish, and to be honest with you, Mr. Lockhart, we had promised to take the boy to the pictures."

"I see. Of course I apologise for detaining you, but my justification is that I wish to speak to you on a matter of supreme importance."

"There's no need to apologise," said Hannah. "God's work is more important than eating or going to the pictures."

Her husband was accustomed to such sanctimony, but he was sure her brother Harry in his enlargement on top of the piano, with the pearl in his tiepin, winked.

Mr. Lockhart, the outsider, was deluded; he stared at her with startled respect; even in the crassest materialist, he reflected, was hidden a pearl of spirituality.

He spoke earnestly, with hands clasped. "What you have just said, Mrs. Rutherford, sums up my religious philosophy. Eating and pleasure-seeking are, I'm sorry to say, the chief preoccupations of most people today. It is my duty, and my ambition, to change that in our own little corner of Drumsagart."

You've been here three months, thought Andrew, and I've been here forty-seven years; yet you calmly say 'our' little corner.

"You're taking on a hard job," he said.

"Yes, a very hard job. I think I learned today just how hard, and I am here to seek your help."

Andrew sat back. He felt there was to be an alignment of forces, the minister and Hannah and the unco-guid on one side, the likes of Tinto Brown on the other.

"I give my help every week," he said.

"Granted, but——"

"At the risk, mind you, of being called a fraud."

Mr. Lockhart had been straining forward; now he sagged back. "Christ Himself has been called a fraud many times," he said. "You are in good company."

"Aye, but in my case it might be true."

Hannah uttered a gratified sniff. The minister, discreeter here between man and wife than between God and any sinner, gave no sign he'd heard: yet amidst his other perplexities he had to decide whether Mrs. Rutherford's vow-breaking disloyalty to her husband was justified in face of the latter's manifest Laodicean attitude to religion. He poked a finger between neck and collar, but really he was seeking more space in brain and soul.

"Self-criticism is a useful exercise," he said slowly, "and I agree it is practised too rarely; but if the result of it is to make one doubt one's religious sincerity, surely one does not remain satisfied at that point? Surely the proper and inevitable course is to regain one's faith and consolidate it?"

Andrew's smile was a rueful how.

"One thing I can tell you," cried his wife. "You'll never do it by hobnobbing with the scruff at the football field."

Gerald peeped in then, his face smeared with chocolate cream. She waved him away.

"And you take my son there to pollute his young mind."

"No, Hannah. I take him because he's fond of football. Into the bargain he's a good wee player himself. I admit he'll hear a rough word or two there, but to avoid that we'd have to flit to a monastery in Tibet."

Mr. Lockhart smiled. "It is true the world is a rough place, Mr. Rutherford, but I must ask you to confess that 'rough' is hardly an adequate description of the language I heard this afternoon. That it would be coarse I expected, but I did not dream it would be so consistently blasphemous." He took a small notebook from his pocket. "I intended to keep a record."

"Don't tell me," said Andrew, laughing, "you jotted down every swear you heard?"

"Hardly. But I did intend to note how often Our Lord's name was taken in vain. It was, of course, impossible, and in any case my soul sickened. I gave up at thirty-five."

"Their swears are meaningless, though; like coughs or spits. No harm's done."

"I'm afraid blasphemy's not a thing I can afford to be so cosy about. Of course I was aware I was hearing only a small section of the crowd. To arrive at an approximate total I should have had to multiply by a hundred at least."

"And it was just the one match too," murmured Andrew. "All over Scotland were thousands of others, with the language not much purer."

"Are you glorifying in it?" cried Hannah.

"No, Hannah."

"It sounds like it to me."

"No one could glorify in it, Mrs. Rutherford," said the minister; "no one save Satan himself, in whose service those profanities are uttered."

Andrew smiled, as if to plead not to bring Auld Clootie, Hornie, or Nick into it.

The minister had seen that smile frequently on other lips, even on those he kissed so fondly, his wife's. "I know I am old-fashioned," he said intensely, "like the Bible itself. I do believe Satan works amongst us, perverting us in many ways."

"All of us."

"Yes, all of us; none is immune from his temptations."

"I'm no hand at theology, Mr. Lockhart, but should we not be left to our own cleansing?"

"Some folk," said Hannah, "enjoy their own filth. What cleansing do they ever do?"

The minister again clasped his hands and in his fervour seemed to be trying to throw them across the room like a football. "Did you know, Mr. Rutherford, there was a famous revival once in Drumsagart?"

"Oh, sure, I kent that. I could show you the slope where the crowds sat."

"Crowds, yes; multitudes in fact. I may say that revival was one of the inducements that brought me to Drumsagart."

Another was, thought Andrew, the hundred pounds a year more.

"On the slope above the swan pond in the public park," said the minister. "They came from all airts. There were, I believe, some wonderful conversions."

"How long did they last, I wonder?"

"I believe the time is ripe for another such revival. We have become in Scotland a race of pagans, we who used to die for our religion."

"And kill too."

"That's your father's talk," cried Hannah.

"It's the truth for all that," he said, remembering the stone box in the old kirk gateway and the armed sentry joining in the forbidden psalms.

"Football is their religion now," said the minister.

"I wouldn't go as far as that. The Scots have always had a violence in their souls. Nowadays they express it at football; long ago religion was the outlet."

"Is it as simple as that, Mr. Rutherford?"

"More or less."

"No. There was an old man yonder." Mr. Lockhart smiled his charity out of a blaze of horror. "He is beyond his allotted span, I should say. He is very close to his Creator and Judge, and yet out of his mouth came stream after stream of dreadful ribaldry."

Andrew grinned. "Had he a crooked stick, and an auld cap with the skip over his ear?"

"Yes, those; and also a laughter, or I should rather say a cachinnation that came not merely from an aged human throat but from the bottommost pit of depravity. Yonder surely is a perfect example of Satan's handiwork."

"I hardly think so. The Deil goes in for smoother material than auld Tinto. Whoever guards the gates of heaven will have little to do if they turn Tinto away. If it's punishment you want to insist on, then let me assure you Tinto's not escaping. In the first place, he was a miner all his days, and now he's retired to poverty. Then he's got some kind of internal disease that causes him agony. He lives on the charity of a poor woman wi' a squad of weans and therefore an uncertain temper. He's half starved. He's in rags."

"Are you asking us to pity yon old scoundrel?" cried Hannah.

"Tinto would thank nobody for pity. But I am asking you not to hate him and wish him into hell-fire: for your own sake as much as for his."

"Don't think," she whispered, "I don't understand."

The minister had been gazing down at his clasped hands; his mouth was very small and firm; he stood up.

"Mr. Rutherford," he said hoarsely, "I came here to ask you one favour. Now I must make it two."

"If I can I'll oblige."

"First, then, I must beg you to consider profoundly if you feel you ought to continue in the meantime as superintendent of our Sunday school?"

If Andrew was taken aback, Hannah was outraged.

"How is that necessary?" she cried. "I'd like to remind you,

Mr. Lockhart, the man that was superintendent before had the name of slipping into a backroom of Malarkin's pub."

"If I am to conduct a revival, Mrs. Rutherford, I must have as my assistants men and women of impregnable faith."

He'll empty the kirk, thought Andrew; he'll empty it, and then he'll have to go cringing to them to come back. He's got the right idea, but in a year's time he'll be as tame a preacher as there is in the land.

"As a matter of fact," he said, "you've anticipated me. I've been thinking of resigning for a while. I never really thought I was suited for the job. The only qualification I had was that the weans seemed to like me."

The minister shook his head resolutely as if that liking, though precious, wasn't enough.

But Hannah was far from appeased. "You can carry everything too far," she said, "and that goes for religion too. I'll tell you frankly, Mr. Lockhart, I don't approve for a minute this notion of a revival. Let folk stew in their own juice. The kirk is always open if they want to go. And what harm have I done?"

As she waited for an answer he had to say: "You, Mrs. Rutherford?"

"Yes, me. Why should I be the victim? Surely you must see that if he's disgraced I'm the one who'll suffer? I haven't many friends in this place, I'm glad to say; but what friends I have are associated with the Church. Am I to have them laughing at me and triumphing over me? It's no good shaking your head either. I know Drumsagart folk better than you."

Andrew ended the pause that followed.

"You mentioned two favours," he said, smiling.

"Yes. I intend to apply for permission to address the crowds at your football matches. I want you to support my application."

Hannah snorted significantly. Andrew had to be content with rubbing his nose.

"Would it be wise?" he asked.

"I'm not afraid of violence."

"Och, nobody would throw as much as a tattie-crisp at you. I meant you might be discouraged in your wish for a revival. They'd resent you. They'd look on it as an unwarrantable interference. They'd argue they didn't march into the kirk on Sunday to lecture you on football."

"Would you support that argument, Mr. Rutherford? Man cannot serve two masters; here it is Christ or Moloch. You must choose your allegiance."

"I'd rather not choose. Suppose you got permission, how would you address them? We send our messages round the park chalked on a blackboard. There's only an old megaphone yonder."

"I could use that."

"At half-time, d'you mean?"

"At any time."

"Not during the game itself surely?"

"Mr. Rutherford, this is to me no jest. The most suitable time obviously would be during the interval."

"Aye, but you'd have Bob McKelvie to contend with."

"Who is he?"

"He's the pipe-major of Drumsagart Pipe Band. They often play at half-time and take a collection. It's a privilege they've had for years."

"No doubt the pipe band is an admirable institution, but my purpose supersedes it."

"Bob would be a hard man to convince."

"Conviction *is* hard. Will you support my application?"

Hannah gave a quick nod, as if to shake off a fly: it was an instruction to Andrew to agree, on condition he was reinstated as superintendent. He saw it and smiled.

He's genuine enough, Andrew was thinking; he really wants to save us all, whether we want it or not; and he thinks he can do it by bawling platitudes through a broken megaphone. He'll be shattered before long, and soured; or, worse, he'll be turned into a simpering nonentity.

"No, Mr. Lockhart," he said at last, "I don't think I can support you."

Hannah frowned: it was a warning that after rejection came bargaining.

Mr. Lockhart smiled. "I'm sorry you see it that way."

"I'm saying no, mind you, because I think it's in your best interests."

"Thank you. Of course I must be the judge of what are my best interests. Well, I must be going now."

Andrew rose to his feet. "I'm sorry."

45

"Mr. Malarkin, I believe, might assist me."

"He might."

"If you'll pardon me saying it, Mr. Lockhart," said Hannah, "I think that religion and drink go as ill together as religion and football."

He bowed his head humbly. "I must beg your pardon, Mrs. Rutherford. I know I have hurt and disappointed you."

"I let nobody and nothing hurt me, Mr. Lockhart."

Startled, he went stiff and erect. "A stoic philosophy. How I wish I could emulate you."

"I'll see you out," said Andrew, and led the way to the door.

On the doorstep the minister, hat in hand, turned. "There's something else I ought to tell you."

Andrew waited sympathetically. Beyond the minister's anxious freckles he saw his withering roses, and beyond them in imagination old Tinto Brown's ravaged face.

"I've been invited to stand as candidate for the Lightburn ward."

"My faither's ward?"

"Yes."

There was a silence. Both smelled the dying roses.

"If you want to enter politics," said Andrew, "why choose that ward? My faither happens to be the best councillor this town has ever had."

"It is right for you to think so," said the young man gently. "Your father has certainly done some material good, but it seems to me, and to others, that that good is more than outweighed by the harm he's done spiritually."

"Harm? What harm? Speak plainly, please. I don't care for insinuations of that sort."

"There's no need to be angry. You wish me to speak plainly?"

"I certainly do."

"It is best. Your father is an avowed atheist."

"Oh, how can you ken that? How can he ken that himself?"

"He boasts of it publicly. But I must hurry now, Mr. Rutherford. I promised my wife not to be long. She's not feeling too well these days."

Rutherford dourly said nothing.

The minister strode down the path. He fumbled with the gate. "Your roses must have been very beautiful."

Rutherford made no acknowledgment. You're not going to betray my father, he thought, and then think to placate me by praising my roses.

The minister had opened the gate but had not yet gone out. He seemed absorbed, perhaps in admiration of the roses. Then he was returning up the path, his face pale, determined, but peculiarly humorous.

"You may laugh at me, Mr. Rutherford, but I shall not mind."

"I'm not likely to laugh."

"Your team, the Thistle, I understand, has been faring very badly for some time."

"Aye."

"Might it not be that, with regenerate spectators, a transformation might take place?"

Andrew frowned; he could not appreciate such humour. "Are you for winning the Cup for us?"

"Who knows?" Mr. Lockhart softly laughed. "The Cup, like the Holy Grail itself, is there for the winning."

This time going down the path he almost ran. It seemed as if he would vault the gate. As he entered his car and drove off, joy and confidence were in the spinning of the wheels and in the clatter of the engine as much as in his valedictory wave.

Watching him, Andrew was thinking: if you wanted to oust somebody from the council, why not Malarkin, the publican? Is it true, after all, what my father says: the kirk has always kowtowed to money and position, and always will?

But as he listened to the noise of the car fading he remembered that whatever Lockhart was as a minister, sincere or hypocritical, saint or fool or sham, as a married man he was very lucky. His wife was not only bonny, she was also a very friendly, honest, sensible woman, who loved him and would stand by him though everybody jeered and though she herself in her inmost heart thought his fervency futile.

47

3

In the main street, in the middle of the pavement, not far from the Lucky Sporran, stood an imitation of the original thirteenth-century Mercat Cross. It consisted of twelve concentric steps dwindling as they ascended towards a column about twelve feet high with a small prancing unicorn at the top. When it had first been set up the council had decreed that sitting on it and even spitting on it were offences punishable by fines of not less than five shillings; but since then authority had tired, time had deposited its own immune scurf, a well-known historian had declared in a Glasgow newspaper that the design was in some details spurious, and the unemployed had increased to such an extent that the benches provided in the main street were no longer sufficient. So the Cross had become an accepted forum; the steps of granite made convenient seats for men hardened by life's kicks. There daily, including Sundays, the Drumsagart vernacular resounded, more authentic and ancestral than the Cross itself. Oaths of ferocity and pertinence were commonplace. Spits of emphasis splashed on the pavement and stayed there to adorn the argument. Sometimes silences fell, during which the traffic rushed by, and despair, meek as mice or beetles, played among the spittle. An elm tree's furthest branches tickled the unicorn, and in autumn wiry black-spotted leaves kept tinkling down. Even in a thunderstorm there might be a quorum.

Football was, of course, the favourite subject. Most were connoisseurs, expert, professorial, knowledgeable, highbrow; many were pedants. All were conversant with, as it were, the classics—that is, the great encounters in the past between famous teams—which set the standards of play. Only a dunderhead was ignorant of the career, prowess, and quirks of any given inter-nationalist. As in literature or music or in any art there are fashions, so in football; and any septuagenarians with ideas obstinately stuck in outmoded principles and techniques were irritants at the Cross. One particularly resented was Tinto Brown. Not only were his opinions antiquated, they were frequently heretical, not to say iconoclastic. Often, had it been detachable, the irascible Tinto would have been stabbed or stunned by the unicorn's horn.

During the days that followed the protest meeting outside the pavilion the talk at the Cross concentrated on Mysie Dougary's Alec Elrigmuir, and more abstrusely on the president's constitutional right to arrange the trial without a vote of the committee. The majority concluded he had been dictatorial, as usual. Under his pretence of good-fellowship he had got his own way. Not even Sam Malarkin's clever dig had deflated him, seeing it wasn't wind he was full of, but sawdust and biscuit crumbs. It was almost to be hoped that Elrigmuir would prove to be not just a crude learner but the most stinking of haddies, a chimpanzee indeed in white shorts and blue jersey. In that case, though Mysie might blush and greet, big Rutherford would not be able to hide his discomfiture.

The minority, led by Tinto, hoped Elrigmuir would be a star, not for Rutherford's sake or Mysie's, but for the Thistle's. Tinto, however, displeased even his own supporters by his perverse and extravagant optimism.

"Do you ken what I'm going to prophesy?" he cried, as he crouched on the top step, with his stick hung by its handle above him from the unicorn's horn.

"Take a peek at him," said one, "a prophet wi' soup on his waistcoat."

"And his fly-buttons loose."

"And the skip of his bonnet ower his ear."

"And a reputation to make the Deil blush."

"And holes in his socks."

"And dirty feet."

"And no hanky, and a damned great need for one."

Tinto snorted. "I'm prophesying that this young chap Elrigmuir will turn oot to be the greatest player the Thistle ever has had. I'm prophesying he'll win the Cup for us; and surely"—here he cackled his old lecher's, boozer's, blasphemer's laugh—"Sam Malarkin will fill it up wi' whisky and let me drain it for him, quick, in case the silver rusts. Then I'll dee. Then you can shovel me under."

More raillery was flung up at him, mostly on the tantalising subject of his reception in the halls of heaven. He gave it all back,

49

with many cackles. One or two behind joking faces thought the old man rash.

Soon he rose up with creaks and grunts, lifted down his stick, and descended the steps. Nobody helped him. They kept their hands in their pockets. Once he nearly skidded. There had been a scene once when, tormented by fiercer stounds of pain than usual, he had been assisted against his passionate wish. He had gone berserk, swinging at them with his stick, spitting at them, frothing, cursing, weeping, and in the end crawling away, a sad, broken, betrayed old man in his long coat that trailed the pavement, and with the skip of his cap set so gallously over his ear.

"I'll tell you where I'm going," he announced, when safely and independently down.

"Where else would a prophet go to but the kirk?"

"Or the graveyard. They're all prophets yonder."

"Or Malarkin's pub. Plenty of profits there."

"I'm going to get the truth oot of Mysie," chuckled Tinto.

"She's snapped a dozen noses off already," he was told.

"She'll not snap mine off." He fingered its warm, swollen rosiness. "This is a nose that was never meant to be snapped off. Providence has been looking after this auld snout; it'll never dee. When the rest of me's gone you'll find it come floating past you here, like a bird, a flaming bird o' paradise. You'll get so used to seeing it you'll just say, wi' a nod: 'There's auld Tinto's nose again', and you'll get back to your blethers." Chuckling, he tottered along the pavement. Soon he turned round. "You'd better come along wi' me, Crutch," he cried to his crony. "At your age, I canna leave you there to have your mind corrupted."

Obediently Crutch, with help from two of the grinning corrupters, got to his feet, adjusted his crutch, and hopped after his friend.

Rab Nuneaton was there. "So Tinto's fond of big Rutherford?" he said. "Do you ken why?"

"Maybe because, Rab," came a blunt answer, "you're not."

"Tinto's thrawn," said a reconciler. "Most folk hae little to say in Rutherford's favour, so Tinto speaks up for him."

"That's not it at all," murmured Nuneaton.

"Tell us, Rab. You might as well relieve yourself; you're bursting to tell."

"Every Christmas," said Nuneaton, "Rutherford slips Tinto a pound note. It's been going on for years."

"Is that so?" asked the blunt fellow. His name was Saunders, and he had a very fat, rather dirty neck, round which was knotted, without the encumbrance of a collar, a greasy crimson crotcheted tie.

"That's so, Jock." Nuneaton's hinney had flattery in it, as well as malice and conceit.

"Then it's to Rutherford's credit," said Saunders in a voice and with a scowl that indicated the ultimate wisdom had been expressed by him on that subject and he would take it ill if anyone, especially Nuneaton, had the effrontery to add a word.

Nuneaton's hinney died away. Saunders was notorious for his violent temper.

A diplomat introduced a new topic: was Russia a slave state, or was it a workers' paradise?

Tinto and Crutch skulked outside the fruitshop in which Mysie served. They keeked in from behind chrysanthemums and cabbages, for the manageress, though a handsome woman smelling of flowers and peaches, seemed sour as goosegogs in her mind. She never saw the gallantry in Tinto's ogles; she called him a dirty old man, meaning more than feet or neck or clothes. She also called him a brazen thief, because she didn't have the imagination to understand that when he picked up a grape or plum, or even a sprig of parsley, and nibbled it deliciously outside the window in full view he was paying homage to her buxom blonde succulence. She just threatened to call the police.

"What money hae you got, Crutch?" he asked.

"Three ha'pence, Tinto."

Tinto puffed out his lips in scorn at such meagre fortune. He himself had nothing. "That makes three ha'pence," he muttered. "All right, it'll need to do. Hand it over. I'll hold your crutch."

Crutch demurred. "What are you going to do wi' it, Tinto? I'm saving up; anither ha'penny and that's a packet of Woodbine."

"And where are you going to get anither ha'penny? Hae you got a rich uncle in America that's due to dee? You've been seeing too many of these films, Crutch; they've softened your brains. Forby, you ken smoking's bad for you. It causes cancer of the lungs."

Crutch's pleasant face clouded. "But you smoke yourself, Tinto."

"I'm defying it, Crutch. You ken you've got a fear of cancer. Didn't your Uncle Erchie die of it?"

"That's right."

"Screaming."

"When I had to lose my leg," said Crutch, "I was terrified it was cancer."

"And it was just gangrene. You were always a worrier, Crutch."

"No, Tinto, that's not true. I was always one for smiling. The teachers at school called me the wee smiler."

"That wasn't yesterday. Rivers of blood hae flowed under the bridges since then."

"That's right. But I need to smoke now. If I don't smoke I get melancholy. Dr. Kiddie said I should smoke."

"Sure he did. Disease is his bread and butter. Crutch, I'm hurt. You're being mean to a lifelong friend."

Crutch could not resist that sudden whimper. He dropped the penny and ha'penny, one at a time, into his friend's hand.

Instantly Tinto straightened himself as much as he could, gave his coat a stroke or two as if it was fur, tugged at his cap, flung one hand behind him with knuckles pressed into his spine, and hobbled into the shop on lordly stick.

Luckily the manageress was having to fawn over a captious customer. Mysie was available.

"Well, Tinto?" she demanded.

"How much are your melons?" His tone was ducal; it hinted he might buy thousands.

She whispered: "Are you in to make a fool of me, Tinto Brown?"

He saw his chance. Hand at mouth, he asked: "This Elrigmuir, Mysie, do you think he's the boy? Will he win us the Cup? Is he big? Can he kick wi' his twa feet? What's his speed like? Don't tell me he's bald, for I don't trust centre-forwards wi' slippery heids, though, mind you, the goalie can never be sure what way the ball's going to skite."

Humour betrayed him; he began to laugh.

The manageress excused herself to the customer and rushed

along. Tinto sniffed and goggled at her, so blooming, so sweet-smelling, so ripe, and yet so bossy, such a waste of woman-flesh.

"You old ruffian," she said, "so you're in pestering us again?"

Haughtily he held up the penny. "I'm in to transact business," he said. "There's more where that came from." He chuckled as he thought how much more.

"Here," she cried, snatching up an apple and pushing it into his hand. "Now get out, and don't show your nose in here again."

"My nose," he repeated in delight, fondling it. Compared to his nose, that Californian pippin was pale.

"Aye, your nose; take it out of here, and the rest of you with it."

Mysie grabbed his arm and pushed him towards the door.

"That nose," cried the customer, "must have cost a king's ransom."

"Listen, Tinto," whispered Mysie, "do you want me to lose my job?"

"No, Mysie, no."

"Well, that's what will happen. Don't come in here again."

"But what if I take a notion for a melon?"

She ignored that, but said: "And he's not bald either."

"You mean this Elrigmuir? Will he score goals, Mysie?"

"Yes, he'll score goals. Now go and sit on a seat in the sun-shine and eat your apple."

She returned into the shop, and Tinto, with Crutch stumping after, made for an empty bench. Along at the Cross the men laughed at his quick repulse.

"Did you spend the whole three ha'pence, Tinto?" gasped Crutch shyly.

"I did not. Here it's back, the whole sum. Put it in the bank."

Crutch sat down beside him. "To tell you the truth, Tinto, I never had a ha'penny in the bank in my life."

"Then you should be ashamed of yourself. By God, it wasn't the likes of you gave the Scots the name of being a thrifty race."

"Had you ever a bank-book, Tinto?"

Tinto chuckled. "Not me. The pub was my bank, and my nose is my dividend. I got this apple from Jackson." He squinted at it, kissed it, and fondled it. "She's got grand breasts," he admitted. "Hae you got a knife?"

"Just the one I use for cutting 'baccy, when I've got some."

"D'you think," asked Tinto, "I'd eat an apple that's been cut by a filthy 'baccy knife? All my life, Crutch, I've been a pernickety man. Many a woman I've refused because she didn't pay enough attention to her hygiene. I'll get George Rankin to halve it. You hold on to this seat. If anybody makes to sit on it cough and spit and splutter as if you'd consumption. You'll need privacy to chew your apple, Crutch, for God kens you're the loudest chewer ever I heard."

"It's my teeth, Tinto. They move."

"Move?" muttered Tinto, as he shuffled towards Rankin's shop. "They damned well gallop."

No customer being in, Rankin the butcher was busy with his cleaver.

"Hello, Tinto," he said suspiciously.

"Still hacking up the deid coos, George?" asked Tinto, with a leer. "I'm in to ask a favour. Halve this apple for me. I got it frae an admirer, and I want to share it wi' poor auld Crutch out there."

Rankin, a brawny red man, glowered at the apple, and then guffawed. "You've got the cheek of the devil, Tinto. There'll be a smell of blood off it."

"I'm no vegetarian."

Still much amused, Rankin took the apple, laid it on a bit of the board less bloody than the rest, picked up a long thin knife, and solemnly operated.

Tinto patted a carcase hanging from a shining hook. "To think," he said, "you once walked in the sunshine and munched daisies."

"Your twa halves," said Rankin, with a flourish of his great beefy hand.

Fastidiously Tinto lifted them. "There's blood on it."

"I warned you."

"Well," said Tinto, "they tell me that where the battle of Bannockburn was fought wheat's growing now. We eat the blood of dead men in our daily bread."

"It's a long time since you left school, Tinto, but I see you're still a scholar."

"Aye. Thanks for halving the apple." As he went out into the sunshine he again patted the carcase. "I'll not be a hell of a long time after you," he muttered.

His despondency continued after he'd rejoined Crutch on the seat. Chewing apple and scowling about him, he muttered comments, ribald, scurrilous, and audible, upon anyone and anything he saw. A woman proudly pushed a new pram: its contents were not her husband's. Another sat on a window-ledge two storeys up, briskly cleaning the panes: outside show, the inside of her house was mucky. Christie's milk-cart rattled by: half the milk was water. The men along at the Cross were heard laughing: blamed the world economic situation for their idleness, but damned well enjoyed it all the same. A seagull flew overhead: a feathered numbskull, why stay in the stagnancy of Drumsagart when there were seven oceans to choose from? The minister rattled by in his car: an ass had been good enough for Christ. The apple had been a gift: Eve's to Adam had been free too, and it had soured the world.

Crutch kept whispering to him to be careful or he'd be overheard. When Tinto responded by raising his voice Crutch giggled. He, who found a simple pleasure in almost everything, enjoyed, too, his friend's witty misanthropy. When he became its victim and was charged with having the mind of a five-year-old lassie whose backside was underskelped he laughed till tears came, and his fingers ran up and down his crutch as if it was the flute he used to play.

"You don't kid me, Tinto," he said. "I ken there's not a man fonder of Drumsagart than you."

Tinto was so astounded by such percipience from a simpleton that he could find no immediate retort, and it was while he sat gaping at his friend that a great dusty van from Birmingham roared into the main street and stopped a few yards away. Out of the cabin climbed stiffly a squat man in a shiny blue serge suit, carrying a small parcel wrapped in brown paper. With his free hand he waved to the driver, who waved cheerfully back and then drove on.

His passenger, on cramped legs and with eyes either myopic or distrustful, came on to the pavement. There, to the amazement of the two old men, he suddenly stooped and rubbed his knuckles on the cement. When he rose again he filled his chest with more than ordinary air and stretched out his long arms, with one fist clutching the parcel.

"In the name of God," yelled Tinto, "do you see who it is?

It's Turk McCabe back again, Turk that disappeared five years ago to seek his fortune."

Tinto scooted across to the hunched, powerful man, who turned to greet him with a massive scowl that slowly faded and revealed behind it a sly, crass smile.

"If it's not auld Tinto," he said. "So you're still to the fore? Nobody's brained you yet?"

"Turk, you're a sight for sore een," cried Tinto.

Turk's grin properly acquired some modesty, with even a smirk of scepticism. He knew he was not handsome. He lacked several teeth. Neither his shirt nor jacket were buttoned at the front, and he wore no waistcoat; the thick black mat of his chest was visible. This had always been his dress, even in January snows. Turk was a famous iron man. Before his disappearance he'd been the Thistle centre-half and every week had saved it from ignominy. Though he'd trained on beer and fags and fish suppers he had never lacked wind or stamina or even speed. His head, an unlikely place for brains, nevertheless had been able to direct him about the field with success, anticipating the wiles of brainier men and frustrating them. In addition, though this was less wonderful, with that head he could propel a ball further and more fiercely than most players could with their feet. Opponents whose pavilion strategy had been to incapacitate Turk had found on the field of play that discreet elbows in his kidneys, subtle knees in his groin, even downright heels on his face, in no way impeded Turk but merely inspired him to impregnable defence and generous retaliation. Although revered in the town because of his effective and courageous play, he had never accepted friends. He had been known to take a toady's drink and then spit in his face. In the middle of a crowd at the Cross he had been alone.

"Sit down on this seat, Turk," said Tinto, acting as Drumsagart's host in the town's best reception room, its broad main street with the trees and flowers and turreted tower.

"I think I will, for a couple of minutes," muttered Turk, craftily peering about. "I can see there's not much changed."

"Hardly a thing, Turk. Auld Sammy Hunter's dead and buried. You used to like auld Sammy."

Turk pondered. "What about his dog, a big Airedale? He called it after me."

56

"Dead too."

"Run over?"

"They had to shoot it. It howled most damnably after Sammy. Folk couldn't get sleeping. It's a wonder you didn't hear it doon in England."

Turk shook his head; he hadn't heard it; but he heard it now. Then he spat, with pensive cunning. "How's my auld lady?" he asked.

"Your mither, Turk?"

"Aye. Is she gone?"

"No, Turk, no. But she's going down the brae fast."

"On roller skates, eh?" Turk grinned at his wit and rubbed his knuckles against his few teeth.

"You'll find her sore failed, Turk."

"I was expecting that. She's no chicken. Still as nippy wi' her tongue? Still sharp in the temper?"

Tinto sadly shook his head. "Not just as nippy, Turk. Nell's too worn out. She's not often seen in the street now. Like me, she's got a stick."

"Is that so?" Turk was impressed; he grinned. "A stick?"

"Aye, and she needs it too. Mine's for swank, but hers is for support. Did you come hame to see her, Turk, before it was too late?"

Turk spat again. "I came hame—to tell the Christ's truth, I don't rightly ken what brought me hame."

"You were in England?"

"Aye."

"Did you like the place?"

"It was all right, except for the beer. I never liked the beer."

"I'm glad to hear you've still got your Scots accent. This is Crutch Brodie. You'll mind of him?"

Turk nodded and Crutch was delighted.

"We're pleased to hae you back, Turk," he said shyly.

"How's the Thistle doing?" asked Turk.

Tinto groaned. "Hellish."

"Bad as that?"

"Worse. We're in tears every week."

"Who's running it? Is wee Wattie Cleugh still secretary?"

"And Andrew Rutherford's president," said Crutch, "and Sam Malarkin vice-president."

57

"Rutherford the auld councillor?"

"No, his son," said Tinto, "the one that manages the Biscuit Factory."

"Big chap wi' a moustache?"

"That's him. He's a good-hearted man, though few like him; but he doesn't count. What we need are new players. What about yourself, Turk? Hae you kept it up?"

"I can still kick a ball."

"Thunderbolts, Turk. I mind them weel."

"Coming up, I won this." Turk held up the parcel, and after reflection began to unwrap it. "At a fairground it was. A prize if you scored three goals wi' three shots."

"Who was the goalie?"

"It said on the bill he used to be an internationalist: fat fellow in a green jersey."

"And you scored the three goals?"

"I won this." Turk held it out with a wistful truculence: he didn't want Tinto and Crutch to think his prize ridiculous, but was afraid they might.

Certainly they found it surprising. It was a small china ornament or toy: a soldier in red coat and blue trousers held the hands of a lady in a white crinoline; they appeared to be dancing.

"You can wind it up and it goes. Look." Turk brought the key out of his pocket and solemnly wound up the toy. Then on the pavement he set down the lilliputian dancers tenderly, and off they went, gliding this way, then that, and swinging in circles.

"I could have taken something else," muttered Turk. "Fags. But I thought the auld lady would like this. Do you think she will?"

"She'll treasure it, Turk."

The dancers stopped.

"Make them dance again, Turk," begged Crutch, his eyes shining.

Turk obliged, and again the three of them in silence watched the performance.

When it was finished they discovered they had an audience. Several people had gathered.

Tinto jumped up.

"Here's Turk McCabe back from England," he cried. "You'll remember Turk, the best centre-half the Thistle ever had?"

"I remember him," snapped a woman called Braid, dustcap

58

on head, purse tight in hand. "I remember him fine. A drunkard who tormented the soul out of his poor auld mither. Is he back to plague her again? Aye, weel I remember your precious Turk. Didn't he do thirty days once for assaulting her? All I can say is, it's a pity he's come back, for we're weel enough supplied wi' trash as it is."

She walked away on stilts of scorn.

"God Almighty!" shouted Tinto. "I think she meant me. Trash!" He turned and screeched after her. "I've seen the day——" But he could not finish, owing to a deficiency of boast rather than of breath. "This town has seen its best days," he said bitterly. "Kind hearts are withered away. Why did you come back, Turk? You see what we're become: apples dropping frae a rotten tree."

"Well," said Turk placidly, with his dancers wrapped up again, "I'll get alang to see her. She's still at the same place?"

"That's right, Turk."

"I never wrote," admitted Turk, "and I never sent her any money. If she's not pleased to see me, don't blame her, though she is my mither. If she turns me away from the door, she's within her rights."

"Where will you sleep if she turns you away?" asked Tinto, passionately concerned for the rejected prodigal. "Crutch here has room."

Crutch gurgled in dismay. "If it was up to me, Turk, you'd be welcome; but I'm just a lodger wi' my daughter Kate. Maybe you remember my Kate? She's got a terrible temper. Sometimes she threatens to throw me oot. 'Oot you'll go,' she cries, 'crutch and all.' She took my flute away; said it drove her crazy."

"I'm in no position myself, Turk, to offer you hospitality," said Tinto, grandly sorrowful.

"I can always toss a brick through a shop window," remarked Turk, as he shambled off, "and get a bunk from the cops."

"Watch out, though, Turk," cried Tinto after him. "Elvan's a dangerous man. Once he's got you ahint the bars you're no better than a gorilla from the jungle to him."

Without turning Turk gave a wave of acknowledgment. Under a tree, in its shadow, he resembled a gorilla, as even Tinto noticed.

"We're all descended from apes," muttered Tinto. "Poor

59

Turk, to think five years ago they were proud if he condescended to take a pint from them."

"It's true, all the same, Tinto; he's never treated his mither well."

Tinto was about to sneer away such ill-treatment as trivial when he remembered his own kindness to his own mother forty years ago.

"Well," he mumbled, "give the man a chance. Maybe he's reformed. Maybe he's back to make amends. He's brought her a present, hasn't he, all the way from England? Well, what is there to be scared about?"

He sat on the seat and in gloomy silence answered his own question. He was scared that Turk, spurned and upbraided by Nell, who still had a squeal left in her, stick or no stick, would end her recriminations by banging her on the head with the toy dancers. There were more ways of earning a bed in a cell than by tossing a brick through a shop window.

4

On Saturday afternoon an observer from the Town Hall turret might have thought at first that the streets below were invaded by ants. There were several points of resemblance: the urgency of movement all in the same direction; the mass of dark clothes with the lighter caps like crumbs of food carried; and the convergence upon the green place at the end of the main street. But there were also some points of dissimilarity: no streams flowed steadfastly in the opposite direction; at the meeting-place there seemed no busyness of work at all, only a communal standing and waiting; and most dissimilar, in the very heart of the surge, at the Mercat Cross, a knot of idlers stood, resisting every seduction of instinct to be incorporated.

The leader of these nonconformists was Jock Saunders. To honour Saturday afternoon he wore a collar round his bulging neck, with, however, the same weekday tie and flea-stained shirt. He had his hands in his pockets, and his very knock-kneed stationariness was a rebuke to that flux of enslavement.

"D'you think," he kept shouting each time he was enticed, "I'm a mug? Am I Carnegie, that I can throw away fourpence on that shower of chanty-wrastlers? Are you all so soft in the heid to think you can turn a team of hams into champs by playing a raw boy at centre and an auld has-been at centre-half? You must all hae turned religious to believe in such a miracle."

He took a hand out of his pocket to seize Rab Nuneaton sneaking by.

"For a man wi' such a spite against Rutherford," he cried, "you fairly subsidise him."

"Just fourpence, Jock; and you ken it's the Thistle I'm subsidising, not Rutherford."

"Off you go, Rab; but never let me hear another snivel from you aboot Rutherford."

Released, Nuneaton hurried to make up for the minute lost. His eyes were on the pavement. "I'll snivel if I like," he muttered, "without asking your permission." But really he wished he had the spirit to stand there independent like Saunders and so be entitled to jeer at the pilgrims. He could not deny himself this escape to the football. Behind him in the house he'd left his wife moaning over swollen breasts, in terror of a new pregnancy; while the rest of his family, penances more present than hair shirt or iron belt, puled and squabbled and complained. He had had to swipe his eldest girl across the face with his cap for asking brazenly for a penny to go to the cinema matinee. If there was no football he felt he'd go mad as men did confined too long in solitary darkness; and it was necessary for him that the Thistle always lost, for in his subtle derogations lay his authority, prestige, and only joy.

Saunders stopped Tinto too.

"It's just as well you get in for nothing, Tinto," he said, "or I'd be rifling your pockets. I've as much right to rob you as the Thistle."

"It's going to be different the day, Jock. I can feel it in my bones."

"Like rheumatics?"

"Like the very opposite. Like the tingle of youth."

But Tinto's voice was hoarse and thick; his face was bleached with pain.

"You should be in your bed, auld man."

"Time enough to dee, Jock, after the Thistle's won the Cup. This young Elrigmuir's going to be a dandy."

"See that beast up there, Tinto?"

Both glanced up at the unicorn.

"I've stood here for years," said Saunders, "and I've never heard it open its mouth once. And that's why, Tinto, it's a damned sight better at prophesying than you'll ever be, you rattling auld blatherskite. Will I tell you what the score will be? Six-nothing."

"For the Thistle?"

"No, for Fernbank."

"Surely, Jock, you're forgetting Turk's back?"

"Turk's as stiff as Granny Chalmers." That lady weighed eighteen stone.

"We'll see," said Tinto, "we'll see," and he hirpled on.

Saunders noticed Tom Kennox without his friend Archie Birkwood. They lived next door to each other and usually went to the matches together.

"Where's big Archie?" asked Saunders. "Don't tell me he's learnt sense at last?"

"He's got a funeral."

"Who's deid so inconvenient?"

"Some auld wife from Lettrickhill. If they hurry, Archie thinks he'll manage it by half-time. What about yourself, Jock? Are you not coming?"

"Not me. I've got myself to bury."

Neither of them quite understood that remark, uttered with coarse laughter, but as Kennox went on towards the football field he found himself repeating it, and it seemed to him to have a meaning deeper than Jock Saunders knew and he himself could fathom.

All the worthies passed the Cross: Nathaniel Stewart, Ned Nicholson, Geordie Bonnyton, Crutch Brodie, and their cronies. Not one of them was willing to reveal by an increase in his pace how sharp as a goad hope was within him, and yet none was able to walk indifferently.

Saunders and his little sect began to feel, against their wills, a sense of exclusion and loss. No amount of self-congratulatory spitting reassured them. In another half-hour the main street would be empty save for women and withering trees, while down at the football field, behind closed gates, the mysterious masculine sacrament would be unfolding, with agony doubtless, but this day with a chance of glory. It might be that something would happen there this afternoon that every Drumsagart man ought to have seen or else his birthright would be forfeited. It might be they would in truth, without picks or spades, bury themselves there at the Cross.

First one weakened, discovered in a crevice of his pocket an unanticipated sixpence, took it out and tossed it up—heads he stayed, tails he went; found it come down heads, tossed it up again, and so won fate's permission. Suddenly he was off, and two with him, leaving Saunders scowling dubiously at the three left, all with fingers diligently ransacking their pockets and with faces more and more pinched each minute. A shilling would buy them wings of treachery.

"If I had it," he said, "I'd give it to you."

They swore allegiance.

"I've no interest in football," said one. "Dog-racing's my game."

"Three years ago," asserted another, "I took a vow to give it up."

"Look at it this way," muttered the third. "It would be money tossed away, time wasted. Fernbank are at the top of the League, the Thistle at the bottom. I've no wish to watch a massacre."

Then the president of the club came along, in a hurry because he was late. Saunders accosted him.

"Expecting a miracle the day, Mr. Rutherford?"

Andrew glanced round and smiled. "Hoping."

"Your boy's not wi' you?"

"No. No, he's at Helensburgh with his mother."

"Visiting his Uncle Harry?"

"That's right. But what about yourself? Are you not for the game?" He spoke shyly, for he wasn't sure whether poverty or principle was keeping Saunders back.

"Not me. But it's beginning to look as if I'll be the only able-bodied man in the town who isn't."

"If we reach the Cup Final, will you come and see us at Hampden?"

"Mr. Rutherford, if you reach the Final I'll crawl on my knees from here to Malarkin's pub and back."

Others passing heard that promise. "We'll keep you to that, Jock," they shouted.

"And at every third step I'll kiss the pavement," he roared.

Rutherford hesitated. It amazed him, and even made him a bit ashamed, that he liked Jock Saunders. According to Hannah's standards, he should have despised the big steelwork labourer. Dirty, lazy, conceited, peevish, negligent of wife and family; yes, Saunders was all that, but he had, too, an independence of mind, a defiant sense of justice, and a raucous unquenchable optimism.

"Well, if it's the entrance money that's keeping you back, boys," he murmured uncomfortably, "that's something can be mended."

Saunders nodded towards his companions. "They're your men, Mr. Rutherford. Half an hour ago they were as healthy as me, but the fever's smitten them. They've got the itch."

Without a word and with a glance away from the men, who to help him glanced away too, Rutherford slipped a shilling to Saunders and then hurried on.

Saunders stared at it, turned it over, and spat on it, but not in aversion: it was his customary salutation to windfalls.

"Why should I gie it to you," he asked, "to squander it on football, which is a luxury? This could buy me a pint, some fags, the wife a loaf, and sweeties for the weans."

They watched the coin, not liking to demand it because of the way they'd got it; moreover, they knew they were renegades.

"Here you are," he said, flicking it to one who caught it smartly though his hands had been in his pockets an instant before. "And if you've got ony decency in you, for God's sake cheer. Even if everybody round you's in mourning, cheer. You're bought men. Your souls are not your own."

They joked: one winked, one laughed, one poked him in the belly. Then they fled.

He was left alone by the Cross.

He was still there when, two hours later, the ants returned, greatly agitated.

Rutherford had not expected to be stopped by Saunders, but when he saw his father waiting for him beside the old kirk gateway he was not surprised; and he knew the tryst was not friendly.

The small shrunken man made his lips thicker than ever with repugnance. Behind rimless glasses his eyes were hard and bulbous. The skin of his neck was very slack, while the knot of his tie had slipped low out of his collar: in each case it looked like a deliberate carelessness.

"Are you for the game, faither?" asked Rutherford cheerfully.

"When I'm seen at your football, Andrew," he replied, in a harsh voice, "the folk in there will be dancing on the grass."

Andrew stared in at the graveyard, but said nothing.

"I want to talk to you about poor Lizzie Anderson."

"Poor, faither?"

"Are you adding stupidity to callousness, Andrew? You ken as weel as I do her mither's a widow, with twa weans still at school."

"Aye, I know that. I thought when you said poor you meant unfortunate, imposed on, to be pitied."

"I meant that too. She's seventeen."

Still staring in at the graves, Andrew frowned. "I can't discuss it now."

"No, you've got your football to attend."

"That's right."

"Don't smile at me, Andrew, when you say a thing like that." His father gripped a bar of the gate and strove to shake it. The whole cruel world was in his fist then, immovable.

"This is the kirk you worship in, Andrew," he whispered. "You're an elder here. You run the Sunday school."

"No, I've resigned."

"You mean you've given up the kirk?"

"Not altogether; just the Sunday school."

"Well, it's always something. I suppose you saw it was sheer hypocrisy to treat Lizzie Anderson the way you've done and at the same time teach weans about Christ. She's little more than a wean herself."

"I'm sorry, faither, I'll have to go."

"You had time to spare for Saunders at the Cross. What's he but a waster, a work-shy, and a toady?"

"He's got his good qualities too. I should have thought you would have seen them first. One thing you should approve: he thinks football's a waste of time."

"Praise him, Andrew. You owe it to him. As you'll ken, he's always got a good word for you."

Andrew had not known; he was surprised and pleased. "I never knew. I seldom talk to the man." He remembered then that Saunders had asked after Gerald, whereas so far his father hadn't noticed the boy wasn't there. "I'll have to go. It won't do if the president's not there to wish the team success before it goes on to the field."

"President! They laugh at you down there, behind your back."

"Not always behind my back."

"Yet you go amongst them as if they were your friends. You hae conceit, Andrew, but it lacks the stiffening of pride. That was a lack you always had; even as a boy." Then by accident, hardly by intent, into his father's wearied, embittered face flashed a resemblance to Gavin, who also at times had been impatient of what he called his brother's spunklessness.

So, thought Andrew, am I despised by my brother the dead hero, and by my father the disillusioned pacifist?

"I'll see you later tonight, if you like," he said. "I'm on my own this week-end, as maybe you've noticed. You've heard Lizzie's side of the story; it's as well you hear mine too."

"I'll be waiting."

It occurred to Andrew that each of them would be having tea alone. He was about to propose they have it together when he thought it would be better for him to have a space of quietness and peace before the discussion, which would likely be harassing. Perhaps in the silent house he would sit down at the piano and finger out some of his favourite tunes.

"Expect me about eight," he said.

"I'll be waiting."

Then they parted; his father made for the I.L.P. den, and Andrew for the football ground.

"So you're more concerned about Lizzie Anderson than about my son," he muttered. "Well, one thing I'll tell you, faither, when I see you tonight: she's going to be no concern of mine."

He was struggling to keep that resolution and not surrender to qualms of conscience about the girl, when he reached the ground, where for the first time in months there were queues outside each of the eight pay-boxes. Harry Lynn, the blind man, was there, singing atrociously and holding out his cap; men dropping pennies in dared not look at that dreadful and prostituted blindness. A young policeman stood by, undecided whether as official to stop the begging or as human being to wish it success.

Many boys were present, pleading with men to take them in; otherwise admission cost twopence. Among them Rutherford saw his nephew Gavin, a year younger than Gerald. The boy was shy. Others seemed able to divine from a man's face whether it was permissible to walk in front of him like his own son and be escorted into the ground. Gavin, on the contrary, was never sure; as he hesitated, the man he was about to beseech was pirated by another boy.

Rutherford watched for a minute, loving the boy for his failure in that game of cocky assertion, and noticing with pangs of sorrow how ill-clad and thin he was. He was said to be clever at school.

Though he knew it must embarrass the lad by making him disobey his father's instruction, he could not resist going up to him and putting his hand on his head.

"Hello, Gavin," he said. "Want to get into the match?"

Guilt instantly appeared on the young face, turning it old and crafty. He was like his grandfather, and someone else. Andrew wondered who that someone was, and then became aware it might be himself.

"Come in with me," he said, gently pushing him forward.

The man in the pay-box couldn't hide his astonishment. "It's a bigger crowd today, Mr. Rutherford," he said, his eyes on the boy.

"Aye, Archie. I hope we're not going to disappoint them."

"I hope so too." If nothing else, thought Archie, we might have a squabble between you and Robbie if he sees you with his boy.

Gavin, despite his terror, was too mannerly and perhaps courageous to run away and lose himself in the crowd. He waited to be dismissed.

"Here you are, Gavin," said Andrew quickly, and handed him half a crown.

The boy took it with a gasp of wonder, murmured thanks, but a moment after was handing it back again, as if it was wet with blood.

"I cannae take it."

67

"Why not, son? Your dad need never ken."

Glancing away, watching for his father, Gavin bit at the knuckle of his other hand "I promised. Last time——" Involuntarily, as he tried to smile, the hand holding the coin went to his leg and touched a large fading bruise.

"Did you fall?" asked Andrew calmly, knowing a belt or boot had caused it, swung in fury as punishment for accepting his last gift, a sixpence, on a wet night outside a chip shop.

Gavin nodded. "I fell." But he again held out the half-crown, with frantic entreaty.

Rutherford took it and walked unsteadily towards the pavilion. "Dear Christ," he kept murmuring, "dear Christ." And on the pavilion steps he met, this time in frank panoply of dark suit and immaculate collar, young Lockhart, Christ's representative, gazing with eager love at the pagan multitude. He had his hands behind his back, but they were not holding a megaphone.

The little scene between Rutherford and his nephew had been observed.

"Look, for God's sake," muttered one man, "there's big Rutherford just gave Robbie's boy some money and took it back."

"Mean big bastard," said another. "What's he up to?"

"Not mean," added a third. "Gutless. He's got cold feet in case Robbie gets to know."

"Maybe," suggested a fourth, who was hardly listened to, "he was frightened for the boy's sake."

But the story spread that Rutherford had given his nephew money and then had snatched it back.

Fernbank was a village in agricultural Lanarkshire, and its menfolk had travelled down in two special buses. Their faces were as red as the rosettes pinned to caps or jackets. Ploughmen, cowherds, carters, and blacksmiths, they had no right in society to show such vulgar condescending glee towards miners, steelmen, and paper-makers like Drumsagart men; nor was their crude dialect ever intended to convey swagger and arrogance. Yet there they gathered in a shaggy phalanx in the centre of the terracing opposite the pavilion, smelling of cowdung, barbarians from their sun-smacked faces to their tacketed shoes, yet assuming a superiority and certitude of victory that would have been intolerable even in the worshippers of the mighty Glasgow Rangers

68

in their own shrine at Ibrox. Unfortunately the Drumsagart men were hampered in their retaliation; not by instincts of hospitality, but by the foreknowledge that soon on the sunny field might be displayed ample justification for this dung-nourished *hubris*.

No Drumsagart rosettes were to be seen, and only two scarves, worn by Mysie Dougary and her grandfather. They had been invited inside the pavilion barrier to protect them from the wrath to come if Elrigmuir failed. Tamas had been given a chair.

Tinto the prophet, licking at the handle of his stick, tasted both sweat and doubt. When someone mentioned to him the new minister was at the match, standing yonder in front of the pavilion, Tinto declared himself absolved of any responsibility. "When I prophesied Elrigmuir would turn out to be a champion," he muttered, "when I said the Thistle would win, I was never told there'd be a minister here. Everybody kens a minister at a football match means bad luck."

"It could be bad luck for Fernbank," pointed out Crutch Brodie.

"He's our minister," snapped Tinto, "so it's our bad luck."

"Bad luck for everybody," growled a bystander. "Take a look at history."

"If that's so," said another, keen to pursue theology even in those hallowed moments before the entry of the gladiators—"if that's so, God pity Glasgow Celtic then, for every time they're playing at Parkhead yonder the grandstand's black wi' priests."

Even if a touchy Catholic had heard no argument could have ensued, for a clamour of voices and ricketies and one bugle heralded the arrival upon the field of Fernbank United in their red jerseys.

Drumsagart was dismayed.

"Look at them," they muttered. "Every damned one six feet and thirteen stone. No wonder they're at the top of the League. They'll kick our chaps off the field. Fed on new-laid eggs and prime steak. Is that the Afton the papers hae been bumming about, him all the senior clubs are after? Looks fast, eh? God help old Turk peching after that one. And just look at that hairy-kneed monster that's centre-half. That one will crush Mysie's Elrigmuir like one of Rutherford's mouldy bannocks. Boys, we're in for a worst slaughter than last week. Only a flood of rain or a storm of snow could save us now, and the sun's shining and the sky's blue."

Nevertheless, despite this daunting muscularity of the enemy, Drumsagart eyes watched for their own team to appear. It began to be rumoured they were on strike in the pavilion, in protest against the size and weight of their opponents; they were banging their heads on the floor, howling for their mammies to come and save them. Though it was a Drumsagart man who started the rumour, the Fernbank contingent took it up, without subtlety or pity, and turned it into brutal insult.

Soon, however, the Thistle trotted out, led by Lachie Houston, with his scalp as laundered as his white pants. Bellows of loyalty and encouragement were mingled with hoots of foreboding at the sight of Turk McCabe, seen now to be balder, fatter in the belly, and altogether uglier than in the past. Moreover his jersey was too short for him and his pants too long; and his boots too big apparently, for the first kick he took at the practice ball was a foozle, which caused him to go down anxiously on one knee and rub the offending toe-cap, as if with lucky spittle.

"Is that you, Turk," shouted a wit, "resting already?"

Affronted, Turk leapt a foot into the air and began to run in a vast earnest circle. As a demonstration of physical fitness it was not convincing, but even the gloomiest sceptics found it hard not to laugh.

Elrigmuir caused disquiet for the opposite reason: he looked so like a football player that everybody, except Mysie and Tinto Brown, was sure it must be some kind of deception. Tall, fair-haired, erect, he moved with speed and grace, and his first practice shot sent the ball whizzing into the net. That could easily be a fluke, but there was no gainsaying his legs were power-ful and had that delicate degree of bandiness so essential to the complete footballer.

The referee appeared, received his meed of jeers, supervised the spinning of the penny, and thereupon blew his whistle to start the game.

Never was there such a start. The Thistle having lost the toss, Elrigmuir as centre-forward kicked off. His inside-left tapped it back to Turk, who banged it prodigiously far upfield, where Elrigmuir at full tilt met it as it fell, controlled it without losing any of its impetus, swung it and himself past the mountainous centre-half, evaded the left-back's desperate lunge, and smote the ball past the Fernbank goalkeeper, who threw up his hands as much in horror at this improper impetuosity as in an attempt to save. It was a goal, and the swiftest and cleverest and most splendid goal ever seen on that field. The archangel Gabriel, wings and all, could not have excelled it; no, nor Alan Morton himself. Even the chawbacons from Fernbank felt the fearful glory in their souls, though they uttered no sound at first and later, minutes later, only profane exhortations to their own team to waken up and avenge that blow, so inhospitable in its suddenness and so ominous in its hint of obliterative power.

In the midst of the Drumsagart hysteria of joy Mysie stood in silence, her hands clasped; while her grandfather was peevish, for using his handkerchief to wipe the moisture from his eyes he'd missed the marvellous goal.

The Fernbank players, nettled at thus being caught napping by these incompetents at the foot of the League, charged down on the Thistle goal. The dexterous Afton dodged this defender and that, manœuvred himself into position for a shot at goal, raised his deadly right foot, and found only air to kick, Turk having nipped in to steal the ball from him and thump it to a far-off harmless place. Convinced, by a scrutiny of the aged ape in the blue jersey, that the theft had been lucky, if not absolutely unintentional, Afton was soon trying again, causing his partisans to shriek in appreciation of his craft, bringing lumps of apprehension into Drumsagart throats, and making the Thistle defenders bungle in panic, except one, Turk McCabe, who remained as cool and as awkward to get round as an iceberg. Wherever Afton's foot meant to be, Turk's was there the instant before; similarly in the contest of heads. Afton was supple and sprang up like a gazelle; Turk ascended as if with the hook of a crane in his back; but he was always that half-inch higher or at that better angle. When he headed the ball, too, it by no means dropped like shot from weary putter's hand; it flew as if spat from cannon.

Twenty minutes passed, and the Drumsagart faithful began to believe it possible that the Thistle might win by that single wonderful goal, provided only that Turk under the stress did not disintegrate into a heap of sweat, fat, beer, fags, and rusty bones.

Then in the twenty-first minute the Thistle outside-left, a long-haired much reviled man who normally pranced about like an inefficient fakir on red-hot stones, found the ball at his feet as a result of a ricochet from an opponent's jaw. He did not, as usual, get rid of it as if it was a wasp's byke, but caressed it with his left foot, went gambolling along the sawdust line, sidestepping two furious adversaries, and at the crucial moment, as if all was predestined, he kicked the ball across in a cunning parabola so that it avoided the heads of all United players and found Elrigmuir's, which flicked it neatly into the top corner of the goal, where it struck the net and thence dropped to the ground to be picked up by the goalkeeper in disgust as if it was a cow's turd.

It was a second goal, equal in beauty to the first, but dearer in that it built another thickness to the wall shutting out defeat. Like men long beleaguered and now hearing at last the Lucknow music, the Drumsagart supporters on the terracing howled hosannahs; while the Fernbank faithful, fed on fat wins for weeks past, spat out in nausea the thin wafer of defeat and contumely.

"Pick me oot ony prophet in the Bible," yelled Tinto Brown, "and I'll show you a better."

Harry Lynn, who was still begging, found his cap showered with thanksgiving pennies and ha'pennies.

In the midst of the pandemonium of glee Rab Nuneaton dismally smiled and remembered how his daughter's eyes had filled with tears when he'd struck her with his cap.

On the field the Thistle players clawed at one another in ecstasy, so that the outside-left emerged from their embraces blinded by his hair and by a blaze of self-esteem. Elrigmuir's shorter hair stood the rumpling well, and so, many noticed, did his modesty. He returned smartly to the centre of the field as if he would rather score more goals than be buffeted with praises for those he'd already scored.

The game became rough. Finding their skill thwarted, the United used their brawn. The Thistle were peremptorily commanded to retaliate; they obeyed. The referee, harming only the grass he trod on, became the most abused man on the field. If he awarded a foul-kick to Drumsagart, Fernbank abused him, while Drumsagart's praise was sarcastic; and vice-versa. Every tootle of his whistle brought vilification; to blow it soon needed much moral courage. His decisions, clear enough at first to himself if obscure to every partisan, became obscure to him too. When two men clashed murderously together and both fell, certainly it was a toss-up who was the greater culprit. The referee was not allowed by the rules to toss up, or hold an enquiry; he had to decide instantaneously, and latterly he could not have said by what principle he decided.

In this mood of confusion, aggravated by ricketies rattled and bugle blown, he awarded a penalty-kick.

Luckily he awarded it to the Thistle, whose adherents were, of course, far more numerous, although it was a Fernbank man who had the bugle. Luckily, too, for his conscience later, it was a just award, as Elrigmuir, well inside the fatal area, had been charged in the back by one United defender while another was in the act of sweeping his legs from under him. Nevertheless Fernbank screeched in protest; the ricketies clattered; the bugle snorted and stuttered sonorously.

Sergeant Elvan had had enough of bugling. Although the taking of a penalty-kick is a crisis on a football field, inflaming all nerves, he ran up to that part of the terracing where the bugler was and roared to him to hand it over or be locked up.

There was an astonishing temporary alliance: both Fernbank and Drumsagart united in rejecting that arbitrary demand. A bugle was a legitimate instrument of encouragement. Did the sergeant think it'd alarm the local Territorials playing soldiers on Drumsagart Hill? Or was he just sensitive about music? If he wasn't careful he'd be hearing the Last Post sounded over him. Let him go to Germany or Russia if he wanted to be a tyrant. His job was to take his big feet so many times round the field; his big ears had nothing to do with it at all.

The sergeant paid no heed but climbed over the wire ropes and pushed up through the Fernbank men till he reached the bugler. This was a stalwart with a red muffler round his neck and slavers on his lips. He held on as the sergeant tugged. He explained the bugle was his, he'd owned it since his Boys' Brigade days, he'd paid for it by instalments, he'd been doing no harm, he was really a trained player, he could give the sergeant a demonstration if he liked. The sergeant said nothing to all that, but kept tugging till he'd wrested the bugle away. A tremendous ironical cheer greeted his success. With the trophy above his head he shoved his way down through the crowd again, climbed over the ropes, and marched haughtily along to his subordinate, Constable Dunsmore, to whom he handed the bugle, and who took it as gratefully as if it was a coiled cobra. Then the sergeant waved to the referee to resume the game.

To Turk had been given the honour and the onus of taking the penalty-kick. During the bugle incident he waited, arms adangle, mouth agape, and head in tonsured dwam. An opponent had slyly placed the ball on the penalty spot, in a tiny hollow, which he hoped might cause the kick to be fluffed. Most men would have gone to the ball, patted it, placed and replaced it, and even prayed to it to fly straight and true, with no grotesque deviations upwards or sideways. Not so Turk. He waited, sober as convict or monk. As soon as the referee blew the whistle, and while the air on the field sensibly thinned through the sucking in of every breath, Turk, as if strolling towards the Lucky Sporran a good hour before closing-time, approached the ball, kicked it, and then blinked at it where it lay behind the sprawling goal-keeper. Thereafter he disappeared under his ardent colleagues, who leapt on him, wielding felicitations like clubs. When he was again seen he was as unperturbed as ever, with perhaps a little sheepishness at the edges of his solemnity.

Half-time came, with the score three-nil for the Thistle. The teams retired to the pavilion, and the spectators began to fight the semi-conflict over again. Into the arena strutted the pipe band, gigantic with moth-eaten busbies, playing "Cock of the North". Their kilts were faded tigers and their sporrans were like fistfuls plucked from long-dead sheep. But never had they blown so imperiously. The whole British army might have been behind them.

Mr. Lockhart, reconnoitring from the pavilion steps, was forced to admit that the band would be a difficult competitor to displace. It did not perhaps play well, nor march with much military precision, but it made an intimidating noise and brought forth from the crowd volleys not only of compliment but also of pennies, which were pecked off the grass and dropped into bags not unlike kirk bags by two small men, assiduous as feeding ostriches, who seemed to be well known and whose honesty seemed to be seriously questioned, judging by the many imputa-tions to the effect that half at least of the tribute would find its way into Mr. Malarkin's pockets, in return for beer and whisky. Certainly the two collectors, who made rude rejoinders, did not appear abashed by those arraignments; but Mr. Lockhart, to

whom scrupulous integrity in pecuniary matters was a virtue
higher than cleanliness, thought he had discovered the Achilles
heel of the band, through which he should be able, for one afternoon at least, to keep them sulking in their practice shed while
here on the battlefield he strove for God. He was about to compliment himself on this conclusion when he realised that, un-
accountably, though his hopes were rising, his heart was sinking.

In the pavilion behind him, at the very heart of the jubilation,
had appeared the worm of a moral problem. Among the on-
lookers had been identified the scout of a first-division senior
club. He had confessed to Sam Malarkin he was present to
report on Afton, but was more taken with young Elrigmuir; in
fact he was prepared there and then, on the strength of his intuition, to make an offer, which would leave the youth richer by
as much as fifty pounds. The Thistle, he added, would be com-
pensated for their loss. Marlarkin as a publican had much
experience of tongues too loose. With his own in splints of caution
he had tepidly praised Elrigmuir and concealed the fact that
the young man was not a Thistle player at all, being merely on
trial.

The thing to do, as all the committee except one agreed, was
to keep the poacher away and have a form ready for Elrigmuir
to sign at half-time. The dissentient was the president. He considered the scheme unfair to the lad, who ought to be told the
position and allowed to choose; otherwise they were cheating
him. The conference was the quickest in the committee's history.
Rutherford found no seconder; even Donald Lowther shook his
head. Elrigmuir was a football goldmine; to keep him murder
might pardonably be done.

Therefore when the team tramped into the dressing-room,
bathed in sweat and triumph, Wattie Cleugh and Sam Malarkin,
after going round patting the damp backs, with two pats for
Turk, took young Elrigmuir into the committee room, laid a
document in front of him, handed him a fountain-pen with
Malarkin inscribed on it in fancy gold letters, and told him where
to sign.

Other committee-men stayed with the rest of the team, while
two outside the pavilion locked the scout in conversation.

Elrigmuir was coy; indeed, he showed more interest in the pen
than in the form.

75

"Maybe I shouldn't," he said, grinning. "What if I'm a haddie? You've only seen me play half a game."

"We know that, boy," agreed Wattie Cleugh, "we know that. Granted you're a bit raw in patches. But we can recognise good stuff when we see it. Sign for us and you'll not regret it. I think Mr. Malarkin will back me up when I say our terms are as generous as any junior club's in the land."

"Some pen this," commented Elrigmuir, with his mouth full of orange. "It must hae cost a quid or two."

"Sign for us, Alec," whispered Malarkin, "and I'll get you one the identical same, with your name on it."

Sam had been trying to see beyond the sweat and glisten of the football genius to the human being, the tasty young fellow of nineteen, the collier, the sweetheart of Mysie Dougary. He saw smooth cheeks, a neck strangely free from extinct or active boils, a skin altogether caressable, lips exciting in spite of the orange juice, a nature unsuspicious and ingenuous, and a brain promisingly simple. Sam felt exhilarated, despite the odour of sweat so rank and masculine. He bent so close his whiskers tickled Elrigmuir's neck; he stroked the young man's back.

"Wattie's right, Alec," he said. "Sign for us, and we'll take care of you. We'll nurse you till you're ready for senior football. There's money here for the right kind, and you're the right kind all right. We'll have you out of the pits. We'll have you rising in the world. Sign that, and it's the first step in the making of your fortune."

"Mind you," confided Elrigmuir, "I like playing football. My teachers used to say it was the only thing I was good at."

"Just sign this," murmured Cleugh, holding the form as if it was a mirror in which Elrigmuir could see his face crowned with Drumsagart laurels and cash. "The rest is easy."

"I don't think I've got any objections to signing," said Elrigmuir. "Will Alec do, or should I write Alexander?"

"Alexander's more legal," said Cleugh.

Elrigmuir laughed. "Some folk call me Sandy. I've a middle name as well: Moffat."

"Alexander will do.

"I'll let you gentlemen into a secret," said the young man as, tongue out, he wrote painstakingly. "I'm doing this for Mysie's sake."

"Ah, sweet bonny Mysie!" Cleugh winked.

"I think the world of her, Mr. Cleugh."

"And so you should."

Malarkin neither winked nor smiled. His hand flew off the youth's back and alighted on the point of his own moustache. His nose twitched.

Elrigmuir paused at g. "But we're not what you would call sweethearts," he said.

Cleugh poked him in the ribs.

On Elrigmuir's frank brow, amidst the smudges left by the ball, appeared a shadow. "It's true," he insisted.

"Whatever you say, Alec. That's your business and Mysie's. You'll settle it between you. Just you finish signing. There's the ref. out on the field already."

Elrigmuir signed. "It's her," he said. "She's not in favour. I don't ken why. Sometimes I think it's because I'm a collier. She denies it. But if it's no that, what is it? I've asked her a hundred times. There's nothing wrong wi' me, is there?"

Cleugh waved the form about to dry it.

"Sure there's nothing wrong wi' you, Alec. There's a whole lot right wi' you. You keep on asking. Women are like that. You ask a hundred times—no good; you ask again and you've done it—you don't ken why, and you don't care. Is that not so, Sam?"

Malarkin's smirk had anguish in it, superciliousness, frustration, anxiety, and sadness. He said nothing, for there were no words to express that mixture.

Cleugh saw nothing peculiar. "Off you go, Alec; and re-member, the sure way to win Mysie's favour is by scoring more and more goals for the Thistle."

Elrigmuir rushed so as not to be last on the field. Last would be conspicuous; conspicuous was boastful, and Mysie had said a thousand times she didn't like boasters. He glanced at her as he passed. Strangers threw invisible bouquets at him, but she pretended to be interested in some gulls high up in the sky.

"You know something, Sam?" said Wattie Cleugh, inside the pavilion. "I envy that boy. He's got a wonderful future ahead of him. He's braw and he's young and he's a grand player and Mysie's a bonny lass. By God, I do envy him."

"Sometimes, Wattie," hissed Malarkin, "you talk a lot of ——" Then he dashed out, curiously, on his tiptoes.

"What's eating him?" asked Cleugh, of himself. Soon he was told the answer. "Well, well," he murmured. "I'll have to keep an eye on you, Sam old girl."

The second half began in catastrophe for Drumsagart. In two minutes the United scored a goal; Afton outwitted the whole defence, including Turk. It was Fernbank's turn to rejoice. Drumsagart blenched, though they also smiled: the poor bumpkins were entitled to this chip of consolation. Afton was good, but Elrigmuir was better. Then Turk stumbled, Afton sped past, the ball again was in the Thistle net. That chip by this addition became a feast, and the Fernbank manners, as they wolved into it, were revolting.

Pessimism spread like plague among the Drumsagart men. Nathaniel Stewart, who had not coughed once during that salubrious first half, now began, crying in the midst of it that Turk, damn him, was out of training, he was letting them down, he should have stayed in England, for though he'd given them all a glimpse of glory, true enough, it was only to strike them blind again.

Rab Nuneaton at last found his ideas flowing. Maybe it was a good thing, he said, that defeat was coming after all, for there would have been no enduring the conceit of Rutherford and the rest of the committee.

Archie Birkwood, arriving in uniform in time to see the United's goals, refused to believe the story of that ascendant first half, especially as it was related in downcast voices. He felt he had come from one graveside to another.

Tinto Brown was silent: so far his demi-god Elrigmuir had hardly touched the ball this half; it seemed to be a case of *ichabod* with him as with old Turk. If the United scored more goals, and this seemed very likely, for they were now furiously assaulting the Thistle goal, Tinto thought that, after a melancholy pint cadged in the Lucky Sporran, he'd creep home to die.

Turk muttered: "Keep the heid." One or two of his teammates heard and felt it would be better advice for him to keep his feet, for twice his stumbles had betrayed them. They did not say so. Turk looked worried rather than villainous, but with a face like his transition could be quick. Really his advice was to himself: "Keep the heid, Turk."

He kept it too, and his feet. There were no more stumbles. Aching with weariness, stiffness, and bruises, he toiled with the selflessness of a saint. Any spectator, such as Mr. Lockhart, for instance, to whom football was not sacred could never have believed that Turk's payment was to be seven shillings and sixpence and perhaps the privilege of suffering again next week. Certainly his superhuman efforts in such a cause made Mr. Lockhart ashamed of his own misgivings about the revival.

Thus the game ended, three goals to two for the Thistle—a harrowing but magnificent victory; and for the United their first defeat of the season. The yokels from Fernbank as they made for their buses still sported rosettes; their bugler on his restored instrument sounded no shamefaced retreat. They were disappointed but not despondent. Indeed, one of them stuck out of the bus window his great empurpled face like a prize turnip and bellowed to all Drumsagart the succinct truth: "We was beaten by a freak." He meant Turk McCabe, and everybody knew it.

The trouble about freaks, as the Drumsagart men confided to one another, was that they couldn't be depended on. That afternoon Turk had played a game that no man in Scotland could have bettered. Next Saturday, though, the magic might fail, and old Turk (for he was thirty-six if he was a day) left to his own natural resources would sag and fumble and miskick and maybe have to hang on to a goalpost to keep from collapse; and next Saturday was the first round of the Cup competition. Some even expressed the opinion that the old state of certain defeat was preferable: to be at the mercy of miracles would shrivel the nerves.

Jock Saunders was at the Cross when the forerunners approached.

"Well, what do you think of that, Jock?" they cried.

"Of what?"

"Of the match, dammit! We won, Jock; we won three-two." The speaker, though he had been there and seen, had to force the words past his own incredulity.

"I heard five roars," admitted Saunders. "I thought the score was five-nothing: for Fernbank."

"That's what we all thought it would be. The United are at the top of the League."

"What happened to them?" asked Saunders. "Did they all eat poisoned fish suppers last night? Did a steamroller run over their bus on their way from Fernbank?"

"Aye, a steamroller did run over them all right. Two steam-rollers: Turk and young Alec Elrigmuir. What a game they played!"

"So it was a glorious victory?"

"Glorious is too tame a word, Jock."

"Yet none of you," he observed, "seem to be in what I would call raptures."

It was true. Looking at one another, they had to admit it. Yet to explain would be difficult, especially with dry throats and palpitating hearts. Later perhaps in the Lucky Sporran some-one might hit on an explanation.

"All the same, Jock, you missed yourself. Yon was the sight of a lifetime."

"I've enjoyed myself here," he said, "watching the leaves come doon."

5

The house where Andrew had been born and in which his father now lived alone was at the end of a tenement above some shops. It was reached by an open stairway in two flights, leading to a long covered lobby at the end of which was the door. On either side of the stairs was a railing of thin green iron bars, as high as a boy's chin, and not far from the foot was a gas street-lamp.

As Andrew went slowly up that Saturday evening, memories of the past thronged round with such a childlike persistence that he had to stop on the landing and try by answering to send them away. Too frequently nowadays he was tempted thus by the past. Everywhere in Drumsagart were objects able to abolish the present for him and surround him with events and persons long vanished: a hawthorn tree that never flowered; a stone dyke smooth with summer sandshoes; the corner of a roof with stars above; a crack in the pavement: these, and many others, could, without warning, by some kind of enchantment, make him turn traitor to the present in favour of the fallacious past. He knew it was a dangerous succumbing: he was a man in his maturity; he was married, and had in his son of thirteen a hostage to time; he had a responsible job and many interests, such as the football team. If he could not rescue himself from these obsessions he might in the end return to find his grasp upon the world, Hannah's world of envy and ownership, weakened to the point of letting go. All his life he had never felt a confident inhabitant of that world. In so many ways it had seemed insubstantial to him; and he had always felt how easy it would be, by a withdrawal of faith, to turn even his loved son into a phantom.

Therefore on those steps, that bridge of the great warship, that snowy mountain of India, that narrow pass in the haunted hills, that scaffold of martyred death, he paused and waited till they became stone steps again, in the dusk of a chilly Saturday evening, in a small town in Scotland, with his father waiting in the house above to charge him with inhumanity towards Lizzie Anderson.

It was not easy to make things as they really were and keep them like that: it was not easy, in fact, to be sure what they really were, for love could shape them one way, hate another. How easy to become lost; and he remembered how Hannah's life was signposted towards what she called success. He had allowed himself to be dragged in that direction too, driven by his desire for harmony with her and by that weakness which made him need to conform, to be like his fellows, to have the approval of the herd, to share with them even their most fatal mistakes. Yet he had not fought in the war but had sheltered within the refuge of his reserved job as engineer making munitions; and it was Hannah, then his sweetheart, with her sin of acquisitiveness disguised as a young girl's natural anxiety to build a home, who had urged him to take as much overtime as possible and not to volunteer for the army. He had been willing enough to oblige her, for he was sufficiently influenced by his father's preaching to hate the war and doubt its justice. He had therefore stayed safe at home and saved money for Hannah to invest. Often he had regretted his choice: no man certainly could be honest and clean-handed in a time of universal bloody war; but he had felt that as a soldier under orders to kill or be killed he could have seen his way more clearly than as an engineer in danger only from his conscience.

Well, it was all past now, he thought, as he went up the rest of the steps and along the lobby. But was it really? Did he not still carry in him unhealed wounds from which seeped bitterness and regret? And would it ever be past for him who could remember so poignantly his returning home from work that cold December night to find his dinner warm as usual in the oven and on the mantelpiece the telegram saying Gavin had been killed? He had held it for minutes in his oily hands. In the scullery Robbie polished his shoes to go out with Isa. His father sat in the green armchair reading. His mother, gently nudging him aside, had lifted the kettle from the hob and gone into the scullery with it to fill a basin with hot water so that he could be washing his hands while she set his dinner out on the table. How in Christ's name could that ever be past?

There was a difference, certainly, in his entering the house. Now he knocked before opening the door, and inside the dark little hallway paused to call out: "It's me, Andrew. Can I come in?" In the old days he'd walked straight in.

His father was reading in the same green armchair. Like himself it was dilapidated. His book was a large one for so shrunken a man and had the great word Capitalism in its title. Andrew smiled. Whether his father was understanding the book or not, he was without a doubt the only man in Drumsagart that night preferring such heavy stuff to the newspapers with their football results and descriptions of the day's games. One of the more modest headlines was: Surprise Defeat of Fernbank.

The table was still littered with the tea-things. The toasting-fork lay on the hearthrug, among many crumbs. The teapot stewed on the hob with its handle towards the fire. On the mantelpiece, with its lid off, was the tea-caddy painted with scenes of Rothesay, against which years ago the telegram had been propped.

The kitchen was so untidy that it conjured up by contrast his mother, who in her own easy-going way had been a fastidious housewife. Cynics might have remarked that Councillor Rutherford, zealous to scrub out a world encrusted with the filth of centuries, was not able to keep his small house clean or even his own person. Andrew was a cynic only towards himself. He felt he could have relaxed here more easily than in his own regulated home, if it hadn't been for the subject to be discussed soon. Immediately, it turned out.

"Well, Andrew, and what excuses have you thought up?"

Andrew grinned at the promptness of the attack. Yet he felt sad at the great change in his father. There was always a whine in his voice now where formerly had been passion. Surely his fight against the world was over. Rest now, in some place like Rothesay say, should be his reward.

"I can well understand, Andrew, you need time to prepare your excuses. What would justify you to your wife and cronies won't do here. I'm glad you realise that."

Andrew stooped and picked up the toasting-fork. "I see you're still as fond of toast," he murmured. "You'll have heard of our famous victory this afternoon?"

"Don't sidetrack me, Andrew. I've no humour to spare."

"You never had, faither." The rebuke was gentle.

"I was never lucky enough to find things to laugh at."

"They were there all the time, though."

"Yesterday I had a visit from Mrs. Anderson. She sat on that chair you're on. You ken what she came to tell me."

"I think so, but maybe she added some things on. You'd better tell me."

"I believed every word she said. She told me her lassie, Lizzie, who's just turned seventeen, has been sacked from your factory and is going to be prosecuted. She told me she and her two other weans who are still at school live in a single-end in Miller Street. You ken what that street's like. She was greeting as she sat there, and not just because you, and the men behind you, are plotting to put her lassie in jail, but because of all the miseries that have been preying on her all her days. She wept in that chair because she's a victim of a society that you and your like have built and uphold. You made her weep as much as if you'd taken your boot and kicked. No, Andrew, you wouldn't do that. None of your sort would. You're too civilised for such brutality; but you're not too civilised to see her, and a multitude like her, rot away in a living death."

The harsh voice, shaken by that unfortunate whine, had kept rising till it suddenly ended in a scream, to be followed by angry sobs and peevish punches at the book.

83

Andrew said nothing. He stared at his mother's portrait on the wall, in a black dress with a white cameo brooch at her breast; that brooch was in his own private drawer at home.

There was much he could say to defend himself, but nothing to soothe his father's grief, if it really was grief and not merely petulance, such as a spoiled child displayed when denied a toy too expensive. He could not help remembering his father had never, in his sight, shed tears for Gavin butchered; yet here he was breaking his heart on behalf of some lying, sleekit, worthless woman. No, no, thought Andrew quickly, taking back that estimate of Mrs. Anderson, whom he had never met and who might well be a decent hard-working woman, struggling to do her best for her family. If she was, Lizzie must cause her many a heartache.

He had to say something. "Do you think it's worth it, faither, upsetting yourself like that? What gratitude have folk ever shown you?"

"Fine advice for a Christian," screamed his father. "You don't ken what suffering is; that's why you've no sympathy. All your life you've been for yourself, and to the midden with everybody else."

"That's not true."

"Aye, it's true. I'm your faither, and I ken you better than you ken yourself. You don't deceive me."

Andrew found he'd bent the toasting-fork almost into a horse-shoe. Smiling, thinking such a shape was lucky, he tried to straighten it and found his hands too self-conscious and weak.

"Never mind discussing me," he said. "Let's stick to Lizzie Anderson. You didn't say why she was sacked. It was for stealing. And it's not right to say she's to be prosecuted. I'm not vindictive. I don't believe in punishment for punishment's sake. She had to go. I couldn't avoid that."

"Aye, you could. You could hae given her another chance. You've no right to fling her out into the world with a brand on her. Her mither needs the money to feed them. To feed them, Andrew, not to throw away on fancy blazers and kilts and bicycles."

Andrew ignored the sneer at Gerald. "How can I take her back? She's a confessed thief."

"So are you a thief, though you'll never confess it; and everybody like you. Why is she so poor she's got to steal?

84

Because you and your kind hae stolen her portion and shared it amongst you."

"Is that not simplifying things a bit, faither?"

"I'm a simple man and I see things simply. You hae more than you need, she has less. You profess to be a Christian. Is it Christ's wish the Andersons should go hungry while you live on the fat of the land? What right in God's een has your son to get every chance in life while the Anderson weans get no chance at all?"

Every chance, faither? he could have asked. You know how it is between Hannah and me. A child can be deprived of more things than food and clothes and a clean bed.

What he did say was: "No right in my own eyes, faither, far less in God's."

"You ken I never had any time for your religion. I vowed once I would never recognise the kirk while it gave its blessing to war; and I think your Christ Himself will never recognise it."

"Not my Christ, I'm afraid."

"So you think you've been a disappointment to Him, as you've been to me?"

"Like most men, I've been a disappointment to myself."

"No, Andrew, I can't let you away wi' that. I don't believe it. You've turned hard and callous enough to enjoy the success you've won."

Andrew laughed. "All right. I'm terrible. I'm beyond redemption. Let's get back to the Andersons. Let's see if there's anything we can do to help them."

His father leaned forward, eager as a child—a malicious, gleeful child. "There are things I've been wanting to say to you for a long time. I'm going to say them now."

"Don't say anything you'll be sorry for."

"Oh, are you threatening me?"

"Don't be daft."

"You're a bigger man than I ever was, in body. You're the biggest of the family, Andrew, in body."

"And the smallest in brains, is that it?"

"In brains, if you like. I meant, in heart." The old man clawed at his own. "In heart, Andrew. When did you last take stock? I don't mean when did you last look at your bank-book? I mean, when did you last examine yourself as a human being?"

"I'm never done doing it," said Andrew, shaking his head.

His father paid no heed. He held up one finger. "Your brother hates you."

With a sudden involuntary spasm of anger Andrew hung the toasting-fork on its hook by the side of the fireplace.

"How in justice," he asked, trying to control his voice, "can you take his part? He's a boozer, a sponger, an idler, and he takes out his spite on his wife and weans. He's all the things I thought you were against."

"I'm taking nobody's part. I'm just taking stock for you. Your brother hates you; and your other brother, if you remember in his last letter—it's still in that drawer there if you want to verify it—he called you—what was it, Andrew? Surely you don't forget."

"I don't forget he was joking."

"It suits you to think that, but when the letter came were you so sure then? If he called you a profiteer, making a fortune out of shells to kill innocent men, did he really slander you, Andrew? Was it not the truth?"

Andrew tried to smile. "Who were these lucky men that were innocent? I'll not believe Gavin despised me before he died. I got letters from him, private letters. He and I had a lot in common. I wish to God he'd been spared. He'd have helped me, for I confess I need help."

His father was silent, not because he had nothing more to say, but because he had something so momentous to say it needed this setting of silence.

Andrew was thinking, as many others had thought and often said, his father had little room to talk: he might not have worked at the making of shells, but surely as storekeeper he had been as deeply involved?

"You were a disappointment to your mither."

Andrew jumped to his feet with a shout, lurched across the room, and stood gripping the chiffonier with both hands.

"You're going too far," he cried. "If I failed my mither, and no doubt I did, for she had her own high standards though she never bragged about them—if I failed her she forgave me. Just as she forgave you."

"Shout as loud as you like, I'm not frightened of your anger."

With a great effort Andrew cast out anger; he turned and faced his father. "I don't want to quarrel wi' you, faither. If this is the mood you're in I'd better go."

"Mrs. Anderson was suffering, Andrew. You showed her no sympathy."

Again Andrew lost control. "Don't you talk," he cried. "Everybody in the town knows you've always been a theory man. You've never really faced the facts. I sympathise with Mrs. Anderson, and I'll tell you why. I sympathise with her for having a daughter who's a thief and a slut—aye, and a young whore into the bargain; and she's only seventeen. Have you ever spoken to her? Lizzie Anderson's a depraved young bitch with as foul a tongue as you'd find in any drunken docker; and don't tell me it's all the fault of society. That's too damned easy an explanation. When I gave her a job, out of pity, do you ken what happened? Other girls protested. They came to me and protested. Some of them were hardly any better off than she was, but they were afraid she'd contaminate them. You can be bad at sixteen, faither, and poverty itself'll not explain it or excuse it. I asked them to give her a chance. They did, and in her gratitude she stole money from their coats. They wanted to hand her over to the police. I wouldn't hear of it, but maybe they were right after all."

His father sneered. "I expected that, Andrew. I expected you to twist it round so that you come out of it big-hearted and generous. It's wonderful how, though you deceive nobody else, you always manage to deceive yourself. Why is it you can find nobody, not even your ain wife, to speak weel of you?"

"I've got friends."

"Name them."

Andrew was silent.

"I'll name some of your well-wishers. There's Tinto Brown. What's he but a rogue and a cadger?"

"Some think he's a brave humorous old man, in constant pain."

"His good opinion can be bought; and so can Saunders's."

"Isa. Does she speak ill of me?"

"You ken she speaks ill of nobody."

"Not even of me, such a monster of iniquity?" As Andrew laughed he caught sight of the small drawer in the chiffonnier where his mother had kept her many receipts, for making elder-berry wine, rowan and apple jelly, carrageen, and other such delicacies. "You had the rearing of me, faither. I was in your charge when I was an impressionable little boy; and I think I was impressionable. Why didn't you make a better job of me? And of Robbie too? Did you not have the receipt for making good men?"

"You're being sorry for yourself again. You're forgetting you passed into other hands, and you let them shape you as they wished. Not only you but your son too, poor lad."

In a rage Andrew swept a small vase off the chiffonier; it crashed to the floor. "Don't say a word against Gerald," he shouted. "Must a wean starve and go in rags before you think he deserves your sympathy? I tell you, I'd rather have my son warm and well without your blessing than cold and hungry with it. All right, say I'm just proving Hannah's smitten me with her view of things. In some ways it's a very sensible view, as you would admit if you weren't so blinded by prejudices. But I would keep coming here happily and humbly even if every time you were to criticise me as you've done this night. Turn on my boy, though, a child of thirteen with a long, difficult road in front of him, as every child has, rich or poor—turn on him, and there'll be no pleasure for me here, only heartbreak and bitterness, and I'd rather not come."

"Please yourself."

"Are Robbie's weans poor enough? Are the Anderson weans poor enough? Do they suffer enough to deserve your interest and pity? It's a damned simple view of human nature to think that poverty's a man's worst enemy. Here." He took out his pocketbook and plucked from it a bank-note: it was for five pounds. That was too much, more than he could afford, and, besides, it would impress his father not by its generosity but by its mercenariness. Nevertheless he threw the note on the chiffonier. "Here. See that this is given, anonymously or any way you like, to Mrs. Anderson. You can deduct from it whatever you think the vase was worth. Good night." And then he was away, crushing the fragments on the floor, banging the door after him, and bumping along the dim lobby, before he began to realise how enormous was the breach he had just made.

Lounging against the wall as if drunk, with fists pressed hard into his thighs, he tried to measure the evil done: he could not, it was immeasurable. He had read once that from a star long ago dissolved light still streamed through space: so surely from an act of evil, though past and forgotten, guilt and remorse continued to pollute the mind; and how, in a world of cynical men, of proliferating sins and sorrows, of cruelty and suffering, and of a rejected God, could there ever be expiation and release?

"If I could pray," he muttered; but he could not—inside and out everything was blank and impenetrable. "God knows, the boy's got his faults." He remembered his son's selfishness with toys, his refusal to part with old ones or share new ones: a refusal applauded by Hannah but not created by her. "They're the faults of most weans." And they became the sins of most men.

Lizzie Anderson at seventeen was still a child.

No prayer came to him in the narrow lobby, no vision of divine help, but instead, bemusing him with its grotesque disproportion and irrelevance, a recollection of the sunny victory that afternoon on the football field, of familiar faces laughing in delight, of Turk McCabe's devoted skull butting the ball out of the Drumsagart goal.

Yet, after his horror and disgust at that inferior consolation, he began, as usual, to feel grateful towards it, for somehow it seemed to inspire him to find other more worthy consolations. If there was happiness in the world there must be goodness; and young Mysie Dougary that afternoon had been very happy. His father this evening was very tired, and tomorrow or soon would apologise; not for his condemnation of Andrew himself, which could stand, but for his slur on Gerald. And Gerald, too, would in the end throw off influences now warping his character and reveal himself as a champion of the meek, a denunciator of cruelty and injustice, free from prejudice and moved by love. In the boy were already traces of such a development; had he not endured without a wince the dab of iodine on his torn knee? And had he not climbed a tree to rescue a cat? That would be Andrew's best ambition realised: after his father's lifetime of courageous opposition, his son's: his own cowardly compliance in between might then be forgiven.

When he came out on to the steps and saw the stars it occurred to him that this present tribulation would in its turn become the past, and he was wondering how it would then appear to him when he noticed someone below staggering in the gaslight towards the foot of the steps, and knew it was Robbie, drunk.

He could have escaped, as once in boyhood, by climbing over the railings and dropping to the ground. Then he had bit his tongue, but now it might mean a broken leg. In any case, if there was shame in the meeting, surely it was Robbie's, who was crawling up before the pubs shut to cadge from his father the price of a few more pints. That five-pound note on the chiffonier might vanish.

He decided to go down calmly, say a word in passing, and hurry on. This was neither place nor time for any attempted reconciliation.

He could not tell afterwards what went wrong. Robbie did not offer provocation; indeed, he seemed so myopically tipsy he wasn't aware it was Andrew till the latter spoke. Nor did that imbecile drunkenness exasperate Andrew; in Drumsagart it was a common enough sight. When he spoke he felt neutral, and indeed his voice was controlled. Yet he said: "Is this you then, the man of high principle, crawling on your hands and knees to wheedle or bully beer money from an old man that needs every ha'penny for food and clothes?"

From his morose and topsy-turvy introspections Robbie emerged, blinking and mumbling obscene curses at first general in their aim. Soon they were for Andrew, as were the brandished fists and the bared teeth. Stink of beer surged on the cold air.

"You're a fine example to your sons," said Andrew.

Robbie seized him by the coat. "Shwine, leavesh my son 'lone," he muttered. "Givesh money and takesh back. Whash y' game? Eh, whash y' game? Who the hellsh think y'are?"

"Let me go." Andrew took hold of the fist gripping him, and though he could have torn it away with ease he did not but waited, his hand on his brother's.

"Your ain son's blurry snob," said Robbie. "So leavesh mine 'lone. No bribery. See? No bribery."

"Your son's worth a hundred of you, you drunken fool."

"Belted him black-blue," muttered Robbie, with mournful relish. "Black-blue. My ain flesh and bluid. Your fault, bastard. Teach him not to take bribes from scabs and black-legs."

Andrew's grip tightened. "Don't tell me you laid a finger on him for what happened today?"

Robbie wished to protest against that grip paralysing his

wrist, but couldn't except by yelps and an involuntary jerking up of his leg.

Andrew slackened his hold. "Did you harm him?" he whispered.

"Belted him. I've a right, he's mine."

"You rotten-hearted, vicious, sodden swine. I could kill you for that. Insult me as much as you like. I can take care of your sort. But I'm warning you, take your spite out on any child and I'll break your miserable neck for you."

In spite of his anger and contempt, the blow was unpremeditated: a moment before he was sure he had his temper under control. Yet it was a fierce blow. It struck Robbie on the cheek, cracked against the bone prominent there, split the taut grey skin, spilled the blood, and sent the whole crumpled, whimpering body reeling backwards to trip over the steps and fall on them.

"You big bloody coward," he cried, in a voice sober and whining, "you ken I'm not fed to fight with you. It's beef and eggs for you, margarine and bread for me." And he began to weep, tenderly exploring his face with his hand.

Andrew rushed away.

6

Every morning now, except Sunday, Mr. Lockhart brought a cup of warm sweet tea to his wife in bed; on Sunday she insisted on rising to put him out to work. They had read in a women's magazine that if she sipped such tea while resting she would be immune from morning sickness. It turned out to be ineffectual in her case, so that when she did get up, cautiously, assisted by him as tenderly as if all her limbs were broken, she was no sooner dressed than the first spasm of nausea came and she had to creep away to the bathroom, while he, forgotten and even slightly resented, hovered near, helpless, murmuring endearments and solicitude, and complaining of Nature's inexplicable callousness.

Nevertheless that half-hour while she lay sipping the tea and he sat on the bed reading his morning's mail, or any uplifting piece of news in the *Glasgow Herald*, was precious to them both. They held hands, though it was inconvenient; they kissed; he sang the Scots air that might have been composed for her: 'Nancy's hair is yellow like gowd'; they whispered about their child that would arrive with the daffodils and the revival; he talked earnestly about the revival; she listened and murmured a word or two, not of scepticism or discouragement, but of loving caution.

On the Thursday morning following the change of super-intendency of the Sunday school he entered the bedroom carrying the tray more solemnly than usual, for that afternoon he was to officiate at a funeral.

Nan knew how that anticipation always made him nervous, subdued, even melancholy. He would glance aside from her into the mirror, by no means to admire his own handsomeness but rather to question his fitness to pronounce the sacred words that were to speed a soul towards its Maker. With his flannel trousers and high-necked woollen pullover, he looked, as he often joked, like a pugilist in training; but only the pugilist part was a joke, the training part was very earnest. If circumstances had been different, if he had not been married, if his wife had not been pregnant, if the century had been the sixteenth instead of the twentieth, he would indeed have spent that forenoon in preparation, fasting and praying and meditating. As it was, only a smiling, rather self-conscious gravity was available to him.

There were several letters, two with Drumsagart postmarks; one of these had immature writing on the envelope. It was not the first time a child had written to him: one had thanked him for the lovely talk he'd given to the Sunday school; another for his visit to her sickbed with sweets and flowers. He wondered why this one had written. The paper was obviously cheap, and he handled it all the more respectfully. He shared Christ's confidence in children; indeed, he felt sure Christ was in every one of them—yes, even in those youngsters who on Sunday had from behind a wall stoned Mr. Rutherford on his way to church and cut his brow. His fingers tearing the envelope paused as he recalled how the big dour man had slipped alone into his pew with his handkerchief at his brow as if to wipe away rain. Rain was now lashing against the window: it had been falling all night, and round the new grave the earth would be cold, slippery, wet, and inhospitable. Rutherford had not mentioned the incident. Others who had seen it had described it afterwards in the church porch and along the rainy streets, with reprehensible relish. John Davis, the beadle, had spoken of it in the vestry as he'd helped the minister off with his robes. Among the boys had been Rutherford's two nephews.

"What is it, dear?" asked Nan gently. "You'll have to remember to put on your overshoes."

"Yes, darling." He lifted her soft, warm, plump hand and kissed it. In every way it contrasted with the sodden desolation of the grave and the violence of so much of life. He kissed it again therefore, in passionate gratitude.

"You must be careful, Harold," she murmured, patting his hair with her other hand. "You know you must look after your throat. Don't stand with your head bare longer than necessary."

"I can't scamp the service, dear."

"Of course not. But on a wild day like this, for the sake of the others as well, you're surely justified in not lingering over it, as you might want to do if the weather was good."

"It may clear up, dear."

"I hope so. Is that the reply from the football committee?"

"No. I think it's from a child; at least it looks like a child's handwriting."

He took out the small square of paper and reverently unfolded it, while his wife, watching his hands, saw also outside the window through the rain the gaunt half-derelict Paper Works, inscribed in huge faded letters with: TOILET PAPER, CARTONS, WRAPPINGS, ETC. She had not yet confessed it to Harold, but she disliked Drumsagart and regretted having left the small Dumfriesshire village, where there had been fewer souls to save but green fields and hills could be seen from the manse windows.

Her husband's mouth was in its tightest knot. He frowned too, as if he'd divined her disloyal regrets. At the same time, committing another disloyalty, she could scarcely keep from smiling at his exaggerated seriousness.

"What is it, dear?" she asked.

"How shocking!" he whispered.

"Is it the reply from the committee then? Have they refused?"

"I do not know whom it is from. It is anonymous, and it is vile."

"Vile? Goodness. May I see it?" She stretched out that hand which he had so recently kissed in gratitude for its innocence and vitality.

"No, no." He drew the letter back. "Don't even touch it. I won't have you defiled."

She could not help laughing at his expression.

Horrified, he gazed at her so sweet and pure in her pink bedjacket; yet she should not laugh.

"I'm sorry, dear," she murmured, "but you look so fierce and disgusted."

"With good cause."

"Please, either read it to me or let me read it myself."

Still he was reluctant: either way she'd be besmirched, and their child within her; but if he read it he could by his tone disinfect it partly.

"And they say," he muttered, "there's no need of a revival in this town."

She knew who they were: his three Protestant colleagues, the Congregationalist, the Baptist, and the Episcopalian ministers.

"It's short," he said curtly, "and the spelling's dreadful. 'Dear Minister, this is to warn you about Rutherford in charge of your Sunday school. Do you know there's a girl in his factory going to have a bairn by him? He's just sacked her to get rid of her. Do you think a man like him should be in charge of a Sunday school?'"

For half a minute after reading it he was ashamed to look in his wife's eyes. If he had looked he would have found them sparkling with indignation.

"What a miserable, sneaking, filthy slander!" she cried.

"Isn't it?"

"Good heavens, Harold! Don't tell me you're thinking for a moment it could be true? Mr. Rutherford's an elder of your church."

He remembered Susanna pestered in the garden. Were there roses in that garden?

"Of course I don't think it's true," he said. "But is it not too naïve, Nan darling, to take it as an axiom that elders, as such, are incapable of sinning?"

"I hope you're going to hand it to the police," she cried.

He had already spoken to Sergeant Elvan, tactfully, about the revival. The sergeant had perhaps too readily agreed it was long overdue. His view of human nature seemed to be that it was a compound of pusillanimity and depravity. He had even hinted, with a cryptic blasphemy, that Christ's own revival had failed. This letter would be like manna to him.

"We must be careful," he murmured. "We must not help to spread pollution. We must take counsel."

"I like Mr. Rutherford," she said stoutly.

"I know you do, Nan, and I've faith in your intuition as regards people. But Mr. Rutherford has enemies in Drumsagart. They would be delighted to have this filth to throw at him."

"They'll throw it all right. Do you think the vicious scoundrel who wrote that is going to keep his foul mouth shut? No, he's going to spout it all over the town. It's our duty, therefore, to make it clear to everybody we think he's a liar."

He shivered at the crudeness of her speech. "He, dear?"

"Surely you don't think a woman wrote that? It sounds like a man."

"I'm afraid, darling, my sex doesn't have a monopoly of sin."

"Let me see it. Don't be silly, Harold. I'm not a child to be so easily corrupted."

She took the letter from his unwilling hand and examined it.

"It's possible it was written by the girl referred to," he murmured. "There *is* such a girl, I'm sorry to say. I know who she is, though I've never met her. She's seventeen, I believe. It seems Mr. Rutherford had occasion to dismiss her—theft was the reason. It could well be this is her way of obtaining revenge. Of course" —and here he smiled: a husband's, not a minister's smile—"an accusation like this can so easily be disproved."

"Can it, Harold? How? I don't see that it can. If the girl is really bad, if she is promiscuous, how can it be easily disproved, if she persists in lying? It will be her word against Andrew Rutherford's, and you've said yourself he's got enemies to believe the worst against him."

"I meant, dear," he murmured, still with that uxorious smirk, "that if she's prevaricating, if she's not going to have a child at all, it will soon be apparent." Gently he laid his hand on the bedclothes near her middle.

She pushed his hand away as if its purpose was indecent. "What if she is pregnant? Likely enough she is. She won't know the father either. I expect it could be any one of a dozen."

"Nan!"

"I prefer to face realities, Harold. It won't be easy for Andrew to convince people he's innocent. Many will want to believe he's guilty just to get gloating over him."

"Now, Nan," he chided, "you're being far too sweeping."

"It's you, Harold, who insists on the need for a revival. And it was you who said Andrew had enemies."

"Yes, yes, but I hope I didn't infer they were all so mean and vile as to gloat over him involved in a sordid misfortune like this."

"But that's what enemies do! That's why they are enemies, surely. Friends sympathise, trust, and help. Enemies hinder and gloat."

He frowned; he didn't like this misanthropic attitude; he had wished her from the conception to the birth to entertain only Christian thoughts and emotions: thus might their child step from the womb into Christ.

"What age did you say she was?" asked Nan.

"Seventeen." As he gave the information rather crossly, horror smote him: seventeen only she was, a child still, with the world's wickedness emptied over her purity like a garbage-can. He could not withhold the bitter cry: "And they say no revival is necessary!"

"What certainly is necessary," said his wife coolly, "is that you let Andrew Rutherford know immediately you've received this letter. You must leave it to him to decide whether the police should be told or not."

"Yes, of course." But he was shaking his head. How was he to tell Rutherford? It could hardly be done by telephone, and he shrank from another encounter with Mrs. Rutherford, especially on such an errand. It occurred to him, with a slow blush, that Rutherford and his wife perhaps no longer lived together as man and wife. If so, it was their own unhappy business and not even their minister had any right to interfere, with advice or reproof; but the desires of the flesh were compelling and if denied legitimate gratification might, except in a man of well-nigh saintly continence, drive him into adultery. Nan might like Rutherford, but for all that he was no saint.

He turned slightly away from her and hardened his voice.

"I know very well," he said, "no man knows better, that we have been commanded not to judge lest we in our turn be judged. I know compassion is our first duty. But this is a world dynamic with sin, and by no means all of it exists in the bosoms of what are called the criminal classes. Sin is not a penal offence in the eyes of man. It breaks only God's law, and God has no prisons, save shame and remorse. Far be it from me, especially in my capacity as a minister of Christ, to presume that Mr. Rutherford is guilty of this abomination, but such things do happen in communities supposedly respectable, perpetrated by men supposedly upright. I wish to be perfectly candid and honourable in this matter; I must be, for a human soul is in peril. Now if I were in a court of law, asked to swear upon the Bible, I could not say I know Mr. Rutherford well enough to be certain he was incapable of such a thing. Here is a Bible." He picked up his bedside copy. "I hope I always strive to tell the truth, but sometimes a man needs help; here is mine. What, then, am I truthfully to say of Mr. Rutherford? I find him secretive, dour, disingenuous, uncooperative, disobliging, superficial, materialistic. I find many of my congregation, including his fellow elders, distrusting him. I find his church-going insincere, his football worship genuine. I find him spoiling his son and turning him into, I'm sorry to say, an unpopular little prig. I find him estranged from his wife. I find him on the one hand boasting about his Socialist father, and on the other hand living as selfishly as any capitalist. I find him with very few friends. I find him engaged in a long vendetta with his only brother. I have found myself obliged to remove him from his position as superintendent of my Sunday school."

She had listened with her head shaking all the time in a disagreement that, in spite of her loveliness and his love, nevertheless slightly vexed him. She had a successful habit of exposing a falseness in his eloquence, sometimes without saying a word. It was, of course, a wifely service and he was grateful; but that gratitude required a self-discipline he could not always achieve.

"I like him," she said.

97

It was not much, but it more than cancelled out his long condemnation.

"Yes, you have said so, dear."

"To be fair, Harold, you ought now to give the catalogue of his virtues. Surely the picture at the moment is unbalanced? Otherwise what must you think of your wife liking such a rascal?"

"I did not use the word."

"You should have; it would have saved you a lot of others. Why did you include his quarrel with his brother? Hasn't he tried to make it up? And wasn't he in the right in the beginning? I've heard you say so. Didn't you say you admired his moral courage in refusing to take part in a strike caused by agitators?"

"I may have said so. However, I was not in Drumsagart at that time."

"Not very long ago, Harold, your opinion of Andrew Rutherford wasn't quite as black as it seems to be now."

"I hope you aren't insinuating, darling, that I've acquired some personal prejudice against him? If so, you are being very unfair. Surely I must speak the truth as I see it?"

"Yes, without condemning."

"It is difficult sometimes to speak the truth and avoid judgment."

"It is difficult to be a Christian, dear."

He smiled, not very cordially, though he took her hand and squeezed it. "You should have been the minister, darling, not I."

"I'm the minister's wife, dear, which is sometimes more important than being the minister."

"Very true." Again he laughed, more warmly, and leant forward to kiss her.

After the kiss she threw the letter on to the floor, with a grimace of disgust.

They refused to look at it and smiled at each other.

"You haven't finished your tea," he murmured, "and it's cold. Shall I make you fresh stuff?"

"Never mind, thanks. It doesn't do any good, anyway." She held on to his hand tightly. "Let's tell each other the truth always, Harold, and let it sweeten our love."

Telling each other the truth, he reflected, usually consisted in her pointing out a weakness or fallacy or pretentiousness in his carefully considered opinion. Nevertheless he smiled, with sweetest love.

Soon he picked up the other letter with the Drumsagart postmark. She had to let go his hand.

"Are you sure, darling, it wasn't a mistake?" she asked, in her most winning voice.

"What, sweet?"

"Asking him to resign? I thought at the time you were too hasty. Now it'll give his detractors more to talk about."

His own voice was a little tart. "I did what I considered my duty. I did not want to do it. I hated to do it. You know how sensitive I am in such matters."

"There was that throwing of stones." She shivered. "How primitive we can become."

"You must not, in your condition, brood on such unpleasantnesses."

"Darling, I've got to face the fact my child's going to be born into a world where good men are still stoned."

"Our child, Nan. I think you are inclined to be a trifle morbid. Of course I appreciate it's your condition; but, all the same, I must confess it somewhat depresses me."

She stared at him. "I'm sorry, Harold." Inwardly she was fuming: My condition! My condition indeed!

"It's for your own sake, sweet. You must concentrate on what's happy and hopeful."

"Does it help much if you keep harping on the necessity of a revival?"

He was visibly huffed. "No, I suppose not. I'm sorry."

"And it doesn't help me either, Harold, to look out of the window at sights like that."

Glumly he gazed out at the Paper Works with its vulgar inscription.

Pity and love drove away her peevishness.

"I'm sorry, darling," she cried. "You're perfectly right; it's my condition. I feel terribly irritable. Don't pay any heed to anything I say."

"But I must, sweet. You're my wife, whom I love very dearly."

"We love each other very dearly, darling, and we always will."

Her fervour roused his. They kissed and fondled and murmured pet names.

"Now let's hear what the football people have to say," she said at last, brightly changing the subject.

"Oh yes."

He opened the letter. It was from Mr. Walter Cleugh, secretary, and stated ponderously that the committee, after considering his application to address the spectators at half-time on the subject of religion, had decided to postpone their answer. There were several factors to be taken into consideration. The pipe band would have to be consulted, and some committee members thought the attitude of the spectators ought to be investigated. A decision would be given before the spring; it was assumed he would prefer to wait for the warmer weather.

He read it out scornfully. "Warmer weather!" he cried, with a glance at the streaming window. "Do they not realise that weeds of sin flourish even in ice and snow?"

"No, dear. They realise that if it's cold and wet the men won't listen patiently to what you have to tell them."

"But it won't be too wet and cold for them to stand for hours watching their miserable football. No, Nan, please don't make excuses for them." Then he adopted his pulpit tone while she smiled and under the bedclothes her toes squirmed. "Must there be comfort, then, before there can be the Word of God? Is this really the land of conventicles? They will demand armchairs in church next. Indeed, do many not sit at home in indolence and listen, between glances at the newspaper, to the service on the wireless? We have to cushion the very words of Christ lest they be too sharp. We have to make Him smug to conform to the prevailing smugness. Is it not shameful? There are times when I feel I would do better to renounce my calling and go into the fields and labour there, like my father—yes, like my father," he repeated, in a cry that was a defiance of the snobbish worldlings who believed it effrontery on his part, a byre-man's son, presuming to intercede between them and God.

Mrs. Lockhart's father had been a schoolmaster. Privately she thought her husband's sensitiveness about his father's occupation revealed a tinge of snobbery in himself. The time was coming when she would tell him so, in love.

"Rutherford was against my application," he said. "He told me he would oppose it."

"Perhaps he thinks he has good reasons, dear."

"No doubt, but spite is a considerable ingredient."

She thought Rutherford opposed because, like her, he was afraid religion might be humiliated and not fostered. After all, he knew the football fans much better than Harold did. As she was wondering how to say this without offence she began to feel squeamish. In preparing to resist it, or thole it if resistance failed, she forgot temporarily Rutherford, religion, Harold, even the child itself.

He was muttering about the hypocrisy of an elder refusing to collaborate in the dissemination of the gospel, when he suddenly noticed her attention was abstracted and her pink cheeks had become yellow. Instantly he was much concerned.

"Are you going to be sick, darling?" he cried. "Please, is there anything I can do? Can I bring you anything? Oh, Nan, my poor sweet little wife!"

She smiled courageously and nodded.

As he dashed away to fetch a basin he had a feeling, apocalyptic in its vividness and terror, of being at the heart of a vast barbed entanglement, from which escape might be impossible though his very soul should be lacerated in innumerable attempts.

7

At the meeting which had drafted the letter to the minister the committee had also deliberated what should be done to strengthen their hold on young Elrigmuir. If possible, he must be persuaded to come to Drumsagart to live, so that he could train with the rest of the team and be protected from the rapacity of senior clubs; but a job would have to be found for him—not a dangerous one like mining, where a sprained knee or broken back was so readily come by, but a light pleasant one with sufficient prospects to attract a courting lad. The president, as the biggest employer among them, was delicately appealed to; he not only refused but asserted with unnecessary and offensive emphasis that if there had been a vacancy in the factory he had a waiting list of married men with families who would come before

Elrigmuir though the latter was twenty times the player he was.

Malarkin had sat all through the discussion with a smile on his lips as though there, too, was a glass of exquisite scented wine about to be sampled. At the opportune time, when brains were empty and tempers full, he remarked, with smirks as of appreciation of that invisible wine, that he thought he could come to their rescue: he needed a new barman, and Elrigmuir might do very well.

Their guffaws were appreciative too, but very coarse: blood they seemed to have smelled and drunk. Oh yes, they roared, Elrigmuir would do very well behind the bar. Not only would he lure in new boozers from all airts, he would also prolong the nightly stay of the regulars: especially if he kept on scoring superb goals, as everybody prayed he would, and took the Thistle up the League and nearer to the Cup. Aye, aye, Sam might look a queer fellow with his perfumed whiskers and fancy clothes, but he was all there, in spite of rumours.

Their mood suddenly was hilarious, bawdy, and confident.

"All the same, Sam," snickered Angus Tennant, "it'll be bad business for you if Elrigmuir draws in the crowds."

"Explain yourself, Angus," chuckled Sam.

Tennant winked to the others; being cross-eyed, he was a fascinating winker.

"Well, you see, Sam, you promised a half of whisky free to every man who came to claim it."

"Man, Angus, you've got a drouthy memory."

"I'm not the only one. It's common talk. I'm warning you, Sam, there'll be thoosands."

Sam was not discomposed.

Neilson the plumber uttered a throaty snarl like a defective drain; it was in good humour, however. "Thoosands drinking from now till the winning of the Cup," he said, "will mean a profit able to cover half a dozen free halfs."

"You think that, Henry?" murmured Sam.

"What I'm thinking," interrupted wee Wattie Cleugh, the secretary, the brainy one, "is: will Mysie stand for it?"

Sam no longer smiled.

"She's a kirk-hand," went on Wattie, "and it could be she has a part in running the Band of Hope. I doubt, then, if she'll approve of her sweetheart serving behind the bar."

"You never know," muttered Donald Lowther. "Look at the Salvation Army lasses. They go into pubs, don't they, to sell their *War Cry*?"

"This is different," murmured Wattie.

"God in heaven," said Tennant bitterly, "would she prefer him doon the pit? Does she want him brought hame squashed on a stretcher?"

"She might," nodded Cleugh, "prefer that to seeing him lose his soul, which is how she might regard it. Women are creatures hard to fathom, as you all ken; with the germ of religion in their brains they're clean gyte. That," he added, with insulting relish, "is a guid auld Scots word meaning mad."

"We ken that, Wattie," said Lowther. "We're as Scotch as you. Are you not forgetting Mysie's a follower of the Thistle as weel as an attender of the Band of Hope?"

"What of it, Donald? It's still possible in Scotland to mix football and religion."

"Is it?" roared Neilson. "D'you think so? Wait till young Lockhart addresses them."

"That business is past for the night, Henry," said the secretary.

Then the president burst into the conversation. It was with the sour objection that bartending was hardly a healthy occupation for a football player, nor a profitable one for any simple-souled youth of nineteen.

"Would you make a drunkard of the boy to suit your ambitions?"

Sam shrugged his shoulders and let the rest speak for him. They did it circumspectly, in a conspiracy of politeness. Rutherford was in a nasty humour these days, and no wonder. Had he not cast out with his father, whom he idolised? Hadn't he struck Robbie and got stoned by Robbie's boys? Hadn't he been heaved out of his post in the Sunday school by the young minister? And wasn't Lizzie Anderson spreading the tale she was bairned by him? And weren't they themselves hatching ways of winkling him out of the presidency before his term was up? After all, if the miracle did happen and the Cup was won, half of the glory would be gone if Rutherford glowered at the top of the proceedings.

Therefore, as he now sat glowering at the top of the table, they outwardly and reasonably, with many 'Andrews' pondered his objection. Sorrowfully they found they must reject it.

He banged on the table with his huge fist, so that the whole pavilion shook and some fag-ends louped out of an ash-tray on to Hugh Neilson's Sunday suit, which he always wore at committee meetings.

"Have it your own way," growled the president.

Accordingly next evening, after training, Sam Malarkin had his car at the ground to carry Elrigmuir up to his house to put the proposition to him there in seductive comfort. Margot was safely, though shamefully, out of the way.

Though flattered by the invitation to step into the big glittering, plushy car, Elrigmuir at first refused. He had to meet Mysie outside the Town Hall; they were to go for a stroll before he got his bus for home.

Sam shoved him in, with gratuitous pats on the bottom.

"What I've got to speak to you about, Alec," he said, "is far more important than any blethers of Mysie's."

"No, Mr. Malarkin," protested Elrigmuir, "that's not the case. Mysie doesn't blether, and she'll not stand for anybody else blethering either. She talks sense all the time. Some subjects she just refuses to discuss: foolish she calls them. One of them's getting married."

Sam was making indeterminate little noises as if his whiskers were being scraped in passion against the steering-wheel. He started the engine and drove off in a frenzy of caution through black shadows. One shadow seemed more substantial than the rest; perhaps it squealed.

"I think," remarked Elrigmuir sensibly, "you've run over a cat."

"There are too many cats in the world," said Malarkin, still in that passion.

"There's one less now. I prefer dogs myself. They're more faithful. Make sure you stop at the Town Hall. I've got to explain to Mysie."

Malarkin had a formula for warding off bad luck: he twirled first the left point of his moustache, then the right, and ended with three slow strokes of forefinger on nose. That it was efficacious was proved by his fabulous luckiness. A joiner by trade, he had during the war run a licensed club, not for profit but for the benefit of the munition-workers parched from forge and furnace. With the profits he had bought the Black Bull, a seedy pub in the main street and turned it into the Lucky Sporran, a tabernacle of coloured lights and mahogany, with carpet instead of sawdust, and on the walls paintings of famous Scottish scenes. Drinking was as soulful there as in any place in the country. A Catholic while fuddled had been heard by arrant Protestants to confess he was never sure whether he was in the Lucky Sporran or the chapel. It was true the atmosphere was hardly secular, so much so that there were men in the town who still preferred the sawdust and battered spittoons and sweating walls of The Howff and the Drumsagart Arms to the splendour of Malarkin's. These were eccentrics, however, pariahs, misfits, degenerates, whose talk never rose above football and women. In the Lucky Sporran, on the contrary, a man had once been flung out into the street for growing too obstreperous during a debate on philosophy.

As they drove slowly along the main street they could see, above the turrets of the Town Hall, the moon curiously small and high, with clouds scudding past but never obscuring it. An attendant star now and then disappeared. Elrigmuir saw also, faithful as the moon, Mysie at the Town Hall. He leant forward and tapped the publican on the shoulder respectfully.

"That's Mysie," he said.

Malarkin accelerated. They shot past Mysie, who would not have noticed them if Elrigmuir hadn't managed to squeeze his head out of the window, skinning his ear in the effort, and bellow, not an explanation, for he himself was mystified, but simply an intimation of his diminishing presence. "I'll not be long," he howled. When he could no longer see her he brought in his head again, almost tearing his ear off altogether in his belligerent eagerness to remonstrate with his kidnapper.

Mysie had seen and heard. She spoke to the ornamental lamp-posts beside her. "He can be as long as he likes," she said. "You'll be here when he comes, but I'll not." Then resolutely she walked away, heedless at first of her direction, until the winking of the moon began to annoy her by making her in some queer way want to cry. Dry-eyed, she turned about where there were only puny stars to see.

Meanwhile Elrigmuir was pressing his remonstrances.

"Are you aware, Mr. Malarkin, she might never speak to me again?"

"Call me Sam. When we're by ourselves, Alec, call me Sam."

"She's got pride and principles, Mr. Malarkin. I worship her. If it hadn't been for her, do you think I would ever have signed for the Thistle? I want to marry her."

"You're a foolish boy, Alec. Don't you see what she's doing to you? She's destroying your self-respect. That's what a woman always does to a man. Look at Andrew Rutherford, for instance; and Angus Tennant, whose Nell's like an elephant in a circus."

"Dependableness," went on Elrigmuir. "She makes a great thing of that. It's more important, she said, than love. You'll have to explain to her, Mr. Malarkin, that it wasn't my fault."

"What are you making all the fuss about, Alec? She's making a fool of you. Surely you know she runs around with young John Watson that's a clerk in the Commercial Bank? All women are snobs, Alec. To them a bank-clerk's a better catch than a collier. Have nothing to do with them. They're cheats and mockers, and they suck a man's soul out of him. But here we are, at the Malarkin mansion."

Elrigmuir sat disconsolately in the car.

"Come out, Alec," whispered Malarkin, holding the door open.

"She's finished with Watson," muttered Elrigmuir. "She said so."

"Of course she said so, Alec. Treachery comes natural to them. I know." He glanced towards the house, glad to see it in darkness. "They laugh at what's sacred."

"You can't say that about Mysie," objected Elrigmuir. "She teaches in the Sunday school."

"There are things too sacred to be taught in the Sunday school."

"And I'll not always be a collier. Maybe I'll become famous as a football player and get signed on by the Rangers or Hearts or Aberdeen, at ten pounds a week, with extra bonuses for wins. Auld Tamas, her grandpa, likes me."

Malarkin shut his eyes against these irrelevancies. He seized the young man's arm and pulled him out of the car.

Elrigmuir saw the moon and was at once despondent. It reminded him of Mysie, and how, while stating she was finished with Watson, she had stressed with shining eyes that it was none of his business, and that if she wished to resume old friendships, with Watson or with anybody else, she would do so without asking his consent.

Therefore he suffered himself to be led through the gate up to the front door. His mood of fatalistic acquiescence excited his host, who could hardly insert the key in the lock. How delicious, Malarkin was thinking, to know that in two or three minutes they'd be seated, far from women, side by side on the low divan in front of the electric fire, with wine and perfumed cigarettes, and calmness, and curtains drawn, and a record on the gramophone of his favourite singer.

As he stepped over the threshold Elrigmuir muttered he couldn't stay long.

"I'll take your coat, Alec."

"There's no need."

"Give it to me." Malarkin pulled it off, wincing as he noticed how shabby it was and how soiled at the neck. "Just go straight into the sitting-room, Alec. Make yourself at home."

Elrigmuir stood in the doorway and gaped in. He was reminded of a play he had once seen; if he walked in he'd be on the stage, with hundreds of people looking at him.

"In you go," said his host, giving him a push.

Elrigmuir stepped stiffly forward, his arms rigid at his sides. When he spoke it was in a strange voice, and somehow the words came out one by one, with long pauses between. "I can't stay long."

Malarkin took him by the hand and led him towards the long, low, elegant divan covered in red plush. "Sit down, Alec."

Elrigmuir obeyed, with somnambulist's precision. No comfort was sought or found in the change from stiff standing to stiffer sitting. His legs were long and stuck out far in front.

Malarkin gave him a pat on the shoulder, and then left him to attend to hostly duties, such as switching on electric fire, pulling curtains, and placing a small table as near as Elrigmuir's ramrods would allow.

"Perhaps you'll excuse me a moment, Alec?" he murmured.

Elrigmuir nodded, as if with a boil on his neck.

At the door Malarkin's twitters grew grim. He frowned at the ivory handle. "If you wish to wash your hands . . ." he began, finding euphemism difficult.

Elrigmuir shook his head.

Malarkin went off happy.

Alone, Elrigmuir began to peer round the room, with stage-frightened diffidence, but also with some of the zeal of prospective householder. In every house he visited now he looked for tips for the home he and Mysie might some day set up together. Somehow, rich though these furnishings were, they did not appeal to him; and he was sure Mysie would have agreed. There was too much velvet for homeliness. The colours were too gaudy. The atmosphere was heavy with scent, as if the enormous yellow flowers on the carpet were real. It just wasn't possible to imagine children playing in that room. Shaking his head, Elrigmuir remembered Malarkin lived with his sister, and from the jokes cracked by the footballers in their bath about her it seemed Miss Malarkin was peculiar. Probably, then, the flamboyance of the room was her doing. Nevertheless it was not homely.

When Malarkin returned in about five minutes, dedicated to hospitality, he disconcerted his guest by having on, over his yellow waistcoat and mauve trousers, a dressing-gown of pale-blue satin. At once the room was a stage again, set for a sinister scene. He did not notice his guest's astonishment and incipient apprehension, but happily and devotedly produced from a cabinet a bottle in a gilt wrapper and two long-stemmed glasses, the bowls of which were so exiguous, two thimblefuls in capacity, that the young man's native derision for a moment drove out his anxiety, and he sniggered.

"Preparing the feast," chuckled his host, who then went swaying across to put a record on the gramophone.

Elrigmuir began to recall jokes made by the footballers about Malarkin himself. He had not understood them at the time, though as a well-bred stranger he had laughed more heartily than most, but now they were becoming more and more intelligible. Complete revelation was hardly possible, but almost came with the music. It was a song whose words he couldn't make out at all, but the emotion in it caused his hair to bristle and his hands to sweat. Crooners he liked, and prattle about love always found him an indulgent hummer, but this low-toned passionate plaint confused and offended him.

"French," said Malarkin.

Elrigmuir's gape, already wide, increased till the record could almost have been slid down his throat. He laughed too, though he felt far from laughing. At the coal-face miners who had been in France during the war had between swings of their picks exchanged stories of fabulous and enterprising vice. Elrigmuir had listened, mouth full of coal dust. Now suddenly in that lush red room the same dreadful taste was in his mouth. He was far away deep in the bowels of the earth, and never again would he see Mysie and the moon.

"Give the French their due," said Malarkin, "they're the boys for passion." He came over and picked up the bottle of wine.

"Not for me, Mr. Malarkin. I don't drink."

"Silly boy. This is no raw liquor to rot a navvy's belly. This is for the angels, to make them dream with their golden heads rested on their wings."

Elrigmuir was so impressed he took the glass; but again its tininess roused his humour. He was reminded of filling the canary's water-dish.

"Temperance is beautiful," said Malarkin, "but abstinence is ugly and mean."

Elrigmuir tasted the wine and grued. It was like water in which scented soap had fallen.

Malarkin filled the glasses again. "Ah," he murmured, gazing through his at Elrigmuir, "life is a long, lonely, and dreary road."

"I don't find it that," said Elrigmuir stoutly.

"You will find it so soon enough, dear boy. Nothing lasts, all is dust in the end. If there is anything to compensate us for the sorrowful journey towards the grave, it is surely friendship."

Elrigmuir thought of Mysie in her clouds of unforgiveness and gloomily nodded.

"Friendship and beauty," went on Malarkin. "I was born with a soul too refined. Was that my fault? I did not even ask to be born at all. Look round you in this room. Do not tell me you expected to find such a haven of loveliness in the coarse brutality of Drumsagart? Am I myself not a surprise to you? They think of me as Malarkin, the comical publican. But the truth is I have a soul as sensitive as a flower." Suddenly he dropped down on to the divan beside Elrigmuir. "You, too, have a sensitive soul. From the first moment I recognised in you a kindred spirit. We must be friends. If we had lived long ago in ancient Greece, Alec, we could have worn white robes or nothing at all, and no-one would have sneered at our friendship.

There is much talk of the beauty of a woman's body; to me it is absurd. I prefer the virile splendour of a man's."

This time Elrigmuir couldn't agree. Indeed, apart altogether from the remote insult to Mysie, he felt exasperated by such a wrong-headed attitude. He had seen the Thistle players in their big bath in the pavilion, and had no more looked for beauty in them than he would have looked for it in lamp-posts. Men's bodies were necessary and adequate, that was all; to see them as beautiful was indecent. Then he remembered how often through the steam Malarkin had been caught peeping, and how the players had joked about it.

"I am not understood in Drumsagart," said Malarkin wistfully, and put his hand on the young man's shoulder.

Instantly Elrigmuir was all over itchy; he had to scratch knee, head, hip, elbow.

"D'you think," he burst out hoarsely, "we'll win on Saturday?"

Malarkin closed his eyes. Wine-drops sparkled like fallen tears on his whiskers. He was silent for almost a minute.

"Alec," he said at last, "there are more important things in life than football."

"That's true," conceded Elrigmuir.

Malarkin became eager and insistent. "You see that, Alec? You agree with me? Then you are indeed a rare spirit, and you and I must be friends. There are men in Scotland, in Drumsagart itself, who put football above everything."

"I think," said Elrigmuir stoutly, "a man's wife and children should come first."

Malarkin shuddered. "Alec," he whispered poignantly, "how would you like to say goodbye to the pits?"

"I don't see what you mean, Mr. Malarkin."

Malarkin came closer. "I mean, there's a place for you in the Lucky Sporran."

"Your pub?"

"My hostelry, my vineyard."

"As a barman?"

"No. Oh, I have heard dull clods criticise such an occupation as though it were menial. What is the truth? Was not Bacchus a god? And did not those who attended him wear only vine-leaves in their hair? Let Rutherford the clod sneer. He is a man without a crumb of beauty in him. How could he have, with his ears so abominably hairy? What do you say, Alec? I shall be generous. I shall pay you ten shillings more than you earn in the pit, and"—here he began to sob—"you shall no longer be in hourly danger of having your beautiful body crushed to bloody pulp like a beetle under the heel of a cruel boy."

"Mysie mightn't like it," announced Elrigmuir.

"What has she to do with it?" asked Malarkin, in a voice faint with disgust.

Elrigmuir was roused. "She's got a lot to do with it, seeing I'm going to marry her some day. I'm being crushed, Mr. Malarkin, and there's plenty of room."

Whatever answer Malarkin could have made to that rude logicality was prevented by noises outside, clip-clops like a horse on cobbles, and a singing equine too. As they waited, host in alarm and anguish, guest in relief and wonder, space grew between them, so that when the door opened and Margot came in, on silver slippers with heels like stilts, one gaped at one end of the divan while the other at the other end nibbled a point of his moustache.

She seemed to have stepped from bath or bed. Her golden hair gleamed about her naked shoulders. Round her she held a fairy's wisp of dressing-gown, pinkly transparent; under it her slim legs, with the knees adazzle, were bare to the topmost thighs. Flesh coloured pants, skimpy as pearl-diver's loin-cloth, and brassiere of pink cords were her only coverings, except for her assurance thicker than brass. She was smoking a cigarette and wore a packet like a third breast.

When she saw Elrigmuir she pretended surprise and even, to her own amusement, drew her gauze closer about her as she hobbled directly towards him.

His eyes raced about the floor like mice, now behind the wine-cabinet, now under the radiogram, and now under his lids.

"I didn't know you were entertaining company, Sammy," she cried, with her sudden wild harsh laughter that mocked both her own duplicity and his too simple chagrin.

He knew she was lying: she had deceived him into thinking she was going out; and here she was again, nude, to steal Elrigmuir from him. He bounced up in pique disguised as dignity.

"I do not think, Margot," he squealed, "you ought to come in here dressed like that."

She puffed his rage aside. "Mr. Elrigmuir's an athlete," she said. "I'm sure he has no objections. He has red blood in his veins. Virile men are never prudes. Do you mind? I'm so warm-blooded I stifle in the house if I wear lots of clothes."

"I thought you said you were going out," said her brother.

She spread out along her gilded brow five crimson nails. "I had a headache."

"Only people with consciences, Margot, have headaches."

She glared at him. "Don't talk to me about consciences. If you ask me, I think I came in the nick of time."

"I don't know what you are talking about. Mr. Elrigmuir and I were discussing business."

"Some business," she muttered, gazing round at the perfumed web. "Play the game fair, Sammy."

Her brother, as he gazed at her invulnerable golden skull, remembered the black cat he had run over. He pressed his cheeks hard with his hands.

She turned to Elrigmuir, squeezing sweetness palpable as condensed milk on to her face. "Is your name Alec?"

He nodded.

"Mine's Margot." She sat down beside him. "Are you living in Drumsagart now?"

"No. I've to catch a bus."

He would have sprung up to dash out and catch it there and then if she hadn't clutched his knee.

"There's no hurry," she murmured. "If you miss the bus we've plenty of room."

"No, no," cried her brother. "You must let him catch his bus. His mother will be worried."

"And I'm on the six-to-two shift," said Elrigmuir.

"D'you mean," she asked, pressing his knee painfully, "you start work in the morning at six?"

He nodded.

"There was a time," said her brother, "when women worked down the mines. A pity they were ever allowed to come up. We talk about progress, but there is none."

She scowled at him. "If I had to earn my living howking coal, I could. You'd starve to death." She turned to Elrigmuir. "Miners are wonderful men. They've got such strong legs."

"I think you should go and catch your bus, Alec," cried Malarkin.

Then the ringing of a bell interrupted them all.

"Answer the door, Sammy," said Margot.

"Who can it be at this time?" he asked.

"Go and find out."

"And leave you here? I certainly will not. If you go upstairs I will open it."

"Do you want me to take a chill?"

The bell rang again. Up shot Elrigmuir, as if it was a referee's whistle.

"I'll go," he cried. "I'm going, anyway. I'll need to catch my bus."

Margot flew after him with marvellous speed on those stilts.

"Leave him. You could be his mother," shouted her brother.

She seized him at the door. There she fuddled him with scent and made him look, not at her fortified face but at the accessible rest. She grabbed his hand and pressed it against her bosom.

"We'll meet again," she whispered hoarsely, "when we've not got that powdered monkey to bother us. Don't believe him. I'm not as old as that. Do you think I look old?"

He shook his head in a confusion of terror, politeness, and lust. Then, snatching back his hand, he pushed past her into the hall. The bell was ringing again as he opened the outside door and saw in front of him on the moonlit steps Mysie Dougary and her sturdy shadow. Before he could even gasp her name the light behind him clicked, and, turning, he saw Margot with her finger on the switch. Sam was nowhere. Mysie, of course, saw too. Then the light clicked out again and Margot's voice was heard cooing, "Good night, Alec, dear."

Courtesy forced him to answer: "Good night, Miss Malarkin." Then he was being dragged by Mysie down the steps and along the path to the gate. There he stopped and tried to go back.

Mysie held on. "It's nothing to me," she said, "but I brought you to Drumsagart and I promised your mother I'd look after you. She must have kent what like a sumph you are. Are you like a moth, then, that must go back to the flame to be burnt?"

"It's my coat," he protested. "I've left my coat."

She muttered something bitter and indistinct.

He heard it. "Aye, that's all I've left. I didn't have a cap."

"Never mind your coat," she said. "Would you walk into a house on fire for the sake of an old coat?"

He glanced back at the house, wondering if the electric fire had been knocked over in a wrestling match between the two Malarkins. "It's not on fire, Mysie."

"It is, with the flames of sin."

"Oh," he murmured, respectfully. It was not the first time he had had a hint that Mysie knew more about the wicked ways of the world than her rosy cheeks indicated.

They walked down the street in the lamplight. Above them the moon winked.

He tried to take her hand, but was not surprised when he failed.

"Yon's a queer pair," he commented.

"Don't talk about them, please. Whatever happened in that house, Alec Elrigmuir, is between your conscience and God. It is no business of mine."

He would have preferred her interest to God's, but he did not dare say so.

"Nothing happened, Mysie."

She said nothing, but sniffed most virtuously and most incredulously.

"Don't be bad-minded, Mysie," he said severely. "All that happened was that Mr. Malarkin asked me to the house to offer me a job in his pub. While we were sitting talking"—he drew in a long breath of cold clean air—"she came in. That was all."

Mysie said nothing.

"It wasn't my fault she wasn't dressed properly."

"You could have left. There was nothing to prevent you."

"There was."

"What?"

He hesitated, doubtful of the thin ice of truth: could he risk saying, Her hand on my knee? No. "Well, she held me."

"Held you? Just what do you mean?"

"I mean she held me. Mr. Malarkin said she should be ashamed of herself, seeing she was old enough to be my mither. Is that true? She's got no wrinkles, but maybe they're all hidden by the powder. One thing, she's not fat."

"Like me, do you mean?"

"You ken I meant nothing of the kind. I don't like skinny women, if it comes to that."

"Don't be disgusting."

He frowned: no doubt he had been disgusting, but he could not see just where.

"What about the job?" he asked. "I told him, no."

"You prefer to be a collier all your days?"

Her sharp sarcasm bewildered him. "No, Mysie. I'd like fine to get out of the pit. Should I hae taken it then?"

"Why ask me? It's none of my business."

"I wish it was, Mysie."

"Well, it isn't."

There was silence from one lamp-post to another.

"Would the wages be better?" she asked.

"Ten shillings a week more," he said. "That's quite a lot, Mysie."

Again there was silence.

"It's disgraceful," she said, "that a man should get paid less for slaving down a pit than for serving out whisky and beer."

He agreed.

"Coal keeps homes warm and happy," she said, "drink destroys them."

"True enough."

"Did he offer you anything to drink in the house?"

He had to confess. "But it tasted terrible."

"You drank it all the same?"

"I had to, out of politeness."

"I've noticed you're a great one for politeness." She referred to his saying good night to Margot, but he missed it.

"Is it a fault, then, to be polite?" he asked, in a huff. "If I was unmannerly that would be a fault too."

"I'll tell you what," she said, "you're such a sumph that if you did take the job as barman you'd develop into a drunkard. Your politeness would be the ruin of you."

He felt that if he'd been holding her hand then he'd have let it go, to show his hurt. "Is that what you think of me, Mysie?"

"On the other hand," she said, ignoring him, "if you stay on as a miner you might become idle, or get killed."

"Last month," he remarked, with gloomy satisfaction, "a rock big as a boat fell on Hughie Johnstone in our pit. He was squashed like a frog under a bus."

"Be quiet."

"No, I'll not be quiet, Mysie. Would you prefer me as a drunkard or as a squashed frog?"

"Be quiet, I said. There's somebody coming I know."

Elrigmuir glanced ahead at the man slowly approaching. "It looks like Rutherford."

"Where's your famous politeness now? He's a friend of mine. Is that why you're going to be rude to him?"

"I'm not going to be rude to anybody," he whispered. "It's just that there are some queer stories going about about him."

"Carried by foul mouths, no doubt."

"Has he got terribly hairy ears?"

"Fool!"

"Somebody said he had. I don't know, and I don't care. It's nothing to me whether his ears are hairy or not. I don't even care if he's got no ears at all."

"Fool!"

"I'm not such a fool maybe as you think, Mysie."

Then their whispers had to die away altogether, for Rutherford was on them.

His gaze had been on the pavement.

"Hello, Mr. Rutherford," said Mysie, very cheerfully. At the same time she nudged Elrigmuir hard to make him utter a similar greeting.

Rutherford looked up. His hands were thrust deep into the pockets of a coat that Elrigmuir was sure must have cost ten pounds.

"You're late, surely," he said.

"I'm just taking your precious centre-forward to the bus," said Mysie.

"You do that, Mysie. Without him we're all lost. Good night." He touched his cap and walked on.

"Mind you," murmured Elrigmuir, "I can see what they all mean."

"Who? What are you talking about?"

"I've heard them all talking about him—the players, I mean, and others too. Nobody seems to hae a good word for him. They say he's selfish, all for himself and his son. I don't know, for I'm just a stranger yet, but that coat he'd on would cost ten pounds at least. I'd hae to howk coal for a month to buy a coat like that."

"I thought I told you he was a friend of mine."

"You just say that, Mysie, because everybody else is against him."

"He's kind-hearted. Do you ken old Tinto Brown?"

Elrigmuir had been introduced, as messiah to prophet. He had been nauseated by the stink off the old flatterer's breath.

"Mr. Rutherford's very good to him," she said. "And to others. But here's your bus."

"Should I miss it and take the next one?"

"There might be no next one. And wouldn't it be the daftest thing to stand and let a bus go by?"

Elrigmuir smiled, and, looking at her, saw she was smiling too. He schemed.

The bus stopped. He made to jump on, turned instead and kissed her, on the cold nose as it happened, and then leapt aboard, waving his hand.

The conductress looked at him with a peculiar smile.

"I'm going to marry that girl," he said, in elation, not caring that half the passengers heard. "And I'm going to play for Scotland some day at footba', for her sake."

Those who heard smiled in indulgence or pity, for a young man without a coat to his back so recklessly in love.

8

When he had encountered Mysie and Elrigmuir, Andrew Rutherford had been arguing himself into a misanthropy. Surely the solution to all his problems of scruple and obligation was simply to toss these into the gutter like fag-ends. If, as at the pavilion tonight, he was cold-shouldered and made feel unwelcome and superfluous, why should he pine and want to cringe like a houseless cur nearer to the fire of folks' approval? Better to stay out in the cold and dark, yelp when yelped at, bite when bitten.

Somehow the meeting with the two young people so evidently in love and yet so evidently in the midst of a quarrel restored to him his faith in people and his confidence that happiness could still be achieved. If he persevered at the pavilion, and if the team continued to do well in the Cup, he would break down the distrust and dislike shown to him. His father had refused reconciliation twice already, though it had been offered with complete humility; but after the hundredth time, or the two hundredth even, there must be an end to an old man's pardonable bitterness. If Robbie had turned their estrangement into an open fight, inciting his sons to throw stones and abuse, even that could be amended by patience, love, and refusal to retaliate.

The more human beings loved each other, the more difficult they found it to forgive faults. Perfection could never be found on earth, not even in the person one loved; but it was forever desired in that person, and every falling short was a mortal blow. Hence the overwhelming need to love Christ, who was perfect and in whom there could be no disappointment. Yet no man who hated or despised or rejected his fellows could ever love Him.

Andrew stopped suddenly as he remembered, in the light of these meditations, the brief scene in the main street yesterday when he had behaved by no means according to this noble recipe.

Robbie's Isa, with her pale-browed madonna-like face, had stopped him on his way home from work. She had timidly plucked him into a closemouth so that they would not be seen. He had been worrying over Lizzie Anderson's accusation, which everybody affected not to believe but which seemed to offend nobody. Therefore, as Isa gazed at him with her eyes dark and large in her pale face, he saw in them an appeal so feminine he instantly hardened against it.

"What is it, Isa? I've little time."

She nodded. There was not the suspicion of a sneer on her face. If she was thinking, why hurry home to a house where he was never waited for, she showed no sign. As she gazed at the cut on his brow she showed only solicitude, which he knew was genuine.

"I had to see you, Andra," she said. "I had to tell you how sorry I am."

"I can believe that, Isa," he said. It was a likely thing to say, a compliment to her pacific nature; but there could be another interpretation, and by the roughness of his tone he hinted at this: was she eager to pacify him in case he stopped her weekly dole of eight and threepence?

She was simple, with a mind as clear as the burn water of her ancestral Highlands; yet she was intelligent too, and understood.

"I hae no pride, Andra," she said.

Though his heart melted in him at that beautiful admission, he kept his attitude ambiguous.

"Don't say that, Isa," he said, with a laugh. "We Scots are great ones for our pride."

"I must take your part, Andra. I ken you're a guid man."

"That's an unpopular view these days."

"I don't care what anybody says."

"You'll hae heard what Lizzie Anderson's saying?"

"She's more to be pitied, Andra, than blamed."

He laughed. "I'm afraid pity for her's a luxury I can't afford."

"What life's in store for her, and her children?"

"Born in the gutter, Isa, they'll be acclimatised to it by the time they're aware of it."

She gazed steadily, serenely, sadly at him. He noticed her hair was turning white, though she was years younger than himself. Far better than most she transcended dowdy, threadbare clothes, calloused fingers, shrunken neck. If ever he was seeking an example of goodness amidst corruption, of kindness amidst hate, of sweetness amidst rancour and spite, he would not have to seek far.

"Don't let them make you hard, Andra," she murmured.

"Easy advice, Isa."

She shook her head. "I ken it's not easy."

He glanced sharply at her: was her goodness not merely an accident of birth like the largeness of her eyes and the paleness of her brow? Had she the same struggles within her as he had? Yes, much harder struggles, for her misfortunes had been greater and her advantages less.

"It's not easy," he agreed.

"It should be easier for you," she said. "You believe in God."

He was surprised, and chose to become angry.

"That's my own business, Isa. Keep that side out of it."

"I'm sorry, Andra. I meant no harm."

"Likely you want to ken why I hit him?"

"No."

"I hit him because he was drunk, and because he was gloating how he'd belted young Gavin for taking money from me. If my money's helping to destroy your family, Isa, maybe I oughtn't to offer any more."

"I'll miss it, Andra, for the boys' sakes."

He touched his brow.

"Don't blame them too much. Gavin was greeting afterwards. He kens it was wrong. He likes you. None of them are bad boys at heart."

"We all start from innocence, Isa."

"You are bitter," she said, and sighed.

"You seem to forget, Isa, I'm married too, and owe a loyalty to my ain family."

"I don't forget it. How is Gerald?"

In anybody else, he thought, the inquiry would have been sickeningly sycophantic. How she avoided it was wonderful: a slim ordinary woman in poor clothes, holding a shopping basket. He ought then to have said what he really wished to say, that while he had a penny in the world she would have share of it.

What he did say was: "He's doing well."

"And Hannah?"

"She's all right too. But I'll hae to be getting along, Isa. One thing Hannah doesn't like is for the tea to be kept waiting." And another thing she doesn't like, he thought, is you, Isa. He wondered again if Isa and he would have made a successful match. When they were young he had had a better chance of her than Robbie. Perhaps it would have failed; a waverer and wanderer in the world of motives like himself had needed the determination and ruthlessness of Hannah. Married to Isa, he would today be still an engineer, probably unemployed, living in a dull street in a room and kitchen with three or four hungry weans.

"Well, I'll think it over, Isa," he said, and, touching his hat, had walked away, deliberately leaving her in doubt.

Now on the lamplit avenue he stopped, and saw his callousness as evil, able to take all beauty from life, the brightness from the moon, the fragrance from roses, and the sweet daffing foolishness from young lovers like Mysie Dougary and Alec Elrigmuir. He must make atonement for this too, and it would not be enough to keep making the weekly payments to Isa through Jordan the factor. Atonement could not be bought; the very hope of buying it was itself a sin. Yet what other store than of money had he at his command?

He trudged on. That way home took him past Malarkin's house. Sometimes young fellows loitered there in the hope of seeing Margot get ready for bed. It was rumoured she could be seen walking about her bedroom almost naked. She knew it outraged the elderly and puritanical and tantalised the young and romantic. She did it just often enough to keep the legend fresh, and just seldom enough to keep Sergeant Elvan from interfering.

As Andrew passed he looked up at the bedroom window; it was in darkness. Margot once at a bowling-club dance had flirted with him; she had been tipsy. Now he wondered if with her, so contemptuous of what were called the sanctities of life, oblivion could be obtained. Hardly, with remorse the clype waiting always behind the door. There were men—like Tinto Brown in his hey-day, for instance—who, seeing no purpose in life and despising religion, sought anodynes in drink and women. Long ago it had been looked on as a beautiful satisfying way of life, according to the paintings of the fat wine-god and his plump pink nymphs. In Calvinist Scotland it was considered degrading. Yet Tinto, bound for the Calvinist hell, despite his dirt, disease, and randiness, could give one a glimpse whiles of that carefree, far-off, mythological life under blue skies and green trees; whereas puritans like Hannah, or himself for that matter, so clean, cautious, and respectable, conjured up only high, narrow stone walls.

As he came nearer home he prepared himself against Hannah's customary grumbles and chidings. It was strange how she resolutely maintained an outward appearance of calmness, dignity, and even fastidiousness, yet by her every word kept revealing the meanness and impoverishment of her mind. Silent in her chair, Hannah was impressive; girning, she became almost contemptible; and yet often as she nagged and showed how empty was her mind, and therefore her life, he felt towards her a great responsibility and compassion. Let her ever admit her insufficiency, let her weep over that emptiness, and they would be brought together closer than they'd ever been, even in their courting days.

Tonight she would be at her worst. That morning she'd received an anonymous scribble, accusing him of being the father of Lizzie Anderson's unborn child. She had read it and then without comment had handed it to him, while she'd gone on to read her other letter, which he thought had been from her brother Harry. When he had handed back the silly little filthy note she had refused to take it. She had shaken her head, with a peculiar smile in her eyes. It was almost as if she'd found the libel amusing. By this time, though, the joke would have turned sour.

Then, unexpectedly, tenderness for her flowed into his mind. For all her faults—and what right had he to assess them?—she was his wife and Gerald's mother. She was the woman he had chosen in preference to Isa and many others. There had been a time when in her erectness of figure and firmness of mouth he had seen courage and endurance. Never bonny in the way Mysie Dougary was bonny, never sweet as Isa in her young days had been sweet, she had nonetheless in his eyes a gracious distinction of body and soul. Recalling it, not in thought but in emotion, he felt moved almost to tears. In many places they had been happy together, particularly at Tighnabruaich in the lovely Kyles of Bute, where they had spent a week in a one-roomed cottage when Gerald was only months old. For that happiness he owed her gratitude. She was not, nor ever had been, the wife he had dreamed of in his romantic adolescence. Always she had lacked feminine softness, always she'd been quick to condemn, slow to pity; always she'd envied success and despised failure. In the early days he had looked on her intelligence as superior; now he knew that, lacking imagination, it was third-rate.

Nevertheless there must be still time to save their marriage, but there must be on his part at least a deliberate curtailment of expectation. He had come too far along life's road with her to believe there was a corner round which he'd trudge to find everything marvellously changed. No, there would be many corners, and he would be lucky to find even the tiniest change round a few of them. In every man's life there was a dreadful moment of fixity, after which the same thoughts and habits and emotions possessed him till he died. Death was well called a dissolution.

He had reached this stoical conclusion, and was padding it with little solaces, turning it into a typical nest of self-pity, when he suddenly realised that he was being guilty of a disloyalty towards his wife more enormous than if he had seduced Lizzie Anderson or had just come from Margot Malarkin's bed. He had no right to judge any human being, weigh that being's worth as if it was easily measurable, reject any hope of reformation, and smugly accept the incurable mediocrity. Far less had he any right when that human being was his wife, married to him for fifteen years. What faults she had, he had contributed to them. To be content with a dreary compromise was a sin against Hannah and Gerald. If human love failed, was there not God's love to revive and strengthen it?

As he pushed open the gate he found himself using the old caution lest it creak and warn Hannah of his coming. Instantly, at that little involuntary demonstration of inveterate distrust and fear, he felt a terror surrounding him, coming from the moonlit sky, from the house, from every corner of the familiar garden— the terror that God's love, which was so necessary, was not available to him. From the gate, along the paved path, through the trellis sweet in summer with rambler roses, by the side of the house, and right up to the back door that terror accompanied him. But there it was miraculously dispelled.

The living-room window was, of course, curtained, and he could not see in; but as he lingered outside, head bowed, heart sick, he heard someone within singing. It was Hannah, who seldom sang, or at least let anyone hear her. The song was a favourite of his, and she had always indicated a contempt for its characteristic sadness. It was the Highland air 'Turn Ye To Me'; and she sang it so mournfully it sounded like a dirge. The wild gleam of love, by the desolation of the dark sea, was extinguished. Yet he sensed she was trying to sing it faithfully, despite her harsh, untunable voice; that she was indeed finding pleasure in it.

When he turned the handle and entered he made enough noise to warn her but not enough to disturb her singing if she wished to continue. She did continue, after a perceptible faltering, which could be attributed to her listening and making sure, like any wife alone at night, that it was her husband who had come in. He felt pleased and grateful that she should recognise the sounds he made, the way he closed the door, cleaned his feet on the mat, switched on the kitchen light, and crossed the stone floor.

Never for years had he entered the living-room with greater anxiety, anticipation, and vigilance. If Hannah, shocked by that anonymous letter so soon after the minister's insult, had determined on her part to make an effort at reconciliation he must take care not to thwart that effort in any way, by word or gesture or even by a wrong silence. Therefore as he entered he remembered to close the door quietly behind him, not slamming it, as he sometimes did to her annoyance, or leaving it ajar. Nor did he show the astonishment and pleasure he felt to see that she was wearing a pink dressing-gown he had bought her two or three Christmases ago, and spurned by her as too gay and frivolous, more suitable for such as Margot Malarkin. Now she wore it over a white nightdress, as she sat in front of the fire, brushing her hair.

As he passed through to hang coat and hat in the cupboard in the lobby he noticed Gerald's suitcase already packed for school tomorrow, and on the sideboard a volume of the encyclopedia. The table was set for supper for two. His hands trembled as he hung coat and hat on their proper peg. He felt shy as he returned into the living-room, where Hannah, more quietly now, as if she, too, was shy, still sang the Hebridean song of sorrow and sea-waves and gulls and gloaming and lover's passionate plea. He pulled his tie straight, wiped his moustache with his handkerchief, and smoothed his hair with his hand, as he had done long ago when he had visited her house to court her.

"Have I kept you waiting for your supper?" he asked. "I'm sorry, Hannah; I was kept a bit late."

The words were false, and threatened to turn the peaceful atmosphere in the room false too. It wasn't only that they contained a lie, for, of course, he could have been home an hour ago, but had preferred to roam the streets in the hope she would have gone to bed. Apart from the lie, his words were altogether too ordinary. They must have sounded to her as if everything was still the same to him as it had been last night or any night for years: thrawn or obtuse or nasty, whatever the reason, he had not noticed her attempt at friendliness. Yet to protest vehemently he was aware of it, and was so much in sympathy with it he could have knelt and laid his head on her lap, would be, within the limits of his nature and abilities, to take too great a risk. All his life he had been clumsy in carrying delicate things.

"I was in no hurry," she said. "After I got Gerald to bed I thought I'd take a bath and wash my hair."

"It's still bonny hair," he murmured.

"Not so bonny now," she said steadily, "though it was my pride once. Plain women have to look after what compensations they've got. I've been noticing there's a lot of grey in it."

"In mine too," he murmured. "Were you and Gerald looking through the encyclopedia?"

"For a while. He was doing his French exercise."

Andrew turned over the pages of the big book. There were pictures of Australian scenes with kangaroos. It occurred to him how often he'd dreamt of emigrating.

"I'll put on the kettle," he said, and went into the kitchen.

She kept on brushing, and resumed her song quietly.

He found the kettle already on the stove, near to boiling. She seemed to have forgotten nothing. As he made the tea his hands were again trembling.

"Three spoonfuls, mind," she called.

He smiled: she liked strong tea.

"I remembered, Hannah."

He carried the teapot into the living-room and placed it inside its cosy, which was really the crinoline, knitted in yellow and green, of a tiny china lady. It struck him it was a peculiarly feminine idea for a tea-cosy, and glancing round the room he found it full of similar dainty ideas.

"Will I pour the tea?" he asked.

"Let it infuse."

"Aye, that's right. I'm always in too big a hurry to pour out tea after it's made."

It was a silly remark, but tonight she let it pass.

"Maybe it proves I'm inclined to rush at things," he said. "I ken this, anyway, I often blurt out the opposite of what's in my mind." He remembered the scene with Robbie at the foot of the stairs.

"We've got to do that, it seems," she said. "I mean, say what we don't think."

"True enough."

She was silent, and he could hear the crackles of the brush through her strong hair. Her face was veiled.

"But I'm going to say now, Andrew, exactly what I think. At least I'm going to try. I ken it's not easy sometimes to find the right words."

"I was just thinking the same thing coming up the road."

"You'd better come and sit here by the fire. We don't want to wake up Gerald."

There had been times when her shouting at him had awakened the boy. Andrew hastened to obey and sat down in the chair opposite her. If he had been a smoker he could have dissembled his awkwardness in searching through his pockets for cigarettes or in lighting his pipe. Without that resource, he clasped his hands on his knees.

She kept brushing, careful not to remove the veil of hair.

"That letter," she said.

He kept quiet.

"It's made me do a lot of thinking. It's a good thing whiles to get a jolt. I've not been thinking much about Lizzie Anderson, though. Everybody kens her for a depraved, evil-minded, lying besom."

"She's all that."

"Even her own mother kens it."

Foolishly he wondered if Hannah had been talking to Mrs. Anderson.

"Everybody in Drumsagart kens," said Hannah again, "that she's a liar as well as a prostitute, young though she is."

He thought in his wife's thorough condemnation of his calumniator there was courage as well as loyalty. In comparison, how feeble and dishonest were his own groping extenuations and fragments of Christian forgiveness.

Hannah suddenly parted her hair and gazed out at him. "I never once mistrusted you in that way, Andrew, and I certainly wouldn't start for the sake of Lizzie Anderson."

"Thanks, Hannah."

"Everybody in this town kens her well for a malicious young liar."

He nodded, but was now uneasy by the repetition, which somehow seemed calculated.

"Isn't that so?"

"I'm afraid it is, Hannah."

Again her face was obscured. For a full minute she did not speak. He thought the tea would be growing cold.

"If she's such a notorious liar," she said suddenly, "why are they all pretending to believe the filthy slanders she and her friends hae been chalking all over the town?"

He was confused, for, of course, there was no answer to her shrewd question. He hadn't known she knew about the chalkings. Had this patience and restraint of hers been imposed to deceive and weaken him, so that when she reverted to her old carping aggressive self he would be very vulnerable?

"There was one chalked on the wall by our gate."

"Surely not!"

"As soon as I knew it was there I went out with a cloth and wiped it off."

"What was it this time?" he asked, with miserable smile.

"It wasn't spelled right."

"Did Gerald see it?"

"I don't know that. Naturally I never asked him."

"Well, anyway, he wouldn't ken what it meant."

"I don't know that either, Andrew. A boy grows up to be a man. His mind's often a secret place, even to his own parents."

"That's true," he whispered, amazed by her insight and frankness.

"This is a dirty-minded town. How can any boy grow up in it and not be defiled?"

"Drumsagart's not any more dirty-minded than anywhere else, Hannah."

"You mean it's a dirty-minded world?"

"I'm sorry to say it is, more or less."

"Don't be sorry. Be glad this has opened your eyes."

"They were never really closed to that sort of thing."

"They could hardly be, seeing you attend so many football matches."

"I didn't mean that, Hannah. I just meant I was a boy myself once and grew up to be a man. My mind was secret too. Maybe it still is, but not from choice now. Such secrecy's a habit that's hard to break."

"The truth of this business is, Andrew: somebody who hates you is chalking foul things about you and writing foul letters about you, and everybody else in this town is enjoying it all as a good joke. They're laughing at the mud on your face."

"Don't spoil your case by exaggerating, Hannah." He laughed.

"They're not all laughing." He hesitated. "I was speaking to somebody yesterday who had a good word for me."

"Who was that?"

"Isa."

There was a pause, filled with danger.

"Well she might praise you, Andrew, seeing all you've done for her. Do you think I don't ken about your arrangement with Jordan the factor?"

He was overwhelmed.

"I've kent for a long time," she said. "I didn't approve, but I thought I had no right to interfere. That was your way of doing good. It wouldn't ever be my way, as you know."

"What other way was there, in this case? If you can tell me that, Hannah, I'll be sincerely grateful."

"Nobody can tell you that. We all hae our own ideas of good and bad."

"Should we, though, Hannah? What's religion for if it's not to give us standards?"

"You're a good man, Andrew," she said, quite sharply.

He was so startled he thought at first she was being sarcastic in a new fashion. When he saw that she was serious he became dismayed, with a sense of softness that affected him to his innermost core of self-respect. He could hardly breathe. His hands were still clasped on his knees. He gazed at her as she calmly brushed her hair.

"But you hae never learned," she added, "that goodness by itself doesn't work in this world."

He shook his head, but did not know himself what the gesture meant.

"There are bad folk everywhere," she said, "and Drumsagart has more than its share. Say what you like, that's it summed up."

"I believe folk try . . ." But he could not finish, though she and her brush waited.

"Everybody in this town kens," she said, "you hae done your best to live according to your principles. Yet today, when it seems you've failed, they show no pity or respect; they laugh at you and seem to take pleasure in believing foul lies about you."

Again she paused. He thought, The tea will be dirt cold; and suddenly he shivered, as if there was a coldness in him too.

"I hear even your faither now refuses to associate with you."

He glanced at her. "Who was saying that?"

"Never mind. It's common knowledge. I can see it's true."

He supposed Geordie Bonnyton, the wee insurance agent,

had told her. He came to the house every week, ostensibly to collect insurance dues but really to have the town's gossip squeezed out of him.

He tried to speak gently. "That's my own private business, Hannah."

"Is your business not mine too? We've been married for fifteen years."

"If you can help me to win my faither's regard again," he said, "I'll be grateful."

"I can scarcely do that. You ken he's got little regard for me; aye, and I've not got much for him. To me he's always been an old, sour, spoiled man. He's talked big, I ken. But wha has listened to him?"

"You said yourself the world was full of bad folk. If they'd listened to my faither, and heeded what he said——"

"They had more to do with their time, Andrew, than listen to him. But that's enough of your faither. I didn't want to bring him into our talk tonight; I had to, as you'll see in a minute. And I don't want to speak about your brother either. Just let me say I ken you and he came to blows, and that you didn't get that cut on the brow from any accident."

"Has Geordie Bonnyton been clyping?" he asked.

She smiled at the child's word. "Clyping? You've done nothing wrong, Andrew, so there can be no clyping. I'm on your side." Her voice softened. "Aye, I'm on your side, and I want to help you, as a wife should when her man's in trouble."

"I wasn't aware I was in trouble. I may have certain problems to solve, but a man's got his own destiny to work out."

"Destiny?" She laughed. "I'll show you destiny." From the pocket of her dressing-gown she took out a small photograph and handed it to him.

It showed a large stone villa set in a spacious garden. It must have been taken on a sunny day. It seemed a very pleasant, peaceful place to live.

She laughed again as she watched his interest. "It's for sale," she said, "in Helensburgh."

"We could never afford to buy that, Hannah."

"That's where you're wrong. Did you notice I had a letter from Harry this morning? That photograph was in it. And do you know what else? An offer to help us to buy it. Harry's been all through it. He knows the owner. He says it's in wonderful condition inside and out." She could not keep a little shriek of eagerness out of her voice; it kept recurring, like a fault in a wireless set. "You can't see the water in the photo, but you can from the windows. There's a wonderful view of the Firth. It's all just been newly decorated. Harry says we'd hardly need to spend a penny on it. The bathroom's tiled from floor to ceiling. You ken how I've always hankered after a bathroom like that. It's situated in a very select quarter. There's a good school, Harry says. The air's healthy. You'll be away from all these foul-mouthed enviers in Drumsagart. Harry says we can depend on him in every way. You ken how fond he is of Gerald. It's our duty to foster that fondness, for Harry's worth a lot of money now, and with no child of his own he's as likely to leave it to Gerald as to anybody. So even if the change didn't suit you and me—and of course it does—we should jump at the chance for Gerald's sake."

He had kept nodding at her enthusiastic description. This was her old mistake, repeated so often before and apparently going to be repeated till she died: that possession of material things brought happiness. Yet somehow her enthusiasm had made her young and susceptible, blazing away the wrinkles of grimness. As he gazed at the photograph as earnestly as any prospective purchaser he felt tender towards her so mistaken.

"Isn't it a fine house, Andrew?"

"On the big side, though."

"Nine rooms and kitchen. I don't think that's too big. We could keep a maid. We must hae ambition for our son's sake. What do you say?"

He searched for words to convey his decision and soften the disappointment. There were no such words in human speech, but still he searched for them.

"You ken I don't like to be any more beholden to Harry. He's done too much for me as it is."

"It's fair of you to admit it, Andrew. But why shouldn't you be able to depend on him? He's my brother, isn't he, and Gerald's uncle? Forby, he admires you."

Shaking his head with a smile, Andrew thought: And he thinks everything in the world can be bought for money, including me; so far, too, he's been proved right. Am I to give him complete proof by accepting this gift of a house? Living near him, deeper and deeper indebted to him, unable to rebel because of Hannah and Gerald, I would become his lickspittle. Maybe, of course, that's all I'm fit for.

As he kept smiling, with brows raised humorously at that bold claim of admiration, he saw the small, bald, brisk man's chubby malevolence and heard his jackal's laughter. No man could describe human corruptibility more joyfully than Harry: it was a joke to him, perennial and inexhaustible. He could in three minutes quote six incontrovertible instances; and he wouldn't need to take the cigar out of his mouth.

"Living in a house like that," said Hannah, "we'd be entitled to hold our places among the best in the land. I can see Gerald a surgeon yet."

"A surgeon?"

"Aye. You ken that's my ambition. Not just a common doctor, a surgeon making up to three thousand a year."

"It's a noble profession, mending people."

"He'll never achieve it in Drumsagart. You've got to have influence as well as brains to rise in the world. There's no influence here. And you ken, Andrew, as weel as me, that here in Drumsagart there's something broken between us no surgeon on earth could mend."

He was greatly moved. "I wouldn't say that, Hannah."

"It's true. But it can be mended easily enough there." She pointed to the photograph in his hand.

He studied it afresh, his hand trembling. "Nine rooms?"

She nodded. "Nine. Good-sized rooms too."

"Room for my faither?" He went on, heedless of her gasp. "I've been thinking he deserves to enjoy his retirement by the sea in comfort."

Still she said nothing, and he dared not look at her.

"Not that he would go," he said, after a long pause. During it he had made up his mind.

"I should think not. He's shown little interest in us. Why should we push in where we're obviously not wanted? Don't keep putting me off, Andrew. I want your answer. Harry asked me to telephone him tomorrow. We've to give our decision quick. What am I to say?"

"There are things in Helensburgh I'd miss."

"Such as?"

He looked at her. "You ken."

She laughed harshly. "Don't tell me," she cried—"for God's sake don't tell me you're thinking twice about going because you'd miss the football? Don't insult me, Andrew."

Of course it was part of his reason. There would be football in Helensburgh too, but it would be different there. From the age of six or seven he'd attended the matches of the Thistle. Those early games, watched through goggling eyes, were like legends to him. It was not just the field with its goalposts and home-made pavilion; nor even the legendary players; nor victories and defeats. It was all these, but much more; it was the quintessence of Drumsagart, his native place. Worthies long since dead had forgathered there, to argue, laugh, cheer, boo, and discuss the history of the town. How could he dismiss it as if it was a triviality? Yet if he did not so dismiss it how could he avoid insulting Hannah?

"I tell you what," he muttered, "give me time to think it over."

"How long d'you think you need?"

"A couple of days, say."

"Just long enough for the chance to be lost? No, Andrew, you'll have to say sooner."

"It's not like one of those profit-and-loss sums," he said, smiling, "that Gerald gets for homework."

"No, this is all profit."

"But, Hannah, I'm Drumsagart born and bred."

"So am I, and I'd leave tomorrow gladly."

He could find no retort.

"Don't insult me, Andrew, with excuses a child would be ashamed of. Hundreds, thousands of men leave the place they were born in. Some even cross oceans."

"Many break their hearts for hame," he said, unable to refrain.

She smiled then, and he imagined he could read behind that smile the accusation that, despite this avowed love of Drumsagart, he hadn't fought in the war to defend it.

"Some weak-minded fools may break their hearts for hame," she said, "but most sensible folk go because they know their native place has nothing for them but poverty and shame, and if they ever return, when they're prosperous and respectable, it's for revenge, to laugh at the place that had no use for them."

"I'll need time to think," he muttered, knowing that whatever time she granted would be used by him to find reasons convincing not to her, for such were impossible, but to himself. "I'll tell you tomorrow morning. Will that do?"

She nodded.

"I'd better make some fresh tea," he said, rising. "That stuff will be dirt cold."

Supper was a strange experience, full of constraint, as though their son upstairs lay not asleep but dead. They spoke softly and laconically about such neutral topics as the weather and Gerald's progress at school. Their very spoons tinkled in a subdued manner. It seemed to Andrew that outside the window were not other suburban gardens and small houses like their own, and beyond these the tenements and works of Drumsagart; no, outside was the great dark, lonely, illimitable sea of the song.

During the meal, and in the midst of his consciousness of that sad, enormous, barren loneliness outside, he became aware again how hope had restored to Hannah some of that distinction he had once cherished as a consolation. She smiled, as if already she saw herself as mistress of that fine house by a sea bright with sunshine and cheerful with yachts. She sat straight as ever, body and head; the skin of her neck was pale and smooth. In the white bridal nightdress and pink dressing-gown, with her hair loosely piled up on her head and flowing down her shoulders, she was, he realised, still more desirable to him as a woman than Margot Malarkin, say, with her slimming tablets and lipstick. Hannah's reluctance as a wife had often been frustrating and even humiliating, and no doubt it had contributed to the breakdown of their marriage; but he had realised that much of her unwillingness and perversity had sprung from a source he must sympathise with—the deep-seated Calvinist conviction that sexual love, like all bodily pleasures, was sinful.

Tomorrow he would deny her; he could not say for certain that his true motive was not revenge: so many times in the past had she denied him. Such eye-for-eye morality would be shameful even towards an enemy; how shocking and unpardonable to practise it against his own wife.

"I'll wash up," he murmured, "if you want to get to bed."

"I'll help."

"Hadn't you better watch you don't catch a cold, seeing you've had a bath and washed your hair?"

"I'm no hot-house plant, Andrew."

Therefore he washed the few dishes and she dried them. Together they returned them to the sideboard.

"I think I'll read a while," he said.

It would not, though, be a book by Walter Scott or Dickens or any such worth-while author he would read; no, it would be the day's newspapers, particularly their football gossip.

She nodded calmly as if to assist him in his pretence that his reading was important and by it he would increase his store of knowledge as well as sharpen his insight into the human heart.

"I'll get to bed, then," she said.

At the door she looked round the room as if there was something she'd forgotten.

"Is it your hot-water bottle?" he asked.

She smiled strangely. "No, that's in."

"I thought you were looking for something."

"No, I was just thinking, Andrew, there's something in this room that's not been here for a long time. It should be here always."

He could find nothing to say.

"I mean, of course," she added, "it should be in our house."

"So it should, Hannah."

"But not here, not here. Good night."

"Good night, Hannah. I'll put out the hall light after you."

She closed the door quietly after her. At once he tiptoed over to it, listened behind it like an eavesdropper, and opened it a little to hear better which bedroom she went into. It was absurd to think she would enter his, but when her own bedroom door closed behind her he felt the old frustrations and spites tighten in him. For a few friendly words she expected him to give up to her and her brother not only his independence and self-respect but also his right to vindicate himself in the eyes of his fellow-townsmen. Her price was his soul.

As he put out the hall light, savagely for all the tininess of the effort, he waited for a minute or so in the darkness; it was somehow like a kind of suicide. In the death of all expectation he felt his scalp tingle with terrifying premonition.

He could not tell that upstairs Hannah, behind her own door, waited too and sighed long and painfully when he at last returned into the living-room.

She was sure now he would not agree to her proposal; and whatever his reasons, he was wrong. If they remained here in Drumsagart, the deep frost in her, in which no flowers grew, would never thaw. She began to sob and warm tears ran down her cheeks.

About an hour later, well after midnight, he went upstairs to bed. Sadness, being exhausted, had turned to resentment. At her door, therefore, he held up his fist, clenched hard, and then let it fall against his brow. Ashamed, but still resentful, he went into his own bedroom, undressed quickly and got into bed, to find an additional grievance there in that no-one had bothered to put in a hot-water bottle for him. In bitter weather, with snow on the roof, he'd known her to have two bags in her bed, leaving none for him.

As he lay shivering it seemed to him the whole world was cold and antagonistic, he had no friends at all. If he gave in no-one could blame him; but if he refused to give in, if he continued the struggle to achieve goodness, if he succeeded in the end, who would ever notice, who would ever care? His father was old and would soon die; his brother was rotten with selfishness; his son was growing up, like all his generation, to recognise material success only; and his wife was a snob and a schemer.

When the door opened he was half-asleep and thought at first he must have forgotten to close it; but as he listened it closed again quietly. Then he became aware of a perfume in the room. Absurdly, emerging from a doze of self-pity, he felt some supernatural presence was in the room, some divine spirit sent to succour him. The perfume was beautiful and familiar. Perhaps his visitor was his mother.

The voice was hoarse, distracted, and pathetic; but it was Hannah's.

"I've come for your answer, Andrew," she said.

He could make her out now, standing with her back to the door, like a ghost indeed in her white nightgown. The scent was the one she'd used years ago.

"Before you say anything," she hurried on, panting, "let

me warn you, let me plead with you, that what I've asked you to do is very important, not just for me but for us all. Otherwise I can see nothing but ruin. Please me in this, and I'll make it up to you. I swear to God I will. If you're agreeable, Andrew, there's no need for me ever to leave this room again."

She waited then, with gasps like sobs.

He began to laugh. He could not understand why, except that he must be in the grip of a hysteria produced by sleepiness, by the unexpectedness of this visitation, by her astonishing words, and above all by that perfume. It was laughter far from mockery. Yet she justifiably thought she was being mocked.

"Are you laughing at me?" she cried, in horror.

"No, no."

"You were. I heard you. You were laughing at me."

"No, Hannah."

"No? What do you mean, no? You're laughing again. Hae I come here to be laughed at, like a cheap whore? I've got pride, mind."

"I ken that, Hannah. I wasn't laughing at you. God kens why I laughed, but it wasn't at you."

"I'm the only one in here besides yourself. Don't lie and make it worse. If you despise me, say so. I crushed my pride to come, and you laughed at me."

"I think I was laughing at myself, Hannah."

"Before I come again you'll be stretched out dead on that bed; and maybe I'll not come then either." She was sobbing as if she'd received not a great insult so much as a great fright.

He still heard her sobs after she'd abruptly gone, leaving the door open.

Stumbling out of bed, he crossed the landing. Her door was closed and locked. He had to speak in a low voice in case he wakened Gerald.

"I'm sorry, Hannah," he whispered. "I didn't mean to laugh at you. I'm bad enough, but not as bad as that, surely. I'll go to Helensburgh. You can tell Harry tomorrow. I'm sorry. I'm sorry. I'm sorry." He repeated that perhaps a dozen times with his brow against the door, but he knew that if he kept up the refrain all night the door would not open to him.

When he went back to bed some of his resentment had returned.

9

The male exodus from Drumsagart on Saturday was zealously planned. A special train was applied for and granted. Several buses were chartered. A few coughing motor-cars were doctored for the journey. Bicycles were oiled, and at least three pairs of boots had tackets hammered into them. Wives watched the preparations in scorn and bafflement: men who hadn't sixpence to spare to treat them to the pictures had the shilling for the train ticket; and workless martyrs, too tired with lounging at Cross or street corner to wash a dish or carry ashes down to the midden, were proposing to cycle or even walk the nineteen miles to Carrick and nineteen back; which made, to mathematicians thirty years left school, an infinity of useless miles. Nor were they assuaged with mumbles of change, of adventure, of a journey past high fields and through autumnal woods, of escape from the eternal bone-rotting idleness. They pointed out that there was to be no change for them; they would have their heads bent over the same sinks, their knees on the same floors, their arms burdened with the same weans, and their brains crazy with the same necessity of making a very little money go a very long way. There could be no answer to all that logic except a shrug, a snarl, or a snatch of cap from peg. Nor was there any answer to the taunt that if the cycle run or the walk were to be in search of work there could be only admiration and respect, and for the resultant blisters, on feet or behinds, tenderest care; but injuries sustained for the sake of football could expect only the salt of contempt.

Those few who could domineer their wives ordered them to shut up. The majority, weakened by tiny spots of doubt and shame on their souls, tried to be reasonable, and when reason failed suffered in patience the marital reproofs. In hardly any case was there a wife exalted to forget the worldly interests of her sex in the glory of Cup-tie victory. But then, had not the Covenanters themselves in their day probably failed to convince their wives that to serve God it was necessary to be imprisoned or harried or killed?

Devout men with a chance of borrowed or free transport let neither pride nor principle stand in their way. Nippy Henderson was such a one. He drove a van for the Biscuit Factory. An incorrigible lover of himself, he had never been able to understand, despite numerous rebuffs, how others might have a different opinion; yet his cunning exceeded his conceit. He reasoned it out that if he took the van to Carrick on Saturday with six passengers, or eight crammed, at a sixpence per head, he would make some money and in addition travel free himself: the petrol would be supplied by the firm. All that was needed was to cajole Rutherford into agreeing, and this he reckoned would be easy, as the big manager these days was as hungry for a crumb of friendliness as a robin in snow-time.

Therefore on Friday afternoon Nippy, in the manner that had given him his nickname, twinkled along to the manager's little office. He kissed his knuckles before he knocked, twiddled his fingers at his nose, and bobbed in on the sharp invitation with his cap submissive at his breast. His face used all his creases of servility twice over.

Rutherford was seated at his desk with his hat and coat on. He looked, thought Nippy, like a gunman in a gangster film, one who served with brainless brawn the master-mind in the background. Nippy felt like such a master-mind.

"Well, Henderson, what is it this time?"

"Begging your pardon for disturbing you, Mr. Rutherford," said Nippy, thinking, with a series of internal winks, was it in here Lizzie was bairned?

"Say what you want, and then get back to your work."

For a moment Nippy was checked in those winks: that internal eye, indeed, had been punched. Arrogant big sod, he thought, bairner of imbecile girls, don't use that tone to me. I was in uniform when you sat at hame coining in the money, you and yon wee fat-arsed brother-in-law of yours.

His voice, however, consorted with his face, over which kept spreading ripples of comical flattery.

"I'll be brief, I'll be brief, as a bride's nightshirt." Then he realised in dismay, behind his chuckles and knee-slaps, that that was the wrong kind of joke altogether. Surely hatred was making him misjudge?

Rutherford scowled. "What the hell d'you mean coming in

here and talking to me like that?" His voice grew louder. "I'm the manager here, mind that. If I tell a man to get out, he gets out."

Nippy was frightened. This was the first time he had heard Rutherford assert his position so fiercely. Hitherto it had been plain to men far less perspicacious than Nippy considered himself that the manager was curiously ashamed. Everybody knew he'd been pushed into the job by his brother-in-law, the fat racketeer; but then most jobs were got by influence nowadays, so why should Rutherford alone be diffident and ashamed? Nevertheless his attitude had been satisfactory to Nippy.

"I'm sorry, Mr. Rutherford," he whined. "You ken me, too big a joker for my ain guid. It slipped oot. My wife says I'll joke at my ain funeral."

Rutherford glared at him. "Or at hers," he snarled. "I hope you're not in to ask if you can have the van for the match tomorrow?"

Nippy bobbed up and down in a mixture of football fan's enthusiasm and underling's deference.

"That's it, Mr. Rutherford. You ken me, safest driver on the road. I'd dearly like to be there to cheer the old Thistle on to victory. We'll need all the support we can get yonder. The truth is, Mr. Rutherford sir, my wife you ken, she's not been keeping well lately, and I thought if I went by train or bus I'd hae to leave a guid hour earlier, and I'd be hame an hour later. Whereas if I went by the van I could sit wi' her till the last minute almost; and of course I could come straight hame."

"If you're so anxious about your wife, why go at all, why not bide at hame and keep her company?"

Nippy tried to look like a man doting on his wife, but could not. His indignation at Rutherford's remark was so huge he couldn't hide it. Rutherford was a fine one to talk about pampering wives; they said he didn't even sleep with his any more. And he was a fine one, too, to give advice about staying at home on Saturday. Hadn't he been given a choice—his old father or football?—and hadn't he chosen football? Wasn't it said of him that he'd sacrifice even his son for the sake of winning the Cup in his year as president? *He'd* be there at Carrick on Saturday; nothing was surer than that.

Despite the flexibility and well-trained loyalty of his features, Nippy was unable to keep some of those thoughts from appearing on his face. He had to seek safety in a fast whimper.

139

"Weel, Mr. Rutherford, you ken how it is. Football takes a grip of a man. Women don't understand. I feel I must be there on Saturday to cheer on our team. After all, I was born in Drumsagart, like yourself. It'll be a great game, and if we win what's to stop us from going on to win the Cup? You did a wonderful stroke of work signing on young Elrigmuir. A shade conceited yet, I thought last week, coming oot the pavilion last to get the limelight, but a grand player for all that, a natural, a world champion in the making. And I don't mind telling you, Mr. Rutherford, though I've nae religious bias—I could swear on my grannie's tombstane to that—still, I'd dearly like to see the old Thistle go yonder and thrash the papish conceit oot of them. We're a Protestant country, after all."

"There's nothing to stop you going and shouting whatever rubbish you like."

"Thanks, Mr. Rutherford."

"But you'll not go in my van."

It's not your van, you big swollen-heidit eedjit, thought Nippy, outwardly fawning. "I'll be mair careful than big Archie Birkwood driving his new hearse. I'll tell you what, let me hae the van and I'll take Tinto Broon and Crutch Brodie with me."

"Would they sit on the floor?"

"I'll get them tins or boxes to sit on. Will it be all right then, Mr. Rutherford?"

"It will not. I said, no van. That's final. Get out now, and be damned smart about it."

Nippy could think of no adequate retort except some very filthy gibe about Lizzie Anderson. He would have given half a day's wages to be able to utter it, but he could not afford to sacrifice the very source of those wages: that would be too high a price for truth. A poor man's principle had to be perpetually in his pocket like the lining, and often was as holey as that.

"I'm sorry if I've offended you, Mr. Rutherford," he snivelled. "It was furthest frae my mind."

"I'd be a damned jessie," shouted Rutherford, "letting the likes of you offend me. Let me tell you this, and you can pass it on to your mates: I've got a reputation here as a saftie—not as a boss who's tried to be decent and lenient, but as a bloody saftie. Well, that's come to an end. You'll see. You'll all see. Now get out."

Nippy got out. Behind the door he made an obscene gesture and then scurried off, bottling his merriment till he arrived in the garage, where two workmates were waiting.

There he let out his merriment, but just couldn't make it sparkle or even fizz. When, with profoundest virulence, he communicated Rutherford's threat of tyranny his mates, too, laughed, but it was the flattest of laughter.

"For Christ's sake," said Davie Morland, who plucked a fag half smoked out of his mouth and threw it away, "what hae we done?"

He repeated it to his puzzled mates. "What hae we done?"

Nippy and the other man, Jimmy Brand, always felt there was a mysterious bit in Davie: he was a Catholic.

"What d'you mean, Davie?" asked Nippy. "All I did was ask for the van, as politely as you like."

"Was he really angry, Nippy?" asked Brand.

"Roaring like a bull; not that I was feart."

"He's a big brute of a man if ever he did get mad," said Brand. "D'you think it's this Lizzie Anderson business that's riled him?"

"We're all to blame," said Morland. "Jesus, haven't we all been sniggering at the man behind his back? Even after he's been to tell us aboot a bonus or an extra day's holiday."

"You sniggered yourself, Davie," muttered Nippy.

"I said so, and I'm saying I was wrang to do it. D'you ken what would be the right thing for everybody in this factory to do?"

"No." They shook their heads, ready to distrust his Catholic suggestion.

"We should get together and apologise. We should at least let him ken there's not one of us believes Lizzie Anderson's rubbish. We should tell him he has our support; aye, and our gratitude for his fair treatment of us."

Nippy and Brand gazed at each other and gave little nods. It was as they'd suspected. This suggestion of Morland's was typically Catholic, with its mixture of submission and confession. As Protestants they instinctively spurned it; that neither attended kirk made no difference; opposition to such monkish notions as kneeling in mystery was bequeathed them, it was in their blood.

"Do you want us, Davie," sneered Nippy, "to walk to him or go on oor knees?"

"Maybe you'll see us all flopping doon on oor bellies like seals in the zoo. If Rutherford changes his policy, who's going to stand between us and yon wee swine Gemmell?"

They shook their heads irritably. What he said was true enough, but such a public display of gratitude towards a man they did not like seemed to them distasteful and even indecent, like crossing oneself in the street or wearing the daub of dirt on one's brow on Ash Wednesday.

"There'll be men and women sacked here, I'm warning you," went on Morland, "and the lucky ones will hae to work twice as hard for less money."

Nippy could find no squib of myriad sparks to throw into the midst of that dismal prophecy.

"I've a guid mind," he snarled, "not to go and see his bluidy team on Saturday."

Meanwhile Rutherford in his office had at last snatched up the telephone and asked for the police-station.

"This is Andrew Rutherford, of the Biscuit Factory," he said. "I want to speak to Sergeant Elvan."

The constable at the other end hesitated. "He's not on duty just now, Mr. Rutherford. As a matter of fact today's his youngest boy's birthday. I don't think he'd want to be disturbed unless it was urgent."

"It's urgent enough."

"I see." He waited. "Could you give me some idea?"

"No."

"All right, I'll try and get hold of him for you."

"Thanks."

Rutherford sat waiting with the telephone gripped far more tightly than was necessary. Once he spoke, an expression of disgust, like a spit, indistinctly uttered and indeterminately aimed.

The sergeant had bought a clockwork train-set for his son's birthday. He was demonstrating it on the kitchen floor when the policeman interrupted. He came to the telephone displeased.

"Hello. This is Elvan."

"Many happy returns to your boy, Sergeant. What age is he now?"

"Nine. It's nice of you, but you didn't ring me up, did you, just to offer your congratulations?"

"No. Though it might make a friendlier world if we were in the habit of doing it."

"A bit inconvenient, I would say."

"It's about those anonymous letters and the chalkings on the walls." He thought he heard Elvan chuckle. "Is it funny?"

"Funny? What do you mean, Mr. Rutherford?"

"I thought you laughed."

"Lawbreaking's no laughing matter to me. It's my bread and butter."

"I hear the Lucky Sporran's full of poets these nights making up rhymes."

"What about?"

"Me."

"Do you want me to go in and tell them to stop it?"

"I want to ask you if you've found out yet who wrote those letters."

"But I thought you said you didn't want any investigation?"

"I said so, but I didn't think that would stop you. Did it?" He was sure he heard another chuckle.

"As a matter of fact it didn't. As you ken, I hae a philosopher's interest in human failings, so I investigated as a philosopher seeing I wasn't to do it as a policeman."

"And were you successful?"

"I was."

"Was it Lizzie herself, the glaikit besom?"

"Lizzie can scarcely wipe her ain neb, far less write. No, it wasn't Lizzie. By the way, you'll be relieved to learn she's not pregnant at all. That was a lie."

"Why should I be relieved?"

Another chuckle. "Well, like everybody else in the town, I ken you are a man wi' great compassion for weans. I've seen you handing oot broken biscuits to them. Think what a life Lizzie's wean would hae been born into; and withoot a faither. That's all I meant."

"I see. All right then, as a compassionate man, Sergeant, I'm relieved."

"Of course it's only a temporary relief. She'll spawn soon enough. Remember what I said to you at the pavilion: guid men are scarce? It could be that oot of Lizzie's brood a guid man could emerge. I admit that's possible, and it's a large part of my faith. I should think, too, it's a chance a Christian like yourself ought to be willing to take."

"I didn't interrupt your birthday celebrations, Sergeant, to discuss Christian beliefs."

"No, you didn't. You wanted to hear who wrote those letters? You still want to hear?"

"Aye."

"It was your brither Robbie. Of course he had accomplices, but he's the main culprit."

"Who helped him?"

"I didn't try to find that out. I suppose Lizzie gave him her story."

"Did his wife help him, d'you think?"

"His wife? I wouldn't think so. She was greeting when I was in the hoose, but women greet for strange reasons. I've seen them greet for men jailed for kicking them. Maybe she did. After all, is a wife not on oath to be a helpmate?"

"I can see, Sergeant, you hae your sense of humour."

"I'm naturally a light-hearted man."

"You're lucky, then. I was a dull stick always. Well, now you ken who wrote them, what are you going to do about it?"

"That's up to you. If you want me to charge him, I'll do it wi' pleasure. It'll be no trouble to me, so don't hesitate oot of consideration for my feelings." There was another chuckle.

"That's very self-sacrificing of you, Sergeant. I don't want him charged, yet. I take it you warned him it's to stop?"

"I warned him."

"Will he stop it?"

"I am no man's keeper, Mr. Rutherford. He's embittered, and he would destroy you if he could."

"I'll take care of that. I think that's all, Sergeant. Thanks for your help."

"I enjoy it; it's my hobby, as football's yours."

"By the way, Sergeant, you're not a Drumsagart man. Where is it you come from?"

Another chuckle, but this time not so confident. "I don't see that it's relevant, Mr. Rutherford; but if it interests you, I come from a wee place called Crosslyon."

"That's in the country, isn't it?"

"It is."

"Why did you leave it?"

Another wary chuckle. "Are you really asking, why did I ever come to Drumsagart to pester you all?"

"No. You see, I'm thinking of leaving here, and I'd like to ken how it feels tearing up one's roots and trying to plant them somewhere else."

"Leaving?"

"It's a secret. It might never happen. Keep it to yourself."

"I'll do that. Well, if I'd stayed on in Crosslyon I'd hae become a ploughman or carter."

"Are there no policemen in the country?"

"Aye, but there's little scope for them. They grow roses as big as cabbages."

"What's wrong with that as a life? Well, goodbye, Sergeant, and thanks again."

"Goodbye." There was a final chuckle.

On his way home Rutherford called in at Sowlas's the undertaker. Behind a counter as smooth and sombre as coffin wood a young girl sat on a stool similarly smooth, for she kept slipping off. Behind her on a shelf lay several graveside ornaments of different shapes, but all corpse-white. Out of fear, surely, rather than callousness she was reading a twopenny paper full of stories where good poor girls married handsome rich men, and where only villains and white-haired saintly old people ever died.

"Is Mr. Sowlas in?" asked Rutherford.

"Yes." She glanced nervously towards an inner door; at the same time she slipped her story-paper into a drawer and took out a notebook. "Can I take down the particulars, sir?"

"I hae nobody to bury, lass," he said, smiling. "Is your name Robinson at all?"

She nodded.

"I thought so. You're like your faither. Surely you ken me?"

She nodded again. "Yes, Mr. Rutherford."

He was pleased. "I think I'd better discuss my business with Mr. Sowlas. Is your first name Molly?"

"Peggy."

"Have you got a sister Molly?"

"No. I've got no sister."

"I must be mixing you up with somebody else. Drumsagart's

not so very big a place, but it's hard to ken everybody. Just tell Mr. Sowlas Andrew Rutherford would like to see him for a couple of minutes."

She walked towards that inner door, as stiff and bristling as a cat towards a dog, and opened it sufficiently to put in her nose. "Mr. Sowlas, here's Mr. Andrew Rutherford to see you."

"Who?" came the reply in Sowlas's voice, so sepulchral that Rutherford smiled. Drumsagart was proud of its undertaker. Matthew Sowlas had not only been born into the trade and bred to it by his father Jonathan, he had also, it seemed, been fashioned for it in the very womb: voice, appearance, mannerisms, gait, all luckily contributed towards the necessary gloomy dignity, so difficult to counterfeit. The very flicker of his sallow eyelids was an act of mourning. In private life he was an ex-provost of the town and was still a councillor. He played bowls in the summer-time, wearing an immaculate panama-hat and white flannels.

"He'll be in in a minute," said Peggy, hurrying back as if from snow and ice to a dying fire.

Rutherford thanked her and waited. She returned to her story, with many involuntary glances which seemed not to be to anticipate her employer's entry so that she could hide the paper: a creaking coffin lid seemed to be in every glance. It would have been the idlest gossip to ask her if she liked her job. Evidently she lived all day in terror even here in the antechamber. No doubt there were occasions when she had to go through into the presence itself, the coffin room, where Sowlas at this moment was artistically and obliviously busy. It was hardly likely she'd prosper in her calling. If she escaped out of it into marriage, would she choose a hearse-driver?

She glanced up, caught him smiling at her, and bravely smiled back.

"I don't like it in here," she confessed, "after it's dark. Sometimes I'm the only one in the shop."

"We all hae our troubles, Peggy."

His remark, he thought, as comfort was typical of the establishment. "Cheer up," he added. "A bonny lass like you should be aye smiling." But again it was dreary comfort.

Then Sowlas came in, wearing a purple smock over his black clothes; his hard winged collar was macabrely white. He carried his long, clean, thin hands stiffly and momentously apart, as if he'd just let slip from them an alabaster angel with wings, costing three pounds. However, there was as much hospitality on his small, high face as decorum allowed.

"I've nobody to bury, Matthew," said Rutherford, proud of the phrase.

"Ah." As undertaker Sowlas was disappointed, as fellow-bowler pleased: he achieved the hybrid expression without the ambiguity of a smile. "Peggy," he murmured, "will you be so kind as to step inside and give Bob a hand. He's nearly finished."

Rutherford took pity on her. "I'll not keep Mr. Sowlas long," he said.

But the fear seemed to have been driven from her face; she smiled. "Is he himself?" she asked.

"Yes, yes. Off you go now."

She went without a shudder or sigh; her eyes shone, anticipating not symbols of death but some hint of eternity.

Rutherford watched her in amazement and joy. "Who's Bob?" he asked.

"Bob Murdoch, my sister's son. I'm supposed to be training him." Sowlas shook his head.

"Is he not taking to it?"

"He has a streak of frivolity in him, I'm sorry to say." Sowlas held up a finger. As they both stared at it they heard giggling from within. Sowlas stepped across, opened the door, and thrust in his little head. "Remember where you are, please. I do not say it is a good thing for the living to impersonate the dead in the matter of stillness and silence; but surely some respect is owed? Surely? Surely?" Then he returned behind the counter and faced Rutherford with a curious twirling on his heels. "Well, Andrew?"

"You've got a fine fleet of Rolls-Royces, Matthew?"

Graciously Sowlas admitted it.

"Well, I want the best for Saturday."

"Is it a wedding, Andrew?"

"No. It's to take me to the football match at Carrick."

"I understand." The voice, though solemn, was calm, but the brow was agitated. "You feel, as president, you ought to make some display of dignity?"

"You can put it that way if you like."

"It's a fair distance, Andrew, through some rough country."

"I'll pay what it costs."

"I am thinking of the car." Sowlas meditated. "Let us be realistic. Carrick is a Catholic niche, is it not?"

"Well, the team's called the Harp, and their jerseys are green."

"Precisely. Please understand I have no bias whatever. In my profession we quickly see the folly of all human prejudice. Do you expect to win?"

"We do."

"It is possible a certain amount of feeling may be engendered in the course of the game?"

"It's possible."

"A head or two might get broken?"

Rutherford knew well where the conversation was heading, but he refused to furnish any short-cut.

"It's happened before," he agreed.

"Supposing you are victorious, may they not wish you godspeed with stones and bottles?"

"There's always that chance."

"My best car cost £3,000."

"You'll hae it insured?"

"Not against violence by football fanatics maddened by defeat. I am afraid that, like an earthquake, would be regarded as an act of God."

Rutherford appreciated the joke, especially as the jester was supremely solemn.

"I take it you're dropping me a hint I can't get your best?"

"That is so, Andrew."

"All right, as long as it's a car with style."

"All my cars have style. True enough, a style more appropriate for occasions other than football matches."

Rutherford laughed. "So you're a heretic too, like my faither. Well, a car I want, and a driver. Can I have Archie Birkwood? He's a good Thistle man. I hope he's not engaged for tomorrow?"

Sowlas pondered. "No."

"Good." Suddenly Rutherford brought his fist down on the counter and laughed. "What's the opposite of the stork, Matthew?" he asked. "The vulture, would you say? Whatever it is, is it staying in its nest tomorrow? No flight over Drumsagart?"

Sowlas's small face diminished in disapproval.

"No disrespect meant, Matthew."

"It so happens," replied Sowlas gravely, gazing at his own clasped hands, "the Angel of Death will be flying tomorrow over our beloved town."

"I said I was sorry."

"The apology is not owed to me, surely."

There was silence. They heard more giggling from within.

"Who is it that's dead?" Rutherford's tone was fierce rather than humble.

Sowlas held his nails high so that to glance upwards at Rutherford's face was the merest elevation. His nails were his pride; between them and a vulture's bony, carrion-stinking talons was no possible resemblance. Nevertheless it could be after he'd answered that Rutherford's dour, heavy, not too intelligent face might be for a moment a more rewarding study. Matthew Sowlas had learnt that to know how properly to observe the decencies of death one had to be an unrelenting student of life in all its brutalities.

"A child," he murmured, "a little girl, twelve years old."

"A white coffin, then?" Rutherford's voice was still harsh.

Sowlas nodded. "Cheapest in the shop, but white. I believe you know her father."

"I suppose I ken most men in Drumsagart."

"You called me a heretic. Him you would call a votary. He worships at your inner temple, I believe."

"You mean he's a football man?"

"He attends every match."

"He'll not attend Saturday's. Who is he?"

"Mr. Robert Nuneaton. Rab, I think they call him. A small man, not very pleased with life, I think. He is unemployed."

"Wee Rab? Aye, I ken him. He's got about half a dozen weans."

"Even so, one's missed."

"I didn't mean that."

"She was the eldest."

"How did it happen? I didn't even ken she was badly. I think I saw him at the match last week. Poor Rab, he'll not be there this week."

"So you already said, but you may be wrong. You do not

give fanaticism its full credit, Andrew, high-priest though you are. He insisted on the interment being at twelve o'clock, which is, you'll agree, an inconvenient time for several reasons. We who tend the dead must eat. When does the game start?"

"Three o'clock."

"You see, he probably hopes to attend."

"Surely not."

"I gathered that impression. When do you yourself intend to set off?"

"About two or quarter past."

"Therefore if you cared to offer Mr. Nuneaton a lift . . ."

"He wouldn't accept. I don't ken why, for I've scarcely ever spoken to the man, but he seems to hae a grudge against me."

"I can tell you why, Andrew."

"Tell me, then."

"You represent success."

Rutherford scowled. "My God. I'm glad he thinks so."

"He's by no means the only one in the town who thinks so. You've done well, Andrew, very well. That, of course, should be a matter for congratulation, but we do not live in an era of generosity. These are mean drab times. I myself have been reprimanded for presuming to maintain dignity and style in my profession. It has been suggested a dowdy shabby equipage is more in keeping. Surely, on the contrary, if our lives lack beauty, we should all the more hold on to the loveliness and the mystery which can attend death, well conducted?"

"I daresay you're right. How did it happen? I mean, how did the lassie die?"

Sowlas shrugged his shoulders; it was like a flap of the vulture's wings.

"Kismet," he murmured. "It seems on Wednesday, while waiting in Freddy's fish-supper shop to buy threepenceworth of chips for the family's supper, she felt a pain in her head. She wandered off home without the chips of course, and no doubt received a scolding for her remissness. During the night she began to scream, and they had to rush her off to the infirmary. She was there less than two hours when she died, in considerable agony, I should say; and I am in a position to say."

"Was it," asked Rutherford, with difficulty, "a tumour on the brain?"

Sowlas gave one characteristically restricted nod, as if in truth the brain was delicate and must never be shaken.

Rutherford was silent. He felt that that little girl, dying in a torment that even after death distorted her face, was at that moment his closest companion in Drumsagart: much closer than Sowlas, now smiling a couple of feet away; closer than Peggy in the inner room cording a coffin and stifling her giggles as Bob tickled her with finger or voice; closer than Hannah, than his father, than his own mortal son. Then he resolutely forced himself to see that such a feeling was in no way pity for the dead child, so lonely in her cheap white coffin, but pity for himself, so robust in health, so well fed, so securely insured, so free from pain.

"Will it be all right, then," he muttered, "for the car at quarter past two?"

"At your house? Is your boy going with you?"

"At the Cross. No, Gerald's not going."

"I thought you were bringing him up in the faith."

"You thought wrong, then. He's not going."

Rutherford turned towards the door. Before he reached it he came heavily back and set down on the counter, with a powerful trembling fist, a ten-shilling note. "Maybe you'll call this presumption. I ken some folk would say I'm using my money to buy me a place in Christ's hert. Let them. Will you buy a wreath for the lassie's grave? Are there to be flowers?"

"A few. A ten-shilling wreath will look quite conspicuous among them."

"What of it? Will you do it for me?"

"Do I put your name on the ticket?"

"There'll be no ticket."

This time he had reached the door when Sowlas called and stopped him.

"Just a minute, Andrew. Can't you persuade your father to withdraw from the council elections?"

"Why should I?"

"He'll be beaten, and he'll take it very sore to heart. Mr. Lockhart is going to be a very redoubtable opponent. He is making religion unashamedly his platform, and you know how influential that still is in Scotland, heathens though most of us be. Your father and I have always been political opponents, but I have respected him, and I would like to see him retire honourably."

"You hope he's beaten?"

With one long finger Sowlas flicked at the note on the counter. He did not speak.

"I take it," said Rutherford, with door open ready to leave, "as I'm hiring the car I'm entitled to invite whomever I like?"

Sowlas nodded.

"Good night." He was about to slam the door shut when he remembered the business the shop dealt in, and he closed it very softly. Yet he felt that softness was not respect so much as a kind of cowardice.

10

Saturday was a fine day for football match and funeral. The sun shone in a pale, beneficient sky; grass sparkled and mud became firm earth again; boots bound in new white laces could swiftly in exhilaration pursue the ball, while shoes could step from the side of the grave undefiled by blobs of clay.

Five attended the funeral in the nearby cemetery; over seven hundred journeyed to the match at Carrick; and the seven hundred included one of the five.

The special train puffed from the station with heads out of the windows cheering and singing. Stay-at-homes, such as heretics, dotards, infants, and women, watched from the main street. Some waved back, a disgruntled boy booed, a few women laughed, more shook their heads, and one old man reminisced about other trains leaving that same station for a more unhappy but nobler purpose. All really were pleasantly affected as they gazed down through the wooden palings at the long red train sliding away into the distance, like a caterpillar, bespeckled with the faces and hands of Drumsagart men.

Geordie Bonnyton, holding on to his sombrero, leaned out to wave to his wife, who had promised to wave back. Detained in the greengrocer's, she was not at the appointed spot. In the same compartment with him were Ned Nicholson, in a new suit and with a large yellow aster in his buttonhole, and Nathaniel Stewart, supplied with a fresh handkerchief to cough into.

They were all happy at that setting-out. They chuckled and chaffed, carefree as sandboys. They were neighbours, acquaintances, fellow-townsmen, born and bred in the same streets, educated at the same schools, whacked by the same teachers, dodgers of the same gaffers, members of the same street-corner clubs, signers-on at the same employment exchange. Here they were off on a sunshiny expedition, to parade in front of strangers their communal Drumsagart quality and to cheer on the team that wore their cherished colours. Their mood was quiet despite their cheerfulness. They were like the Drumsagart sparrows that so cheekily perched on the lions' heads adorning the Town Hall under the turrets; but if their team won this first round, then the second, and the third, and so fought its way into the final, they would roar like the lions themselves, challenging all Scotland.

Into one of the other compartments Harry Lynn had clambered, trampling on everybody's polished toes and gasping stink into everybody's washed face. A blind man must always be made welcome everywhere; yet they knew he had no ticket, they were sure he was going to beg, and most of them, being trade unionists, thought he had no right to compete with the Carrick beggar, who was sure to exist. Moreover, his clothes were covered with detachable filth, and they were tricked out in their best, which in some cases certainly meant only an extra brushing of a suit and the ironing of a tie; but none relished his slavering contact. The two who had him crushed between them were in no way propitiated by the winks of sympathy.

Once during the journey Harry rumbled into song. They had all heard it before, they had all slunk away from its dirge-like raucousness. Now they had to listen to it right through in that small space, wondering all the time if it was a professional offering or a contribution gratis to the entertainment of the company. At the end he snatched off his cap, revealing great islands of dark-green scurf on his scalp, and dangled its arrogant noisomeness in front of their noses. At every tinkle he gave a different, but no less repugnant, snort of thanks; a ha'penny got twice as loud a snort as a penny; and a washer dropped in by a jocular engineer was greeted with a doglike whine that dismayed them all and caused the joker to pluck out his washer and replace it, in his contrite haste, with a sixpence. The exclamations of annoyance at his highwayman's rapacity, though much louder than the chinks in his cap, were quite ignored by Harry. When one man asked what he meant to do at Carrick when he was asked for his ticket, he released a cackle fit to chill the blood of a public executioner and pointed to his eye-sockets, where, taking the place of eyes, were gatherings of creamy pus. They were all saddened, as well as scunnered: the sights that Harry had lived among for over fifty years without ever seeing them were, after all, Drumsagart sights.

Four buses had been chartered, and each one as it sped down the main street received its meed of brandished baskets from the housewives, who, though convinced that the journey was neither heroic, adventurous, nor even necessary, nevertheless agreed with one another that after twenty or thirty or in some cases forty years of married argument there was little hope now of educating men to recognise what, like the price of food, was important, and what, like spendthrift football, was of no consequence whatever.

The bus carrying the team and all the committee members, except Malarkin and Rutherford, passed unsaluted. It left early while most people were at dinner. Indeed, on the main street it met the Nuneaton funeral, and all hats and caps had to be removed at once, on the order of Turk McCabe. One committee-man, hypersensitively bald, who wore his hat even in his house, was slow in making this small show of respect. Turk called to him, the first time amiably enough, but the second time with the threat that if the hat wasn't off before he counted three he'd go up the bus and knock it off. In the silence that followed, while the black velour was rising and the pale scalp was coming into view like the moon from behind a cloud, Turk remarked that he meant no harm, it was just that all his life he'd been in the habit of raising his cap in honour of a white coffin; only if it was white, he added, for you never knew who lay deservedly stiff inside a black one—it might be a miser, a pussy-foot, or some fat wife who alive would have sniffed at him as if he was dead. The incident lasted a minute only, and after it Turk seemed well content, gazing out at the passing scene with interest and intelligence, and even whistling an amicable tune. The rest, however, players and officials, sat for another minute like mourners.

Alec Elrigmuir did not travel with the team; this was an irregularity to which Wattie Cleugh, the secretary, and Scoosh McLean, the trainer, had assented with long faces of foreboding. The other players might have been expected to be jealous of this privilege given to their youngest and newest colleague; but no, it amused them, and was the cause of many guffaws, which, exasperatingly, had to be moderated in Turk's hearing. Owing perhaps to the innumerable thuds of ball and boot on Turk's skull, he frequently displayed a hebetude in the seeing of a joke, and behind that hebetude was discovered an erratic prudishness. One innuendo about Malarkin's predilection for Elrigmuir, or any fair-haired youth, would have Turk scratching his chest and, as if in response to that vigorous tickle, slowly simpering; but another, and in the whisperer's opinion less scandalous, would outrage Turk, who would spit and curse and assert that, though he had never won any prizes at Sunday school and had seen the inside of at least four jails in different parts of the country, there was nevertheless a limit to what he could stomach. The popular explanation was that Turk's reaction depended not so much on the amount of beer in his stomach as on the degree of sourness of that beer. It was not a question of whether he was drunk or sober. Few men could boast they had seen him indubitably drunk: that was a rarity like seeing a two-headed kitten or a tribe of rats flitting.

Secretive as a mouse, Sam Malarkin had planned to take Alec in his car; to have the handsome young man beside him, in the midst of the stimulating sunny uplands, would be to have exquisite sensations travelling across his mind, like sunshine and shadow over the moors. Unhappily, Alec refused at first, with indeed some of the viciousness of a cat assaulting a mouse; and at the most plaintive stage of Sam's entreaties he had consented, but only on a condition feline in its cruelty: Mysie must accompany them. How could Sam explain her presence would be anathema? There were no squeaks in the language subtle enough to convey that without self-annihilation. He had to agree to Mysie's presence. His plan so far agley, he had raised no objection when his sister Margot unexpectedly proposed going with him too. She said it was a lovely day for a car ride. It turned out to be a foursome therefore, with Sam and Margot furiously avoiding leg-contact in the front; in the back Alec and Mysie were not quite so squeamish in the matter of legs, but were entirely abandoned as to hands. Mysie was the instigator, for she early seized Alec's hand and held it hard, with a matching determination on her rosy face under the blue tammy.

Far more sensational than train or bus or quadrangular car was Rutherford's taxi. It arrived at the Cross at two o'clock, as glittering in the sunshine as the freshest spittle there. Archie Birkwood, after consulting his wife Teena, had decided not to wear hearse suit or cap; instead he wore his Saturday-afternoon flannel trousers and sports jacket, with a white cap. To secularise the car had not been so easy. It glittered as it stood; it glittered as it went; inside and out it represented opulence, dignity, and good taste. In the end Archie had accepted the suggestion of his seven-year-old daughter and had placed on the car's huge aristocratic nose a small rosette in the Thistle shade of blue, with specks of crimson.

There was, of course, no danger of embarrassment. Archie had been well schooled in the disregarding of incongruities: the coming to blows of man and wife over the grave of a son; the catcalls from behind adjacent tombstones of a wife divorced for drink and adultery; the finding of two bird's eggs on a green wreath; the crash and splitting open of a coffin on an icy day— these, and similar contretemps, had happened during his career, and he had impressed Mr. Sowlas by his sobriety during them all. Others, since migrated to more suitable callings, had sniggered nervously; but Archie had reinforced his professional gravity with some private melancholy. He it was who had walked to the madwoman hooting at her dead ex-husband and, taking her by the hand, had led her firmly towards the cemetery gates. He had been given a three shillings a week rise a month later.

Now he stood calmly beside the great magnificent rosetted car, smoking a fag-nip plucked from behind his ear and gazing up at the face of the Town Hall clock, larger than his own, more perfectly round, but not more patient. He was eager to see the match at Carrick from the kick-off, but was confident the car would not let him down.

Now and then he gazed along the street to see if his passengers were coming. He had been told by Rutherford who these were to be, and he had nodded, with the merest scratch of his ear to indicate an astonishment that would have shaken off any ordinary hearse-driver's ears like apples in a storm. Did Mr. Sowlas know? he had asked. When the answer had been negative, he'd tickled the other ear and nodded again, though a tempest of loyalty was raging in his soul.

Ought he to inform his employer? He had consulted Teena, whose response astounded him, accustomed though he was to that tearful distraction she called her sense of humour. First she had burst into a laughter that altogether diminished her feminine appeal by displaying her false teeth, moistening her eyes with false tears, loosening her hair, flattening her nose, and even causing her breasts to sag lower in her jumper. For a full two minutes by his watch she had been unable to give him a sensible answer. Indeed she had to stagger up out of her chair to go about the kitchen as if in cancerous pain, holding on to table, to dresser, to sink, and even to his own long-suffering solemnity. When she could speak she had said in tears, weakly, it was the funniest thing she had heard of for years. Didn't he think so? When he had shaken his head, as in truthfulness he must, it had started her off again, and all through the making and eating of tea she had giggled and wiped her nose and dabbed her eyes, and once had stuck, with her knife in the butter, helpless in the contemplation of that most comic taxi-load. Wasn't it as well, Teena, he had asked then, that he didn't laugh so readily as she? If he did, would they have butter on the table at all? No, they would have been lucky to have margarine itself; some families were reduced to dripping.

Nevertheless he smiled when Rab Nuneaton, slinking from tree to tree, came up to him and hoarsely asked if he was late. Archie knew very well Rab had been burying his daughter that morning, and like many others had wondered if the little sour-faced man would make an attempt to go to the match. In Archie's opinion such an attempt would be reprehensible; he would certainly not abet it; and here it was now about to be made, with typical cunning.

"Late, Rab?" he asked, still smiling, rising a little on his toes. "For what?"

Nuneaton gazed with even bitterer penetration than usual at the pavement.

"The taxi," he muttered, "I was told it was leaving at quarter past."

"That's right, Rab; but what's it got to do with you?" Archie, a big man like Rutherford, spoke with what he considered would be Rutherford's scorn.

"I'm going wi' you, Archie . . . if you don't mind." The addition was in humility, not in sarcasm.

Humble or sarcastic, he could not endear himself to Birkwood. "This is a private party, Rab," said the latter. "It's got nothing to do with me. I'm just the driver. I take my orders. I can't offer a lift to any Tom, Dick, or Harry."

"I was asked."

"Wha asked you?"

Nuneaton dug the words out of his thrapple. "Mr. Rutherford."

Archie frowned. "Are you at the kidding, Rab? It would be a daft thing to try. I'm a man not easily taken in. Forby, Rutherford'll be alang himself in a minute."

"Surely to God you don't think I'm in any mood for kidding?"

"If you want the truth as far as God's concerned, Rab, then I'm bound to tell you I don't think you should be in a mood for football."

Nuneaton glanced up; his eyes were wet; tears, somebody who didn't know him would have thought; hypocrisy and flyness, thought Birkwood, who believed he knew him well.

"That's my business, Archie," he said. "There's a crowd of folk in this town don't like me. I ken that. This is their time. They've got me doon, and they're kicking me. What am I to do, for Christ's sake? Am I to sit at hame, with the wife demented and the other weans greeting? A man can only stand so much. I was fond of my wee girl, Archie. Maybe you heard me shout at her whiles, maybe you saw me warm her ear, but I was fond of her for all that."

Birkwood turned his back on that snivelling appeal. He had caught sight of Tinto Brown, Crutch Brodie, and Jock Saunders approaching. These were to be his passengers. He had not been officially told about Nuneaton, and therefore still discounted him.

"Women are bitter," muttered Rab. "She said if I went to the match she'd never forgie me as long as she lived. Women are bitter and don't make allowances. Why did Rutherford offer to take me? Was it kindness? Some say he's a kind man, though I must say I've never noticed it. Was it to torment me, d'you think? But what good will staying at hame do? If I wasn't to go to the match I'd go for a long walk; and then I'd brood and drive myself crazy, and I'd come hame and say things I'd be sorry for. They tell me, Archie, when your lassie was being born you were at a football match. Is that right?"

Archie frowned; he did not approve of the attempted camaraderie in the worried voice.

"I 'phoned at twelve o'clock," he said. "They said, no news, 'phone again at two. I 'phoned at two; they said 'phone again at five. Five was after the match. I 'phoned at five; they said, 'phone again at eight. I 'phoned at eight and they told me it was a girl; she had been born at a quarter past six. I think the cases are different, Rab."

"You think I shouldn't go?"

"To tell you the truth, Rab, I don't like to advise people on such matters. They come to me thinking I'm an expert. Well, maybe so; but I still don't like it. In your case, Rab, I'll make an exception. I don't think you should go."

"But, Archie, at the footba' I think I'll find my balance again. It'll clear my heid and my mind. I'll come hame a better man."

"What if the Thistle loses?"

"Win or lose, Archie. It's the company. It's the freedom. It's the peace."

"There might be little peace yonder. Carrick can be a tough place to visit."

"I meant peace in my mind."

"I've given you my advice, Rab—take it or leave it. These are important matters. It's really a branch of religion. You've got to decide for yourself. If your decision turns oot to be wrong, likely you roast; if it's right, you're in clover."

"After the funeral," muttered Nuneaton, "the minister went into Ferguson's for tobacco for his pipe."

"You can't go by that, Rab. In an affair of this kind he's neutral, like a referee."

Then Archie turned away to greet the genuine travellers. He examined them with little moans of condolence for his old but splendid limousine. There had been some pitiable effort on their part to make themselves presentable. Crutch's crutch, for instance, had had the stuffing shoved back into the arm-rest; Tinto's face was newly washed, with tide-marks of dried soap on it; and fat Saunders wore a raincoat, not new but new on him, and so short and tight that his baggy knees and grubby cuffs were unusually conspicuous.

Crutch and Saunders had the decency to look ashamed as they squinted at the shining immaculacy of the car; but Tinto began to twist and jerk his withered features in imitation of some monocled duke accustomed to such cars. Flakes of dried soap dropped off. Heaving up one leg on the running-board, he perched there and glowered all round Drumsagart, like a great man revisiting his birthplace and finding it unworthy of having produced him. That was all very well, thought Archie, while the others and several spectators sniggered—that was all very well, but there was a smell off him, it must have been years since he had a bath, and hadn't he a disease that stank too?

"Here's Andra Rutherford coming," murmured Crutch, pointing.

Archie noticed how silvery with dried nose-wipe Crutch's sleeve was. Would it come off on to the cushions? A pity to use a two-thousand-pound car to carry this tuppenceworth of humanity. More than ever he failed to see what Teena had found to laugh at.

Rutherford was crossing the street.

"Good," said Archie, aloud. This was Rutherford's menagerie; let him manage it.

Rutherford, of course, was suitably dressed. He wore a tweed suit under his raincoat, and in accordance with football etiquette he had preferred a cap to a hat. Small, irascible men finding their view blocked by a hat had been known to skite it off. Geordie Bonnyton had had his squashed down over his ears at least three times, and he was only five feet two. No matter how small a man was, there was sure to be another smaller behind him.

Caps can be barometers of their wearer's moods. Rutherford's, though not as jaunty as Tinto's, had nevertheless a hint of defiance in the way it sat on his big head. He marched up to them, too, as if they were beholden to him, and not the other way round. Archie Birkwood was satisfied. A few days ago he had heard Mr. Sowlas describe Rutherford as a remarkable man, one who could crush the whole town in his fist if he chose; and here was corroboration of his employer's opinion, which to Archie's feudalistic mind was as it should be. True enough, he had himself condemned Rutherford recently, but as a judge of a football player only, not as a man. It was likely, too, he now admitted, he had been wrong in that; after all, it was Rutherford who had had the courage and initiative to propose giving Alec Elrigmuir a trial. Moreover, Archie could not remember having seen or heard Rutherford laugh much: and a grave man was a sound man, just as a lifelong joker like Tinto was as chaff in the wind. With women it was, of course, different; their brains were lighter, no-one could expect them to be as serious as men.

Tinto had a speech ready. He wasn't sure whether to deliver it comically as monocled duke or plainly as himself: which way would be the more sincere? He fumbled for words and was flummoxed by shyness.

"This is guid of you, Andra," he managed to say.

His two cronies nodded.

Rutherford fisted their gratitude away, like a goalkeeper punching the ball from under the bar. It was a good-natured, yet extravagant and reckless gesture.

"Nane of that," he said. "I'm glad of your company. You're all welcome. So you've made it, Rab?"

Nuneaton crept closer. "I've no juist made up my mind yet, whether I should go."

"You've not much time left."

"Is he going?" demanded Tinto.

Archie whispered, "Seems he was asked."

Tinto whispered back, but not so cautiously, "Better withoot him. He's a hoodoo, and a snake in the grass, a viper."

Jock Saunders frowned. "Hae you considered it thoroughly, Rab?"

"As thoroughly as I'm capable. My heid, it's as if twa iron hands were crushing it."

"If I was a religious man," said Saunders, "I'd say they were God's hands. I'll gie you my opinion, Rab, whether you're insulted or satisfied. If I was in your position, wi' a wean new-buried, I wouldnae be thinking of football."

"What would you be thinking of, Jock?" The query was quick as a viper's tongue.

Saunders swelled, so that his raincoat shrank to jacket size. The knot of his red crotcheted tie, already huge, seemed to expand with him, like a goitre under his chin. He scowled. "I would be thinking of more important things than football," he said.

"What things?" insisted Nuneaton. "I want to ken. Naebody will tell me onything."

"Never mind, Rab," murmured Crutch Brodie, gently. "Come wi' us. I cannae see what harm's in it."

"Thanks, Crutch."

Tinto snorted but said nothing.

"Let's get in," said Rutherford then, sharp and sudden. "We want to get there before the kick-off. You first, Tinto. Up you go." He helped Tinto and then Crutch. Saunders he let climb in unaided. "Well, Rab, what about it?"

"They'll shout after me in the streets," said Rab, in anguish. "But I don't care. A man's got his ain life to lead. If there is a judgment in the end, he's got it all to bear himself." He hurried forward and entered the car. There a seat had been prepared for him by Saunders apart from the others. He crouched on it, mumbling and nibbling at his nails.

Archie climbed in, Rutherford sat beside him, and off they glided, to some sarcastic cheers and a few sincere boos. Tinto put first one thumb and then the other to his nose.

In five minutes they were out of the town among fields of stubble and derelict pit-bings.

"They say Scotland's one of the maist beautiful countries in the world," muttered Nuneaton. "You wouldn't think it here."

No-one was provoked.

"Are you all comfortable?" asked their host.

"We're fine," they cried.

"I should think you should be," said Archie. "There's many a duchess would envy you luxury like this."

Tinto was incensed. "I never got married, as you all ken; but if ever I had my wife would hae been treated like a duchess frae honeymoon to daith-bed."

Rutherford laughed loudly; Archie winked approvingly at the rosette in front of him, wrought by Teena's hands; Crutch sighed; Saunders frowned; and Nuneaton let out a little yelp.

"You were a dirty-faced collier all your days, Tinto," pointed out Saunders. "How could you hae afforded it?"

"It's surely no a matter of money," chuckled Tinto.

"You forget, Tinto," said Crutch wistfully, "a man micht want to treat his wife as if she was an angel, never mind a duchess, but how can he keep it up if she keeps making a fool of him?"

"How does Tinto ken," asked Rab Nuneaton, "how a duchess is treated? Does she never quarrel wi' her man, duke though he is? Is she never dissatisfied, wi' her lap full of pearls? You're a theory man, Tinto; all your life you've been a theory man."

Rutherford passed a packet of cigarettes behind. "You all smoke?"

They assured him eagerly they did. They winked at one another in a truce.

Saunders took the packet and handed it round. Archie asked for his to be inserted between ear and head. Tinto took one as if, himself a duke, fat Saunders was his duchess. Crutch was clumsy and had to be helped. Rab had one almost out when he changed his mind and pushed it back in again. His lips remained shaped for it.

"What's up?" asked Saunders.

"Is it not your favourite brand, Rab?" asked Rutherford.

"I've made a vow."

"A vow?" It was Tinto, zealous as priest. "What vow? I've made thoosands."

"And broken them all," laughed Crutch.

Rab was miserable; he gazed out of the window. "I've vowed to gie up smoking."

"Economy?" inquired Tinto.

"But these are free," chuckled Crutch.

"Is it," asked Saunders, "because your lassie's deid?"

Nuneaton nodded.

"Penance?" asked Tinto, and shook his head. "I don't believe in it now. I once did penance. I'll not tell you why, but I'll tell you what I did. There was a nail sticking up in my pit boots, so that every step was an agony. For days I refused to hammer it doon. My sock was soaked in bluid."

"Were you not smoking last night when I spoke to you, Rab?" asked Rutherford.

"That's right, I was."

"Did you make the vow, Rab," asked Crutch softly, "at the graveside?"

Rab nodded.

Saunders suspected the vow had been made only a minute ago when Rab's fingers had touched the fag and realised it was Rutherford's; but he did not know how to call the little man a liar and a cheat without in some way shaming the dead girl.

"See that you keep it," he said.

"No." It was Archie's confident voice. "No. Vows made at the graveside are very seldom kept. I think I can speak as an expert. I once cleeked a man away frae his wife's grave; he was greeting like a wean and saying how much he'd loved her. Then he made a vow that he would never marry again. He would hae gone down on his knees if I hadn't stopped him: it was a wet day and the ground was glabbery, and he'd his best suit on. However, what I want to tell you is, he was married again within the year. I could tell you his name, but you'll understand that in my job secrets are sacred."

"For God's sake," moaned Nuneaton, "change the subject."

Since they were smoking contentedly they could be magnanimous. They changed the subject and discussed football. They made no attempt, however, to blow all the smoke out of the windows. Indeed, Jock Saunders found himself once puffing it deliberately in Rab's neck. He was displeased by his own wickedness.

"Will we win the day?" asked Crutch.

"Hae I not prophesied it?" cried Tinto. "It's as sure as the setting of the sun."

"Are we going to win the Cup?" asked Rutherford.

"We are. This is our big year, and I'm telling you, without fear or flattery, I consider it's due to you being president."

His two cronies concurred. Archie and Rab abstained.

Rutherford laughed, yet they all thought he sounded pleased. "There are some who'd lock you in a padded cell for a remark like that, Tinto."

"I'm over seventy, as you ken," said Tinto earnestly, "and all my days I've been a sinner. Am I not qualified to tell what guidness is?"

"Like Rab here," said Rutherford, "I'll hae to ask you to change the subject."

"Will Alec Elrigmuir ever play for Scotland?" It was again Crutch who obliged.

"No." It was Rab Nuneaton's swift, sure denial. "He's a flash in the pan. Brilliant at the moment, yes. Will it last? No. I'll tell you why. No brains. Hae you talked to him? He's got the mind of a boy of twelve."

Tinto gaped like a prophet denounced.

"I only saw him in the second half last week," said Archie, "and I must say he didn't strike me as anything outstanding. Turk was the man who won the game for us. All the same, if the boy's no good, what are we on our way to Carrick for?"

"I didn't say he was no good," muttered Rab. "I said he's brilliant, but like a rocket; it reaches its height, and then it's dark and drops to earth again. I'm not the only one wi' that opinion. Just speak to him, that's all. He's so saft he's damned near half-witted."

"You'll be a genius, Rab?" It was Tinto's voice hoarse with indignation.

Rab grinned. "I never said so, Tinto."

"You think it, though?"

"I'm a failure, Tinto; you ken that."

Suddenly Tinto seemed to lose interest. He grunted and leaned back on the cushions, with eyes shut, as if to meditate in peace.

Crutch understood; he knew the pain must have begun again. "Is it starting, Tinto?" he whispered.

Tinto opened one bloodshot eye. "Mind your own damned business."

Crutch nodded and gazed out past Rutherford's hairy ear at the radiant sky.

"If we win the Cup, Tinto," murmured Rab Nuneaton, "will you live to see it?"

Jock Saunders smoked.

Archie Birkwood saw that the speedometer read fifty-five miles an hour, and he sang softly: "Pack up your troubles in your old kitbag."

Rutherford, too, was gazing at the sky and at the spacious moor over which the road undulated. Once he saw a rabbit by the roadside, and a bird like a hawk in the distance: prey and hunter. Heather now whitened with age covered the moor. Somewhere out there had been long ago a skirmish between Covenanters and their persecutors: there was a monument to three men killed. He could see no house, no human being, and he felt that if he stopped the car and wandered alone over that wide expanse under the shining sky, with only rabbits and birds as his companions, he would not only be healed in his mind but would acquire a faith with which to return among his fellow human beings. But that faith, like the heather, would wither; nor would it, like the heather, inevitably grow again. Rather like garden roses untended it would first be blighted and then would perish. How did a man tend and nourish faith? Rab Nuneaton in his sorrow had whined that nobody ever told him anything. It was true, for all the whine. Scotland was a country where faith lay rotted like neglected roses, and the secret of resurrection was lost. We are a dreich, miserable, back-biting, self-tormenting, haunted, self-pitying crew, he thought. This sunshine is as bright as any on earth, these moors are splendid: why are not the brightness and splendour in our lives? Seeking them, here we are speeding at fifty miles an hour to see what—a football match, a game invented for exercise and recreation, but now our only substitute for a faith and purpose. Hannah is not right, he thought, but she is not any more wrong than I am. I should have gone to Helensburgh. Maybe I have flung away the only chance I'll ever get of mending my life with my wife and son, and my reason was probably false.

"You used to have a car, Mr. Rutherford?" chatted Archie.

"That's right."

"You gave it up. Not fancy it?"

"No. I was afraid it'd make me too fat."

Archie indicated the little space between his own belly and the steering-wheel.

"The wife gets worried," he said. "Thinks that if I'm ever in an accident I'll be stuck in here, not able to get out." He reflected. "Women are queer that way."

"What way, Archie?"

"They're optimists."

Rutherford grinned. "You'll not find many men to agree to that. Are not women always expecting the worst to happen?"

"No. Not in my Teena's case, anyhow. There's she thinking how I could escape if there was an accident. Now I ken, and you ken, if we were to hit a milk lorry coming round this corner there'd be precious little of us left for even Mr. Sowlas to make a tidy job of—and I'll say that for him, given a chance at all, he does make a tidy job. Folk grumble at the cost of funerals, and I suppose there are profiteers in the business, as there are everywhere else. But I can vouch for it Mr. Sowlas gives them their money's worth. Teena doesn't see it the way we do. She sees me being spilt oot, and so her worry is my belly might wedge me in. That's the optimistic angle, isn't it?"

"It is."

"Another thing, she's always harping on the theme that my job's a steadier one even than a schoolteacher's. She means folk must die and be buried. In a way that's optimism too. She's always laughing, is Teena. Talk about a canary in a cage. If you're ever at the pictures and there's a comic on you'll hear her all right, rising above everybody else. Folk laugh when they hear her though they've been seeing nothing funny in the picture themselves. I tell her the management ought to give her a season ticket free. I suppose it's a gift she's got. Maybe it balances the fact that I'm a bit on the serious side myself. We get on weel."

"I'm sure you do."

Something in Rutherford's remark, just short of cordial, caused Archie to ponder. His mind was as slow as his car was swift; there was no accelerator he could press. Then he recalled that Rutherford and his wife were reputed not to get on well. Thus he had been guilty of indiscretion. There was no way of atoning; apology, he could see, would only make matters worse. What really vexed him was that a man in his job ought to have more tact; as Mr. Sowlas said, a good undertaker practises on the living.

"We'll soon be there," he said at last.

11

Carrick was one of those infrequent towns in the West of Scotland where the Catholics outnumber the Protestants, not merely as regular church-goers, which is everywhere common, but as countable souls. Lying amidst excellent potato country, it had for generations attracted howkers from Ireland, some of whom had stayed and multiplied. Poles, too, had been imported to work in the nearby coal-mines; these had converted their names into Scottish equivalents, intermarried with the Irish, and had produced, in addition to a church described by indignant Protestants as 'damned near a cathedral', a breed of black-haired footballers whose feet knew innumerable jesuitical wiles and whose hearts every week were on fire to avenge Boyne Water by means of goals. Their team, Carrick Harp, was celebrated. Their field was called Tara Park, and from it a fine view could be had of the soaring and sculptured church. Indeed, one side of the terracing was known to visiting infidels by such names as Orange Lodge or Boyne Bank or just Wee Scotland. Standing there, a man watching the play had his back to the chapel.

For a few it was never easy to know where to stand, whom to cheer, and what to hope. These were Carrick men, Protestant or agnostic or Laodicean in religion, but fervent in football. Most of them, after wrestlings with conscience, had given their allegiance to the Harp.

In the same way Drumsagart Catholics supported the Thistle. For them, of course, a visit to Tara Park was the supreme test, and a few shirked it by staying at home and helping their wives to shop; but at least fifty among the seven hundred invaders came determined to stand sideways to the great crossed church, so that while shouting for the Protestant team they could not be accused of abandoning their religion. The position was further complicated for everybody by the fact that in the Harp's team were three Protestants, while the Thistle's right-back and inside-left, called Connelly and Murphy respectively, were practising Catholics. A Catholic, therefore, by bellowing to some jerseyed nuisance on the field that he was an Orange bastard might be traducing a fellow Catholic oftener in the confessional than he; and similar blunders were possible among the Protestants.

The players were indeed the martyrs. But it was understood by everybody, and partly admitted by themselves, that as soon as they consented to put on a jersey and run out on to a field, admission to which had to be paid for, then they forfeited all rights as citizens or Christians or even human beings. It had been known for a footballer once, provoked by a shower of scurrilities perhaps over-enthusiastic but none the less constitutional, to loup over the barrier, seize his slanderer by the throat and punch him hard. No-one could possibly approve or condone. Other spectators had rescued their colleague and thrown the player back onto the field, where the referee had instantly ordered him to the pavilion for ungentlemanly conduct. A policeman had appeared to ask the assaulted spectator if he was going to make a charge. He had decided not to, though his nose was swollen, and he was universally applauded for his forbearance and charitableness.

As Carrick greens and Drumsagart blues filed into the ground through the narrow pay-boxes, and surged towards their favourite stances, they tossed at one another much badinage, lusty but not rancorous. Before the contest there was always this truce. Each faction was sure its team would win, and felt for the other not only generosity but even an affectionate gratitude. Drumsagart, for instance, thought that Carrick was going to provide the first foothold up the towering precipice where, like a grail, shone the silver Cup. Carrick thought contrariwise. The only time when it was possible for such contradictory hopes to exist side by side was before the match began. Moreover, it was a bright, crisp afternoon, ideal for football; and Drumsagart in holiday mood was for the time being accepted by Carrick as guests.

Good will, of course, is never unanimous. Hence Nathaniel Stewart, in a spirit of theological controversy, contrasted the Carrick pavilion with the Carrick church; the former, as he truthfully though coarsely said, was more like a tin piss-house than a pavilion, it was a disgrace to football; while the latter was far too boastful with its hugeness and its big statues niched in the walls.

Rab Nuneaton, too, as he hid himself among Carrick men,

silently condemned those statues as no better than stone idols; the Virgin, clasping her baby, especially displeased him, for she seemed, shining up there in the sunshine, to be rebuking him for being at a football match with his daughter hardly cold in her grave.

One or two Carrick men similarly disgraced the truce. One did so at the pitch of his voice. He seemed prematurely drunk and kept waving two pound notes in the air with a challenge, luridly worded, to any Drumsagart man to cover them; he would give the benefit of a draw. When no-one accepted the wager he took it not so much as an indication of Drumsagart lack of faith or poverty, which would have been triumphant interpretations, but rather as a personal affront which must be expunged by blood. Those round him, mostly Carrick men, were wonderfully tolerant of his howlings, which interfered with their own calm conversations; but when he took off his cap and jacket and squared up with his fists to his invisible affronters they lost their communal temper, ordered him obscenely but idiomatically to go elsewhere, and helped him to re-dress by slapping on his cap peak-backwards and throwing his jacket about him without consideration either for his elbow or the bottle in his pocket, both of which collided. He withdrew in pain, fury, shame, and infinite bitterness.

In front of the pavilion, on a bench that rocked, sat the notables. Mysie and Margot were there, placed together by an hospitable Carrick official, who was not to know they were as doe to wolf, as rose to canker. Beside them sat the lesser Drumsagart committee-men, who had tried to shove into their team's dressing-room and found it as crammed as the Black Hole of Calcutta. Nevertheless they still felt piqued at being pushed out again into the fresh ample air. Inside was fate, and inside, too, were fate's darlings, Rutherford, Malarkin, and Cleugh, administering to the team who knew what foolish, indeed what pernicious, last words of advice? Even Donald Lowther felt disgruntled and did not object when his colleagues blamed the president. It was undeniable Andrew these days was acting far too brusquely. No doubt he had his troubles, but did not a good man become better under adversity? Would it not have been plain Christian policy for Rutherford to stay out here on the bench entertaining Mysie and Margot, rather than to thrust his way in, using his strength and weight, simply to pat Turk's back, say a daft word of encouragement to Lachie the skipper, and shake young Alec Elrigmuir's hand, as if he was a sultan of the East and owned them all? What made it more galling was that the players laughed at him, and at Malarkin, too, for that matter, behind his back. The intelligent members of the committee, the same sound men whom the players respected, were the very ones excluded. Of course such was the case all over, in every department of life. This was the salve with which they rubbed one another's smarting pride.

Then out on to the field, which sloped and had grass as a bald man has hair, ran the referee. He was a dapper man in freshly laundered white shirt and black pants, and his creamed hair shone like a helmet. Conversant with the religious aspect of his hobby, he had remarked rather wittily to his wife as he was leaving the house that morning that it would be more appropriate for a Moslem or a Buddhist to arbitrate in a contest between Catholic and Protestant. She had been too apprehensive for his sake, too intent upon urging him to consult the police beforehand, to point out that as a man of no religious views whatever (for in ten years of marriage she had heard him express none apart from football) he was as well fitted as anyone to referee. Here he was, then, in the centre of the field, with his foot on the new ball, waiting for the teams to appear.

They appeared, just as Nippy Henderson had been informed that Rutherford had come all the way in one of Sowlas's Rolls-Royces. Therefore amidst the tumultuous applause were his imprecations on what he saw as the most atrocious display of hypocrisy ever committed. Rutherford had refused him the use of a rusty van and himself had come in a Rolls-Royce. He could not adequately express his horror and wrath, and, besides, not a soul round him was listening. If he had dropped dead in his passion no-one would have picked him up, though they might perhaps have instinctively avoided trampling on him. He turned traitor in his bitterness and hoped the Harp would win.

Each goalkeeper had been presented with a mascot, a green harp of cloth and wire for Carrick, and a thistle for Drumsagart. These they reverently placed behind them. The Carrick goal-keeper kissed his first, which evoked from his followers a roar of appreciation, and which caused their Drumsagart rivals openly to criticise this Catholic love of idolatry but secretly to wish their own goalkeeper had had the grace and abandon to kiss the thistle.

The game was about to start, the truce to end. Tense as a man lighting a fuse, the referee blew his whistle: the explosion was instantaneous and prolonged.

It was a memorable and historic game. If football can be legitimately regarded as a religion, as many claim, then this was an exhibition of purest evangelism. From the minds of the worshippers malevolence was driven out and philanthropy took its place. The Drumsagart committee-men forgave their president. Nippy Henderson forgave him, too, and repented his treason. Rab Nuneaton found tears at last in his eyes. Tinto Brown, alarmed by an exceptionally vicious bout of pain just before the game started, found an anodyne in the thrills, the beauty, the exciting grace, and the suspense. While that drunken Carrick man, who had fallen asleep in a corner after emptying the bottle which had numbed his elbow, dreamed benevolent dreams. No doubt the conversions were temporary, as in all religions, but while they lasted they were genuine and proved redemption possible. To keep it permanent is a problem that has teased redeemers long before football was founded.

Apart altogether from the mystery of the play, the scene was beautiful. The sun never for a moment faltered, but kept flooding the field with invigorating and paradisean radiance; seagulls sported in it, exhilarating little spurts of purity. The green jerseys of the Harp and the royal-blue of the Thistle, with one goalkeeper's sweater crimson and the other orange, wove lovely swift patterns. Goalposts, preternaturally white, brought gasps as ecstatic or awful as any altars; and at the core of everything was the ball, potent and magical, whether it merely rested or flashed into netting or skimmed the gleaming grass or soared up among the gulls or at the toe of an ingenious dribbler sped this way and that, evading other questing toes.

Each team excelled itself; and the result was football transcendental, full of fast attacks, audacious defence, subtle stratagems and subtler counter-movements, individual juggleries, much heroism, and seven great goals. No wonder the watchers' faces were transfigured; no wonder normal animosities were stifled. The Angel of Football, in which all believed but which few had ever seen, was hovering over Tara Park that afternoon. One team must lose, and its followers must be disappointed; but it would be a defeat and a disappointment far more soul-satisfying than many victories and fulfilments. If Carrick won, then Drumsagart would wish them well during the rest of the competition; if Drumsagart won, then Carrick would pray for them to reach the final round, and would be at Hampden Park in Glasgow to cheer them on.

Drumsagart won, by four goals to three; and everybody agreed that, among the many glories of that afternoon, none outshone the fleet, intrepid, and inspired play of young Alec Elrigmuir. It was he who transformed the other four Drumsagart forwards; he had so much genius and was so unselfish he shared it lavishly with them; and though he scored all four goals no-one, not even Rab Nuneaton, could accuse him of self-glorification. Once when he was injured, by accident, both trainers scooted out to attend to him as he lay squirming, and not a single voice roared out the time-honoured advice to dig a hole and bury him. On the contrary, everybody was concerned, and on the bench in front of the pavilion Mysie and Margot forgot their jealousy in a common anxiety. When he rose again it was a resurrection heartily applauded.

Turk, too, was pre-eminent. Perhaps he was not so whole-heartedly acclaimed by the Carrick faithful, as these could not quite get rid of the suspicion that in his agility, his knack of position, and his incredible stamina was something not altogether orthodox. Before the game they had mocked his crude appearance, and without originality but with unconscious heresy had nicknamed him the missing link. Now, when they saw him playing with such inexplicable effectiveness, they suspected sorcery: only with diabolical help could so ugly a man play so well.

As for the referee, he was hardly noticed; and this neglect, so rare and so desiderated, in a Cup-tie, filled him with awe. One or two of his decisions were disapproved—in this matter there could be no perfection even in a millennium—but he was all the time more and more aware of a sense of uniqueness, so that he ran about elated on his toes, with muted whistlings and gestures like benedictions.

That night in the Glasgow newspapers four times the expected space was given to accounts of the game; the headlines were bigger and blacker than those announcing many senior games; and concluding the many superlatives spouted by one reporter was his affirmation that Drumsagart Thistle must now be regarded as among the favourites for the Cup.

Alec Elrigmuir was famous. His photograph appeared as it had been snapped at half-time, and somehow, perhaps because of his bashfulness, it had not been the superb conquistador of the football field who had been delineated but the apprehensive simpleton of Malarkin's couch. Nevertheless dozens of Drumsagart scissors were busy cutting that picture out, for it was without doubt the first of a long and honourable gallery.

Mysie, however, when it was shown to her, had no praise, only blame for the photographer for perpetuating so imbecile an expression, and for Alec for ever wearing it. He needed a guide or manager, she declared; well, she herself would take on the job, no matter how much Rutherford or Cleugh or the two Malarkins objected. Alec eagerly replied the job was hers for a kiss. It was a high price, she answered, especially as he was in danger of again looking like that photograph; but she would pay it. She did, and immediately after, repudiating his claim for another, informed him she now regarded them as engaged; the ring could follow. Therefore she could issue conditions. As he nodded, in blissful surrender, she insisted that the chief of those conditions was that he must keep away from Margot Malarkin. He promised, he swore, he vowed, and then he asked for another kiss. After a moment's candid calculation, with eyes wide open, she consented.

In all the Sunday newspapers, which circulated throughout the whole country, the descriptions of the game were just as fervid; but in one, to Drumsagart's astonishment, was the photograph, not of Alec Elrigmuir or Turk McCabe or Lachie the captain, but of Rutherford, with the caption: 'Mr. Andrew Rutherford, the genial chief of Drumsagart Thistle.' Everybody agreed he must have either bullied or bribed the photographer. A few cut out the picture to have it to hate; Rab Nuneaton was one. But Tinto Brown cut it out in love and pinned it alongside Alec Elrigmuir's above his bed, in company with at least a dozen film actresses, plain and coloured, lush and voluptuous, in bathing costume or negligée.

But now the paramount question in Drumsagart was, and would continue to be, collecting excitement as a snowball collects snow: would the Thistle win the Cup?

12

In the weeks that followed the victory at Carrick, Cup-tie feeling in Drumsagart surged from fever to frenzy. No-one was immune; even male heretics and contemptuous wives were smitten; neither disbelief nor common sense availed as prophylactics. Everything else in the town's life lacked spice or significance. During the council elections, for instance, the attendances at meetings were the smallest ever known, in spite of the vastness of the issues invoked by some of the candidates. Five appeared in the schoolroom, where the Reverend Mr. Lockhart had intended to purge politics with religion; while one less turned up to hear Councillor Rutherford's jeremiad on his own lifetime consumed in vain in the service of justice, peace, and humanity. When the voting took place it was found that the minister had won by sixteen votes, and that less than twenty per cent of the ward electorate had voted. His victory, therefore, had a sting in it, but not so venomous as the old man's defeat.

Doctors found it more efficacious to sit down and chat to their male patients about the Thistle's prospects than to prescribe medicines. Teachers were granted the attention of boys during grammar and arithmetic in return for allowing them to write essays or draw pictures on the theme of Alec Elrigmuir's scoring of the winning goal in the Final. Coalmen peching up three flights of stairs with hundredweights on their armoured backs spoke of the Thistle as they couped the bags into bunkers in a shower of black dust. All shopkeepers got in a stock of optimistic conversation; and George Rankin, the butcher, outsmarted all rivals by offering to supply free every week to every Thistle player, while the team was still in the Cup contest, one pound of his prime steak. The succulent gifts were displayed in his shop window before being handed over.

Sergeant Elvan, arch-heretic, found himself being accosted frequently by the most beery-nosed of the Lucky Sporran clientèle. They were never quite drunk enough or impertinent enough to be arrested, but they slunk up to him and spoke to him in a variety of sly tipsy ways about the Thistle and the Cup. Through grabbing one and threatening to lock him up for the night, he discovered that in the pub a plot had been hatched, whose purpose was to wheedle or startle or trick out of him a good wish for the team. The winner was to receive a bottle of whisky, which had to be kept, however, and drunk communally without glasses on the famous Hampden slopes on Cup Final day. What, asked the sergeant, if the Thistle was knocked out before it reached the Final? Then, said his informer gloomily, they were pledged to pour the whisky, to the last drop, down a stank.

Harry Lynn had made up a song of his own, with its subject the winning of the Cup. It rambled but it rhymed, and when he first sang it to a jigging tune in the Lucky Sporran he was rewarded with a couple of pints of beer. Next night that tribute was repeated; but the third night, and the six succeeding nights, it was gradually reduced to half a pint. Thereafter he was reminded that singing for drinks, no matter how hallowed the subject of the song, was prohibited by by-law, and so would he mind leaving? It was not a pleasant sight, said Malarkin the publican, to see a blind man drunk. Noted drunkards solemnly agreed. Harry whimpered an assertion of his rights: having no eyes, his mouth was one of his chief sources of pleasure; besides, in a free country why should he not get drunk, provided he molested nobody? He was sadly but ruthlessly led out. Perhaps it mitigated the desolateness of the expulsion that it was Alec Elrigmuir's hand that clasped his arm and slipped a sixpence into his pocket at the door.

The sorrows of individuals had to be endured without the bitter-sweetness of limelight, unless, of course, they could be related to the master issue of the Cup. Tinto's disease worsened rapidly until there were days when he couldn't rise from his bed of fleas; it was questioned if he would live to see the Cup being borne in glory up the main street. Ned Nicholson's wife died at last, and nobody noticed whether he laughed or cried at the graveside. Rab Nuneaton had another child, a boy of three, perhaps his favourite, extinguished as unexpectedly as the girl, so that for days he sat in front of a mirror squeezing his head with his fingers all round seeking the murderous parental tumour. Old Tamas Dougary's sight failed rapidly: he was shown public sympathy because it meant that on the brink of the ever-lasting darkness he had been cheated out of the brightness of Alec Elrigmuir's winning goals. Crutch Brodie took an ulcer under his crutch arm and it refused to heal. Andrew Rutherford found the atmosphere in his home turn from cold to icy, from indifference to antagonism. Hannah now would not make his bed or wash his clothes, although she still prepared his food. Gerald, who had done badly in the term examinations, became openly impertinent, except when his mother was present. Harry, however, wrote a letter of congratulation on the Thistle's successes: these had brought Drumsagart into the news and were excellent free advertisements for Drumsagart bannocks.

In the second round the Thistle were drawn at home against a mediocre team from Ayrshire and skelped them by six goals to one.

In the third round they had to face a crack Glasgow team; but, encouraged by hundreds of their followers, who had fearlessly escorted them into that enormous lair of gangsters, shawlies, and keelies, they scraped through by a single goal scored by Elrigmuir ten minutes from the end. It was a narrow but heroic victory, for their opponents in those last ten minutes, in a desperation deprecated at the time but afterwards sympathised with, kicked and hacked, shoved and bumped, elbowed and kneed, spat and swore, wept and bled, all in vain. At the finish Turk McCabe had a bloody knee and a split scalp, while Elrigmuir of the golden limbs limped. Luckily his injury was slight. As for Turk, he drank more beer that Saturday night than he'd done on any single night before; but it could not be said the result was buoyancy and joy. The beer, of course, was all a sort of sacrificial offering, sent up to him in his corner and received without so much as a snarl of acknowledgment. Nobody thought fit to remonstrate. It would have been wonderful to have Turk publicly thank one; such an incident could have been related proudly to one's grandchildren; but if it had happened it would have meant a change, a softening, a departure of grace in Turk, so that in the next round he would have played like any hairy-chested misanthrope of near forty who drank too much beer, smoked too many fags, and carried too big a belly. Therefore he was left sacredly alone until at last he went home. There was a volley of good-nights, but he answered none. One or two followed him lest he should slip on the icy pavement and shatter his already split skull. But he reached home safely, and there took down from the shelf the china dancing couple. While they danced on the kitchen table his mother crept about preparing his supper. Never yet had she thanked him for the gift, and he had not forgiven her.

The fourth-round tie was against a team invincibly named Livingstone Caledonia; the Thistle won by two goals to nil.

The fifth round was to be played on the Saturday two days after Hogmanay. Christmas was over. Mr. Lockhart's experimental carol-singing on the steps of the church at midnight had been a fiasco because of tempests of sleet. Rutherford had been there, singing as loudly as anybody, with his head bare and his face uplifted. Yet the other carollers knew, and the audience under straining umbrellas knew, that if he had Christian gratefulness in his heart while his voice sang deeply of the birth of God's son it was remarkable, and not just because of the heathenish weather. All the town knew the factory had been sold, he was on a month's notice, his father was ill, and his wife had left him, taking their boy to live with her brother in Helensburgh.

One cold wet forenoon a day or two before Christmas Harry had driven into the factory yard. His wife Mabel was with him, but she remained hunched up in the big car, like a drugged bear in her fur coat. Harry, too, was armoured against the cold in a leather coat with fleecy lining and fur collar. Andrew, who was moping at his desk, felt guilty at being caught idle by his employer; a moment after he felt furious at his own timidity.

Harry did not take off his hat, though he pushed it back on his brow. "I'm not staying long," he said.

"Sit down, anyway."

"No." Suddenly Harry showed his gold teeth in a wide grin. "It's a bit late in the day to congratulate you, Andrew, but I'd like to tell you that this is the first time I've ever come into the yard without catching somebody playing football or tossing pennies or skylarking in some way."

" That's stopped."

"It went on, though?"

"There are times," said Andrew dourly, "when, in the course of his job, a man finds himself with little or nothing to do. I used to let them kick a ball about. Am I not a patron of the sport in the town?"

Harry burst into a laughter that seemed ready-made. "That's a good one, Andrew: a patron of the sport. Makes you sound like a member of the Jockey Club."

"Now they skulk in some corner or in the lavatory."

Harry turned his head aside as if to consult some omniscient companion. "Better that," he said. "Better for discipline if they don't enjoy their idle spells. I can see you've stepped up some grades in the hard school of life. But, as I said, it's a bit late in the day for congratulations. You'll hae heard we're going to sell out?"

"There've been men here doing everything but calculate the smell from the ovens."

Harry looked serious and sniffed briskly. "I have never liked the smell of baking oatcakes," he said. "Shall I tell you why? Maybe I've told you before."

"You hae."

"I'll tell you again. When I was a boy"—he struck the air with his fist at the level of a boy's face—"I used to come here for the smell; not because I liked it, but because I was hungry. When I bought the place it was partly as a revenge."

"I thought when you bought it there was a stipulation it had never to pass oot of Drumsagart hands?"

Harry laughed. "How could there be any such stipulation in a business deal?"

"A promise, then. Did old Bannatyne not let it go cheap because you promised never to sell it to strangers? Didn't he say he wanted the name Drumsagart bannocks kept?"

"Even if there was such a promise, Andrew, would you consider it ethical to miss the chance of a nice profit for the sake of humouring a doited old man, who's dead besides? Did I say you'd stepped up some grades? I was too hasty: step down again. Tell me, man, is it I'm the bad teacher or is it you're the dunce? Other men I've coached have passed. You can't say I'm all theory; I've put into pretty successful practice what I preach."

He held up his hand as his brother-in-law muttered something sour about principle. "I've never argued with you, Andrew, and I'm not going to. My banker speaks for me; I stay quiet. I've helped you because you're Hannah's man, and I'm fond of Hannah. At the same time I'm not going to try to interfere between you. I've always thought there must be something in a man who gets himself as unpopular as you have managed. Hannah tells me you're so daft about Drumsagart you'll not leave it. Or is it you're so thrawn you'll not give them the pleasure of thinking they've driven you out?"

As he waited as if for an answer there was the blare of his car's siren.

"Mabel's getting impatient," he said.

"Before you go," said Andrew, "has there been any understanding about the folk who work here? Are they to keep their jobs?"

"No such understanding, Andrew. I don't reduce my profits by raising snags of that sort. The less favours asked the better. That goes for you too, Andrew. They'll want the management changed at least."

"I wasn't asking about myself."

"The more fool you. You'll be out in the street in a month's time. What will you do?"

"That's my business."

"It's also your wife's, and your son's."

"I was a good engineer before ever I let myself be shoved in here. I can be one again."

"Your hands are soft, Andrew, and your knowledge will be rusty. Besides, are there not as many engineers idle as are working?"

"I have friends."

"You mean Aitchison of the steelwork? Don't depend on him. No, the truth is, Andrew, you come into my orbit. Be content to stay there for your family's sake. I'm putting it, Andrew, with as much tact as I can."

There was another blare of the siren.

"Tact's a thing Mabel lacks," he said, smiling. "But I'm overdue. I told her I'd be five minutes, no more. We're on our way to see Hannah. I think she'll be telling you something tonight. As I said before, I'm not going to interfere between you." He paused at the door and showed his gold teeth in another big grin. "You're in my orbit, Andrew. Whenever you want me you'll find me bright in the centre. In the meantime, good-bye and merry Christmas. Oh, by the way, I was sorry to hear about your faither. That's genuine, I was sorry. When I was a youngster, poor but full of ambition to be rich, I remember listening to him giving a speech—just outside your football park it was. Every single word he said about the cruelty and injustice of poverty and hunger was as genuine as the pearls on a millionairess's neck. But I looked about me at the crowd he was addressing, and I said to myself: Oh, you're clapping him all right, but not one of you really believes a word he's saying, and not one of you is going to lift a pinkie to help him. I didn't clap, but I went away with my mind made up, and it's been made up that way ever since. He's an old man now, and I'm grey-haired myself. I'm sorry to hear he's ill. But was I right or not? Didn't they turn their backs on him in the end, as if to say the old fool's drivelled long enough? I mean no disrespect by that. I admire your faither; all his life he's championed the poor, and he's stayed poor himself. He's proved himself genuine. Friends of his hae climbed up over the backs of the poor to fine well-paid official jobs; some are M.P.s. But don't you be patterning yourself on him, Andrew. You're not in his orbit; you're in mine. When you admit that to yourself, and act up to it, you'll be a happier man. Good-bye, then. I'll be hearing from you."

Then he was gone, and in another minute or two Andrew heard the car swing round in the yard and dash through the narrow gate. As a driver Harry was much superior to him; as a maker of money; as a pathfinder through the world; as a husband; and perhaps—who was to judge?—as a man.

He got up and went for another fault-finding inspection of the factory.

That evening when he got home he found his tea set for him as usual on the table, but this time Hannah did not, with a grim nod towards those ministrations, go out of the room into the sitting-room, where Gerald would either be doing his home lessons or practising the piano. She stood over by the wireless set, in a place not often occupied by her at rest, so that she seemed a stranger there, as perhaps she intended. Her hair was as rigorously disciplined as ever, but was much greyer than he had thought. She could not control her face so well; its twitchings, formerly indistinguishable from inward smilings, were now unmistakably nervous, the consequence of self-esteem baited, in the narrow cage of the soul, by frustration and disappointment.

It was the day of publication of the *Drumsagart Pilot*. He picked up the newspaper, intending to read it as he ate, but when he saw that she was still in the room, grudging a single word yet wishing to speak, he put the paper aside discreetly, as if, after all, he preferred not to read. Even if she had not been going to speak, if she had just been going to stand there all during his meal, he could hardly have read. Reading at table, according to her code of etiquette, was disgraceful; reading anywhere, he had sometimes thought, except, of course, reading for profit, such as Gerald's studying. There had been an argument once over *The Three Musketeers*. Hannah, displeased and perhaps worried by the boy's remoteness, had become strangely angry when she learnt he was reading it simply for pleasure, it was not a prescribed book to win marks from at an examination.

The boy could be heard thumping at the piano. Well, thought his father, it's to be hoped he's smart at Latin and science, for he'll certainly never make his fortune as a musician. Then that childish spitefulness brought overwhelming remorse. He munched at his ham and eggs, not tasting them, and gazed at the silver sugar-bowl.

"I'm leaving you, Andrew," she said.

He did not reply, though she gave him a clear space; but after a minute or so, feeling obscurely that to keep on eating would be to show boorishness, he put down his knife and fork. Afterwards the tiny rattle of a fork against a plate was to have the power to evoke in him a great barren, paralysing sadness.

"Harry was here today," she said.

He nodded.

"I'm glad it means so little to you," she said. "It's all settled. We're going at the week-end."

"We?"

"The boy's going with me; that's to say, if he wants to go."

Slowly he clenched his fist and at the same time put on a smile as aggressive; yet within him was no fight at all.

"I could do something about that," he muttered.

"Harry's got lawyers you could never afford."

"So it's all been discussed, lawyers and all?"

"Aye."

He unclenched his fist and picking up a teaspoon tapped it on the table. "Does Harry think justice can be bought?"

"Justice was never mentioned."

"No, it wouldn't be. I could bring you all down on your bended knees if I liked."

"Never," she said, but not defiantly as if in answer to a threat; contemptuously rather, rejecting a boast.

"The boy's got a mind of his own," he muttered, knowing it was not true. Gerald had the mind they had instructed him to have, and in later years of manhood that mind would have developed according to their further instructions. Still, if the boy's training was left to him, what could he teach?

"Get on with your tea," she said. "There's no sense in letting it get cold."

Sensibly, he took that sensible advice.

"What you've just said," he murmured, with a smile, "is hardly the maist appetising of sauces."

"Wholesome food needs no sauce."

As he was wondering whether her remark had a deeper meaning or whether it was merely more common sense, she went to the door, opened it, and called: "Gerald!"

"What is it, Mum?"

"You know when I call you it's your place to come at once, not to shout 'What is it?' If I had no reason for calling you I wouldn't call."

Andrew thought as he tried to eat, Well, there would be some good instruction for the boy, even if it was just in the small things. He realised by the shaking of his hand holding the teacup that he was dreading the entrance of his son; and that this disquietude had for some time been replacing the pleasure Gerald's approach and presence had given him. Now he was afraid not merely that the verdict on his son's face would be unfavourable but also that it might be insolently so. If it were, then all the unhappiness and worry of the past weeks might suddenly burst out, and he would say or even do what he would regret eternally.

Hannah put a hand on Gerald's shoulder as he came in; with the other she straightened his tie.

183

"You'll say what you're asked to say," she said, "and nothing else."

"Yes, Mum." Perhaps there was no insolence on the handsome young face, but there was surely the smooth effort to keep it off.

"Hello, Gerald," said his father.

"Hello, Dad."

"Was that you practising?"

The fatuous question was given a careful nod.

"You're still a fair bit off being a Paderewski." Andrew smiled, although he knew he had intended some malice by the remark.

"Who's he, Dad?"

"A famous piano-player."

"I never heard of him."

"That's surely strange. I thought just as every budding football player dreams of being an Alan Morton some day, so budding pianists dream of being a Paderewski."

"Attend to me, Gerald." His mother's voice was purposely flat. Though she considered the talk about music as cheating on her husband's part, she was herself determined to play fair. Her son's future depended on the decision he was being asked to make.

Gerald struck a listening attitude.

"Ask no questions," she said. "What you've to do is to answer them."

He nodded wisely.

"I've just been telling your father that on Saturday I'm going to Helensburgh to stay with your Uncle Harry and Aunt Mabel."

"For good, Mum?"

"For good, I think. Now, what we want to know is, what do you want to do? Do you want to go with me, or do you want to stay here with your father?"

"Is Dad not going?"

Hannah turned and stared at Andrew. "I don't think so. Are you?"

He was confused and startled, so that he answered far more harshly than he meant. "I wasn't aware the offer was still open."

"Then it is. It must always be."

Gerald began to gaze about with polite inattention; this part of the conversation did not concern him.

184

"Well, that's good to know," said Andrew, and laughed.

She said nothing, but seemed to wince at his laughter.

He tried to become serious. Inwardly he felt falling to pieces and hardly knew what he would say.

"Harry would tell you about the factory?"

She nodded.

"I'm on a month's notice."

"He told you he would never see you stuck."

"But he wasn't a bit concerned about the rest of the folk. As far as he was concerned, they could be tossed out on the scrapheap. He's made a profit; they can rot."

"Aye, they can rot. Your answer's still the same, then. We're wasting time."

He half rose from his chair and banged his fist among the dishes. So factitious was his passion he was careful not to do any damage.

"Aye, my answer's still the same, Hannah, and it always will be. I ken your ambition's to see me led about by your brother like his prize poodle; but that's a sight you'll never see."

"There's no need to shout. Gerald, you've had time to think. What do you want to do?"

He pretended to ponder, as if either decision must cause him pain.

"What about school, Mum?" he murmured.

"If you stay here you'll keep attending the school you're at, provided your fees can still be paid. If you go with me you'll have to start a new school."

"I wouldn't like to do that," he said.

"I don't want to say anything to influence you unfairly, son," said his father, "but I'd like you to remember that you were born here in Drumsagart. This is your native place, your source of strength. If you leave here you might find yourself weakened in a way you'll never make up."

"That's rubbish, of course," said Hannah. "What is it to be, Gerald?"

The boy glanced down at his twiddling fingers; it was as if he was saying: Thumb, mother; forefinger, father; and so on to his little finger, mother again and finally. He threw up his head and cried in a clear voice, "I want to go with you, Mum," and he made to seize her hand.

She shook it off. "Are you sure?"

"Yes, Mum, I'm sure."

"I can see," said Andrew, "it's been well rehearsed."

Gerald turned round with shocked mouth and eyes, but he was really amused and could not hide it.

His mother gave him an angry push. "There's nothing to smile at. Get back to your practice."

When he was gone she turned to her husband. "There was nothing rehearsed."

"It looked like it."

"The boy's not a fool. Maybe he didn't get the high marks in the examination he should have, but he's not a fool for all that. He's been noticing for some time there's something wrong between us. This hasn't come as a surprise to him."

"It has to me."

She frowned at him, puzzled.

"Oh, I admit we've made a mess of things," he said, "but I don't think it ever entered my head it would come to a separation. I thought our sort didn't do things like that. We're sound Scots working-folk, not riff-raff or nobility. If we make mistakes and canna mend them we thole them."

She was silent so long that when he glanced up at her he half expected to find her relenting in tears. Instead, she wore as embittered an expression as he had ever seen on her.

"I can't be as cool as that about it," she said, with forced slowness. "You've insulted me, you've laughed at me as if I was in your estimation no better than a woman off the streets. Yet I've said I'm prepared to forget that, to go against my whole nature and subdue my pride. What are you asked to do in return? Leave here and go with me and our boy to Helensburgh. Here in this town I've been accounted a success. They nod to me with respect, they touch their bonnets, they leave others to attend to me, they say nice things to my face. I'm not concerned with what they say behind my back. When I walk in the garden, am I wondering what the worms are thinking? I've been a success here, where you've been a failure. Go down into the main street, stop anybody, man or woman, and ask if for your own good you should stay or go. You know better than me what the answer would be. I've wondered often what your true reason must be for preferring to stay here, though everybody, including your own family, despises you. I know the reason now. It's because you want to be rid of me. If that's your reason, and I can see no other, then it makes sense, and I'd have been obliged if you'd admitted it long ago. I would hae known that I was like a body waiting for a train when the last one's gone. Now I can leave you with a good conscience. The truth is, Andrew, we were never matched. When we got married, that was a mistake; maybe—if it's any comfort to you to hear me say it—I was chiefly to blame. But now the situation's not tolerable, whoever's to blame. You say: thole it. I can't any longer."

She paused then.

He had been watching her all the time and had seen the bitterness soften to suffering, regret, and perplexity. Her voice had never escaped her control, but it had become strangely deep and eloquent. He was greatly moved.

But he was bewildered too. Was he, on the point of losing her, finding out what was finest in his wife? And was that the only circumstance in which he would ever find it? If he were to surrender to her now, would he hand her back to her old complaining, bitter self? Were she and he prisoners of their own natures? And was there to be no escape ever, in Drumsagart or Helensburgh or anywhere?

Looking round the room, he remembered how in every detail of its furnishings and decorating she had been far more interested than himself.

"But this is your house, Hannah, more than mine," he said.

She glanced about, and her hand went out involuntarily to touch on the wireless set a vase of hand-cut crystal she had chosen herself with much pride.

Her hand came back to join the other on her breast.

"There are more important things than vases or furniture," she said.

He stared at her in amazement.

"We'll go on Saturday," she said. "We'll slip away while you're at the match. Harry's coming with his car. Maybe later we can come to some arrangement."

He found himself shaking his head.

"Well, maybe not," she said. "It's best to be honest. I'm sorry if your tea's been spoiled. I should have waited, but I couldn't." Then she left the room.

He still kept shaking his head, in denial not merely of her whispered hope they might later come to an arrangement, but of all hope.

For a long time he sat at the table with his face covered by his hands. Many inchoate thoughts drifted through his mind. One kept taking shape and persisting; he had to beat on his brow to try and scatter it: it was that there was nothing noble or even intelligible in his attitude; it was fatalistic and self-destructive. There could be some kind of salvation in going to Helensburgh with Hannah and Gerald. There was the beautiful Firth; there could be the sense of newness and cleanness, after the old Drumsagart slough was shaken off; and surely in walks on the hills or along the shores, in steamer voyages, in rowing-boats, there could be a renewal of the relationship that had existed between him and Gerald up to a year or so ago? As for forfeiting his independence and surrendering himself body and soul to Harry, had he not already done so? He was in Harry's orbit true enough, and there was no use struggling against his ordained place.

Why, then, would he not go, at least not yet? He could not put it into words. He seemed to be like the lonely sentinel in the stone box in the old kirk gateway; he was on the edge of a great dark, empty sea of sorrow; he was the small boy in the picture in his school book more than thirty years ago, waiting in an antechamber with his mother, dressed in black, for an interview with some mysterious person in authority, while a tall soldier in a helmet stood silent guard. . . .

He stayed, therefore, and sang carols on Christmas Eve in the sleet on the steps of the church.

13

It is an axiom throughout Scotland that to win the Junior Cup a little luck is essential. Skill, stamina, courage, and morale are necessary; but teams which have these qualities in abundance find them unavailing without this other tiny ingredient. Nor can it be cultivated. Amulets can be carried in waistcoat pockets, from miniature Buddhas to whippets' teeth; prayers can be offered into the froth on beer; ladders can be avoided; boys can be employed to drive away from the precincts of the field all black cats; wives can be ordered to stitch magical emblems on to scarves; and ministers can be prevailed on to mention the team in pulpit addresses. These propitiations can all be made, indeed must be made, but as they are being made elsewhere at the same time by opponents there is in the laboratories of the occult a cancelling out. A team, therefore, in its progress has to be like any individual man: it must wrack heart, soul, and limbs; if it is lucky, it will succeed; if unlucky, it will fail. God can be praised or blamed thereafter.

For the fifth-round tie two days after Hogmanay the Thistle had to journey to Aberdeenshire, to play a team called Forgie Bluebell, which contained three internationals. Nearly every newspaper prophet forecast their defeat. Nor could they expect hordes of their followers to be present to stimulate them with applause or abuse. The fare was too much for dolemen; and workmen found themselves impoverished after the Ne'erday celebrations. Thus only three buses travelled: one containing the team and officials, the others the plutocrats of the town. A few went by train. Half a dozen set out to cadge lifts on lorries; of these only two arrived in time to see the game.

Archie Birkwood was one of those who travelled by special bus; his fare, however, was subsidised by a syndicate of stay-at-homes. It had been ascertained that not far from the Forgie football field was a telephone kiosk; Archie's duty was to rush out at fifteen-minute intervals to telephone the score to the public kiosk at Drumsagart Cross. As these calls would be costly, and he might also have to be at the expense of paying readmission money several times if the gatemen didn't co-operate, as many stay-at-homes as possible were enrolled in the combine, at a penny per head. Unfortunately a paid due brought the right of criticism. Many objected to the choice of Archie as too fat and lazy, they were afraid he'd find the dash from game to telephone too strenuous and would leave them all at the Drumsagart end listening to a long silence. Others declared he would be excellent at announcing disaster but disastrous at announcing joyful triumph. The majority, however, after much discussion, agreed

189

with the organisers that Archie, having no imagination or humour, would describe plainly how the game was going.

Nathaniel Stewart, as the originator, was appointed chairman of the organising committee. It met in the Lucky Sporran, and, according to cynics, consumed beer bought out of the fund. There Archie, who was a teetotaller, received his instructions and pledged his word not to let down the hundreds depending on him. He pledged it with appropriate sobriety, but added that if in one of his races to the telephone he broke his leg he hoped he wasn't expected to crawl the rest of his way on his belly; and, moreover, if he found the telephone in use they would all just have to content their souls in patience, for he wasn't going to involve himself in any altercation or fight, in alien country. They sent him apart while they considered these scruples. One or two feared he seemed lukewarm and pointed out there was nothing to prevent his claiming the telephone was in use just to save himself the bother of leaving the game, especially if this was at an exciting stage. Gravely they sipped beer and that possibility, and cast keeks at Archie where he sat apart waiting for their conference to end. If a man could not be trusted in such a cause, they decided, there was no hope for humanity: the Thistle might just as well be beaten; the town might as well be burnt to the ground or decimated by smallpox; beer might as well taste like water. Recalled, Archie was exhorted to do his best, to remember that two hundred miles away hundreds of his fellow townsmen would be as dependent on him as any corpse: let him in this enterprise show the same loyalty and efficiency as he did in his daily task, and they would be more than satisfied. He went home proud of their faith in him. Teena rather spoiled his dedicated mood by smelling beer off his raincoat, and indeed there was a large stain on the elbow where he'd rested it on a table. She pretended to weep because he'd turned drunkard and for nearly half an hour he wasn't sure whether she was pretending or not. As for her amusement over his election as courier, that was long since exhausted, but while it had lasted it had been as extravagant as that over the taxi-load to Carrick.

The committee pressed on with its arrangements. A team had to be chosen to receive the news and relay it amongst the crowds waiting outside the kiosk. Nat Stewart proposed his own ear as the one to be nearest the receiver. It was opposed as slightly defective. He denied that. The demurrers insisted. In a fury he banged his ears but proved nothing. A trial was arranged. Nat stood glowering at one end of the long bar, a committee-man stood at the other end and said faintly but distinctly: The Thistle are winning two-nothing. Others further off than Nat heard it, but he obviously did not; gnashing teeth could not help his straining ears. He protested, he grew pale with passion, for a few minutes it looked as if he might take a hæmorrhage; but even if he had, and he had had to be tenderly carried home all bloody and laid in his bed, the decision would still have gone against him. What would be the use of all the expense and planning if the man receiving Archie's news interpreted it wrongly? God in heaven, he might inform them the Thistle was winning when the truth was they were being beaten, so that hundreds of cheers would ascend instead of groans and prayers; and, conversely, he might pass on the news the Thistle was losing when the truth was they were winning, so that some old Drumsagart man might drop down dead in a stroke quite needlessly: it would be a kind of murder.

Nat withdrew, on condition that no other member of the committee be appointed. It was a condition vehemently and variously opposed, but in the end it was agreed to. The question of the outsider was then debated for several sessions. Nominations were flung forward and hurled back. Unanimity was unattainable. There was talk of the whole project being scrapped and the pennies returned. One committee-man resigned. Then at last a man whom they all equally distrusted was chosen; this was Jock Saunders. His chief qualification was that, as an ex-bookie's runner, he was an expert with the telephone. When he was informed the honour was to be his he uttered no thanks, sought no explanation, and remarked it was as well he was to be stationed in the kiosk, otherwise if the afternoon was wet he wouldn't be leaving the fireside.

Alas, the afternoon was wet, very wet—filthily, scandalously, brutally wet, after a dry grey morning. At half-past two a cloud burst over the town. The rain swished down into the main street as if the fire brigade was practising with its hoses from the Town Hall tower. Everybody was confident so thorough a deluge couldn't last; by three o'clock, when the game in far-off Aberdeenshire would be starting, the sky would be clear again and the gutters would be bubbling merrily. But cloud after cloud continued to burst over the Cross; the hoses of that squad of invisible and imbecile firefighters on the tower continued to be trained on the kiosk under the bare elm-tree.

Nat Stewart, in an unbuttoned raincoat, appeared at five to three with two of the committee at Jock Saunders' door. He invited them in, with no warnings or apologies that the table was littered with soiled dishes, his three-year-old son was enthroned on a chamber-pot in front of the fire, and his wife was drawing a fine comb through her seven-year-old daughter's hair, with a tray held under the girl's head to catch the numerous but infinitesimal quarry. She, sensitive housewife, was affronted at being thus surprised. Leaping to her feet, she flung glances at her husband as baleful as Medusa's, and indeed he seemed turned to sceptical stone as he listened to the reproaches and entreaties of his visitors.

"Supposing I got dry to the kiosk," he said, "what guarantee hae I got it doesn't leak? There are panes missing."

"It's got a concrete roof, Jock; it'll not leak."

"I hope it does," cried his wife, still mortified, "and droons you."

He rasped his chin. "How am I to get there dry?" he asked. "I mean, just look at yourselves. You're drookit."

"Are you coming, Jock? It's after three."

"See," he said, "you're hoarse already. Do you ken what I think? I think this afternoon's going to gie Sowlas and Birkwood a lot of customers."

"A pity you couldn't be one of them," shrieked his wife. Though she had removed the monarch behind a sofa, where he bawled, and had thrown a newspaper over the dishes, she was still venomous with shame.

Her travail was unheeded, and would have been had she been lying on the sofa in childbirth. The deputation and her husband had imperative business to settle.

"For the last time, Jock," asked Peter Goldie, "are you coming?" Then he sneezed.

"We picked you," wheezed Nat Stewart, "and we had to gie you the chance. If you don't want it, there's hundreds dying to take your place."

Jock sneered with sinister unshaven sapience. "I can see

how it is," he said. "If it's not me, who is it? There might be wrangling." He nodded then like some king offered the crown not for his abilities to rule but for contumelious compromise. "Oh, I'll oblige you," he added, "though I deserve pneumonia for my daft good nature. Betty"—this was to his daughter, clawing her head in a corner—"run doon to Grandpa Riddrie and ask him for a loan of his umbrella for your dad. Hurry, sweetheart."

"Aye, hurry, lass," gasped the officials, standing in three separate puddles on the linoleum.

"I'll get ready," said Jock, and proceeded to dress, calmly and portentously, as if indeed in kingly robes. "My shoes," he remarked, as he put them on, "let in if I stand on a spittle. This tie," he went on, as he fixed it fastidiously in front of a cracked mirror, "is the wrong colour. I hear Forgie Bluebell play in red, though I never saw a red bluebell in my life." He laughed loudly at his joke, but had to turn on his three courtiers to scowl the merest of grins out of them. "Hae patience, gentlemen. The first call is at quarter past."

"It's ten past now."

"Ample time. Archie'll not be punctual. Keep the heid, as the executioneer said to Mary, Queen of Scots." As he spoke he was putting on his own huge head a cap much too small. His arms stuck so far out of his raincoat sleeves he looked like a comedian in a film who'd fallen into a pond and whose clothes were visibly shrinking. The comedian, however, would have been dismayed and crestfallen. Jock was haughty; the sleeves were ermined-tipped, the cap a jewelled crown.

Betty arrived with an umbrella taller than herself.

"He says it's got a hole in it," she said shrilly.

Her father took it and shot it open, taking them all by surprise. His wife yelled, the deputation cursed, for of course it was bad luck to put up an umbrella in the house.

"For God's sake," asked Nat Stewart hoarsely, "do you want to ruin the Thistle's chances?"

"I had to see where the hole is," answered Jock, "and I can see it's where I'll be under. That's a damnable thing to lend a man an umbrella with a hole in it at such an inconvenient place. Well, let's go. Liz, hae the tea ready for quarter to five, prompt, and see it's hot."

"And I'll hae it sugared wi' arsenic, you big gomeril," she cried.

Outside on the landing he paused. "Did she say arsenic?"

"Aye, Jock. For God's sake, hurry."

"Am I to hurry frae my ain door, Peter, after my wife's just threatened to arsenicise my tea?"

"She was just annoyed wi' you for asking us in wi' the hoose unredd. All women are like that."

"Do all women threaten to put arsenic in the tea?"

"Mair or less. Come on, we're late; it's fully sixteen and a half minutes past."

They descended the stairs and marched deliberately out into the downpour. Jock put up the umbrella, on which the rain instantly beat like a drum. As he had calculated, the hole was so placed a small cataract began to shoot down his neck. He bore it stoically, merely observing that doctors might find it necessary to be out on such an afternoon; anybody else was a God-forsaken lunatic.

They arrived in a main street as wet as the bed of a burn. Men huddled in doorways and closemouths were like fish or larvae sheltering under rocks. No women were to be seen. They had apparently decided that not even the quest for food justified venturing out.

The fish or larvae flapped fins and uttered watery cheeps when they saw Saunders under the black umbrella hastening towards the kiosk. By the Town Hall clock the time was twenty past. Several fanatics were gathered round the kiosk, where there was no shelter; Rab Nuneaton was amongst them. The door was open, but no-one was inside. The reason was not that it was then a hallowed place, reserved for Saunders the anointed; nor that, being small, it could accommodate only three at most, leaving the rest to be drenched—no, the reason was Sergeant Elvan, who, gleaming in raincoat and helmet, barred the door.

He continued to bar it when the three officials arrived, with their elected under his black umbrella.

"Has Archie phoned yet?" shouted Nat Stewart.

"There's been nothing yet, Nat," cried one. "But you're not to be allowed in."

"Who says so?"

"I do," said the sergeant. "This is a public telephone. It's got to be kept clear for general use."

"Look," cried Stewart, indicating the gloom and wetness all round. "Is it likely there'll be a rush on the 'phone this afternoon? Is this a toon of mermaids?" He began to cough in his rage.

The sergeant frowned solicitously at him. "I ken what's afoot," he said, "and I don't want to be a spoilsport. But I can't get beyond the law."

"Even in weather like this?" asked Jock Saunders, not arrogantly, but rather as if his purpose was serious anthropological research.

With the rain cascading off his helmet, the sergeant nodded.

"If it was the last hour on earth," pressed Saunders, under his black umbrella, "and you saw a fellow stealing, say, a concertina frae a pawnshop window, would you arrest him?"

Then before the sergeant could reply the telephone rang.

"That's for us," shouted Nat Stewart. "It's Archie."

Those who heard cheered. Pushed towards the kiosk, Saunders resisted till he'd carefully lowered the umbrella. The sergeant's arm across the door reluctantly withdrew. Saunders entered and picked up the receiver.

"Is that you, Archie?" he asked. "What's the weather like up there? Here it's a flood. Your coffins'll be floating doon the main street if it keeps on much longer. Snaw? You're haeing snaw?" He took away his mouth to inform those waiting in frenzy for the score that in Aberdeenshire there was snow on the ground. "Is that so, Archie? Well, it'll not suit you. You've not got the build for that sort of thing." Again he took his mouth away. "Archie's complaining," he said. "He says the telephone's nearly a quarter of a mile away, and the snaw's two inches thick on the road."

"What in Christ's name is the score?" yelled Nat Stewart. "The game's twenty-five minutes started. Are there ony goals?"

"Goals? I'll ask him," promised Saunders, and was as good as his word. "Is there ony score, Archie? They're waiting here wi' their een bulging. Is that so? Well, well, there are going to be sore herts. But even at Bannockburn somebody was bound to lose "

Stewart reached in and grabbed him. "What is it?"

"It's one-nothing for the Bluebell."

Then as Saunders returned to his conversation with the far-off Birkwood the dismal news was spread. Those round the kiosk yelped it to those in the nearest doorways and closemouths; thence it fled like plague to the furthest ends of the main street. A few, smitten by blackest pessimism, slunk off home. The rest decided to perish there in the rain.

The first conversation in the kiosk was over. Archie was trudging back through the snow to the football field. Jock was blowing his hand, cold from contact with the telephone. A dozen men tried to speak to him at once. "Was that all he said, Jock? What the hell's the maitter wi' Turk that he let them score? Has Alec Elrigmuir done nothing? Was it a good goal or a fluke? Was the Thistle pressing for the equaliser? What's the ground like? Did Archie not say it was a damned disgrace to play in inches of snaw?" They beseeched Jock to give them comforting answers, and they stared in at the black telephone with fear, hatred, despair, and anguish. Dry in the kiosk, Saunders watched them soaked outside.

"If you'd let me get a word in edgeways," he said.

"Shut up," they all roared. "Jock's got something to tell us."

They were silent, except for hectic breathings, snuffles, suppressed sneezes, and bronchial grunts. A bus streamed by on the street. Rain stotted on the pavement and on the roof of the kiosk.

"Archie said," said Jock, "there was a great shout from the park. He didn't ken if it was a goal for us or another for the Bluebell."

"A great shout?"

"It must hae been, if he could hear it a quarter of a mile away."

"If it was a great shout, then it must hae been a goal for the Bluebell. How could oor men, three or four dozen of them, raise a great shout?"

"Was it a joyful shout?"

"He didn't say."

"It could hae been a great shout of lamentation from the Bluebell supporters. In that case it must hae been a goal for us."

"Archie said," remarked Jock, "the Bluebell are playing great football. He said the Thistle will need a lot of luck to win."

"Archie Birkwood never had a cheery word for anybody in his life," muttered Rab Nuneaton.

"You get the name of being sparing wi' them yourself, Rab," said Saunders mildly.

Then Crutch Brodie came hobbling up to the kiosk on his crutch. He wore a sou'wester and an oilskin coat, and looked, as somebody muttered not in jest, like a sailor whose leg had been snapped off by a shark. He wanted to have it verified that the score was one-nothing against the Thistle. It was verified.

"I promised Tinto Broon to keep him in touch," he panted, and hirpled away.

"News like that's liable to kill auld Tinto in the state he's in," remarked someone.

Then they all settled down damply to wait for the next call in fifteen minutes.

That call never came. Half-past three went by and the telephone did not ring. Suppositions were many and melancholy. It was believed the Bluebell must have scored more goals, putting the Thistle in a hopeless position. Archie had therefore decided it was hardly worth the trouble plodding through the snow to tell them what his silence told them far more eloquently. More crept home. The rest hung on in the stoic assumption that, already wet to the skin, another quarter of an hour would make no difference. Archie would surely get in touch again at half-time. All admitted they were mad to stay out there in the cold and pelting rain. Some tried to justify it by pointing out how as miners they sometimes had to work up to the knees in water; if they had to suffer for their employer, why should they not suffer for their own pleasure?

Jock Saunders lounged in the kiosk, tapping his teeth with his finger-nails. Now and then he complained that when he'd undertaken that duty and when he'd started that afternoon his nerves had been as steady as the man's who'd walked across Niagara Falls on a tightrope. Their nervousness had affected him. If the telephone rang he would jump, and his heart in his breast would jump too, reducing his life by months. Nor would he be consoled or soothed by hearing good news from Archie. From the beginning he had insisted, and still did, that the winning or losing of the Cup was of much less concern to him than his ingrowing toe-nail. What recompense then could he expect for this shortening of his mortal existence?

Though several heard him through the open door, it was a soliloquy. Their minds were in distant snowy Aberdeen.

"You look as weans look," he said, "when they stare in the window of a sweetie shop. Mind this, if your weans are ailing for lack of proper sustenance, the winning of the Cup by the Thistle will not revive them. If your wife's a nag, she'll still nag. If you sometimes hae the ambition to stick your heid into the gas-oven, you'll still hae it, whether the Cup's in Drumsagart or Forgie. What's this Cup after all? Is it like the lamp Aladdin found? If you rub it, does a jouker in a turban and a face as crabbit as Tinto Broon's spring up beside you and offer you the world? Even then I doubt if it wad bring you happiness."

Then the telephone rang at his ear. He snatched it up and peevishly listened. He said nothing. Streaming faces gaped hungrily in. Fingers plucked at him. Hoarse voices cajoled. From the doorways and closemouths crawled the dozens of bedraggled, shivering men to gather round the kiosk. The sky was dull. Shops were lit. Cold, damp, and dark possessed the street. Only there in that kiosk by the unicorned Cross might there be light, warmth and splendour. They pressed round it, striving to see Jock Saunders in communication, not with a blue-nosed Archie Birkwood, but with Fate.

The fateful crackles ceased, Jock wiped his nose with the back of his hand, hung up the receiver, yawned, scratched his neck, and grinned.

"It's a boy," he said.

No joke was ever less appreciated.

"All right. It's a draw at half-time, one goal each."

They cheered as well as inflamed nostrils and flowing noses permitted. They said huskily that news was as good as hot mustard baths to them. Reverently, they asked if Alec Elrigmuir had scored.

"Aye," said Jock, "it was him. In a breakaway. Archie warns you all not to get too confident. He thinks only a miracle can save the Thistle. He says if you ken any prayers you've to say them."

In sad consternation they gazed at one another. They knew no prayers likely to be efficacious; and in any case were their knees not sodden?

"Surely to God they can hold oot?"

"Turk will never weaken."

"Alec Elrigmuir might steal anither goal."

"If we get a draw oot of it we'll beat them here at Drumsagart."

"Archie said," announced Jock, "that he'll 'phone again at time-up. He declares it's unreasonable to expect him to rush through snaw. He says his feet are wet."

"I hope you told him, Jock, what we're suffering here."

"He asked if we thought he was a member of the Canadian Mounted Police."

"Why the hell did he ask that?"

"Because of the snaw."

"I always said so—he's a big glaikit numbskull."

"Well, lads, that's the position," said Jock. "No more calls till time-up. That'll be aboot twenty to five. You can go hame and sit by the fire. That's what I'm for doing."

He pushed his way out and was putting up his umbrella when Crutch Brodie arrived beside him.

"Would you like to do a good turn, Jock?" he asked.

"Am I a Samaritan?" muttered Jock.

"It's Tinto. You ken he's badly. He'd be pleased if you went doon and gave him the news aboot the game."

"Crutch, the news is it's a draw so far, one each."

"But you can fill in the picture for him."

"I'm sorry, Crutch. Football's not my topic. I'm going hame for a cup of tea. But tell Tinto I'll be paying him a visit one of these days."

Crutch watched him hurry away. "Poor auld Tinto," he murmured. "They all promise to visit you, but nane of them do it except me." Then he hobbled away to where in the dark, cold little room his friend was lying semi-conscious.

Many took Jock Saunders' advice and hurried home to dry by the fire while their wives made them cups of tea and scalded them with sarcasms. Most, however, continued to absent themselves from such domestic felicity. With so much suspense in their souls they had to forsake comfort and stay out in the wilderness. Some crowded into Isaac Purdie's billiard-saloon, where the fug of smoke, steam, breath, and soaked clothes sent a few to sleep in spite of the crush and the yabble of football speculation. Others shivered in closes or pends, through which chill winds swept constantly. Some in twos and threes insinuated themselves into dry nooks, such as the library and Paleri's café and Baldy Logie's barber shop. A few congregated in the public lavatory. Nat Stewart and another stood sentinel in the kiosk. Rab Nuneaton slipped into the stone box at the kirk gate and waited there alone, half sheltered from the rain. Crutch Brodie crouched by Tinto's bed. All concentrated on stifling time till twenty to five when Archie would speak again.

At half-past four the concourse round the kiosk was denser than it had been all afternoon. Cravens, hitherto hugging the fire, now came out for the last excitement. The rain was still heavy. It was, as Jock Saunders grumbled, shoving through them, as if the kiosk was a spilt pot of jam and they were all flies. In another couple of hours the newspapers would have come from Glasgow with the score in the stop-press columns; or it might be heard on the wireless. Surely any man who'd waited for a mother to die or a child to be born had the patience to wait for the result of a football match? No wonder, he muttered, the young minister was said to be bitter about the apathy towards religion compared with the tremendous enthusiasm for football. I'm neutral, said Jock; but if I was to become enthusiastic it would be for religion, not for football; the rewards, if the truth's being told, are not to be compared.

Sergeant Elvan was back at the door of the kiosk.

"You look, Sergeant," said Jock, as he put down his umbrella, "like a bloke that's been waiting all day for his lass and she's not turned up."

Saunders was one of the few men in the town after whom in the sergeant's judgment-book was written a question-mark instead of the double lines of finality. As a corner-lounger, an ex-bookie's runner, and the possessor of a single shirt, Saunders at first sight was fit to be damned; but he was capable of a judicial aloofness, and his criticism of human folly was often coincidental with the sergeant's own. Therefore at this jest about being jilted Elvan smiled.

"It'll depend on your news," he said, "whether a lot of them here will think their lasses are away for good."

"Do you hope the news is good or bad, Sergeant?" asked Saunders.

"It's all the same to me."

"Is it all the same to you, then, whether your fellow-men are in joy or misery?"

They both laughed, and Saunders entered the kiosk. The sergeant held the door open for him, and then shut it.

"Everybody keep back now," he cried. "You'll hear soon enough."

Nat Stewart, his cap black with wet, snatched it off and crushed it in his fists. It was not to squeeze the rain out of it but to express his resentment at this arrogant interference by the law.

"What the hell has it got to do wi' you?" he cried.

From the crowd there rose a mutter of hostility, too damp to burst into flame.

"I just want to make sure there's no stampede," answered Elvan amicably. "Saunders is in there. He'll give you the news when he gets it. I don't see what there's to complain about."

"Don't you?" yelled Stewart. "It's just this; I object on principle to you and your like shoving yourself in where there's no need for you. Do you remember the General Strike?"

"Why do you use up your strength," asked the policeman, "in such useless anger?"

They were interrupted by a disturbance on the edge of the crowd. A woman with a small blue umbrella seemed to be trying to push her way in. Eagerly Elvan thrust towards her.

"What is it?" he demanded. "What's going on?"

"She wants to use the 'phone," muttered one. "As if there weren't other 'phones!"

"Look at the time," said others. "The game will be over. Archie'll be ringing us up ony minute now. If we're not careful we might miss him. After all, we've waited for hours in the rain; she's just arrived. Fair's fair."

She was in tears. "I'm a widow woman," she said, with inspired irrelevance.

They continued to frown and protest, but gave way to let her through, escorted by the sergeant.

"This morning, you see," she explained, weeping, "my lassie Nan was taken to hospital wi' diphtheria. They told me to 'phone at half-past four. I'm late because it's wet."

"It's wet all right, Mrs. Woods," they agreed, anxious in some way to establish kinship with her, despite their irreconcilable disagreement over the use of the telephone. It was impossible to expect her to see their point of view; the gap was wider than that between Catholic and Protestant, Tory and Communist.

"Is Saturday afternoon not visiting time?" asked one.

"Visiting hours are frae six to seven."

"If she 'phones," muttered another to his friend, "do you see what's going to happen? Archie will be told the number's engaged, he'll not wait because he'll be in a hurry to catch the bus hame, and we'll not get the result at all."

But they had all seen the threatening void.

"Well?" said the sergeant to Nat Stewart. "You ken what she wants. What about it?"

She appealed to the perplexed masculine faces.

"I don't want to cause ony trouble," she snivelled, "but you can see how anxious I am."

"There are other 'phones in Drumsagart," suggested Rab Nuneaton.

"What's a wean mair or less?" muttered Nat Stewart.

Even his fellow committee-men gasped and shook their heads. At the same time they glanced up at the clock.

"I might have waited a minute or so," said Elvan grimly, "but not after that."

He made to tug open the door but Stewart pulled his arm away.

"Can she not wait five minutes?" he cried. "We've waited more than ninety."

It was obvious many agreed with him, though none had the courage or shamelessness to say it.

"Five minutes of this poor woman's worry causes me more concern," said the sergeant, "than if you'd been waiting ninety years to hear how many times a chunk of leather was kicked between a couple of posts."

"It is ninety years really we've been waiting," cried Rab Nuneaton. "The Thistle hae never won the Cup yet."

"I'll wait," said Mrs. Woods. "Surely I can wait five minutes?"

She was applauded by all except the sergeant.

"Not if I can help it," he said.

"How can you help it?" cried Nat Stewart. "If the woman says she'll wait, what's it got to do with you?"

"But what if my lassie's lying dying?" she suddenly wailed.

Then the kiosk door opened and Jock Saunders stuck out his head.

"What's all the fuss aboot?" he asked. "It's bad enough wi' traffic scooshing by and catarrh in the lugs withoot a riot as well."

Fifty explained it to him. Haughtily he silenced them all but one; this was the sergeant, who briefly told him.

Jock rubbed his chin. "Seems to me there's only one thing to be done."

"And what's that?" demanded the sergeant.

"'Phone the hospital. What's the number, Mrs. Woods?"

She told him.

"Gie me your tuppence. I'll get them for you and you can talk to them."

She handed him the two pennies ready in her glove. Before he withdrew into the kiosk he glared round the crowd, as if defying anyone to frown or boo.

"You damned traitor," said Nat Stewart.

Jock gazed at him sadly. "There are some things mair important than football, Nat." Then he patted Mrs. Wood on the shoulder and went for the telephone. He had his hand on it when it rang. Lifting it, with a scowl, he put it to his ear. After listening for about ten seconds he snapped "Is that so? Goodbye" and replaced the instrument. As he waited for a second or two before picking it up again to call the hospital they surged forward outside, despite the sergeant, and roared in if that had been Archie talking and what had he said. Jock turned his back on them. As he put in the two pennies and gave the hospital's number he might have been alone for all the attention he paid to the crowd bellowing at him. When he came out, after handing over the telephone to Mrs. Woods, he closed the door behind her and held up his hand for attention. They gave it to him, expecting that he would repay them by telling them the score.

"She's in there 'phoning aboot her girl in hospital wi' diphtheria," he said. "Gie her a chance."

They gave him a growl.

Someone yelped, "For God's sake, tell us the score, and let us get hame oot of this rain."

"As soon as she's finished," he promised, and went on angrily, as the growl was repeated, "If you don't keep quiet you'll hear no score from me. You were asking that poor woman to wait five minutes. I'm asking you to wait just one."

They quietened.

Nat Stewart, close to Saunders, whispered, "Did we win, Jock?"

Saunders shook his head. "I'm not saying."

"Tell me, Jock. I'll keep it quiet."

Saunders jerked his thumb behind him.

They waited.

"This is meat and drink to you," muttered Nat Stewart to the sergeant.

Mrs. Woods came out. She was weeping more sorely.

"Bad news?" asked Saunders humbly.

"She's ill. They said she's quite ill."

He patted her. "She'll get better."

"She'll need to," she sobbed as she went away. "She'll need to, for since her faither dee'd she's all I hae."

Saunders waited till she was clear of the impatient crowd.

"That woman," he cried, "is away hame broken-herted."

"For Jesus' sake," shouted somebody, in some kind of disgust.

"I don't want to find oot who shouted that," cried Saunders, "for I'd think it necessary to skite the words doon his throat." He showed a flash of anger. "Is there anybody here says I couldn't do it?"

No-one there said any such thing.

"I'll tell you the score," he said. "But no demonstrations. Just disperse quietly."

"Did we win?"

He paused, cleared a space to put up his umbrella as if he'd suddenly remembered it was still raining, and then from under it announced contemptuously: "Aye, you won. You were lucky too. Bluebell one, Thistle two. Elrigmuir scored two minutes from the end."

In spite of his appeal they cheered. It was useless asking them to stop. He merely shook his head. Nat Stewart burst into a delirium of triumph; he seemed to think the victory was over, not the Bluebell two hundred miles away, but the sergeant and Jock Saunders beside him. He mouthed at them with spit flying, until some of his friends dragged him away.

Slowly they dispersed. Soon only the sergeant and Saunders were left by the kiosk.

"Did they win?" asked Elvan.

"You heard me."

"I thought maybe you'd misinformed them. They deserved it. Did you hear them cheering, with that poor woman breaking her heart?"

"Tell me, Sergeant," said Saunders, turning to him, "when you sit doon to your Sunday breakfast of ham and eggs and sausage, are you considering that there are millions starving?"

Elvan smiled, suspecting a joke. "Hardly. But it's not the same thing at all. Granted there are folk starving in India, say, but that's thousands of miles away. Mrs. Woods was among them, they could see her tears, she could hear them cheering."

"You forget there are folk in this very Drumsagart damned hungry at times," said Saunders, and walked away under his leaking umbrella.

The sergeant, gazing after him, noticed he had large holes in both his heels.

14

The raid on the public-house was subtly planned. Mr. Lockhart did not make the mistake of just walking in off the street. Even Christ, after all, had been heralded for centuries.

He chose the Lucky Sporran not only because it was owned by a member of his church but also because it had the largest clientèle. Malarkin at first was not delighted by the proposal; Mr. Lockhart had not expected him to be: beer and piety were in the last analysis incompatibles. But the publican was honourably overcome by the Christian; Malarkin acquiesced on condition that the address would not exceed five minutes, would contain nothing exceptionable to Protestant, Catholic, agnostic or atheist, and would have in it somewhere a hopeful reference to the Thistle, which in a few days was to contest the sixth round of the Cup. A pure evangelist would never have agreed to such conditions;

but then a pure evangelist in these irreligious days would never open his lips to utter the name of Christ, so frequently and blasphemously soiled in the public streets. It was not a fair fight, thought Mr. Lockhart, rejoicing: one expected diabolical tactics from the Devil; but it was none the less one's duty to show that on God's side there was generalship too.

Malarkin chose the evening, the Thursday before the Cup-tie; on Thursdays most of his customers were looking for tick, which made them amenable. He himself appeared behind the bar, wearing a black jacket over a mauve waistcoat. Most of the regulars were present. Some drank at the bar; some stood round the fireplace; some were seated at the little tables; and one glowered and grunted like Genghis Khan in a corner, drinking in noisy gulps pints sent up to him by admirers, who were rewarded with surly nods. This was Turk McCabe. His fellow genius, Alec Elrigmuir, wrapped in white apron, was amateurishly carrying pints; these were accepted from his hand reverently as if his other hand asked no payment. Rab Nuneaton was there, trying to be allowed into the conversation at the fireplace; he had been in for nearly an hour and had drunk so far only half of a half-pint of beer. A more interesting, though hardly more profitable customer was Robbie Rutherford. He was entertaining a group at one table with remarks about his brother, who everybody knew was now living by himself, was out of work, and was apparently as savage as a bear with an arrow in its rump. Sam thought that after the minister had gone it might be worthwhile standing Robbie a pint to have a private account of the Rutherford situation; it was known, for instance, that the old man was ill—some said insanely so—but nobody was sure whether he had forgiven Andrew or taken him back into favour.

At a quarter to seven Sam lifted a handbell and rang it. They paused to look at him. Already they had remarked on the sombreness of his dress. One had asked if his grannie was dead; another, less audibly, had conjectured that Margot had run away with a Negro.

He leant both elbows on the bar, with his fingers twirling his whiskers to still finer points.

"Sorry for interrupting your talk, lads," he said. "I've got a surprise for you."

"A free round, Sam?"

He smiled the demurest of rebukes at that grossest of impertinences.

Some guffawed.

"There might be a free half-pint in it," he said, and was astounded himself, for a second before he had not known he was going to make this reckless offer, this extravagant libation. Religion was insidious: he must be careful.

They gaped; some had to return to their glasses to ease throats rasped by astonishment.

"If the Thistle win the League as well as the Cup? Is that it, Sam?"

"No, George. I mean this very night, at ten past seven or thereabouts."

"What's the celebration for, Sam?"

"Is Margot getting married?"

"Who said that?" he cried sharply.

Nobody owned up, and the culprit's friends, though displeased with him for risking their free half-pints, protected him.

"A joke, Sam," said a conciliator. "In bad taste, but a joke. You ken what some men are like when they've got beer in them."

"Don't blame the beer."

"No, it's damned good beer; the best in Drumsagart."

"You know the Lucky Sporran code of honour: no references to women."

"That's right, Sam." They looked about for Ned Nicholson, who could recite blue jokes for two hours without ever telling a stale one; he was not present. "That's right, Sam. True enough. Purest pub in Christendom."

He frowned, and then smiled: it was a gibe, but it was also his cue. "Christendom," he repeated, with a glance at the clock. "Here's my surprise for you, lads. Tonight at seven o'clock, that's in about seven minutes, you're going to have a visitor."

"Who is it, Sam? Alan Morton?"

"We don't need Alan Morton here when we've got Alec Elrigmuir."

That was applauded. Elrigmuir simpered at his feet. Then Turk in his corner blew his nose. As far as they could see, in their circumspect glances, he used no handkerchief. It was not possible to say whether he was expressing derision or jealousy; or indeed whether he was just clearing his nasal passages of beery phlegm.

"The visitor is the young minister, Mr. Lockhart," said Sam.

There was silence. Then someone sniggered. Another laughed. Then all buzzed.

"He's the one that chucks out bosses of Sunday schools if they're frauds," cried Robbie Rutherford. "He'll get my welcome even if he's in to preach on temperance."

"Hardly that," giggled Rab Nuneaton. "I don't think Sam would approve of that agenda."

Malarkin was displeased. No doubt the country was a democracy, and it was true a public-house was the most democratic of meeting-places; but he could never stomach being called by his Christian name, in its diminutive form too, by a rag of a man like Nuneaton, who wore no collar and tie, whose trousers were patched, and who, after paying threepence for a half-pint of beer, stayed for over two hours, enjoying more than threepenceworth of light and warmth. Besides, Nuneaton always called Rutherford Mr.

"I'm expecting you all to give the young man a decent hearing."

"I'm broad-minded," shouted one. "I'd drink wi' the Pope himself spouting."

"No sectarian talk," cried Sam.

"There'd better not be," said Mick Flynn, gripping his beer-mug as if there were two thoughts in his bald head: the first to smash the glass, the second to jab the jagged remnants in the scoffer's face.

"No offence meant, Mick. I hae no religion, and envy nobody that has."

Mick's grip slackened ever so slightly.

"I'm as loyal a supporter of the Thistle as there is in the town," he said, "but I'm proud of my religion."

Then from Turk's corner came a growl. "Will yous eedjits shut your gubs? I was listening to Sam. You go on, Sam. Tell us what the young bloke's going to say."

"Well, Turk, I think he's going to tell us what sort of work the church does."

"Curing lepers?" asked Turk.

Sam was astonished. "That, among other things. He wants more men to come to church."

"Would he put a bar up against drinking?" asked one.

"Sure he would," said another. "He'd tell us it was a great sin. They've done it before, that crowd: their motto is, misery. I ken them. I used to go to Sunday school."

"Shut your traps," roared Turk. "Nobody asked you to speak."

For a moment they looked as if they might uphold their right to express their opinions.

Turk stood up. "Listen," he said, "all of you, listen. I never had any time for ministers or priests; they went one way, I went anither. Their preaching was nane of my business; it's still nane of my business. But my mither's getting auld and she's taken to singing hymns she learned at school. She's not got long now, poor auld girl, before she snuffs it. What I want to say is this—if anybody here tries to make a mug oot of the minister, then he's trying to make a mug oot of my auld mither, and that's something I'll not stand for."

They all thought he was the expert at making a mug out of his mother, he'd been doing it since he was born; but none said it, and all applauded his filial loyalty.

"Well spoken, Turk," said Sam. "It does you credit. Remember then, as soon as the minister's gone, if he's been given a good reception, there's that half-pint for every man at this moment in the house. Newcomers excluded. Bob and Alec"—these were his barmen—"count the faces."

Bob and Alec were doing so, and the faces were making sure they were included, when the door swung open and in came, not the young minister, expeller of sins, but Tinto Brown, the old sinner risen from his deathbed.

After the first startled gaze there was an outburst of pitying and contemptuous laughter. Tinto, ashamed because he had no money to justify his entering, glanced up from the floor, so often now the direction of his eyes, and uttered a snarl far too feeble to be characteristic. Indeed, in it was contained a plea to be left alone, not to be laughed at; to be allowed to sit quietly by the fire and listen to their talk.

"Whit's so funny?" he squealed, and tried to wave his stick at them. "Is it my faut I've to drag aboot wi' me a carcase that's deid and nobody will bury?"

Malarkin shook his head to that appeal. "I think, Tinto, you should get back to your bed."

"I've just crawled oot of it. I need a change from girning weans and the stink of my ain decay."

"And you've brought it here," cried one, "to scunner us off our booze?"

Tinto made an effort to be complaisant. He tortured his face into a smile and held out his withered palsied hand with friendliness in it like a bright flower.

"All I'm here for, Tam," he said, "is just to hear you all talk." He sniffed. "This is hame to me."

"This is a public-house," said the publican, "not a convalescent home. If men talk here, they must drink too; and they pay for their drinks."

Tinto's pride flared up; the flower turned to a thistle; he flung it at them. "To hell wi' you all," he cried. "I'll go. I ken when I'm not wanted."

They waited for him to turn and go; some smiled in shame.

Suddenly Turk McCabe sprang to his feet and, shouldering through the throng, rushed to the door, where he seized the old man's hand. "Come in to the fire, Tinto," he cried; "and if any man here says no, let him step ootside to the pavement and take off his jacket. I don't forget you were the first to welcome me when I arrived back in Drumsagart. When others cursed at me and ordered me away again you took my part."

Tinto was unwilling, but it made no difference. He was almost carried up to the fire and placed so near it that he singed. Turk had to kick chairs aside to clear room. Then he turned his fiercest scowl on the bar and ordered a pint.

"For Tinto," he said. "For this auld man."

"For me, Turk?" asked Tinto, in tears.

"For you, Tinto."

A certain question was not spoken, yet it was heard as clearly by everybody as if elephants in chorus had trumpeted it: who was to pay for this pint? Alec Elrigmuir looked at Bob Bankhead, who looked at Sam Malarkin, who looked, or tried to, at the points of his whiskers.

Turk grew impatient. "What's keeping that pint?" he cried.

Tinto turned as shy as a little girl. "Ask young Alec to bring it," he whispered.

"Sure, Tinto, just as you like. Alec, he wants you to bring it."

Malarkin had nodded, Bob Bankhead had drawn the beer.

He slid it along to Elrigmuir, who took it and was carrying it to the enraptured old man huddled at the fireplace when the door again opened, and this time came in, not a newcomer to be debarred from the bonus, but the cause of the bonus himself, the Rev. Mr. Harold Lockhart.

After much solitary cogitation, for he refused to consult even Nan, he had decided to wear his uniform of black cloth and immaculate white collar. From smart walking in the cold wind his cheeks were red, his eyes bright, and his step assured. Indeed, afterwards it was to be said he entered the pub as if, not heaven exactly, it was the way in.

He held a small Bible in his gloved hands. Beaming round, he caught sight of the host and greeted him cordially. A few of the men he knew by sight; to these he gave affable smiles; to everyone a hearty good-evening. Alec Elrigmuir, as a member of the church, newly introduced by Mysie, was granted the warmest of salutations, although he was at that very moment handing over a glass of beer to the most scurrilous enemy of the kirk in Drumsagart, that confessed reprobate, that self-approving anti-Christ, the old rapscallion they called Tinto Brown.

Tinto was the only one not expecting the minister. He thought the newcomer was some ordinary drouth, and so ignored him. Besides, was he not taking a pint from the hand of Alec Elrigmuir, the young football wizard, whom he'd more or less discovered, in whom he had had faith while everybody else disbelieved?

"Thank ye, Alec son," he said. "Do you mind if I toast ye?" He tottered to his feet, held up his glass in shaky hand, and quavered: "To your success——"

"Quiet, Tinto," murmured one.

Then Tinto realised there was strange silence. Mouth whitened with a great moustache of froth, he peered round and soon saw the minister, smiling awkwardly at him.

"What's this?" cried Tinto, in a voice that chilled the blood of many who heard. They said afterwards they'd thought Tinto had seen the ogre of death and was going to drop there by the fire in a puddle of beer. Nobody laughed though in speaking he kept blowing off bits of that false moustache.

Turk reassured him. "It's all right, Tinto. You're not seeing things. It's just the minister in to tell us aboot the work of the church." He winked at the minister.

Tinto was trembling. "I ken they burst their way into the room where a man lies dying," he said. "I ken they stand dominant ower his coffin, but I thought we were safe from them in pubs."

"No, you've got it wrong, Tinto," explained Turk patiently. "The minister's just going to gie us a chat aboot the work of the church, like curing lepers, you ken."

Tinto glared round. "Let me get oot of here," he cried.

Mr. Lockhart felt the same sick whirl in his stomach as on the night Nan had fainted and he had thought her dead.

"You misjudge me," he murmured.

Tinto turned at the door. "What your kind's been saying for centuries has been the curse of Scotland and of the whole world. When was there ever a war you didn't bless? Tell me, when was there ever a better Christian in this toon than auld John Rutherford? And when the auld man was doon, stricken doon by the ingratitude and foolishness of folk, wha kicked him, wha stamped his face into the muck of bitterness?" His voice grew shriller. "You all ken I'm a damned sight nearer my Maker than any one of you. If He's what your kind hae represented Him to be, when I meet Him face to face there'll be mony things far frae complimentary I'll hae to say to Him; and then, nae doubt, wi' your sanction and to the soond of your hallelujahs, He'll whistle up His son, young Christ, to strangle me wi' His bare hands for all my sins. Till then, leave me in peace." Then he was gone.

Turk wisely scratched his chest through a gap in his shirt. "It's age," he said. "It fankles the brain. Same with my mither. Same with us all some day." Catching sight of Tinto's forsaken pint, he reached forward, lifted it, held it up, said "Christ pity auld Tinto," and drank deeply.

Mr. Lockhart was so physically, morally, and spiritually shocked that Malarkin, alarmed, swithered about offering him a glass of brandy.

Mick Flynn sidled up to the minister. "Minister," he said, "I'm a Catholic, and there are more of us in this pub. I want to tell you that though there's much we disagree aboot in the way of religion, when it comes to that auld atheistical rubbish that's just crawled oot we're on your side."

His co-religionists nodded.

Turk let out a bellow. "I'm damned if I'll stand for that," he shouted.

"Quiet now, Turk," said Malarkin. "Remember who's here."

"I'll not be quiet when I hear auld Tinto called rubbish. Was it rubbish that welcomed me back? Anybody who says it was is entitled to his opinion, but on condition I'm entitled to try and knock it, and his teeth wi' it, doon his throat; and it's all the same to me whether it's an Orange or a Papish throat." He kicked over a chair. "Don't think I'm ignorant. I ken some Bible. We got it hammered into us at school. 'I am become a sounding brass or a tingling simple.' That's Bible."

Malarkin leant over the bar and advised the minister to postpone the address. Turk might become violent and assault somebody or damage the pub. If Elvan had to be summoned he'd take pleasure in arresting Turk, who was, of course, indispensable for the Cup-tie on Saturday. Did Mr. Lockhart not agree?

He did. "How fiendish a view of Christ!" he whispered, staring at his own hands.

"Don't be blaming us all for what Tinto said," urged Malarkin. "Maybe he's new to you; to us he's been a nuisance and a disturbance for years. He'll be taken care of."

That innuendo caused Mr. Lockhart's hands to flee behind his back. "There is compassion in God's heart even for the most horrible blasphemers."

"He'll be taken care of," repeated Malarkin, who was reflecting that while the minister remained there, peeping daftly at his hands, the business of the pub must be suspended. "It's most unfortunate. Who'd have thought Tinto would choose this night to rise from his bed? We'll be luckier another night."

"No." The minister's voice was low, but the agony in it made the publican pout. "No, we shall not be lucky any night." Then, without a good-night, he was gone.

Rude, thought Sam, and rum, too, for a parson. But it's his business, just as selling liquor's mine. He returned briskly to work. "Shop open, lads. Order your drinks."

"What about that free half-pint?"

"There was no address."

"You're welshing, Sam," cried one, in the tone of a man who, living in the midst of degeneracy, was disgusted but not surprised.

"Any reasonable man," said Malarkin, "must agree that the

conditions were altered. Mr. Lockhart will come back another night. The offer will be renewed then."

"If he comes back," said Rab Nuneaton, with a snigger, "I hope auld Tinto's here again."

There immediately broke out loud and thirsty debate on that wish of Rab's. Religion was inevitably brought into it, on the high controversial level of retribution after death. Those who maintained there would be punishment in hell were confident that Christ personally would not administer it. On earth the gaffers never did the dirty work; the judge who ordered the flogging was far from the screams and the weals when the cat cracked.

Turk had been smouldering in his corner. Suddenly he broke out as if invisible men were holding him. He punched those transcendental faces, kicked those ethereal shins. "I'm going hame," he cried. "Get oot of my way."

Those visible men did so, nimble as dancers.

"Good night, Turk," they called. "Watch yourself on the slippery pavements. To bed early, that's the stuff. We'll need you on Saturday."

At the door, which he opened with a lunge of his shoulder, he turned. "A shower of tingling simples," he muttered, and disappeared.

There was no doubt that, great man though he was, worth every pint of tribute, licensed to insult them as he wished, nevertheless it was a relief when he went.

"Somebody should follow him," they said, "in case he falls."

"Or in case he makes his water in the gutter and gets arrested by Elvan."

"Or takes a notion to jump on a bus and disappear again."

"True," they said, "we should take care of him, for without him we've no chance of the Cup."

All nodded, all shivered at the prospect of losing the silver grail, but none left the warmth and brightness. Soon they returned to their eschatological argument, leaving Turk in the care of whatever saint protected football players.

15

As Turk slouched home under the stars he brooded on religion and the destructiveness of age. In a few more years his own head would soften, so that it would never be able to repel a football whizzing into goal. When that happened he would be turned out of the Lucky Sporran without pity or a single pint. To grow old, he reflected, was hellish.

His own mother, for instance, was growing so absent-minded it was like lunacy. Sometimes when he went home after an evening in the pub he found she'd gone to bed, having forgotten about his supper. Nor could she be coaxed or bullied into rising to make it. She lay on her back in the set-in bed in the kitchen, with her wrinkled face above the clothes, staring at the ceiling so steadily he'd been forced to examine it thoroughly, but had seen nothing except a spider's web in the corner. Deliberately she had left him in the predicament either of making supper for himself or going without. Usually he chose the latter, as the more honourable and masculine course; but he had at the same time pointed out to her that if he mentioned her negligence out in the street there would be men wanting to lynch her, for she was trying to weaken him whose strength was so valuable for the winning of the Cup. She was, he decided on this night of religious recollections, like the wife in the Bible who'd cut off her man's hair and so betrayed him to his enemies.

That night she had not gone to bed. When he keeked into the kitchen, there she was on a stool in front of the fire, combing her long white hair and crooning to herself. The table wasn't set, but at least the kettle sang on the hob.

Throwing his cap on to the coal-bunker, Turk sat on his favourite chair, bumping her to the side; then he removed his boots and put his stockinged feet up on to a less hot part of the hob. There was a hole in one sock, exposing his big toe; but as he waggled it, to draw it to her attention through her veil of hair, his grin was not too censorious or self-pitying. She was an old woman, and there had been a time when she had faithfully darned his socks.

"You would be at school about the same time as Tinto Broon," he said. "Were you ever in the same class?"

"Wha?"

He roared, for she was sometimes genuinely deaf: "Tinto Broon. Were you in the same class at school wi' him?"

"He was in the penny-buff," she said, with disdain, "when I was in the fourth standard."

Turk ruminated. "What I'm wondering is, what gave him such a spite against religion? He never got married."

"I mind him at school," she said. "Always girning, always blaming somebody, always wanting the first shot at the ropes or the ba' or whatever the game was. I don't think he was fed."

"That might account for it." For another minute Turk meditated on Tinto's impiety. Warmth passed through his feet into his whole being. Ice of misanthropy melted in him. He gazed at his mother's white hair and thought it braw.

"What about a bite of supper, old girl?" he asked.

She paid no heed, so absolutely he was sure it was because of thrawnness, not deafness. Yet she was old, and age fankled the brain.

"I'm hungry, Mither," he said amiably, "and I'll hae to get to bed early. You ken I'm in training. Saturday's the sixth round of the Cup. See these toes?" He waggled them. "Ken this?" Solemnly he paused. "Ken this? There are men in Drumsagart wad kiss these toes." He turned sad. "If I had had a chance I could hae made myself a great name at football. I could hae bought myself a pub. I never was given a chance. I'm sorry to say, old girl, you were a bit to blame."

Through her hair she was gazing at his feet.

"I bear no spite against you now," he went on, "but you'll remember that when I was a youngster, playing football, you ca'd me up to go for a packet of salt or half a pound of margarine. The other kids went on playing, but I had to go to the shops. Then when I left school I was shoved into the steelwork. I should hae been nursed."

"I nursed you," she whimpered, "I nursed you." And she stroked her old breast.

For about a minute he tried to see himself a babe at the breast; not sure whether the recollection was pleasing or revolting, he soon dismissed it. "Keep to the point," he said. "I meant I

216

should hae been nursed when I was a young fellow, like that Elrigmuir. Look what's happening to him. He's being nursed in Malarkin's pub, fetching a pint or two on a tray. What happened to me? I had to carry hundredweights of steel and iron. It ruined my balance. It stiffened my back. But worst, it thickened my heid. I'm a good player yet, mind you; but if I had been nursed I could hae been famous. I could hae bought my ain pub." He sighed several times. "But what about the supper?"

She had been binding up her hair with combs and pins. Now she rose submissively and began to set the table. There were margarine in paper, milk in bottle, jam in jar, and bread in loaf.

He watched sombrely. "I'm not grumbling, but I should be better fed. Are ye sure I get a' my steak?"

"I get nane of it."

"No, but what about that brute of a cat I've seen you cuddling? Are you sure it gets nane? A damned disgrace it would be if a cat was to get the steak Geordie Rankin's gieing me to build up my stamina for the Cup-ties. No wonder auld Tinto's against religion."

She put her skinny hand on the handle of the kettle.

"It's not boiling," he said. "That's a fault of yours, old girl. You're too impatient to let the water boil. I'd hae thought you'd made enough tea in your day to ken the water must be boiling. I've heard it said folk never learn."

In agitation she lifted off the hot lid.

"I said it wasn't boiling," he said patiently. "Shove it on the fire."

It was a large iron kettle heavy in itself, and it was full of water. She had to take both hands to heave it on to the coals.

He watched, waggling his toes.

"I think," he said, "once I've won the Cup for them I'll go back to England." He turned and glanced at the dancing partners on the shelf. "There was a barmaid yonder fond of me. She was fat. But she had a kind heart towards me. I might do worse than settle doon wi' her. She liked me. Is that it boiling now?"

She nodded.

"Make the tea then. Mind my feet."

The teapot, with the tea ready in it, stood on the hob close to his feet. She lifted up the kettle to pour in the water. Sustained by a faith that had its roots in infancy, Turk did not draw back his feet a quarter-inch. He was watching therefore, the nearest and most intimate witness, when the stream shot out, not into the teapot at all, but curving over it on to his feet. He howled and snatched away his scalded toes. The water continued to pour and hiss where they had been.

Still howling, and reproving his mother's carelessness with heartfelt profanity, he rushed and leapt about the kitchen. Once he had spilled hot tea on her cat, and it had behaved precisely like this.

He stopped, crouched to pull down his socks to inspect the agonised flesh, and was so overcome by the sight he closed his eyes and involuntarily prayed: "For God's sake, what about the Cup?"

His mother picked up her stick, wrapped herself in her black shawl, and left the house. By the time she'd gone down the stairs and reached the street Turk was through at the room window, roaring out of it the news that he was crippled.

Some men came running. They saw her.

"What is it, Mrs. McCabe?" they cried. "What's Turk saying? Is it the drink? Has it softened his brain at last?"

"The kettle skailed ower his feet on the hob," she said.

"Don't say, for God's sake, it was boiling water?" That was a screech of incredulity, with undertones of doom.

"Boiling all right. He said it was nae use making tea wi' water that wasn't boiling. It was boiling."

"Fetch a doctor," bellowed Turk. "Fetch me a doctor or the Thistle's out of the Cup."

One man rushed off for one doctor, another for another. A third went to rouse the committee. The rest dashed into the close to run up the stairs and see the calamity for themselves. One stayed behind in the street, weeping; true enough, he had been lachrymose earlier with drink.

Mrs. McCabe crept along the dark streets, cowering into her shawl. As she passed the school she remembered how, long ago, a small, serious-minded tomboy in pigtails had played in that very playground. She put out her hand and touched one of the railings. For a minute or two then, bewildered, she was not sure who was there: whether an unhappy old woman remembering in tears or the stubborn, daring little girl about to clamber up, heedless that the boys saw her breeks. One boy she saw particularly, with glossy brown hair, freckles, dimpled chin, and small neat ears. Then she had played with him at many boyish games—at moshie, girds, running, and even football—and had surpassed him in them all. Later they had tried, for more than twenty years, to play that other more complicated, still childish game without rules, marriage; and again she had played it better. But he was dead now, and all his mistakes and laziness, his infidelities and meanness ought to be forgiven if they could never be forgotten. Yet could she swear that one of the reasons she had poured boiling water over her son's feet was not because, in his appearance as well as in his domineering laziness, he had reminded her too much of his father? She had miscalled Tinto Brown and yet her own wickedness was the blackest in the world.

She tottered on, weeping, and soon came to the police-station. Like one familiar she rang the bell and walked in.

Sergeant Elvan was seated at ease at his desk. His tunic was unbuttoned and he was smoking his pipe. In one hand was a screwdriver and in the other the toy locomotive he'd bought for his son's birthday. Parts of it lay on the desk.

She stood in a corner, peeping out of the shawl.

"It's me again," she said.

He looked hard at her, forgetting to puff his pipe. Then, with remarkable delicacy for so big and gaunt a man, he set down locomotive, screwdriver, and pipe, and came over to her. Gently he took her shawl and pulled it aside. On her face he saw only the marks of age. Last time he'd seen the bruised cheek and swollen eye of filial cruelty.

He stood with his big hand gently on her head.

"What is it now, lass?" he asked. "Has he turned you oot into the cold?"

"I walked oot."

He glanced down at her stick. Her legs seemed to be twitching. "Come and sit down, lass," he said, and assisted her to the chair. As she began to weep he grew angry. "Has he been using his precious feet on you this time? Has he been using you as a football to practise on? Give me the chance and I'll show him, and the rest of them, just what place football should hae among civilised folk. Week in, week out, now, it's nothing but football. Their weans are half starved and run about in snaw, slush, and rain in shoes and clothes not fit for summer. Their wives squirm and squeal in pain to bring them mair weans. But they sit like lords in pubs and discuss the football. Give me the chance, and I'll show them the reality."

She wept more sorely in spite of his hand comforting her head. That little girl who had climbed up the spiked railings more agilely than any boy had squirmed in pain once to bring forth another girl, who had lived half an hour and been buried in secret for cheapness.

It occurred to the sergeant here perhaps was his chance. He subdued his eagerness.

"Why have you come here, lass? Is it to charge him wi' cruelty?"

"I'm here to gie myself up," she sobbed.

He scratched his own thin grey hair. "Why, lass? What hae you done?"

"Whatever he's done, whatever he's been, he's still my son."

He nodded. In being given such a son she had been wronged; but there was no culprit apprehensible.

"What's he done this time?"

"If he cut his feet on the street," she sobbed, "I bathed them and bandaged them."

He frowned. Maternal love, often illogical and exasperating, was a fact of nature, like death; it had to be accepted.

"But what's happened to bring you here, lass? Surely you ken this is a police-station?"

"I ken that fine, for I'm here to gie myself up. You've to put me in jail."

"What for? What hae you done, lass?" For a moment he wondered if she'd deepened Turk's sleep with a hatchet. He hoped not, for her sake.

"I coupped the kettle ower his feet."

"What?"

"He had them on the hob. He was taking his ease and telling me to hurry wi' his supper. He was saying strangers would kiss his feet; he'd nae mind of the times I kissed them. God help me, I think he looked like his faither. So I missed the teapot a'thegether wi' the water; it went ower his feet."

The sergeant realised he was grinning; sternly he bade himself remember he was a police-officer.

"Had he on his boots?" he asked.

"He always has them off when he's got them on the hob. It's a habit his faither had too. There was a hole in his socks. He never said a word, but he was making oot I should hae darned it. Maybe I should."

Again that grin appeared. He became afraid he might guffaw. Not only would that shock the old woman, it would lower his own dignity.

"And what happened to his feet, lass?"

"What would happen to your feet if your mither skailed boiling water over them?"

"Are they badly burned?"

"He louped high enough."

"But his football? It'll be interfered with, surely?"

"That was a' his worry."

"It would be, it would be." The sergeant felt he must go out of her presence for a minute or two to get rid of a shameful rejoicing surging up in him. "Well, Mrs. McCabe," he said, "I'm sorry to hear about this accident."

"It was nae accident."

"You're bound to be upset. I tell you what, just rest there while I go through and see if my Agnes has a cup of tea ready."

"I'm no' here for tea," she said indignantly. "They say you're a great man for doing your duty. They say you'd jail your own mither if she broke the law. Weel, jail me."

"In good time, lass. You've had an awful shake. You're still trembling. A cup of tea will do no harm, even if you are my prisoner."

When he was at the door leading through to his living quarters she cried him back. "Are you for leaving me here wi' the door unlocked? I could be escaped when you came back wi' the tea."

"That's so," he said, smiling. "I forgot that. We can't have you escaping."

He locked the door and put the key in his pocket.

"I'm beginning to think," she said, "you're no' the man you're cracked up to be." She meant it as disparagement, not praise.

"I'm getting auld, lass; like yourself. Absentminded, you see."

"I could gie you thirty years," she muttered contemptuously.

His wife was seated by the kitchen fire, knitting and listening to the wireless. He startled her by the way he burst in and began to stride up and down, laughing moderately, but banging his fists together in front of him like cymbals. She could not help laughing.

"What's the matter, Dan?" she asked.

"Make a cup of tea, Agnes. I've got a guest outbye."

"Is some poor soul in trouble?" She put down her knitting, rose, and went into the scullery to put the kettle on the gas stove.

He stared after his plump, placid, red-haired wife. She was much too soft-hearted. If a wife-beater was brought in Agnes would sympathise even with him, or find excuses, or murmur that she had two boys herself: only God knew how they would turn out. She attended church; indeed, she was knitting a jacket for the minister's baby when it was born. Agnes took religion seriously in her quiet way. Openly he shook his head at her simplicity of heart and asked her what would happen to the flock if the wolves weren't deprived of their fangs; inwardly he looked on her spontaneous pity as a kind of compensation.

"You know I don't like you to look so pleased, Dan," she said, as she set a tray with cup and saucer and some home-baked cake.

He laughed and laid his hand on her hair. Remembering that he'd just been stroking old Mrs. McCabe's hair with that same hand, he hurriedly withdrew it. The quick withdrawal hurt her.

"I'll tell you why I'm pleased, Agnes. I've got no prisoner. It's old Mrs. McCabe the tea's for. Our precious Turk's mither."

"What's she here for?" She was still hurt and huffed.

"To give herself up. Do you know why? Do you know what she's done? She's just gone and spilled some boiling water over his sacred feet."

"Deliberately?"

"I don't know. She says so, but she's gey near eighty, and a bit doted at times."

"If it was an accident it's a pity; if it was intentional it's shocking. Either way, I don't see it's anything to rejoice about."

"Aren't you forgetting, Agnes, he struck her once? You were the very one who bathed her cheek."

"That was years ago. For a man that's so set on forcing folk to be good, Dan, you're terribly reluctant to take what help they give you. This Turk, isn't he improved?"

"Not much that I can see. He's still a lazy, beer-swilling, mooching, dumb-witted brute. The one thing you can say in his favour is that he can play football."

"And can give folk pleasure by playing it so well. I've heard your own sons sing his praises."

He frowned: it was true, his two boys were now Thistle supporters; Turk was their hero. Though he still had his hands in front of him, there was no clang of triumph left in them.

"If he's improved by as much as this even"—Agnes showed the pink tip of her finger—"give him the credit for it." Suddenly she showed her pinker tongue in horror. "Is that why you were so pleased? Because his feet are scalded, he'll not be able to play football and so his team will be beaten?"

"All right, Agnes. You've struck it. That's why I am so pleased. I want their team to be beaten. I want them all, from Rutherford downward, to be made understand they're men now, not weans any longer. It's time to put away toys. Not that football's a toy to most of them. It's a religion. It consumes their souls. I've seen them weep with joy, weep! When did you last see anybody weep for joy in church, Agnes?"

"There's not a woman in Scotland doesn't know the importance of football is exaggerated. But I'll tell you something, Dan, that you don't seem to have noticed. If they're crazy for football, then you're becoming just as crazy against it, and the one's as bad as the other."

"There's not a cooler man on the subject in the country," he cried.

"Cool? You came barging in that door like a boy with a new drum. And why? Because a silly doted old wife has scalded her son's feet with boiling water. If that's not being crazy, Dan, I'd like to know what is. But there's your tray ready. Take it through to her; though, mind you, if she spilled that water deliberately she's not got my blessing."

He stared glumly at her.

"You're angry, Agnes, because I laid my hand on your head and then snatched it away again."

"Ho! I never noticed it if you did."

"Don't fib. You did. I didn't do it because you were contradicting me. I hope I'm not as childish as that. Just a minute or two before I'd laid my hand on the old woman's head, trying to soothe her. Well, she's old."

She was pleased with his explanation, or rather with the humility with which it was expressed, and for a moment or so she seemed about to become her usual smiling, amiable, indulgent self; but visibly her intention changed.

"So you're a snob too, Dan?" she asked.

He grabbed the tray.

"You'll spill the tea."

"Women," he muttered, as he went out. "If there is on God's earth an excuse for football it's women."

Later that night, when he turned into the street where Mrs. McCabe lived, he chuckled defiantly to notice several motorcars there—one of them Dr. Kiddie's—and also a number of people hanging about the McCabes' closemouth.

"The wake's begun," he said.

His companion halted. "They'll attack me," she muttered.

"There'll be no attacking."

"You don't ken what wild beasts the football makes them."

"I ken that very well." He gave a nod in the direction of Agnes seated at home, knitting again. "Come on, lass. Nobody's going to lay a finger on you. They'll be taking Turk away to hospital."

"I hope so. He deserves the best of treatment."

This time, though he cast a thought towards Agnes, no nod went with it.

As they approached the mourners at the closemouth saw them.

"There she is, the auld witch!"

"She's been arrested!"

"It's burnt she should be!"

"Is it?" shrieked a fourth voice, defiantly feminine. "For years he's treated her as if she was his slave. Thank God she's got her revenge at last."

Again Mrs. McCabe wished to stop, but the sergeant gently pushed her on up to the hostile crowd. At first they were pleased with him, thinking the old woman was his prisoner; except the woman who'd shrieked, a termagant called Harper, who seized him by the arm.

"For Christ's sake," she shouted into his face, "are you for jailing the old woman?"

"No, missus," he said calmly. "I can't very well jail a body for an accident."

"That's right," she cried. "That's what I said."

"It was no accident," they shouted. "She did it on purpose to keep him out of the game on Saturday. Do you ken what this means? It means we'll lose the Cup."

The sergeant roughly shoved them aside. "To me," he said, "one hair of this old woman's head's more precious than a hundred silver cups won for football. And if I hear of anybody attempting to molest her, or even to shout after her in the street, by the living God I'll hae that man so deep in jail Carnegie himself couldn't bail him out."

Then, heedless of their rebellious mutters, he began to assist the old woman up the narrow, ill-lit, sour-smelling stone stairs.

She peched and had to rest often.

"It's my turn this week," she said.

"Your turn?"

"Aye, of the stairs."

"Don't tell me you still scrub these stairs at your age."

"Wha else would scrub them if it's my turn?"

"Some neighbour's girl."

"I've taken my turn for more than sixty years, and I'm not going to be beholden to anybody now."

"Has Turk never offered to do them for you?"

"For God's sake, he's a man."

"Even so, he's far abler to scrub stairs than you."

"Men don't scrub stairs," she said peevishly, as if explaining to some dense foreigner. "If I was ever to go upstairs and saw a man on his knees scrubbing them I'd kick ower his pail, the jessie. And I'd be obliged if you stopped using the name Turk. Gordon he's called."

He smiled. "I never knew that, Mrs. McCabe."

"Naebody seems to ken it. What sort of name is Turk for a Christian?"

They arrived at the door. She had no key. The sergeant banged so lustily she complained.

It was Angus Tennant who opened the door. Misery had already occupied the vast unintelligent spaces of his face; now at the sight of the sergeant hope, and at the sight of Mrs. McCabe, aversion, sought to invade: all three, misery, hope, and aversion, contended on the heavy brow, the big slack nose, the thick lips, and in the cross eyes.

"Is the ambulance come?" he asked.

"Not that I ken of," said Elvan. "In you go, Mrs. McCabe. It's your hoose. So an ambulance has been sent for?"

Tennant shrank backwards. "Aye. You should see his feet. They're pitiful, tragic, sordid. I doubt if he'll ever play again."

"I'm sorry to hear that," said the sergeant, with a grin that broadened as they went into the tiny kitchen and found it crammed with men. Four or five committee-members were there, including Cleugh and Rutherford. Scoosh McLean, the trainer, crouched by the bed, where Dr. Kiddie was busy. There was a hospital smell but a mortuary gloom.

The sergeant pushed one or two aside to instal Mrs. McCabe in a chair by the fire. He noticed the grate was still in a mess from the fateful spilling.

The pushing had been unnecessary. All recoiled from her as if, an enchantress, she could with a wave of her stick turn them into frogs; and indeed in some of them the metamorphosis was already happening, so beady their eyes, so agitated their thrapples, so sad their croaks.

The sergeant caught a glimpse of Turk's face in the bed; the eyes were closed, perhaps the cheeks under the bristle were pale, but the apelike resemblance was in no way diminished.

The doctor turned and gave the policeman a curt nod. "What the devil are you doing here, Sergeant?" he asked. "Has somebody sent for the minister as well, and Jordan the lawyer?"

"I'm here, Doctor," he replied, "to see fair play. Well, Mr. Cleugh, what's the damage?"

Usually a humorous, discreet, percipient little man, the secretary seemed then to have been stunned into an obtuseness as great as Tennant's.

"He'll be out of the game for weeks."

"Is that all? I mean, they'll get better? He'll walk again?"

"You ken, Sergeant," said Cleugh bitterly, "what this means to Drumsagart."

Tennant thrust in his face. "This is the worst disaster that's

226

struck Drumsagart since the flooding of the Birkside Pit," he said simply, believing it with all the crassness of his heart.

Therefore the sergeant's ferocity astonished him all the more. "You damned fool," said Elvan, "shut your mouth. Are you comparing a bunch of blisters with the drowning in darkness of eight men? If I had my way of it, stupidity of that sort would be classified as a crime, with the penalty not less than twa years."

Sure of the support of his fellow committee-men, all substantial citizens, Tennant blustered. "Don't talk to me like that. I'm no street-corner lout. I'm a ratepayer. I've got some influence in this town. You think you're God Almighty, but you're just a sergeant, not even an inspector. Your superiors will hear about this. All these gentlemen are witnesses."

"Is a man to be jailed for expressing an opinion?" inquired Wattie Cleugh.

"Aye, if his opinion's so daft as to be an insult to common-sense. I didn't say the sentence would be served in jail: a school of correction would be better, with prayers and fasting and reading the Bible."

"Still sounds like your jail," muttered Hugh Neilson.

The sergeant turned towards Rutherford, who avoided his gaze. The president seemed not to have shaved that morning, and his shirt collar was soiled. So the rumour was true enough: living alone, he was neglecting himself, at least outwardly; it could be, of course, he spent the days of solitude purifying his soul.

Mrs. McCabe sat amidst them as if blind, deaf, and dumb. She should have had a placard pinned to her and a tinny on her lap.

"Listen," whispered Cleugh to the sergeant, "I'm not a vindictive man as a rule, but what are you going to do about this? In your calendar of crimes is wilful scalding not included? Maybe not, eh, if it's a football player that's scalded, a Drumsagart player, one vital to the winning of some honour and pleasure for the town? If a boy scalded a cat, would you be after him? You would that, to the gates of hell, and beyond."

The sergeant grinned down at the broad, earnest face with its sharp ears and its missing twinkles.

"It was an accident," he said.

"I don't believe that. According to Turk, it was deliberate."

"What do you want me to do, Mr. Cleugh? Drag her by the hair along to the jail and give her a good kicking there to teach her football players are sacred?"

"I want you to do your duty."

Again the sergeant turned to Rutherford. "And what's your opinion, Mr. Rutherford? I used to think you tried to combine fondness for football with common sense and decency: a combination as rare as roses and snow."

They all waited for the president's, the rose-lover's, answer. Hunched into his coat, he glared at them. Most of them, already sufferers from it, would have pardoned his surliness if he had let it loose then upon the sergeant; and the sergeant would have sympathised with it if it had been turned against football. Rutherford, he thought, carried in his breast sorrow and torment that had their origin in human folly and deficiency, but which, for all that, did not altogether forfeit pity. A man parted from his wife and child could be seen against the background of human loss and grief and irremediable weakness, with Christ nailed to His cross nearby; but if into that background pranced some bare-kneed cretins kicking at a ball, though the agony would remain no-one could be moved by it, any more than one was moved by a rat coughing up its poisoned guts in the dark.

As Rutherford hesitated Mrs. McCabe spoke. "I used to play with your mither, Andra Rutherford. Many's the time I held hands wi' her at ring-a-roses."

He gazed at her.

"And many's the time," she added, "I stopped her in the street, carrying you in the shawl. You were dour even then."

"I since hae had reason to get dourer."

The sergeant snorted. Committee-men grinned behind their hands, except Angus Tennant, who nodded eagerly.

"You mean the likes of what's happened tonight, Andrew?" he asked. "It would make an angel dour."

A voice sounded from the bed. "Whit about a fag?"

They all felt for their packets. Tennant was the first to produce his. He rushed over to the bed.

"Is it all right, Doctor?" asked Cleugh.

"Do him good." The doctor intercepted the packet and took one himself. "Do me good."

Turk sat up in bed. "You ken what?" he said. "I'm going to play on Saturday."

They cried out as at a possible miracle.

"Don't be a damned fool," said the doctor.

"I'm not going to let the team down," insisted Turk. "I can stand pain. It's settled then, I'll play. Scoosh can get me a pair of football boots a couple of sizes too big."

"How long, Doctor," asked Hugh Neilson, "before he's fit to play again? I mean, we've still got Alec Elrigmuir. Granted in Turk's absence we might lose three or four goals, but why shouldn't Alec score just as many. We might manage a draw."

"That's so," agreed the optimists.

"What if we lose six?" asked the pessimists.

"What if you lose sixty?" It was the sergeant, the grinning sceptic. "It's only a game."

There was an interruption from the bed.

"There's one thing sure," said Turk.

"What's that, Turk?"

"No miscalling the old girl."

They gaped.

"What she did she had to do. It's a bygone."

"A bygone?" Dr. Kiddie whistled. "Those feet must be hurting like hell."

"We were discussing religion in the pub tonight," went on Turk. "All right. The thing's over and done wi'. It's a poor world if a man cannae overlook his mither's fault."

Mrs. McCabe added to their consternation by beginning to sob.

"So if I hear that anybody's said a word against her," said Turk, "I tell you, the first use I'll put my feet to when they're better will be to kick that somebody from one end of Drumsagart to the other, even if it's one of you. Spread the word, will you?"

Sergeant Elvan replied. "I'll spread the word."

Turk grinned out at him. "I bet you brought her alang in case I socked her one. That's finished."

"I'm glad to hear it, Turk."

"Gordon's his name," sobbed Mrs. McCabe, but nobody heard her.

"In fact, Sergeant," said Turk, "I'm obliged to you for looking after my mither. Will you keep looking after her till I'm better? Can I depend on you?"

"You can certainly depend on me."

"Will you shake on it?"

"With pleasure."

Then the sergeant went over to the bed and shook hands with Turk, while Mrs. McCabe quietly sobbed and the committeemen's faces turned simple, puzzled, and resentful, like children confronted by a kind of sum they had never been taught.

16

No basket ever carried more eggs than young Alec Elrigmuir did hopes that Friday before the sixth-round tie. From the moment when his landlady's son roused him, with as much devotion and faith as any medieval squire his lord for the battle, to the time when he went down to the football pavilion for the last ritualistic rub-up he was treated like a being apart, consecrated, to be spoken to as an oracle, and listened to in awe even if his remark was only a mutter he'd do his best but it was a pity Turk couldn't play. Everybody saw him enhaloed, aureoled, empanoplied; and therefore no one noticed he was unhappy.

All the members of the committee were at the pavilion that night. After a last round of the players, exhorting each to put forth that bit extra to compensate for Turk's absence, they retired to their own private cell to consider, as generals, tactics for the field of conflict tomorrow. Rutherford was obstinately present. Every night he came to the pavilion, saying little, ignoring the snubs that grew less and less sleekit, and disconcerting them all with sudden fierce spurts of his former affability. The players grumbled that he made them nervous: one minute he glowered in a corner as if plotting arson, next minute he was over offering to rub a stiff knee although he had no skill at all as masseur. They were privately assured intrigue was afoot to remove him from the presidency and so deprive him of his right to enter the pavilion. It was not easy to expel a president: there was no procedure explained in the constitution of the club; but the matter was being studied by agile brains.

That Friday night he sat in his chair at the head of the table. Again he was badly shaven; again his collar was soiled. His fist lay clenched in front of him, the gold ring prominent.

The crucial question was, who should take Turk's place? One proposal was to play Lachie Houston, the captain, at centre-half and try young Bill Seedie at left-half; another was to keep Lachie at left-half and give Bill the important centre-half position. It could not be settled quickly. The argument was passionate and involved much expert analysis of the technique of the game.

Rutherford said nothing but sometimes smiled as if it was all much talk about a trifle. Such a smile might be expected from an Elvan or a Saunders, but never from their president. At last Donald Lowther boldly asked him his opinion.

"My opinion, Donald?" Rutherford seemed surprised, and indeed not clearly aware about what his opinion was being asked. They suspected his thoughts had been elsewhere—in Helensburgh, for example, or in a certain house in Drumsagart; which was all very well, but if he wished to mope over his wife and son, or his sick father, surely there was a more suitable place than the committee-room during the planning for tomorrow's vital match.

Before he could find wits enough to answer there was a knock at the door and in came Alec Elrigmuir, dressed in a red jersey and very brief white shorts.

They were delighted to see him, although as a player he really had no right to interlope upon executive business.

"Well, Alec?" they asked, smiling as fondly as any owner at potential Derby winner. They thought he looked not only splendidly fit but also extremely handsome.

Sam Malarkin's ogle was particularly possessive.

"In to tell us, Alec, it's at least four goals tomorrow?" he cried.

"No, Mr. Malarkin. I'm in to tell you I'll not be playing tomorrow."

Wattie Cleugh, with his quick mind, recognised it as a joke whose revoltingly bad taste was excusable only in a hero of nineteen.

Angus Tennant, on the other hand, gawked at the fair-haired youth in the red shirt and white breeks as if he was a messenger from those gods who lived not on sunny Olympus but in darkest Erebus.

"I've got a sore back," muttered Alec.

They saw that he was in earnest. They moaned, whimpered, yelped.

Even Rutherford looked concerned.

"A sore back?" repeated Cleugh.

Alec nodded, gazing at the floor.

"Where?"

One hand went behind the straight, stalwart back and crept about, seeking the pain. At last it found it.

"Here," he muttered.

They gaped at one another. Cleugh held up his hand to plead with them to leave the questioning to him.

"When did it get sore?" he asked.

"A day or two ago."

"Why didn't you report it before this?"

"I didn't like because of what happened to Turk. I thought it would get better."

"Look at me, Alec. Look at us all. Look us straight in the eyes, son. We represent the men and women of Drumsagart, who are looking to you to bring the Cup to them. You are our hero. Now, lad, answer me this: is your back really sore, or are you, God help us, becoming temperamental? We deserve the truth, Alec. You've got to give it to us."

Elrigmuir still looked at the floor.

"It is sore," he mumbled.

"He's a football player," interrupted Rutherford, "and accordingly isn't credited with much brains. But surely he kens whether his back's sore or not. Even a wean of three could tell you that."

"That's not a helpful thing to say," complained Cleugh.

"I believe," murmured Malarkin, "there's something else."

It was Rutherford, nevertheless, who revealed the truth. "Have you and Mysie cast out?" he asked.

Some were about to rebuke him for another impertinence when they saw that Elrigmuir, with a groan or a sob, had suddenly turned upon them his back with the dubious pain.

Malarkin was furious; not with Elrigmuir, who was his barman and protégé; not even with Mysie the cruel seductress; nor with Rutherford for his insight—no, not with any namable human being; but at the same time he was so furious he could have ripped off his whiskers and screamed.

Wattie Cleugh, however, was laughing in relief.

"So that's all it is?" he asked.

"What mair could there be?" said Rutherford. "A sore back's easily mended."

"Don't exaggerate, Andrew. Alec's only nineteen, and Mysie's no older. The world never comes to an end at that age. What's more natural than a lovers' tiff? It's like a sunny shower, and when it's past everything's brighter than before. Most of us are married men; we quarrelled, too, for the fun of it when we were courting."

"That's so," agreed Angus Tennant.

One or two couldn't help smiling. Nell Tennant was now like the back end of a dropsical elephant; she had never been slim. It was difficult to picture her ever, with squinting Angus, taking part in a sparkling disagreement like a sunny shower; though, true enough, she wasn't unlike the huge swollen clouds that drifted off over the horizon.

"Have we hit on the truth, Alec?" asked Cleugh. "Have you and Mysie fallen out?"

"We're finished for good."

Cleugh laughed, and winked with confidence at his colleagues. "Don't think you're the first man who's said that," he cried.

"Sometimes," muttered Rutherford, "it turns out to be the truth."

They frowned, irritated with his intruding his own case, which was altogether different.

"What's the cause of the difference, Alec?" asked Cleugh, soothingly.

It was obvious the young man was swithering whether or not to tell them. They waited, nodding to one another in hope. They conjectured the quarrel was about his talking to another girl, her talking to another boy; his wanting to go to one picture, her preferring another; his being late for a tryst; her trying to be too domineering. There could be, of course, an infinity of amusingly trivial causes, such was the pleasure of young love.

He turned, and they saw tears in his eyes.

Though they smiled, a coldness crept into their hearts.

233

"I'll tell you," he said, "and I don't care whether you keep it a secret or not."

"With us, Alec, it'll be as safe as wi' the dead."

"I hope you don't mind, Mr. Malarkin?"

Sam, thinking he was addressed as patron, shook his head. "You'll find us sympathetic, Alec."

"As the dead," muttered Rutherford.

Nobody heeded him.

Alec was silent for nearly another minute.

"I don't care," he said at last. "I'm finished wi' everything—wi' football, wi' Mysie, wi' Drumsagart. I'm leaving. I'm going back to the pit."

"That's hardly the job for you if you're going to be subject to sore backs," said Angus Tennant.

He was astonished and aggrieved to receive so many scowls and see so many teeth.

"I can tell the truth," said Alec. "I'm in a trap. I'm in the pit and the shaft has fallen in. Nobody can dig me oot."

"Don't say that, Alec," cried Cleugh. "We'll dig you oot, be sure of that."

The youth shook his head. "It was Miss Malarkin," he muttered.

Had Margot herself appeared then, nude or in transparent negligée, greater commotion could not have been caused. Her brother squealed like rabbit in a snare. Lewd expectation got among the committee-men's fears like a dog among sheep and made them gallop.

"I think," said Malarkin, choking, "this ought not to be discussed in public."

"This isn't public," replied Cleugh. "Lock the door, Angus."

Angus locked it and then scurried back to his seat.

"I think," said Cleugh solemnly, "everybody in this room believes that the most important consideration for us is the winning of the Cup."

"Not for me," sighed Elrigmuir.

"Nor me," muttered Rutherford.

"We are elected officials," said Cleugh, with a touch of severity, "and therefore we must place public welfare before our private affairs."

"That's right," said a committee-man, usually tongue-tied.

"You often read of actors carrying on wi' the show though their hearts were broken."

"I'd rather say," said Cleugh, "that no sodger on the battle-field drops his gun because he's had bad news from hame."

Malarkin rose to his feet; somehow his face resembled a painted clown's. "Are you going to discuss this," he whispered, "nakedly?"

"Weel," smiled Cleugh, "we'll try to wrap a rag or two o' decency round it if it needs it, Sam. Alec must play tomorrow, come what may."

Malarkin appealed to the youth. "Alec, I want you to leave here and come with me. What you've got to say has nothing at all to do with these gentlemen. I agree it's important you should play tomorrow, and I think if you and I were to go where we can talk it over we can reach an understanding."

"No," cried Cleugh, also on his feet. He even rapped the table. "Alec is our signed player. He's under contract to us. Surely he kens, and you ken it too, Sam, that if he refuses to play for us tomorrow, while he's physically fit to do so, he could jeopardise his whole career. In fact I shall go so far as to say he'll never have a career as a football player if he breaks his contract."

"Didn't I tell you," said Alec, "I was never going to kick a ball again?"

Angus Tennant, speaking for most, said impatiently, "Tell us what's happened, Alec. If we ken we can help." He licked his lips.

"I'm not blaming Miss Malarkin," muttered Alec, beginning to blush. "I ken she's older than me, but it was as much my fault as hers; and it was Mysie's fault as well. If I kissed her she complained."

"Who?" asked Angus.

"Mysie. If I squeezed her hand just, she complained. She let me hae a kiss as you would let a wean take a sweetie out of a poke."

"You shouldn't be telling us this, Alec," said Rutherford. "This is between you and Mysie only."

"Sometimes it's better to confide in others," said Cleugh. "Keep it bottled up and it turns to poison. Does a man that's seeking directions ask them from another who's lost, who's wandered in the middle of the moors?"

"Does that," asked Rutherford slowly, "refer to me?"

"It does, Andrew, I'm sorry to say."

"You'll be a damned sight sorrier if I was to break your neck for you."

Donald Lowther was the peacemaker. He pushed Rutherford back into his chair and scolded Cleugh. "For God's sake remember," he said, "that while we're destroying ourselves wi' animosities Muirvale Athletic this very night are banding together to knock us out of the Cup tomorrow. Fate's fouled us already by haeing Turk's feet burned. Let us be men, let us be faithful to each other, let us kick fate back. Now I think the position's this. Alec here in some way has compromised himself."

"In what way?" asked Angus Tennant. "I mean, how can we advise him if we don't know exactly what's happened?"

He had supporters. "That's so," they muttered.

Donald's yellowish face showed some pink. "I was having consideration for Sam here," he said, "and for Alec, as weel as for the two ladies."

"We ken what you're hinting at, Donald," said Hugh Neilson, "but you might be exaggerating."

"I was in bed wi' her," said Alec.

One man laughed, but it was in hysteria; another sighed, in envy; a third winked, in ambiguity. But all gazed in respect at the nineteen-year-old in the red jersey and white shorts. They had seen him often in the bath and had admired his fresh virility. Was it fresher now, or had Margot soiled it?

Malarkin jumped up and staggered to the door. Forgetting it was locked, he turned and turned the handle; remembering, he unlocked it and fled.

Scoosh McLean, the trainer, who had been eavesdropping outside, now thrust in his wizened, sly face. He had his usual towel over his shoulder and he stank of liniment.

"I'll hae a last slap at that thigh of yours, Alec," he said.

"We're busy, Scoosh," said Wattie Cleugh. "Get out and shut the door."

Scoosh nodded. "It's a bad thing for discipline," he muttered, "if one player's shown favour above the rest. They're talking oot here."

"It's not us that's been showing the favour," whispered a committee-man. He got no-one to smile.

"We're running the team, Scoosh," said Cleugh sharply. "Tell them that."

Scoosh nodded again. "Harmony," he murmured before he vanished.

Angus Tennant rushed to lock the door again.

Then the conference was ready to resume business.

"Well," said Cleugh, "we're obliged to Sam for leaving. It means we can talk frankly, like men of the world. So, Alec, that's what you've been up to? Well, well. But you've not to be getting it into your head it's an enormous sin. It's natural. Let's put it this way: you're young and virile, you were enticed, you couldn't resist, you took your pleasure, you're sorry. Experience. Send the bill to experience. As far as we're concerned, we've heard about it, we've reprimanded you, and we've forgotten it. You should play a lot better now you've got the burden off your mind. What do you say, gentlemen?"

They all nodded, but Angus Tennant had a honest grin, which seemed to say he would like to ask Elrigmuir how it was done.

"How can I play?" asked Alec plaintively. "It was for Mysie's sake I signed for the Thistle. Drumsagart's nothing to me. Now she's finished wi' me I don't want to stay here. I want to go back hame. I want to go back to the pit."

Wattie Cleugh smiled a secret male smile. "Mysie?" he whispered. "What's Mysie got to do wi' it?"

The others were in the secret. "That's right, Alec," they said. "Leave Mysie out of it. The less she kens the happier she'll be. No woman has the right to ken all a man's business. True enough, it might be safer not to make a habit of such enterprises, but one's allowed every man. Never let dab to Mysie. Tell her when you're baith eighty. Win the Cup for us, boy, and you'll see then how Mysie'll kiss you. Some young lassies are like that, Alec, they think chastity's a sheet of ice; when it's broken, look out!"

"She kens," he said, when he could get in a word.

"How does she ken?"

"Because I told her, that's how."

They stared at one another, admitting without speech that the abominable slander was true, no longer able to be denied: Alec Elrigmuir was a genius on the football field, off it he was a sumph. No wonder it was said he had failed to pass his qualifying examination at school.

"What in God's name made you tell her?" cried Cleugh.

"I did it so I could tell her," said the youth. "I wanted to cast it up to her. She gave me nothing, Miss Malarkin gave me everything." He was coy over the last word.

"I bet she did," sighed Angus Tennant in an ecstasy of envy.

Cleugh, the leader, had to hide his dismay. He laughed. "That complicates it a bit," he said. "But the chief thing to keep in mind is that we're going to win tomorrow, and you're going to score the goals that'll make us win."

"No."

"Now, Alec, it's not going to help if you're going to behave like a wean in a huff. You've committed a man's sin; face it like a man. If Mysie forgave you you would play?"

"She'll never."

"But if she did, would you play?"

He nodded. "Maybe."

"Alec, you're going to play whether she forgives you or not. But we'll interview Mysie and point out to her what's at stake. She's entitled to her private principles, but she's not entitled to wreck public hopes. Surely she's got a duty towards auld Tamas. He's just hanging on till he hears we've won the Cup. It would be a miserable daith for him to be told we'd lost. I can't think she'll be as selfish as that."

"Would it do any good interviewing Margot?" asked Angus Tennant.

Then there was a hammering at the door.

"Is that Sam back?" asked Wattie Cleugh.

"Wi' Margot to apologise maybe?" suggested Angus.

It was Scoosh's voice. "There's a boy wanting to speak to Mr. Rutherford. It's his nephew Gavin. Seems auld John's taken a bad turn."

Rutherford sprang to his feet so violently he knocked the table against their knees. He went out leaving them rubbing.

"If Robbie's there at the death-bed," murmured Hugh Neilson, "it might be a sight worth seeing."

"We've got our ain business to attend to," said Cleugh. "I hope, all the same, you noticed that the president left withoot a word of encouragement to us. I admit it's right a man should hurry to the side of his father who's dying, but his duty to the living

238

ought not to be neglected. I would say, in passing, that Andrew's resignation is now overripe."

They concurred.

Cleugh then turned back to Alec Elrigmuir.

"You see our difficulties, Alec?" he said. "Well, you're the one, and the only one, who can help us to get over them. The hopes of Drumsagart lie in our hands, and we lie in yours."

"I cannae play," muttered Alec. "My mind's made up."

Some of them were convinced he meant it and were dismayed; at the same time they felt exasperated by his unmanliness, his lack of gumption, and his defeatism. Wattie Cleugh could not afford to show the qualms he felt. He stood up, laughed, and patted Alec's back. If he thought a scourge more deserved than tender palm he hid it well.

"We'll have you playing tomorrow, Alec," he said, "though the sun should drop out of the sky."

"It has dropped out."

"Then we'll put it back. Just you go and let Scoosh give you that slap he spoke about."

Elrigmuir departed. They let their consternation appear on them like Hallowe'en masks.

"I think he needs his back kicked," muttered Hugh Neilson, "but where would that get us?"

"Margot should be tarred and feathered," said another, "and run out of the town."

"I blame Mysie," said Angus Tennant. "She's holding us up to ransom. She doesn't take me in either. Don't tell me she's annoyed because Alec's misbehaved himself wi' Margot. What's annoying her is Margot's got what she thinks should be her ain exclusive property; only she's too damned stuck-up and respectable to admit it openly. If she'd humoured the boy this would never have happened?"

"Have you noticed, gentlemen," said Wattie Cleugh, "how it's women causing all the trouble? First, Turk's mither; then Mysie and Margot. It would seem what started in Eden's still going on."

"I wonder," murmured Donald Lowther, in the midst of the bitterness and disgruntlement, "how old John Rutherford is? For me, anyway, Drumsagart will never be the same without him."

"If he's dying," said Angus Tennant, "he'd go out happier

if he kent of our difficulties this night. All his life he's never had a good word for football."

"And I would say, speaking impartially," said Cleugh, "that it's brought more happiness to people than politics ever have."

"Or religion, for that matter," added Tennant.

He was surprised to find nobody approved. Looking at their stricken faces, he became aware himself of invisible vast forces stirring in the little room, with success sweet as flowers to give or disaster black and foul as death.

"I might get the young minister to speak to Mysie," said Wattie Cleugh, "if all else fails."

17

It was the first opportunity Andrew had had of speaking to his nephew about the stoning. Every time Gavin had seen him he had fled in obvious shame. Now this night the boy was a prisoner by his side, bound to him by a common grief. It was a chance not only to ease his own heart and win back even to his old position of precarious faith and reluctant disillusionment but also to give the boy an exhibition of adult understanding, of magnanimity, and transmuting love. He saw it as such an opportunity as plainly as he saw the illumined clock high in the tower, but there was never any likelihood of his accepting it.

He was no longer interested in his own or any other person's motive for any action whatsoever, good or bad. During the past weeks, almost against his will, certainly without much conscious effort on his part, this fatalism had been created in him as naturally as milk in a mother or venom in a snake. Whatever he saw or heard or read about, even if it was a deed of individual heroism against tyrannical authority or an act of compassion such as formerly would almost have brought tears to his eyes, now turned in his mind into something separate, indifferent, lacking all fruitfulness. Had he been trying, with the alchemy of self-pity, to achieve such transformation he might have been horrified into some reaction by the completeness of his success; but it did not seem to him in his apathy that he was responsible at all.

He spoke to the boy harshly.

"Who sent you for me?"

"My mither."

"Is your faither there?"

"Aye."

"Has the doctor been?"

"Aye."

"Did your grandfaither speak to you at all?"

"No."

Gavin stopped at the corner leading to the dark street near the gasworks where he lived.

"I've to go hame," he muttered.

"Did your faither say so?"

"It was my mither."

"She seems to be in command. How's Bella, your sister?"

"She's all right."

"How can she be all right? The last time I spoke to your mither she said your sister was ill. It was the sort of illness, too, that doesn't get better as soon as that. Is she still in her bed?"

"Aye." Then the boy, with a grimace of hatred and a muttered good-night, turned and ran down the narrow street.

Rutherford stood grinning. He raised his head high, pretending to believe that when the boy was at a safe distance he would look for a stone to fling, or at least some obscene abuse. None came. The quick forlorn steps grew fainter and fainter.

"He's forgotten," said Andrew aloud. "It's possible even for viciousness to forget."

Then he continued towards his father's house. The time on the Town Hall clock was five to nine. Not far along the main street under a lamp-post a group of little girls was playing. As he passed them they were dancing in a ring round one who crouched in the middle pretending to weep, and they sang in shrill sad voices a song he remembered girls singing when he was a boy.

> "Oh, what is Mary weeping for,
>   Oh, weeping for,
>   Oh, weeping for?
>   Oh, what is Mary weeping for
>   On a cold and frosty morning?"

Then they danced round in the opposite direction and sang with even more vigorous melancholy.

> "Because her mother's dead and gone,
> Oh, dead and gone,
> Oh, dead and gone,
> Her mother she is dead and gone,
> On a cold and frosty morning."

He lingered to watch what they did then. They stopped dancing in a circle and instead stood swinging their linked arms; their voices, though now to convey consolation, were even shriller and more sorrowful.

> "Stand up, Mary, and wipe away your tears,
> Choose the one you love the best,
> And that's
> Jean Nuneaton."

In response to the song the girl in the centre had stood up, dried away her tears, and danced forward to choose her successor, Jean Nuneaton, one of Rab's girls no doubt.

All of them, thought Rutherford as he went on, ought to be in their beds; their parents were putting off as long as possible the exhausting task of calling them up and putting them to bed. But what difference did it make how a child was reared? His own niece, tubercular, could not play such games in the street: she soon might die. The weeping for her would be real, just as the children's weeping was feigned: tears, true or false, nourished no greenness in the heart; withering was early and continuous until death.

His mood was still despairing as he went up the stairs and along the dark lobby to his father's house.

Isa answered his soft knock.

"Am I too late?" he asked.

"No, Andrew." She had lately been weeping. "But I don't think he'll last the night. Did Gavin find you all right?"

"I'm here. What about the doctor?"

"He said he'll be back again in an hour or two, but it seems there's nothing he can do. Your faither's not wanting to live, it seems; he's making no effort."

"Why should he?"

She gripped him as he made to enter the kitchen. "Robbie's here," she whispered. "He expects you. There's to be no quarrelling here."

"I'm not here to quarrel," he said roughly.

She held on to his coat. "What's come over you, Andrew? You're changed. It was a mistake parting from Hannah and the boy."

"That's my business, Isa. I'd be obliged if you kept out of it."

She still detained him. She was so close he could feel her trembling. Her body was very soft.

He pushed her away and went into the kitchen. The gas was turned down low. By the fire Robbie was crouched, bareheaded. He turned as Andrew entered and gave a cocky, impudent gesture with something in his hand; it looked like a book. Andrew made no acknowledgment and went straight to the bed, where, behind curtains, his father lay asleep.

For some minutes he gazed down at the shrunken, defeated face. The nose seemed longer than ever because of the shrinkage round it; in spite of the moustache the mouth was like a woman's or a child's, not only in its smallness but also, somehow, in its pettedness, its weary plaint that something wept for had never been granted. He did not see the face then as his father's, but rather as the man's who for so many querulous years had persisted in the belief that human beings were improvable and one day would live together in love and trust.

He became aware Isa was beside him, weeping softly; she had her face turned away.

"What is it?" he asked. "Old men must die."

They came away from the bed.

"It's not like you to say that," she sobbed. "You were always so fond and proud of your faither; and he deserved it. You've no idea how many folk hae stopped me and asked after him."

"Such sympathy's cheap."

They were speaking in whispers, which seemed to magnify her sorrow and his vindictiveness.

"Sit doon," said Robbie. "I put on a good fire. We might be here all night."

Andrew sat down, still in his coat.

243

Robbie seemed amused. "If it was to be a public funeral," he said, "there would be hundreds at it." He chuckled; there was a smell of beer off him.

"Anything for an exhibition," said Andrew.

Robbie nodded cheerfully enough, though he didn't understand. "But he's to be cremated. He said so. He's always said so. You ken that."

"I thought at the end he might have wanted to be put beside my mither."

Robbie fingered his nose. "What difference does it make?"

"None."

"Cremation's healthier."

"Were you sent for?" asked Andrew.

"That's right."

"Were you found in the pub as usual?"

"Now, Andrew," said Isa shyly, "you promised. None of you has any right to criticise the other. Where were you found yourself? In the pavilion, discussing football."

Robbie nodded, satisfied with that judgment.

A silence fell. Isa crept over to the bed and peeped in.

"No change yet," she whispered.

Andrew noticed that what Robbie held in his hand looked like a bank-book.

"What are the Thistle's prospects tomorrow?" asked Robbie. "Everybody thinks withoot Turk they've no chance. He's not playing, is he?"

"No."

"There was a rumour he was going to play, bandages and all. I couldn't believe it. Bad auld bitch, his mither."

"Young Elrigmuir's not playing either."

"What?" Robbie's interest was engrossing; he quite forgot his father in the bed behind him. "Is he injured? I never heard a word of it."

"He's not injured."

"Then what's up? He can't sign for any other team while the Thistle are still in the Cup."

"He and Mysie hae fallen out. His heart's crushed as a consequence. It seems he was in bed wi' Margot Malarkin."

Robbie almost guffawed. "Was he, by God?"

Andrew turned and looked at Isa. Blushing, she shut her eyes.

"Margot likes them fresh," said Robbie. "So Mysie's huffed? Well, the way to cure that is for her to let Alec into bed wi' her."

"It might help," agreed Andrew, again staring at Isa.

This time she stared back. "Do you think so?" she murmured.

"I remember," said Robbie, "somebody in the Lucky Sporran reading us a letter Rabbie Burns once wrote aboot Jean Armour. It was gey coarse. He said that the best peacemaker between a man and a woman was—I'll leave you to guess; and you'll be right."

"Are you not scolding us, Isa, for such talk at such a time?" asked Andrew.

She said nothing but kept staring at him. It was he who looked away.

"Is that a bank-book you've got?" he asked.

"Aye." Robbie winked at his wife.

"I didn't think you possessed such a thing."

"It's my faither's. He gave it to me."

"For young Gavin's education," murmured Isa.

"I thought," said Andrew, "my faither always condemned banks. How much is in it? Half a crown, as a sort of snub to them?"

"More than that," said Robbie, sniggering softly, "raither more than that."

"Let me see it." Andrew held out his hand.

Robbie hesitated.

"You'll get it back." Andrew took it. There were many entries. He turned the pages and found, to his astonishment, the sum was one hundred and sixty-three pounds. "Good God!" he said.

Robbie took the book back. "I was a bit surprised myself," he said smugly. "There must have been a bit of the hoarder in my faither too."

Andrew sat smiling.

Robbie misunderstood. He smiled too. "Bit of a shock, eh?"

Isa understood. "Your faither worked hard all his days, Andrew," she said. "He was entitled to provide for his old age."

He said nothing but still smiled.

"Often we've to act against our principles," she added, with a shiver. "Have pity, not blame."

"One hundred and sixty-three pounds," he whispered.

"Sounds a lot," remarked Robbie. "But it's far from enough, considering what we've got to do wi' it."

"It might be the means of saving wee Bella's life," whispered Isa.

"We could buy her the things she needs," said Robbie virtuously. "Maybe we could move into a hoose wi' a garden."

"One hundred and sixty-three pounds," repeated Andrew. "I suppose, in his position, he'd get backhanders nobody ever heard about."

Robbie became irritated. "It's not a fortune," he said. "Dammit, it must be chicken-feed to you. They say Harry Gemmell's worth ten thousand."

"I ken what's in your mind, Andrew," said Isa.

"Do you, Isa?" He grinned at her.

"I think I do. And it's not fair either to your faither or to yourself."

"Fair?" asked Robbie. "What are you talking about?"

"This is no time to look for perfection," said Isa, "and to be bitter if you don't find it. Your faither's deeing."

"Bitter, Isa? I'm not bitter. I'm the very opposite." He laughed. "As Robbie says, Harry Gemmell's got ten thousand."

As they were gazing at him, wondering what he meant, there came a sigh from the bed, followed by a loud choked gurgling.

Isa sprang up and rushed over. Her husband, bank-book in hand, was close behind. Andrew sat on by the fire.

18

While old John Rutherford was dying Wattie Cleugh and Angus Tennant, representing the committee, sought to interview Mysie Dougary. One or two members had gone home, under oath to keep the secret even from their wives. Others waited outside Mysie's house.

They fidgeted on the doorstep. In their possession was a bomb, set to explode. Only Mysie could make it harmless, and she might refuse. For pride's sake she might allow everybody to be blown to bits.

Moreover, increasing their fidgets, they knew her father, Martin Dougary, alias Brag or Bum, was a fuzzy-haired eccentric, who might welcome them in and co-operate like any normal parent, but who, on the other hand, might look on their visit as some kind of insult. Though his father had been revered as a footballer, he himself had often backslidden in the faith.

"Leave Brag to me," said Wattie. "For God's sake don't cross him."

"I'll not open my mouth," replied Angus.

Mrs. Dougary opened the door. They smiled with relief. She was a stout, brisk, cheerful woman, far from witch-like but capable, so it was said, of reducing her lion-imitating husband to a mouse. They noticed she did not see the bomb they carried. Nor did Brag, who was sprawled out on a chair by the fire, with his eyes closed, listening to some peculiar music from the wireless. It was not jazz; it was not even roaring symphony; it was, thought Angus with involuntary grin, like the squeals of half a dozen hungry cats being walloped with a tin frying-pan.

"You call it chamber music," said Mrs. Dougary wearily. "He says it's the highest-class stuff. Listening to it's supposed to make the brain grow. It's given me toothache."

"Chamber music?" Angus grinned again. It was well named chamber music; about a couple of dozen were being rattled together.

"I never thought music could gie a body toothache," sighed Mrs. Dougary, "but this stuff does."

Mr. Dougary opened first one fierce eye then another. Then up shot one hand to clutch his fuzz of white hair, followed by the other. Next moment the entirety, the whole five-feet-four of indignant culture-seeker was on his slippered feet.

"Can a man not get improving his mind in his own house?" he cried, and darted forward to switch off the wireless set.

Silence like heaven descended, with Mephistopheles in a knitted cardigan glaring in the midst.

"We must apologise," said Wattie humbly. "It's Mysie we really want to see."

"She's gone to bed long ago," said Mrs. Dougary. "She said her heid was sore."

Her husband went snorting back to his chair.

"This is a queer time for two married men to come asking after my daughter," he said.

"We appreciate that, Martin," said Wattie, "and we're sorry. If it hadn't been so urgent we would never have disturbed you. This is an official business, on behalf of the committee. The truth is, Mysie and Alec have had a cast-out."

"Another one?" he cried, and held out his arms as if to embrace thousands.

"This is the worst, Martin," said Angus eagerly.

"The latest is always the worst. That's surely the elementary logic of love, about which, Angus, I can see you ken nothing."

"Now, Martin, I've got four of a family."

"What does that prove beyond your ability to procreate, shared by beetles and monkeys alike?"

"It proves, surely," said Angus, with a smile out of which confidence kept slipping, "I'm not what you would call an ignoramus in matters of love."

"Maybe it should prove that, but it doesn't. I've known men with a dozen of a family, and they were such ignoramuses. Forby, they say one rat in a year can father twa hundred. Fertility proves nothing."

"Don't get him started," said Mrs. Dougary wearily, one hand over her cheek. "I'm not up to it tonight. Is it really necessary for you to see Mysie?"

"They'll explain their business first," said her husband. "Sit down and do it."

They sat on the edges of chairs.

"It seems," said Wattie carefully, "Alec is so upset by this latest quarrel he's not just fit to play tomorrow."

"It's not that he's not fit really," put in Angus. "He just refuses."

Wattie flicked his ear with terrible warning.

"It's the sixth round, Martin," he said, "and you ken what's happened to Turk McCabe."

"Meg here," said her husband, with malice, "has expressed the opinion it should have been Turk's heid was scalded."

Without being unmannerly they contrived not to look at their hostess.

"I'll go up, anyway," she said hastily, "and tell her you're here." She departed.

"Tell me," said Mr. Dougary, "in plain language, without exaggeration, understatement, or misrepresentation, what's it about this time? Last time it was about the colour of Alec's tie."

But they had decided in conclave not to tell her parents. These might put their parental feelings before their patriotism; they might rather the Thistle lost the Cup than that their daughter should be cajoled into forgiving and later marrying a simpleton who had let Margot Malarkin make a fornicator out of him.

"Jealousy, I think," said Wattie delicately. "You ken what a hero Alec is these days. I believe lassies blow kisses after him in the streets."

Mr. Dougary said nothing at all. At first his abstinence was a relief, but soon it became an obstacle. Wattie did not know what to say next; Angus Tennant did.

"Could you tell us, Martin," he asked, —"and I hope you'll not think me impudent for asking—are Mysie and Alec serious about each other? If we ken that, maybe we can assess the situation better."

"It is an impudent question, Angus; but I'll answer it. I do not know. Any faither that tries to plumb the depth of his daughter's fondness for any young man is a bull in a china shop. You've heard of a bull in a china shop, Angus?"

Angus hesitated, himself a bull in front of expert matador. "As a saying, Martin, I've heard of it. I've never actually, mind you, heard of any actual bull in a shop."

"What about a butcher's shop?"

Angus laughed. "You're trying to kid me."

Wattie jumped in to rescue his colleague. "We hoped you might be able to persuade her for us, Martin."

Dougary leapt up and began to toast his backside at the fire. "I'm going to tell you this, straight and plain. I'm her faither, and I have the tact to keep out of my daughter's private life. You're strangers, and you're blundering in; likely you're trampling sacred objects to bits."

Wattie winced. "There's justice in what you say, Martin. But for God's sake Alec must play tomorrow. Otherwise we're doomed. Think of your faither. Think of Tamas."

"Maybe I'm thinking it's time he put his mind on higher things than football. I don't want my faither, on the other side, to be associating wi' the likes of Tinto Brown."

"But, Martin, all I'm asking is: if Mysie's thrawn, will you talk to her?"

"I will not. Haven't I just explained to you my philosophy in such matters?"

Angus Tennant was interested apart from football. "But, Martin, surely you'd interfere if your girl was going to marry a wastrel, a thief say, or even a Chinaman?"

"I would not."

"You'd let her marry a Chinaman?"

"I would."

Angus, confused by the miscegenation conjured up by himself, shook his head. "It doesn't seem to me natural," he muttered.

Then Mrs. Dougary came in. They turned to her, eager and humble as argonauts consulting an encountered goddess as to the way to the Golden Fleece. Hand against cheek, she shook her head.

"She flatly refuses to speak to you," she mumbled.

Angus Tennant lowered his head. "That's us sunk then. We might as well face it."

"I asked her," added Mrs. Dougary, "what was between her and Alec this time. She said if she was to be burnt alive for it she wouldn't tell. I told her she might say that to her faither, not to me. He's the speirer in this family; he's the one that likes to ken what's going on."

Her husband, betrayed, was furious. "That's a lot of nonsense, Meg, and you know it."

Cleugh and Tennant made for the door. Mrs. Dougary accompanied them.

"She said I'd to tell you you weren't to molest her at her work tomorrow. If you do she'll go straight to Sergeant Elvan. She will too. She's a determined one."

"That's one man," muttered Cleugh, "will be pleased."

Before she shut the door after them she said, "I don't mind telling you this: I'm not very keen to see Mysie married to a football player. If there's anything in the world more aggravating than to have to hang on the wall of your sitting-room a picture of a football team, then I don't ken what it is. I had to put up wi' that for years. Good night."

"Good night, Mrs. Dougary. We hope your toothache gets better."

But when they were out on the street again Angus Tennant asked what had she meant about hanging a picture on the wall.

Cleugh was too preoccupied to pass on the knowledge.

They reached the lamp-post, where some committee-members were waiting for their news.

It was soon told.

"So," said one, "that's that. I only hope," he added morbidly, "we don't get beaten by a fantastic score like seven-nothing. We'd be the laughing-stock of the country."

"When it's all over," said another, "we'll hae to consider what's to be done about young Elrigmuir. A kind of court-martial will hae to be held. Isn't he deserting us in the middle of the battle? With Turk it's different; he's wounded."

"There's one hope left," said Wattie Cleugh.

They waited.

"The minister," he added.

"The minister?" Angus Tennant frowned in the lamplight. Religion to his pagan mind was a mystery: an archbishop in his robes was a kind of civilised witch-doctor. He had heard of miracles; he had had them read to him out of the Bible by a teacher to whom they were as authentic as the multiplication table. But still he could not see how young Mr. Lockhart could, as it were, put things in reverse as was sometimes done in the cinema: Alec Elrigmuir would be pulled out of Margot's bed, Margot's clothes would fly upon her, out of the door Alec would race backwards, and everything then would be at the point where the divergence towards sin had taken place. Thus perhaps God could do it; but young Lockhart lacked even the suspicion of magic. Not only was he losing his congregation fast as any tree its leaves in a windy autumn, but he was also involved in the ludicrous human predicament of having his wife conspicuously pregnant.

"How?" he asked.

"Mysie's a member of his church," said Wattie testily. "He might have influence over her."

"If she was a Catholic," muttered one, "and Lockhart was a priest she'd damned soon do what she told him."

They brooded over that damnable but tempting obedience.

"Well," said Wattie, "Angus and me will get along to the manse. There's no need for you fellows to hang around any longer. We'll get into touch wi' you if anything turns up."

They exchanged sad good-nights and went their separate ways.

There were lights on in every window in the manse. Two cars were at the gate; one was the minister's, the other Dr. Kiddie's.

"Her time must have come," said Angus.

Wattie had no children; he went right past the cars, through the gate, and up the path. Angus came unwillingly behind.

"This'll not be a very convenient time, Wattie," he said. "It's after ten, and maybe there's a wean being born."

Wattie paid no heed. He was like a man entranced; indeed, before putting out his finger to press the bell he spat on it. Tennant dared not ask why.

It was a flustered maid who came to the door.

"Is the minister in?" asked Cleugh.

"Aye, aye. But nobody can see him now. The mistress is having a baby. Did you not see the doctor's car at the gate? The nurse is here as well. It's expected any time."

"Our business is very urgent," said Cleugh. "Please inform the minister that Mr. Walter Cleugh, secretary of the Thistle, would like to speak to him for a minute or two."

"I'll go," she said, "but I don't ken what he'll say."

They were left on the doorstep.

"Right enough," said Angus, "it might take his mind off the birth."

"I understand," said Cleugh, "these things can go on for hours, days even."

"That's so, Wattie."

Wattie was silent for a few moments. "I've heard," he remarked, "that every time we sneeze a thousand babies are born in China."

Angus retreated into the fastnesses of his mind to chew over that statement. He could not see any connection between a sneeze and birth in China; as far as he knew nature operated there in the same way as anywhere else; and to confuse him further there was that sinister saying of Brag Dougary's, that if his daughter wanted to marry a Chinaman he wouldn't stop her.

The maid returned. "You've to come in," she said, inhospitably.

Clutching their caps, they followed her into the house and into the minister's study. Angus had expected to find him praying, and was shocked therefore to find him not only standing

252

but wearing flannels and pullover. What was the good, he thought, of having influence with God if you were too slack to use it? If he'd been the minister he'd be on his knees, in his blackest suit, in his whitest collar, with the Bible beside him, begging for a quick and easy delivery, a healthy wean, and good fortune for it in the world; whereas Mr. Lockhart, on the contrary, looked like a boxer just out of the gymnasium, except that he held a daffodil in his hand.

"We must apologise for bursting in on you at such a time, Mr. Lockhart," said Wattie Cleugh.

The minister took a quick sniff at the daffodil and listened upwards. "Sit down, gentlemen," he said. "But you will excuse me if I keep standing."

Just like a boxer, thought Angus, louping about, unable to sit.

"This is a worrying time for you," murmured Wattie.

"Every home at one time or another passes through the shadow of Bethlehem," said the minister.

Tennant was lost, but Cleugh in a clear light saw his own childless hearth; he grunted.

"We'll not trespass on your time longer than's necessary," he said. "What I'm going to say may shock you. You know Alec Elrigmuir, our centre-forward?"

Mr. Lockhart nodded.

"He and Mysie Dougary are, or were, sweethearts. They've parted, it seems, and as a result he declares he will not play tomorrow." It was obvious the young man was not listening. Cleugh spoke louder as if to a man he'd discovered was deaf. "Tomorrow's the sixth round of the Cup. It's vitally important we win. You ken as well as I do how low this town's morale has been in the past two or three years. We've had more than our share of unemployment and poverty. To make it worse our team, the Thistle, has had a terrible record of defeats. But that's been changed in recent weeks. We've climbed up the League, and we've fought our way through to the sixth round of the Cup. If we win we're in the semi-final, and then the Final."

Angus had been listening in admiration of his chief's eloquence; he couldn't have put the case better himself.

Mr. Lockhart's attention, alas, had not been so close.

"Do you expect to win?" he asked politely.

It was an old, well-bred, deaf man's question. Still making allowances, Wattie raised his voice a little higher. "We did expect to win, but Turk McCabe, or Gordon as I think he's called, got his feet scalded in unfortunate circumstances. If Alec Elrigmuir calls off as well we're utterly destroyed, utterly."

"Why should he call off? Were his feet scalded too?"

"No." Wattie paused after that definite negative with its sweeping away of all nonsense. "No. He and Mysie Dougary have fallen out. I'm now going to tell you why."

"Yes, please do, Mr. Cleugh."

"It seems the young fool"—here Angus Tennant nodded at the folly, but smacked his lips at it too—"allowed Miss Malarkin to lead him into the path of sin." This time Angus's nod was of sorrow at sinfulness, but still salacity kept sliding in and out of his soul.

"Precisely what do you mean, Mr. Cleugh?" asked the minister, in the bright tones of one pretending interest. He sniffed the daffodil; he listened upwards; he held his wife's hand; he kissed her damp brow; he heard her groans.

"I mean precisely this: they were in bed together."

"Indeed."

"Aye. It seems he blurted out a confession to Mysie. You may think he did right there; me, I think it was a bad blunder. Anyhow, she's jumped up on to her high horse, as women do; and she'll ride to her destruction unless she's stopped. That's why we're here tonight. You might be able to stop her. Maybe she thinks her attitude's religious. But I never yet heard of any commandment that said: Thou shalt not forgive."

Mr. Lockhart heard the last word. "Forgiveness is divine," he murmured, and prayed that Nan, in her travail, would forgive him.

"Will you talk to her, then, Mr. Lockhart?"

"I shall certainly do so."

They were not sure he meant what they meant.

Then they were interrupted by a voice from upstairs. It was Dr. Kiddie's.

"Is there a dram in the house?" he shouted. "You're the father of a handsome boy."

Without an apology the minister rushed out of the room. He dropped the daffodil.

Wattie Cleugh rose up and Angus Tennant did likewise. The latter was grinning amiably; he was in at the birth, as it were, eligible for that dram if it existed; indeed, he picked up the daffodil and put it on the desk.

Not so Wattie; he felt excluded. "Come on," he said. "There's no help here," and he led the way out.

19

All surmises as to why Rutherford and his wife parted had been, of course, handicapped by the necessity of being disparaging to them both. She was the sort of barren-minded woman any warm-hearted man would flee from; but few were willing to pay him that compliment. If he had shown some restraint in comparison with her, several reasons were more likely than a sense of decency: his shyness, for example, was the kind produced by cowardice; or his stupidity was so thick it prevented him from exploiting his financial advantages; or conscience to him was like a serpent coiled round his every movement; or his contempt for his fellows was so well developed he had no need or desire to exercise it. Nevertheless the restraint had been there, and it had made him rather less obnoxious than her. Rid of her, he might have been expected to mellow, at least a little; but no, he had become much more offensive, as if, incredibly, she had been a sweetening influence. It might be he missed his son; and of course he was no longer manager at the factory, where, under the new management, the familiar blue-thistle wrappings for the biscuits had been abandoned.

If the effect on him of his wife's desertion had been difficult to understand, that of his father's death was utterly baffling. Had the old councillor been a saint instead of an unrepentant atheist, and had not only his own benediction been given but also those of a hundred attendant angels, the revolution in his son's character might have been comprehensible. As it was, it became known that Rutherford, though in the same room, had not seen his father dying; he had sat by the fire with his back to the bed.

Robbie's reason, confided to cronies in the pub, was that his brother was in a furious huff because their father had left him not a ha'penny. In spite of probings, Robbie did not add how much had been left. However, this account of death-bed resentfulness and jealousy only darkened the enigma. Had Rutherford turned more dour, truculent, and outcast it would have been plain enough, a sum in psychology as easy as two and two; but no, instead of dour he became frank and uncomfortably cordial; truculence was replaced by bonhomie; and instead of sulking by himself like a scarecrow he marched out into the sunlight, like a farmer in a field sowing seed. The restraint was quite gone: the bud had burst and become the full flower; and everybody was astonished, and rather ashamed, to find it was a rose. Had a man won fifty thousand pounds in a football pool he might have been expected to bloom like that.

The feud with Robbie was over, although nobody noticed any change in Robbie. They travelled in the same Sowlas taxi into Glasgow to see their father cremated, and afterwards, over lunch in a restaurant, with Harry also a mourner, Andrew put a proposition to his brother that increased the latter's shifty shyness till it became almost a physical ailment like itch or wryneck. Andrew proposed that, as he was now going to Helensburgh to live, Robbie and his family should move into his house; and he added he was sure Harry would find him a job either in Drumsagart itself or nearby: Harry, as Robbie knew, had many contacts. Harry kept nodding, like a magnate; but he murmured modestly he would do his best.

Later Andrew and Harry returned by car to Helensburgh, and in a long conversation came to a satisfactory arrangement. Harry showed neither surprise nor triumph at his brother-in-law's capitulation. He was accustomed in business to having men hum-and-haw, but in the end, if they were sensible men deserving of success, they accepted his view. He did not even say he thought Andrew had taken far too long to see where his best interests lay; it was always better to let a man take his natural time and so make his foundations of surrender firm.

The sun was shining, red rhododendrons and yellow daffodils were in bloom, and the Firth itself shone below like a great blue flower, with the purity of the air its fragrance. Hannah, Gerald, and Mabel were waiting on the steps of the house. Hannah and

Mabel wore black dresses, Gerald had a black diamond sewn on to his sleeve.

Later that night, in their bedroom, anxious, too, to make concessions, Hannah at last agreed to his proposal about their house in Drumsagart. It meant, for one thing, that they themselves were never going back. When he said he was going to resign from the presidency of the club she thought there was no reason why he should give them the satisfaction of seeing him resign: let him finish his term. He supposed he might do so, although now that the Thistle were out of the Cup the office held neither honour nor interest.

It was true the Thistle were knocked out, but nobody in Drumsagart could blame the president. In the early hours of Saturday morning, coming straight from his father's deathbed, he had roused Alec Elrigmuir and persuaded him to play by offering him, so it was said, as much as fifty pounds towards the furnishing of a house for himself and Mysie. The latter, he assured the youth, would never be so foolish or unnatural as to prefer principle, which turned sour in a week, to a walnut bedroom suite or a sitting-room suite in real hide. Fuddled with sleep and penitence, Elrigmuir was convinced. He played; he scored two goals; but unhappily Muirvale Athletic scored three. Mysie was not reconciled and the Thistle were out of the Cup.

The town was disconsolate: it lay at the foot of the green Drumsagart Hill like a huge black cat of ill fortune and gloom, with one white speck on its face, representing the cheerfulness of Sam Malarkin. Sam had prayed for defeat, and felt his prayer had been answered. He had also prayed, contradictorily, for the punishment of Margot: nothing had been done about that yet. Indeed, she sang and once boasted to him about her conquest of Elrigmuir. An arithmetical calculation had shown Sam that free drams for all-comers would have cost him hundreds of pounds. Therefore amidst the rancidness of defeat he was an oasis of balm.

Tinto Brown, still dying, turned his face to the wall. Nathaniel Stewart took to his bed, determined that nothing, not even cure, would assuage him. Rab Nuneaton found when he sat down to the feast of misery that he had been cheated: what at a distance looked like ambrosia turned out in the mouth to be dust. His wife was again pregnant: the gift of life, so abhorred, had been thrust upon them.

Archie Birkwood, who lived by death, now found every burial symbolical. As the coffins descended and the worms wriggled at his feet he remembered that the glory of the Cup was buried too. When his wife Teena began to tease him for being so depressed he rose and went out of the house. She was snivelling when he returned an hour later, with the smell of beer off his breath. Never again, she was warned, would she insult him with laughter.

When old Mrs. McCabe appeared in the main street somebody noticed how short her shadow was, and added that in the old days witches were said to have no shadows at all. But for her two protectors, Sergeant Elvan and Turk in hospital, she would have had at least curses thrown at her. Doddering along on her stick, peering in at the shop windows in search of the cheapest food, she forgot she was the principal cause of all those dejected faces.

It was the president who resurrected hope. At the first committee meeting after the defeat he reminded his fellow members that it was possible, without magic, to have the tie replayed. They knew what he meant. If they could prove that any player of the team which had beaten them had been at the time ineligible, for any one of a number of reasons, then they could protest to the Association, which would order an inquiry and the tie would be replayed. Protests were often lodged but infrequently sustained. Suspicions would buzz round a certain player thick as flies, but cunning and brazenness could swat them away to the satisfaction of the inspecting authority. Such a player was Jack Muldie of the Muirvale team. Other teams defeated by Muirvale had poked and delved in archives and men's minds but had failed to produce evidence that he was taboo. If they had failed, with their expert and frenzied inquisitors, how was the Thistle committee to succeed? Rutherford had asserted they could at least try. This was the reformed Rutherford; the other, the former, had often opposed protests as being unsporting and mean. If a team was beaten fairly on the field, he had insisted, it ought to accept that and not go seeking some quibble, some trifle of faulty or omitted registration, some paper mistake, by means of which another chance could be obtained. Now here he was demanding they spare neither effort nor money in search of some such quibble. A man could hardly have proved his conversion more convincingly.

He conducted the campaign. First those journalists who dealt with Junior football were notified that Drumsagart were hot on the scent of a protest and were confident they would show themselves more persevering bloodhounds than all others for whom the same scent had gone cold. These statements appeared in four national newspapers and of course were read in the enemy citadel.

Then committee-members were sent to the other clubs who had previously tried to establish the ineligibility of Muldie. They returned with the assurance, given to them by secretaries with bloodshot eyes, that they were not seeking gold at the foot of the rainbow or chasing a will-of-the-wisp; but, alas, no one could tell them exactly what they were seeking or where it was to be found. One secretary half-jokingly had said it ought to be permitted to kidnap Muldie or one of the Muirvale committee and put him to the torture. In some secret way the regulations had been broken. Surely, with a town's happiness at stake, the breaker of those regulations ought to be made to confess? What was the use, that secretary had asked, of living amongst the advantages of the twentieth century, if you could be tamely cheated out of your rights by certain men's silence? In more primitive times that silence would have been shattered like bones.

"Aye, but," said Rutherford, when they were listening to that report, "there wasn't any football in those days."

"The English soldiers," muttered Angus Tennant, "kicked Wallace's heid about like a ba'."

"I propose," murmured Sam Malarkin, "we drop it. We've done our best, but we've failed. I propose we give Andrew here a vote of thanks for his endeavours and then we drop it. There's always next year."

"I'm inclined to second that," said Wattie Cleugh, who resented Rutherford's usurping of the leadership.

"Before we take a vote on it," said Rutherford, "why not send somebody into Muirvale itself?"

"A spy?" asked Angus.

"Something of that sort. If he sat in the pubs yonder he might pick up something."

"Sounds reasonable," said Hugh Neilson.

"It would be a waste of money," cried Sam.

"Not the club's money," said Rutherford. "As it's my idea I'm willing to foot the bill."

"I can see nothing wrong wi' that," said Angus Tennant.

"What about you Donald?" asked Sam, seeking a supporter.

Donald was a man of conscience. "Protests are legal," he said. "I see no harm in using information got in that way. It would be different if we were using bribes."

"All right," said Sam. "I withdraw my objection. But who'll be sent?"

"Ned Nicholson," replied Rutherford promptly.

"Ned?" they said, surprised. "Well, right enough, he'd be the very man. If there was a scrap to be found he'd find it."

"He's not a committee-man," objected Sam.

"None of us could go," said Rutherford. "We might be recognised."

A majority agreed with him.

"I'd send Harry Lynn if I thought he'd hear anything," said Angus Tennant.

"Will Ned be willing?" asked Malarkin, remembering that Rutherford and Nicholson didn't get on well together. "He's an awkward man to handle."

"He'll go."

"You seem very sure, Andrew."

"So I should be, Sam, seeing I've already discussed it with him."

"Oh ho. Was that not ultra vires?"

"It was gumption, Sam, good Scots gumption. Why should I waste the committee's time with a proposition that wasn't feasible?"

"True, Andrew, true," they agreed.

Malarkin looked at Cleugh, saw he would support no rebellion, and surrendered with a snigger.

At the close of the meeting they slapped Rutherford's back in congratulation, and at the bus-stop Donald Lowther stood beside him and said, "Changed days, Andrew. I'm glad to see you get your due."

Rutherford laughed. "Donald," he said, "I always had faith in my fellow men."

Lowther frowned. "Don't have too much, Andrew. I'd keep an eye on Malarkin."

Rutherford spread out his hands. "Donald, I'm a man that's seen the unpleasant side of folk."

"You have, Andrew."

"If I say then I have faith in them nobody can accuse me of being a simpleton that's ripe for a rude awakening."

"Well, Andrew," said Donald hesitantly, "I have always thought of you as a simple-minded man at heart. Don't misunderstand me. That's a compliment."

"Thanks, Donald. Well, here's my bus. Good night."

"Good night, Andrew. How are Hannah and the boy?"

"Fine. Both fine. Never were better. I'll tell them you were asking for them."

"Do that, Andrew. You're lucky, mind you, to be living by the sea. It must be bonny there at this time of the year."

"Beautiful, Donald. I could have been there years ago. I don't know what kept me back."

Then the bus came and he boarded it. Lowther walked slowly home, gloomily but not covetously comparing his own lot with that of the president. He had four pounds a week and lived up a close in a two-room and kitchen house, with a steelwork to look out on to; whereas Andrew might be drawing twenty pounds a week and lived in a mansion within its own grounds, with hills behind it and the sea in front.

In the bus Rutherford found himself, as always when alone now, biting at his nails and trembling. He pulled a newspaper from his pocket and tried to obliterate himself in its daily trivialities of death and theft and threats of war.

Nicholson's mission was unsuccessful. He visited all four Muirvale pubs and found the talk impregnably about victory; there was no way in for apprehension about Drumsagart's protest hunt. Secret schemer of their downfall, he felt ashamed, he said, when they insisted on standing him drinks to show him, a stranger, how noble was Muirvale's heart, and how, on the sideboard of the town as it were, the silver Cup would look in its proper place. He came home to report that neither blatherskite nor traitor existed in Muirvale.

It seemed hope was dead. As the committee-men waited for Andrew Rutherford to arrive they chatted sorrowfully with Ned, who was there to make his official report. On the field some players were running round the track, while others were practising shots at goal. Football, like life, must go on though hope had died. This season must be completed in bitterest anticlimax, and next season must be prepared for. Unfortunately, at the season's close, when dead hope might at last be buried and new hope born, it was certain they would lose young Elrigmuir, after whom the Senior Clubs were already flocking. As it was, he still stayed in Drumsagart to try and win Mysie back; but it was rumoured she had gone back to her former sweetheart, the bank-clerk. Certainly she no longer attended the Thistle matches; in which defection she was not alone. If Elrigmuir went, then without a doubt the Thistle would become a weed in the wilderness again. Turk McCabe's feet were healing with marvellous speed, but it was quite likely that as they put on new skin they would shed their old football skill. Turk was a meteor; whereas Elrigmuir was a star that would shine for years, alas, above other fields than this.

They were interrupted by the arrival through the gates of a motor car, small but splendid. It came as close to the pavilion as it could, so that they could see who the driver was as he got out and slammed the door carelessly as if he'd been a car owner all his life. He was their president, Andrew Rutherford. They noticed he had on a new suit.

"I never," said Angus Tennant, with a benevolent squint, "saw such a change in a man in my life."

"Auld John was the encumbrance," murmured Hugh Neilson sagely.

"Ach, Andrew was always all right," said Ned Nicholson, with a giggle. "I ken I used to miscall him as much as anybody, but I kent all the time there wasn't much wrong wi' him. To tell you the truth, I whiles thought he took far too much snash from us all."

"He's got the strength of a bull," said Angus Tennant.

Sam Malarkin hissed at all this hypocrisy. He wanted to ask them how much had Rutherford paid them for these good opinions. It used to be only outcasts like Tinto Brown and Jock Saunders and Harry Lynn that Rutherford bribed; now it seemed to be everybody. Even Wattie Cleugh, see, was greeting him with a chuckle and a nip for his new suit.

Sam found himself, even as he was blaming Cleugh, saying

that on such a fine night it must have been a pleasant run up from Helensburgh.

"Well, it should have been, Sam," said the president, "but, to tell you the truth, my driving's so rusty I damned near knocked over a traffic policeman in Dumbarton. If I hadn't on this new suit I think he'd have booked me."

"Pity it wasn't Elvan," said Angus Tennant.

They all laughed as they went into the pavilion. On the table in front of the president's chair was a letter. Cleugh picked it up and handed it to him.

"It's for you, Andrew," he said.

"Thanks, Wattie." Rutherford glanced at the postmark, which was indistinct. "It looks damned like Muirvale," he said. "Did you make any contacts, Ned?"

"Sorry to say, no, Andrew."

They crowded round to look. In excitement they agreed it did look like Muirvale. Maybe, they said, a letter of commiseration from the Athletic people; maybe even, in a display of unprecedented sportsmanship, an offer to divulge the incriminating information about Muldie.

"Well, there's one good way of finding out," said Rutherford, laughing. "And that's to open it and read it. Your places, gentlemen. Ned, find yourself a place. You're co-opted for the night. Excuse me while I investigate."

They sat down and lit cigarettes and pipes, but watched him all the time. The smile never faded from his face, but there seemed to be subtle changes in it. It was a short letter, a single page of a smallish notebook, yet he took three times as long to read it as was surely necessary. Of course, they thought indulgently, Andrew had always admitted he'd been something of a blockhead at school.

"Is it in Chinese, Andrew?" asked Donald Lowther.

Angus Tennant felt a strange desire to sneeze; he had to take out his handkerchief in case.

Rutherford gave a little start and seemed surprised to find them all staring at him. It was well acted and they laughed. His was the loudest laughter.

"Do you ken what this is, lads?" he cried. "This is our protest. Just listen. 'Dear Mr. Rutherford, I saw your name in the paper. If you want a protest against Jack Muldie I'm the one can help you to get it. If you're interested, I'll meet you in the Glasgow Central Station beside the Shell at seven o'clock on Tuesday. Bring your treasurer with you."

He stopped. They waited for him to go on.

"That's the lot," he said.

"But who wrote it?" asked Angus Tennant.

"It doesn't say, Angus. There are some crosses where the signature should be."

"Crosses usually mean kisses," commented Angus.

"So it's anonymous?" observed Malarkin.

"That's right, Sam," said the president, "and you'll all allow I'm an expert on the subject." He led the laughter and seemed to stare at each one in turn to make sure he was laughing heartily enough. "By the way," he cried, "how's the daft bitch Lizzie keeping these days? '

"Still as worthless as ever, I'm afraid," said Donald Lowther uncomfortably.

"I nearly had a family yonder," said Rutherford, "but it turned out to be a bagful of slander. I hear wee Rab Nuneaton's wife's expectant again. Rab will be pleased; it'll make up for the lassie he lost."

Angus Tennant was the only one who thought the words were meant to be sincere. "You're not just on the mark there, Andrew," he said, with a grin. "Rab's near demented. He's got it into his heid God's got a spite against him."

"He used to think I had," said the president.

"Without wishing to interrupt," said Wattie Cleugh, "I'd like to suggest we return to the very interesting subject of this letter. Is it a hoax, do you think? Did some joker in Muirvale write it? If we turn up at the Shell in the station yonder, will we find some fellow with a Muirvale rosette in his jacket and his fingers at his neb? Or will we really meet somebody willing to sell us information? That hint about the treasurer seems to indicate money's wanted."

"There's one sure way to find out, Wattie. Go and see."

"That's so, Andrew."

Malarkin leant forward. "If it came to handing out money, where would it come from? It would look a queer item on our balance sheet."

"There's another point comes first," said Donald Lowther.

"Well, Donald, what is it?" asked Rutherford.

Lowther looked at his friend miserably. "I'd have thought it would have occurred to you, Andrew, even before it occurred to me."

"What are you talking about, Donald?"

"It's just this: I don't like having anything to do with a rotter that'd betray his ain team. We're out of the Cup, and I've got as sore a heart as any man here; but I'd rather stay out than sneak back in with the help of a coward and a traitor. If there was a man in Drumsagart would do this to the Thistle, what would we think of him?"

"Is there such a man, Donald?" asked Rutherford.

"I suppose there is, Andrew, God help him."

Rutherford was rubbing his hands. "Donald's got a scruple," he said. "Is there anybody else infected?"

"Infected?" muttered Lowther. "Is it a disease?"

"I think," said Malarkin slowly—"yes, I think I agree with Donald. We've a duty to keep the sport as pure as we can." He looked at Tennant and Cleugh, offering them his patronage if they supported him.

Cleugh shook his head.

Tennant winked. "Dammit, Sam, to be truthful, I'd deal with the Deil himself if it would get us back into the Cup. All's fair in love and war; this is war."

"Well spoken, Angus," said Rutherford. "I couldn't put it better myself. Is there anyone else with Donald's qualms? If he can win a majority, then of course I'll tear this up and we can forget the Cup for another season."

"For any season," muttered Hugh Neilson.

"As you say, Hugh. Well, who agrees with Sam and Donald?"

No one else put up his hand.

"We carry on then," said Rutherford. "That right, Donald?"

Lowther nodded. "I might resign," he muttered. "I'll think over it. I ken this, if we get our protest this way and then win the Cup I'll be ashamed to look at it."

"You think that now, Donald. But remorse is a bird of passage; it never stays long in any nest. Sam brought up a good point, though, about the money. If this offer's genuine, how much do we pay? I'm willing as a donation to the club, to put down twenty pounds of my own money."

"Twenty quid!" Angus Tennant whistled in admiration, but Donald Lowther suddenly clasped his head in his hands.

"Got a headache, Donald?" asked Rutherford.

"Aye, Andrew. You ken I'm subject to them. Bessie says it's my eyesight: I should wear specs."

"Nell tells me," said Angus Tennant, "my brains were shovelled in in the beginning, so it never affects them how they're shoogled about. I never have headaches."

"I'm proposing then," said Hugh Neilson, very serious, "we accept Andrew's very generous offer, and that he and you, Wattie, go and interview the fellow who wrote the letter."

"Seconded," cried Angus Tennant.

There was no amendment.

"It's settled then," said the president. "Wattie and I try to meet our mysterious correspondent, and get from him, as cheaply as we can, any relevant information. I hope you've noticed he doesn't say how we'll recognise him. D'you think he'll have a placard on his chest, saying: 'I'm the Judas from Muirvale'?"

They all laughed, except Donald. It was suggested solicitously he should take a couple of aspirins.

20

Like a second honeymoon, Harry had said, with glittering grin. Mabel had laughed or hinneyed, randily, with her belly tight against the black silken dress. Hannah had smiled like a bride indeed, more grim and proud perhaps than bashful, but pleased with her bridegroom. He, clapping Harry on the shoulder in mock rebuke, was as usual sitting remote in a corner watching himself, all judgment suspended, every faculty of observation heightened to miss not a detail of this phenomenon of a man reformed, of self-distrust become crass typical assurance, of diffidence become a jackal's bark never noticed in the pack.

Everywhere now he spied on himself, even when he was alone; and there was no communication between the spy and the man spied upon. Nor was it simply a case of his old Drumsagart self watching, with fraternal malicious interest, this new self: it was much more peculiar than that, for the watcher showed a steadfastness and impartiality never at any time characteristic of him. Sometimes he imagined it was not himself watching but God; but that was the sort of foolishness forever renounced.

In flattering Harry, in thanking him, in accompanying him to his various businesses in the city like a sycophant, he was not acting a part; he was the same Andrew Rutherford who at the door of the taxi had toyed with Rab Nuneaton's grief. Nor was his adulation of Gerald assumed: he took the boy on motor runs, steamer trips, rowing-boat expeditions, and bought him whatever he asked for, until Hannah protested. Well, he had always spoiled his son, but shame in the presence of so many poor and deprived children had acted like a brake; now it was removed and the spoiling was accelerated.

It was similar with his treatment of Hannah, though here shame had not been the inhibition; it had been something deeper than shame, a self-disgust which had caused him to see a kiss between them as an act of treachery and hypocrisy, though he had nearly always managed to disguise it as native awkwardness; but once or twice she had seen it for what it was and had shown herself betrayed and humiliated. Bodily displays of affection between them had dwindled to stray touching of hands, and then had ceased altogether. Now he could kiss her, fondle her, make love to her, and feel it was all sincere. That disgust must therefore have gone or become strangely quiescent. Certainly her suspicions, at first very wary, making her indeed as nervous as a bride, were gradually lulled until they soon disappeared. So much so that once, while they were making love, she had gasped that if she hadn't been so old, past the age now, there was nothing she'd like better than another child, a girl this time. She had always wanted a girl, she said, although it was the first time she had ever uttered the wish. He had believed her, and afterwards, lying watching the moonlight on the ceiling, with his hand in hers, he remembered the girls singing in the street and he dreamed of the girl they might have had.

It seemed to him strange that by abandoning his faith in humanity, or at least by realistically reducing his expectations of what human beings were capable of, he should have become more popular, better understood, more sympathetically tolerated, made to feel more at home.

Never before an entertainer, gauche even in telling a funny story with a moral to the assembled Sunday school, he now found himself in that household considered as fine a turn as Harry Lauder, on the subject of Drumsagart's football problems. Seated by the window, looking over the rhododendrons and through the trees to the water red with evening, he had Harry cackling, Mabel hinneying, and Hannah sternly smiling as he described the vicissitudes of the Thistle, its prolonged stuntedness, its marvellous growth, its unhappy beheading: there were so many comical episodes—the scalding of Turk's feet, the confession of Elrigmuir, the visit to the minister at the time of the birth, the defeat, the public despondency, the quest of a protest, and finally this letter from Judas.

They had their favourite episodes: Harry's was Turk's scalding; Mabel's was nineteen-year-old Elrigmuir in bed with forty-plus Margot; and Hannah's, strangely enough, was the birth of the Lockhart baby. She seemed to show an envy of Nan Lockhart, not merely for the new child but also for her fair hair, her youth, her pleasant disposition. They asked him to go over the tales again and again with more ridiculous detail. He always obliged, exaggerating the absurdities and the pettiness, while Hannah nodded and even took his hand, to hear him so loyally and so courageously admit, by implication, that her estimate of Drumsagart had been right, his own wrong. Perhaps he was seeing more amusement in the antics of those poverty-blighted fools than really existed, but in the end he was saying what she had always said, and what she had always wanted him to say: Drumsagart was a place to turn your back on if ever you wished to advance in the world.

Wattie Cleugh had on his Sunday clothes, from hat to shoes, as he stood in the station entrance waiting for the president. He was dressed thus not only to impress the man from Muirvale but also to prevent himself from appearing beside Rutherford like labourer beside works manager: there was the honour of Drumsagart to keep up. Yet when at last he saw the president stride towards him among the crowds he knew that after all, despite his wife's pressing of his trousers and his own sprinkling himself in his bath with talcum powder, he was still the common man. Since the night was chilly, Rutherford had on a huge thick overcoat with luxurious pile; his light-grey hat was almost as wide-brimmed as Geordie Bonnyton's, but splendid where Geordie's was grubby, and worn with arrogant confidence, whereas Geordie's was always pulled down over his ears as if its ambition was to blot out his eyes too. Even on the fashionable city street Rutherford looked superior and masterful. His very good nature, as he greeted Wattie, was overbearing.

"Well, Wattie," he asked, "have you been in to take a peep at spy-corner?"

Cleugh smiled faintly. "No, Andrew. I thought I'd wait for you. I see there's a train in from Muirvale at 6.57. He may be on that one."

"What's it now?" Rutherford glanced at his wrist-watch, while Cleugh wondered if the gold pocket one ticked there under all that opulent cloth. "A quarter to. You must have been early."

"Aye, I asked away from work half an hour early."

"Right then, we'll go on up into the station and stand where we can get a good view of the Shell. It'll be a bit warmer there, anyway." He seemed to glance at Wattie's raincoat, his best, but thin.

"I can't say I feel it cold," said Wattie.

"That's your guid thick Drumsagart blood."

They went up the iron steps into the station. There were about a dozen persons gathered round the Shell in the centre.

"We'll stand here, where we'll be conspicuous," said Rutherford. "Likely he's seen my picture in the paper and he's going to go by that."

"Likely enough, Andrew."

The vastness of the place, the large number of strangers, their position out in the open, intimidated Cleugh; by himself he would have watched from a dark corner.

Rutherford looked all round boldly. Then each man at the Shell was scrutinised. None stared back significantly, none approached.

"Well, I don't think he's there yet," said Rutherford.

"If ever he comes."

"Oh, I fully expect he'll come, Wattie. There are such creatures as traitors, you ken."

"I suppose there are."

"What sort of a man do you think we're looking for, Wattie? I've got it into my head he'll be a wee, furtive, miserable chap like Rab Nuneaton, who thinks he's got a grudge against life, and this is his way of getting his own back."

"I've never really tried to picture him," said Cleugh, "but I wouldn't be surprised if he was like Rab. Rab could easily be our traitor if we were ever unlucky enough to hae one."

A woman strolled past them, reeking of scent and shoogling her bottom; her glance towards them was as brassy as her hair. Cleugh, thinking her a city prostitute, was thrilled and terrified.

"Traitors and whores," chuckled Rutherford. "You can't say life lacks variety." He laughed more loudly. "I'm laughing at young Lockhart yonder with his feather-duster," he said.

Cleugh didn't quite understand and waited for the rest. No more came, though Rutherford kept grinning.

"We had an accident in the town yesterday," said Wattie, to break the silence.

"Somebody hurt?"

"Aye, Tom Lennox. You might not know him: a quiet man. He drove a dustbin lorry."

"Red-haired fellow, always smiling?"

"That's him, that's him exactly. Another lorry crashed into his. I don't know who was at fault. But he's in Glasgow here, in the infirmary. They don't think he'll live."

"Well, well. Is he married?"

"Aye. He's got two of a family, a boy and a girl. He stays next door to big Archie Birkwood. Oh, and by the way, Andrew, guess who's dead?"

Rutherford, with his eyes on the destination board, grinned. "There are a lot yonder ripe for the journey, Wattie. Who is it?"

"An auld friend of yours: Tinto Brown."

"Oh." Rutherford looked so hard at the board that Cleugh examined it, expecting to see the name Muirvale perhaps, or even Drumsagart; but neither name was there.

"So he's gone at last?" said Rutherford.

"Aye, on Saturday night. Somebody said just when the pubs were cheeriest. He was buried yesterday. The parish had to do it: quick and cheap. I believe there was one mourner: Crutch Brodie, in tears they tell me, and down on his one knee."

"He was better away," said Rutherford, with a sudden quiet passion. "Latterly they were laughing at him. He was better away. He was in pain too."

"Agony, from what I hear." Wattie laughed. "It seems, deid though he is, he still wants to ken how our protest gets on. So Crutch was saying. Mrs. Campkin's to get into touch with him and let him know. She's the spiritualist medium, you ken, that has meetings every Thursday in the Tabernacle Hall. I went to one once out of curiosity. I came away scunnered. Tinto said if there was anything he could do for us he'd do it. That was a joke, mind you: for, by God, if there ever was a man died withoot influence it was Tinto Brown."

"I liked him," said Rutherford. "I liked him."

It was such a feeble thing to say, almost a bleat of grief, that Cleugh glanced up in surprise. On the big solid face an expression appropriate to that bleat could be seen. It restored to Cleugh much of his own confidence: why be shut up in one's own sense of decency in a world where men with cars and twenty-pound overcoats pretended, with lumps in their throats, to grieve for old broken-down miners buried in paupers' graves? In such a world, it seemed to the secretary, nothing was in its right place, everything was torn loose, and to a wide-awake man opportunities were as plentiful as in war.

"Well," said Wattie briskly, "there seems to be a train in now. Maybe it's the one from Muirvale. We'll see if anybody deliberately takes up his stance at the Shell. Most folk arriving in Glasgow hurry out to continue their journey on trams or buses, or taxis if money's no object."

Himself keenly now, Rutherford stonily, they watched the stream of people from the platform. No-one resembling Rab Nuneaton was amongst them; no-one with treachery for a face halted at the Shell.

"It's beginning to look," said Wattie, "as if we're on a wild-goose chase."

But just as he'd finished speaking he felt a tap on his back. Rutherford's was tapped at the same moment. They swung round to find confronting them no cringing cadger without collar or tie, no monster with misery malforming his face like leprosy, but an ordinary citizen, no different from dozens then in the station, almost Drumsagartian in his respectibility, with his collar obviously ironed by his wife. His cap, too, was almost white, the colour of purity; even his shoes were polished.

Perhaps, thought Cleugh, he's deep in debt; perhaps he needs money desperately for his family's sake. No wonder he looks so ordinary: he is marching with the world.

"Are you Mr. Rutherford?" he asked, in a voice that, even there in the great hall of the station, was subdued and domestic.

It might be, thought Cleugh remembering the malevolence of women, he was ordered here by his wife.

"That's me," said Rutherford, harshly.

"Well, I'm the man you're here to see." The stranger held out his hand.

Cleugh took it before he realised Rutherford was not going to. He snatched it back then and waited for his leader to speak: he was himself again, a mouse in a roomful of baited traps.

Then, after the slight had been administered, Rutherford held out his hand contemptuously. The stranger took it. Perhaps, thought Cleugh, he's not aware Andrew's insulting him; perhaps he's insensitive, as a traitor ought to be.

"I'll confess to you," said Rutherford, laughing, "that I was minded not to shake hands with you at all. But surely if to sell secrets is bad, to buy them's no better?"

The Muirvale man muttered something. Though Cleugh, who was about the same height, held his ear close he couldn't quite make it out. Rutherford, seven inches above them, made no effort to hear.

The Muirvale man repeated it, with a frail smile. "I don't think what I'm doing is bad."

It seemed to Rutherford a joke. "That's it," he said. "There never yet was a man to condemn himself; or a nation either, for that matter. The human mind's got a marvellous slippery way of justifying itself. When we were weans hardly able to talk we lisped our excuses. But we can't stand out here as if we were honest men. I propose we go into the tea-room there and find a table in a corner. This, by the way, is Wattie Cleugh, our secretary and treasurer. What name are we to call you? You signed yourself with three kisses."

"I've been worried about that. I should have put my name."

"If you've lost your shame of it, what is it?"

"William Muldie."

"Muldie?" squeaked Wattie. "Are you related to Jack?"

"He's my brother."

As they entered the tea-room Cleugh again felt boldness surge into him: he skipped among the traps, choosing which one to set off and plunder. The treachery then had its roots in a feud between brothers. How delicious, and yet how dangerous! He dared not look at Rutherford. On Muldie's pale smile, though, he could feast without fear.

In the tea-room Rutherford asserted himself as the master. He selected their table, summoned the waitress, gave the order. When they were seated, bareheaded, he took out a packet of cigarettes and offered them. Cleugh and Muldie took one. By removing his cap Muldie had revealed a rather absurd baldness, the kind a wife laments and tries to camouflage. Rutherford struck a match for them. His hand was very steady, but Muldie's shook.

"So Jack's your brother?" asked Rutherford.

"Aye. But that doesn't need to be discussed."

"Would you rather discuss terms?"

Muldie nodded.

"We're not millionaires in Drumsagart," said Rutherford. "We've got more than our share of poverty and idleset. You'll take that into account. Are you working yourself?"

"I don't think we need discuss my personal affairs, Mr. Rutherford."

"It might be necessary. I mean, if you were down-and-out your price might with reason be higher than if you're comfortably off."

"I'm not starving."

"Well, name your figure."

"Just a minute, Andrew," said Wattie. "Wouldn't it be better if we first saw—at least got a peep at—Mr. Muldie's wares?"

"That's sound business sense, Wattie. After all, he could tell us a damned lie, couldn't he, that would need investigating? By the time we'd investigated it he'd have eloped with our money. Are you married at all, Mr. Muldie?"

"That doesn't come into it," whispered Muldie.

"No? You'll pardon my curiosity. I was just showing a friendly interest. In business it helps if you ken a man's background."

Then they leant back while the waitress set their teas on the table. As soon as she was gone Rutherford said: "Why did you choose us? There were five other teams hungry for information. Why did you favour us?"

Muldie shook his head.

"You're not connected with Drumsagart in any way, are you? Did your forebears come from there? Or is your wife of Drumsagart stock? It'd be nice if we were connected. It'd change the nature of this transaction. We'd be friends helping one another, instead of dealers in treachery."

Muldie made to rise.

"Oh, sit down, man," said Rutherford. "Don't be so thin-skinned. We're all rogues here together. We can surely laugh at each other's rascality. Wouldn't it be fine article for the *Sunday Mail*, say, if a reporter was under the table taking it all down in shorthand? It would be the stink of Scotland; and yet, mind you, I'm prepared to believe negotiations of this sort are not uncommon."

Cleugh noticed that Muldie could hardly trust himself to carry his tea to his mouth, without spilling it. It was a good time to go straight to the tender point.

"What information have you, Mr. Muldie?" he asked.

"I can tell you what'll give you a replay," replied Muldie, smiling, and yet looking at the tablecloth as if it was a shroud.

"Tell us then, and we'll judge for ourselves."

"I'll want my expenses; and a bit extra."

"First," said Cleugh, "we must have some means of assessing what we're buying."

With trembling hands Muldie took out a pocketbook and from it produced a photograph and what looked like a letter. He placed them on the table.

"Four seasons ago," he said, "Jack Muldie was in England."

"I think that's known," murmured Cleugh.

"He went really to look for work, but while he was there he signed on for an English team, a third-division Senior team. He played about nine games for them. When he came back to Scotland he was never reinstated as a Junior."

Cleugh looked at Rutherford. "If it's true," he said, "and we can prove it, it's a sure protest."

"But is it true, Wattie? Other teams have searched. They must have gone through the lists of every English team. Why didn't they ferret him out?"

"He played under a different name," said Muldie.

"Why? Is he ashamed of the name too?"

Cleugh shook his head and clutched Rutherford's arm: this was not the time for personal animosity.

"I take it," he murmured, "Jack was leaving the door open for the time when he would return to Scotland?"

Muldie nodded. "He's fond of football; it's about the only thing he is fond of."

Rutherford fed on that last bitter whisper as if it was a choice grape.

"Don't they ask to see birth certificates in England?" he asked.

"It might be omitted, Andrew," said Cleugh.

"You think then, Wattie, we've struck the goldmine? We'll be able to go back to Drumsagart and make them all rich again, rich with hope of glory?"

"We might well be able to do that, Andrew."

"Well, we'll take a look at the evidence," said Rutherford, stretching out his hand.

Muldie withdrew the letter and photograph.

"You don't trust us?" asked Rutherford, laughing.

"I trust nobody. That's a lesson I've learnt."

"You've been to a good school then."

"Two things we need to know," said Cleugh. "The name of the English team, and Jack's fictitious name. After that we could easily verify the whole story."

"Here's all the proof you need," said Muldie, indicating letter and photograph.

"It's a well-hatched plot," remarked Rutherford. "How long have you had these ready?"

"For two years."

"So you've been biding your time? Or is it your conscience, on the see-saw so long, has sickened at last?"

"I don't think, Andrew," murmured Cleugh, "that aspect comes under our jurisdiction."

"Surely it does," replied Rutherford. "Would it not be good for our friend's soul if he gave us the information for justice's sake? If he takes money, as much as a ha'penny, he has no answer to the charge of traitor."

Cleugh flicked his ear: this was a tricky game, surely, trying to choke the wolf in a man with soft soap about conscience; safer in the long run to satisfy his greed.

"To some extent Mr. Muldie's in our power," said Rutherford. "If we gave him away to the Muirvale folk, his life there wouldn't be worth living. In Drumsagart we're a kind-hearted breed; yet look how some of us wanted to savage Turk's old mither."

"I'm not a Muirvale man," said Muldie.

"Your letter was posted from there."

"That was to deceive you."

Perhaps it was an impulse, regretted a second later, but Muldie suddenly flung the letter on to the table. Rutherford instantly picked it up and read it; then he handed it to Cleugh, who also read it. They grinned at each other: they knew now the English club's name, and Jack Muldie's nom-de-guerre.

"You must realise, Mr. Muldie," said Rutherford, "there's nothing to prevent us getting up and walking straight out."

"I trusted you."

"I thought you said you trusted nobody. I complimented you on it. I didn't try to persuade you that distrust was a bad thing to nurse in your mind."

Muldie avoided looking at them. "I thought it might be worth twenty pounds to you."

Cleugh nodded: in a sharp world it was a reasonable price for a replay.

But Rutherford was getting to his feet. "I don't think so," he said. He pulled out his wallet and took a note from it. Only when it fell upon the table did Cleugh see it was only a pound. He couldn't help grinning; he, too, was standing, ready to withdraw.

"Keep your letter and photo," said Rutherford. "We can build up our own case." Beckoning with forefinger to waitress, he paid the bill with a ten-shilling note and told her to keep the change. It represented so handsome a tip she was thunderstruck. "I mean it," he said. "My friends and I have just done a fine stroke of business, and we're feeling generous."

As they hurried away out of the station Wattie glanced in

through the window. Muldie was nibbling at a cake. The pound still lay untouched.

"That was a bargain, Andrew," he said.

"I would hae given him nothing, but then he'd hae been able to console himself he'd done it out of duty and justice. There's nothing like cash for calling a man's bluff and for taking him straight to the bottom like chains bound round his feet. One pound, or twenty, or twenty thousand, down he goes for ever."

The bottom, Cleugh understood, was degradation; and of course it was the public talk of ministers, moralists, and hypocrites that money defiled. Yet, as Hugh Neilson said in almost every conversation, L.S.D. was today the King of kings.

That night, while getting ready for bed, standing meditatively in shirt tail, Wattie remarked with a chuckle to his wife: "Maybe there was justice in it; but, by God, it took a hard heart to do it."

21

Standing by the Cross, on the beautiful May afternoon, with the Town Hall clock striking three, Sergeant Elvan saw that he was the only human being at that precise moment on the main street. Not even on the dreichest, wettest Sunday in the murk of December had he seen the town so deserted. Yet the sunshine was warm and mellow, the leaves of the elms and poplars glittered in a pleasant breeze, yesterday's rain had laid the dust and cleansed the air, starlings and sparrows twittered in the trees, and high above an adjacent field a lark sang. It was an afternoon for old men to warm chilled bones on the benches in the fragrance of the flower-beds; for young mothers to push their prams with their sunburnt babies sleeping or chuckling at their own toes; for adventuring boys to be setting out for the pond under Drumsagart Hill to fish for minnows; for little girls to wear large white hats and very short dresses; for the philosophers at the University of the Unicorn to take off their caps and let the sweetness of the sun through to their bitter brains; for the matriarchs, grim, resolute, and compassionate, battered bulwarks against the incessant seas of despair, to stand at the doors of shops, clutching their purses, discussing prices and the latest births. Yet the street was as empty as if that morning, instead of old Davie Masters with the brush he sang to, Death had swept it.

The sergeant looked at the nearest flower-bed. In the midst of tall tulips, crimson, yellow, mauve, and pink, was an enormous many-headed thistle. It was not there through an accident of the wind or because of the negligence of the town council's gardeners; it had been carefully dug out of a field and replanted in that place. In every flower-bed was a similar thistle, a weed given royal supremacy over the lovely tulips. There was a clue here as to the vacuity of the street.

In George Rankin's butcher-shop window was another clue: a piece of silver cardboard cut into a peculiar shape. Across the street, in Robert Hutton the tailor's window, was still another hint: a large photograph draped with broad blue and thin red ribbons; it showed a dozen proud men with their arms folded and their knees bare. Further along, in Will Henderson's photographer's window, was another picture, this time of one footballer only, life-size, in colour: he had fair hair and had a ball at his feet. It was said that this spectacle in his window had brought Will more business in the last month than in the whole year previously.

The sergeant began to walk along the street. A cat ran miaowing out of a closemouth to rub itself against his legs. He bent down to stroke it.

"Whether they win or lose today," he said, "you'd be wise this night to find a cellar to hide in." A bumble-bee hummed by to bury itself inside a red tulip. "They'll be as thick as bees yonder," he murmured, rather wistfully, as he went on; for he knew his own two boys would be buzzing as loudly as any. "And to think," he added, but without much conviction, "it's all based on fraud and trickery."

Thicker than bees they were at Hampden Park that afternoon. Towards that famous Mecca they had been heading since one o'clock by bus, train, private car, taxi, motor-bike, lorry, van, invalid chair, bicycle, and foot. Stour was swirled up at all the entrances by feet anxious to get through the turnstiles early and so be able to take up a good position near the front. Beggars, blind, maimed, or imbecile, some with war medals, sang outside pay-boxes. Harry Lynn was one of them, with a Drumsagart blue-red rosette in one lapel and an Allanbank yellow-gold one in the other. Newspaper placards were everywhere, promising to tell that evening the whole story of the Final to those thousands hurrying to see it with their own eyes. Ice-cream barrows and carts were busy outside the gates. More mobile, and far more vociferous, were the sellers of chocolate and chewing-gum: their stereotyped cries—"P.K., a penny a packet; Duncans' Hazelnut, penny a bar"—were as indigenous there as the cooing of doves in tranquil woods or the laughing of hyenas in African prairies. Peddlers of rosettes were impartial, having on their trays both the Drumsagart and the Allanbank colours. In their shouting, though, was a hoarseness of desperation, for after the game, though one part of their stock would be snatched up, the other part would be as unsaleable as eggs marked rotten.

Those crowds swarming into Hampden were different in many ways from the usual crowds attending the important Senior matches there. They were made up largely of family parties, with many women and children. Being from various country towns and villages, they spoke in broader accents, with more Scots in their vocabulary than American. They were more sedately dressed. Their faces were redder, their hands thicker, their hair shorter, their humour more homely, their passions much less fierce. One old man, rolling along the pavement as if it was a ploughed field, saw a cartful of dung outside a house gate; it was being sold in bagfuls. He went over, sniffed at the dung, thrust a finger into it, and then announced to the scandalised merchants: "By God, you've been gey sore on the sawdust." He continued towards the football field, more indignant at the fraud perpetrated on the soil than on these city gardeners. That avenue had seen millions of football fans hurrying towards the shrine; his kind, however, was unusual, being met only once a year, in May, when the Junior Cup Final was played.

The contestants this year were Drumsagart Thistle and Allanbank Rangers from Ayrshire. Of course everybody from Allanbank came to see the Rangers win, and everybody from Drumsagart prayed for a Thistle victory. The large majority of spectators at the outset were neutral. Some were there to support the team which had knocked their own team out of the competition; others to see that team itself suffer defeat. Many would make up their minds as soon as they saw the actual players on the field; Turk McCabe was to engage the sympathies of a large proportion of these for his side. A few would decide aesthetically: they would cheer the team with the bonnier strip. Still fewer would all during the game favour neither team but would applaud good play whoever was responsible. One section, small but violently outspoken, came not to support Allanbank but to revile, abuse, and asperse their opponents—in short, to wish them to the blackest corner of hell: these hailed from Muirvale and still burned for revenge for that infamous but successful protest.

A section of the vast grandstand had been reserved for Drumsagart fans able to pay the higher prices; another, at a judicious distance, for the affluent from Allanbank. These sections from a little way off looked like gigantic rosettes in the rival colours, so many were the flamboyant favours sported: scarves, handkerchiefs, ties, tammies, and even blouses were in the sacred colours; and at least one man wore a blazer in the Allanbank yellow and gold.

Of course the majority of Drumsagart people were not in the grandstand. They could not afford to be, for one reason; and for another, just as genuine, they deprecated the snobbery of sitting in comfort watching their team strive; they preferred to stand amongst their indigent fellows, who were, after all, the experts, the custodians of the inmost mysteries. There was, therefore, one part of the terracing which needed only the Mercat Cross to be erected in its midst to become another Drumsagart. Nat Stewart was there, out of his bed against the doctor's orders, his wife's tears, and his own premonitions of death. Others present were Rab Nuneaton, ashamed to be in Glasgow wearing his Drumsagart rags; Ned Nicholson, who had been offered a seat for the grandstand by Rutherford but who preferred to be with his cronies; Jock Saunders, with his crotcheted tie round a throat as eager to pulsate with cheers as anybody else's; Crutch Brodie, for whom a place at a crush barrier had been cleared, so that he could lean on it and take some weight off his leg; Nippy Henderson, who kept reminding everybody about the free dram at Malarkin's that night; and Tinto Brown, who was not there in body, being now two months buried in the paupers' corner of Drumsagart cemetery, but whom everybody felt to be there in spirit.

In the grandstand were many Drumsagart notabilities, present out of a sense of history rather than from any zest for football. They seldom attended the matches at home, but here at Hampden Park, Glasgow, this mighty open-air cathedral, where world-famous teams and personalities had appeared, here this afternoon it was Drumsagart's occasion; and Allabank's, too, of course. Therefore the Provost was there, with his wife and daughter. Most of the councillors were present, among them Mr. Lockhart, who, however, preferred to look on himself as a shepherd from other pastures. Nan was beside him, immensely interested and delighted; she kept assuring him the baby, in Nurse Brodie's charge, would come to no harm. He, too, was immensely thrilled, not so much by the actual scene around him as by an imaginary one, this tremendous bowl crammed to its full capacity of 140,000 souls, assembled not to watch football but to listen to the word of God and sing hymns. He did not presume to see himself as the preacher at so stupendous a conventicle: he had not done well enough at far humbler Drumsagart Park to justify that ambition; but he could readily see himself by the side of the inspired evangelist, a staunch lieutenant in the war against paganism. He was interrupted in this stirring reverie by Nan's hand nipping his arm and her voice whispering, in excitement, glee, and malice: "Look, Harold, yonder's Mr. and Mrs. Sowlas. For goodness' sake, look at her hat. It's like a wreath."

Margot Malarkin, in one of the most expensive seats, sat beside a man whom nobody knew, but whom everybody wished to know. He was elderly, about sixty perhaps, with silvery hair and a pale hand oftener than not on her knee; but he gave off an aroma of wealth, with his clothes more suitable for Ascot than Hampden Park, and nothing was surer than that among the many cars in the car-park his would be the largest and the most magnificent.

Another couple to attract much attention were Mysie Dougary and John Watson, the bank-clerk. It was agreed, after inquisitive inspection, that Alec Elrigmuir still had a chance. He was known to be in love with her still; which was wonderful, which was as good as a story in the *People's Friend*, which helped the Thistle, for it inspired Alec to prodigious play (in the semi-final he had scored three goals), but which, all the same, confirmed the belief, now universally held though seldom uttered, that off the football field he was simpler than a man ought to be.

Archie Birkwood had brought his daughter and his wife. There, amidst all that laughter before the game began, she was given full licence; but, to his disappointment rather, she did not take advantage of it. She laughed, but temperately; she stood up and waved her hand to friends, but not as if she held in it the flag of victory.

Robbie Rutherford and his two boys had been sent complimentary tickets by the president. They were dressed in new clothes and already looked healthier from the change of house. Isa was at home looking after the sick girl.

The committee-men, of course, were in the best seats in the centre; and at the very altar, as it were, in the directors' box, was Andrew Rutherford, the president. With him he'd brought his wife and son, and also his brother-in-law Harry and his wife. It had been hoped for a time that Harry would buy his place on that eminence by supplying the pipe band with new accoutrements; but the warm possibility had turned to a cold doubt. Therefore he unmeritedly sat amongst the mighty, who included Glasgow's Lord Provost; while standing below in the enclosure, handy to an exit, were Bob McKelvie and his men in mufti, ready at the final whistle to dash out to their waiting bus, be rushed to Drumsagart, and there be waiting to greet the team with proud lament if beaten, with shrill and boisterous paeans if victorious. If they had got their new outfits they might have been out there strutting and piping to entertain this crowd of thousands, instead of the band of the King's Own Cameron Highlanders, which, though proficient enough, blew from duty rather than love.

To shrieks, bellows, and buglings of acclamation the teams trotted out side by side. They did not at once sprint towards their respective goals, but lined up leaving a lane between them, down which in a minute or so came walking the Lord Provost wearing his chain of office and accompanied by the Allanbank president, who presented his players, and by Andrew Rutherford, who presented his. The Provost had an amiable smile and a handclasp for each player; but for one he had an involuntary laugh. Turk McCabe had not shaved; his hair was cut close to the scalp; his shorts were so long as to be misnomers; and he wore an expression of simian melancholy. At the Provost's laughter he showed his two or three teeth in what was really reciprocal mirth, but which looked rather like resentment in the tree-tops. The Provost was a man of humour; outwardly impartial as his position demanded, he became at heart Turk's man and in the ensuing game applauded his every valiant rescue; which meant he was applauding often.

Presentations over, the teams made for the goals for some preliminary practice. Photographers waylaid one or two to snap them. Alec Elrigmuir had three snapping him like crocodiles at the same moment. It was noticed that when one approached Turk to confer on him this accolade of being photographed on the field of play, in the presence of forty thousand roaring devotees, he was repulsed either by word or glower, or by both, so precipitately did he run backwards in his retreat. The crowd roared appreciation of Turk's modesty. Without having so far kicked a ball, he was already a favourite. A thousand witticisms were launched as he set out on his usual circular canter. Many guessed this was his way of praying.

To the Allanbank goalkeeper ran a boy in a yellow-and-gold jersey with a horseshoe of yellow-and-gold ribbons; to Sam Teem in the Drumsagart goal scooted the nephew of Ned Nicholson wearing a bright blue tall hat and carrying a thistle of the same colour almost as large as himself. Other worshippers leapt over the barriers to rush out on to the field and shake their champions' hands. Nathaniel Stewart was one of them. Despite the remonstrations of a policeman who followed him about, he insisted on shaking the hand of every Drumsagart player. To Alec Elrigmuir he said, "Alec, son, I'll be dying soon. Win for me today, win for me today, and I'll die happy." Alec politely said he would do his best. To Turk he merely said, "Turk, for God's sake"; and Turk answered by winking.

Then the field was cleared of these interlopers, the coin was tossed up, Lachie Houston guessed wrongly, causing tremors in the hearts of his Drumsagart followers, the players took up position, Alec Elrigmuir kicked off, and the great game, the Cup Final, was on at last.

Had one team, Drumsagart say, scored several goals early and prevented their opponents from retaliating, many souls that afternoon would have been spared the vertigo of suspense. Drumsagart souls would have kept on soaring, Allanbank souls plunging: there would have been no soarings, hoverings, and plungings in sick succession, time after time, while hands covered terrified eyes or teeth bit into scarves or eyes glistened or mouths watered or hands were clasped or legs stiffened or bottoms sprang off seats or seats were sprinkled with the tin-tacks of mortification.

It would have been known in advance that the dancing that evening on the wide pavements of Drumsagart would be natural and joyous, while the jigging in Allanbank's school playground would be half-hearted or hysterical. It would have been known, too, that the Drumsagart feast of ham and egg in the Town Hall would have the mustard of success, whereas the Allanbank boiled ham and tomato and lettuce would have lurking amidst it the maggot of disappointment. Above all, it would have been known that Drumsagart beer would be an elixir, preserving that time of bliss for ever; whereas in Allanbank pubs at the bottom of every glass would be found the frog of disenchantment, with its eyes wide open.

All that could have been known and prepared for had Drumsagart—or Allanbank, of course—scored those early goals.

But for a long time neither side could score, though one or other came very close to it almost every minute. Excitement ran among the players, teasing them into blunders that had the spectators shrieking, leaping to their feet, hammering their heads, moaning, laughing, and utterly silent. Alec Elrigmuir three times struck the crossbar with the ball, and once, from four yards, with the Allanbank goalkeeper flat on his face as if chewing daisies and the other Allanbank defenders reeling in horror at the anticipated blow, he hit the ball with all his juvenescent might and high over the bar it flew. Drumsagart howled, Allanbank smiled. Mysie Dougary turned like a wounded vixen on John Watson, who had, in company with thousands of Drumsagart well-wishers, cried: "Oh you mug!" He was not a mug, she screamed, he was excited—that was all; he was worried too, but he would win the game in the end even if she had to go to the pavilion at half-time to tell him there was no need to worry any more. Young Watson scowled, for he was not so simple as Alec.

Among the Allanbank players excitement that hampered them

284

had an ally, as grotesque as Puck and as supernatural in his endeavours. Turk McCabe, though his feet were still tender, played as though a goal scored against the Thistle would be his own death warrant, would be the signal for him to go back to the weird underworld from which he'd obviously come. Immortal though he was, he sweated, suffered, slaved, and bled more than any human. Not even the dragon guarding the Fleece in the woods of Colchis showed more devotion.

Half-time came without scoring; but three minutes after the restart Allanbank scored. While their followers were trying to express their glee, with voices, hands, eyes and lungs all inadequate, and while Drumsagart players and spectators alike were shivering at this first touch of the icy finger, Turk McCabe snatched the ball from an Allanbank foot, and instead of kicking it upfield as he'd done so often he began to charge towards the Allanbank goal as if he knew his immortality was fading and could be revived only by a goal nullifying that other. Allanbank players drew back, expecting him to pass the ball to one of his colleagues; they could not believe this freak had any virtue outside its own penalty area. But when he was within their own penalty area, and when at least three of them were hurtling themselves at him, he slipped the ball aside to Elrigmuir, who, football genius, was in the right place to kick it with wonderful élan past the Allanbank goalkeeper.

It was Drumsagart's turn now to find their rejoicing limited only by the coarseness of flesh. Mysie Dougary was on her feet, shrieking like any harridan and waving her tammy. Her rival, Margot Malarkin, shrieked too and dug her nails into her escort's knee in a way to bring tears of anguish to his mildly lewd eyes. Mrs. Lockhart bounced up and down on her seat, so that her husband, remembering her fragility, was forced to chide her gently.

In the directors' box Hannah Rutherford was astonished and moved to see on her husband's face and hear in his voice a joy so spontaneous and innocent she knew, as deep in her heart she had suspected, there had been something a little false in his new delight in her company. Yet strangely she was not offended; rather did she feel an unprecedented pity for him and a fresh flow of affection. Perhaps it helped her to see on her other side that their son, too, was transformed by joy.

On the terracing, in Drumsagart corner, men who for years had disliked and distrusted one another were shaking hands. Even Rab Nuneaton, for whom friendly contacts had been so long loathsome, was taking any hand presented to him, and he was listening to yells of happiness in an unfamiliar voice that emerged from his own mouth.

On the field Turk and Alec were being pummelled by their team-mates. A congratulatory thumb poked into Turk's eye, a fist struck his scalp like a hammer; but brushing these off as if they were confetti, he shouted hoarsely "The Cup! The Cup!" as if it was a mystical slogan.

Excitement that had made them clumsy in the beginning now made the players swift and fiery. The ball flew like hawk, skimmed the grass like hare, bounced like kangaroo; it had in it not mere air but the hopes, fears, frenzies, and ecstasies of that great crowd. It went everywhere—up on to the terracing even, into the grandstand, into this, that, and every section of the field —everywhere except into one or other of the goals.

Watches were in hands now; minutes, half-minutes, seconds were being counted. People anxious to be away early to avoid the homeward crush lingered, throwing backward glances, walking a step or two away, turning again, waiting, watching, groaning, sighing, and gasping. It would be a draw, everybody said; it would have to be refought next Saturday. Look, the referee was staring at his watch for the sixth or seventh time; his whistle was going to his mouth to blow for time-up. But look again. Look at young Alec Elrigmuir. He was on the ball, he was sidestepping the centre-half, dribbling past the right-back, swerving round that other player, and banging the ball well and truly past the goalkeeper.

Allanbank was stricken. Yellow-and-golden women wailed; children wept; and men whined: "No. Offside. Time was up. Foul." But there was no remedy. The referee was blowing his whistle for the end, no god descended, and all Drumsagart was abandoned to ecstasy and cacophony. On the field the players were being punched and kissed by hordes of fanatically grateful followers; among these was Nat Stewart, so overwrought he found himself shaking the hand of an Allanbank player. On the terracing, when other more restrained Drumsagart rejoicers wished to shake hands with their Allanbank rivals the latter declined with shudders, saying never in sobriety could they be magnanimous enough.

In the grandstand the committee-men, captains in victory, were loving one another. Angus Tennant even, with devilment in his love, kissed Sam Malarkin's cheek, which tasted, he said afterwards, like a jujube. It was the kind of daft thing expected of Angus, but nobody could have anticipated it would put Sam into such a towering pet. Indeed, Sam's wan peevishness all that evening was to be attributed wrongly to the loss of whisky, as enervating to a publican as the loss of blood.

In the directors' box Rutherford showed no restraint. He kissed his wife, lifted up his son above his head as he'd done when the boy was an infant, shook hands rapturously with Harry, and slapped Mabel's bottom.

"We've done it, Hannah," he cried. "We've won the Cup."

She smiled and nodded: her thought was, What money is it putting in your purse? But she did not, as formerly, sharpen that thought and wield it; she kept it blunted and sheathed; and she found, to her surprise, she had acted not so much virtuously as happily.

"I could greet," he cried. "I feel so pleased I could greet."

It was Harry's turn to smile: his meant, So you're a wean yet, Andrew, in many ways? Well, weans are amenable, especially happy weans.

"If only old Tinto could hae been spared to see this," cried Andrew.

Hannah noted that it was the old drunkard rather than his father he wished still alive.

Then the players, still in their shorts and jerseys, and with the grime and sweat of battle, came up the steps in single file. Lachie Houston led them. From the Lord Provost he received the Cup, which he immediately held on high, the silver grail at long last achieved, so that the Drumsagart people roared their homage. Then every player got handshakes of congratulation, first from the Provost, and immediately after from their president, who had words as well for them. "Well done, boy. Champion work, Jim. Tom, you played like a hero," and so on. He did not, as most did, praise Turk McCabe and Alec Elrigmuir above the rest; and the rest noticed it and were grateful.

He insisted on shaking the hands of the Allanbank players, too, though they seemed to think it was an act of supreme supererogation. To the Allanbank officials he was generous in his commiserations. They had to accept them, but one incontinently muttered: "We should never have been playing you anyway: a poor Cup that's won by a protest." Rutherford overheard and for a moment experienced his old dismay. "That's true," he said, to the person nearest him.

It was Hannah. She hadn't been attending. "What's true, Andrew?"

He began to laugh and laid his hand on her shoulder. "Never mind, Hannah. Whoever rejoices, there are bound to be some with sore hearts. We're just not built that we can all be happy together."

She understood now, for all round were mourning Allanbank faces. "No, but we that can manage to be happy, Andrew, are not to be expected to give it up till everybody joins us."

"No, Hannah. That's right."

It was at last, she thought, the formula they had been searching for for years, reconciling their different points of view. Hampden grandstand was a queer place to find it.

"Would you mind very much," he asked, "if I didn't go straight back home with you? I'd like to be in Drumsagart tonight and see the celebrations. Maybe you would like to come yourself? Maybe you would all like to come?"

"Not me, Andrew," she said, smiling. "But I've no objections if you want to go."

"Thanks all the same, Andrew," said Harry, "but I think I'd be out of place in the celebrations. I've enjoyed myself here this afternoon, I've met some interesting and useful people, and the Thistle won. I think I can call it a day."

"What about you, Gerald?" asked his father.

The boy gazed at his mother.

"It's up to you," she said. "It'll be a bit of a rabble there tonight, but surely your father can look after you."

He saw she was no longer on his side against his father; and he felt sorry for himself.

"I don't know," he muttered.

"It'll be great fun, Gerald," said his father. "There's to be dancing to the pipe band, and fireworks, and——"

"No. I want to go home."

His father was disappointed. "All right, son." He looked at them all and laughed. "Am I being thrawn?" he asked. "Should I just go home too? Mind you, I'm the president."

"You go to Drumsagart," said Hannah. "Likely it'll be your last visit there for a long time."

So he went to Drumsagart, in the bus carrying the conquerors. Part of the roof had been slid back, and by standing on a seat a man could display the Cup to the passing world. That was a duty as much as a pleasure, but it was also less convenient than sitting comfortably in a seat; therefore it was honourably shared among the players. Only Turk refused: on the ground that it was a damned stupid way of travelling in a bus, one might as well be on a motor-bike. He had to be excused; his determined, surly common sense in the midst of the exultation was a pity, but it couldn't be helped: Turk was a force of nature, like a volcano, say, and if he chose to erupt that night after consuming gallons of whisky, so that Elvan and at least three bobbies dragged him to jail—why, then, it would all be part of the saga of the winning of the Cup.

The other hero, Alec Elrigmuir, was drunk already. He had to be restrained from climbing out on to the roof of the bus. Going through villages on the road home, he threw pennies to children, some of whom cheered and some of whom searched for clods to throw back. Everybody knew it was not just because he'd scored the winning goal, nor because six Senior clubs had begged him to play for them, but because Mysie Dougary had come shouting for him at the dressing-room door, had kissed him though he was naked from the waist up, and had called him her Sandy.

Rutherford sat amidst that busload of familiar men, noticing how happiness had purged them, as it had purged him, of all characteristic meanness and selfishness. This really was how men were, how they would wish to be always if circumstances allowed them. He had been wrong to think they had begun to respect and even like him because he had thrown away all his scruples about accepting their own standards of conduct and belief, which were the standards of pigs round a trough, every man for himself and to hell with the hindmost. Surely that respect and liking had been granted simply because he had given them a chance to respect and like him. Hitherto he had been too stiff, too remote, too entangled in prejudice and illusion. Here was the proof, his hand being shaken every minute, his back slapped, his part in the general victory loudly acknowledged.

When the bus, with dozens of vehicles following it, like coaches a great hearse, came into the main street there was Bob McKelvie ready with his swollen-cheeked men. To the shrill braggadocio of 'Scotland For Ever' that vast procession crawled along to the Town Hall, where from the lofty flagpole was flying a blue flag with a crimson thistle in the centre. Along each kerb were hundreds of townspeople waving, cheering, and laughing. Boys went wild, fencing each other with stolen tulips, or hooting at the team from the tops of trees. It was not thought likely even Sergeant Elvan would be at his normal work that evening.

It seemed to Rutherford from inside the bus, with tears almost in his eyes, that his native town, evergreen, deep-rooted, but sombre, had suddenly burst forth with bright flowers.

When the bus stopped at the Town Hall entrance the crowd began to roar for speeches; but for quite ten minutes more everybody had to wait in an explosive, sentimental, derisive, hilarious patience while Bob McKelvie and his pipers exhausted lungs and repertoire. When the last ululation had died away into the sunshine the speeches were made from the top of the bus. First was Lachie Houston, who let the Cup speak for him.

"Here it is, folks," he shouted, and held it up.

The applause was excessive; at least so Mr. Lockhart thought, now back at the manse, soothing the baby in his arms.

Alec Elrigmuir was called on. "I'll tell you this," he cried. "I'm glad we won. And I'll tell you something else: me and Mysie are going to get married soon."

Again the response was loud enough to waken all babies within half a mile and to make impossible the hushing of those not asleep. Mr. Lockhart had to come away from the window, and found himself uttering the ungracious wish that Nan had stayed at home to attend to her fundamental duty instead of going out to see the fun, as she called it. It seemed she was fond of pipe music.

Wattie Cleugh spoke. "This is a proud, proud day for Drumsagart," he said, and went on saying it in a dozen different ways until at last even pride wearied.

Other players were shouted for: some refused; those who obliged were very brief. Turk at first was a refuser. The crowd kept roaring for him. At last he sprang up through the hole in the roof of the bus. When he was seen they cheered him so mightily that what he was roaring at them was not at first heard, although he kept repeating it, more and more vehemently. Then suddenly there was a hush. They were ready to listen to the blue-chinned scowling oracle.

"You're a shower of mugs," he roared.

Apparently he could have chosen no more successful address: they cheered, whistled, clapped, and shrieked; one boy stole a great bang at the big drum.

Other committee-men spoke. Angus Tennant persevered in spite of the affectionate abuse flung at him, based mostly on the crookedness of his gaze and the fatness of his wife.

Then suddenly, at the end, when the band was getting ready to pipe the team into the Town Hall for the victory feast, there rose up a shout for the president, for Andrew Rutherford, for the man who'd got the protest.

He was afraid to speak, lest he should break the spell; yet he was afraid, too, not to speak, lest he should be admitting to himself that the spell, of friendliness, of neighbourly goodwill, was illusory; and there was always the danger that if he managed to find the right simple words someone would toss at him one disenchanting shout of spite or envy or contempt or even of hatred. Rab Nuneaton was in that crowd; so was Nippy Henderson; and many another who used, with good enough reason, to miscall him. Would one of them now, in the presence of the whole community, in the sunshine and the laughter, utter such a word?

No-one did. He found the right simple words. He was clapped as cordially as anyone else had been. When with the others he followed the pipers into the hall tears were again near his eyes.

It was a jubilant feast, even if the ham and eggs were a little cold, and Turk McCabe out of a morose silence jumped to his feet, hammered on the table for attention, passionately accused them all of having made use of him without ever having really been fond of him, and announced his intention of returning to England as soon as his mother was dead and buried.

The dancing afterwards on the pavement in the shadows of the trees became perhaps too boisterous as the males became drunker. These had all signs on their right wrists, conspicuous as they flung up their hands in corybantic extravagance. This sign was a tiny thistle in blue indelible ink, and it was proof not merely that the bearer was a true Thistle follower but also that he had been to collect his free dram of well-watered whisky at the Lucky Sporran, where four extra barmen had been engaged, and where the proprietor, in the midst of a bonanza of business, was pale and captious.

Jock Saunders was reminded of his pledge to creep on hands from the Cross to the Lucky Sporran and was challenged to make it good. He regretted he could not: it would make the knees of his trousers baggy. As these trousers had not been pressed for years, and indeed had knees not of the original cloth, his plea was accepted, amidst an uproar of appreciation like the simultaneous ripping of thousands of tight trousers.

Sergeant Elvan had been taken to the pictures by his wife; they almost had the place to themselves.

But Andrew Rutherford had to remember he no longer lived in Drumsagart; he was a visitor now, who had to keep his eye on the clock and his mind on the last bus. Therefore shortly after nine, during an impromptu concert round the Mercat Cross, at which he'd sung 'The Wee Cooper of Fife', he slipped away without saying goodbye to anyone, or at least to anyone alive. This might well be, as Hannah had hinted, his last visit here for a long time: the Drumsagart phase of his life might be ending; in that case he could hardly leave without saying farewell to his mother.

The cemetery lay out in the country among the fields, approached by quiet hedged roads. The bing of the now derelict Birkside Pit was close beside it, growing green like a hill. From the top of the bing the tombstones looked like the seagulls that were often to be seen in the neighbouring fields. Yet the white birds seldom came amongst the graves, perhaps because the geometrical paths and headstones, the decaying wreaths, and the general circumscription made too great a dissimilarity to the vast moving sea. Tits, sparrows, finches, starlings, and even the black crows, all earth-dwellers like man himself, found sanctuary there, fat worms, and crumbs left by picnicking mourners.

Rutherford met no-one on the way. Few people were so disorganised in their mourning as to be driven by it to huddle over a grave on a Saturday night. Most waited for the more propitious Sabbath when Christ in all the compassion of Sunday-school tracts might be imagined there, shaping promises with His mild bearded lips. This Saturday evening especially, with the celebrations in the town, nobody could be expected to languish there in loneliness.

Therefore as he went through the tall iron gates and made up the red path towards his mother's grave he saw no-one, only birds, butterflies, and on the green grass of one grave a black-beetle. He remembered how in boyhood, if someone had squashed such a beetle, everyone would spit, drawing a hand across his throat, and say: "Not my grannie." So far as he knew, boys still went through that ritual; but he had never found out what it meant.

For nearly half an hour he stood by his mother's grave, making no significant gesture, such as touching the small headstone, or plucking a blade of the grass, or reaching up for a leaf of the birch tree that grew near; thinking no important thoughts about himself and his leaving Drumsagart; revolving few memories of her. He just stood there, hat in hand, more still than the tree which the breeze stirred. Yet he did not feel this visit, this fare-well, was being a failure: he had not come to weep, or pray, or beg for pity and forgiveness; he had come for a rest, a recupera-tion, a breathing space, and he was sure, as he softly walked away again, that he had found it.

He was almost at the gates again when he remembered there was Tinto Brown's grave to see, in the paupers' corner. He stop-ped, undecided. There was not much time to spare if he wanted to catch a bus to Glasgow and then a train to Helensburgh. Perhaps it would be better not to go away with the two graves confused in his mind. Yet would it not be unpardonable, on this night of victory, to be here so close to the friendless old man and not at least whisper the news to him? Whether Tinto would hear it or not, whether he was now a communicable creature of light and air, or whether he was a mess of rotting old flesh and bones under the heavy subsidised earth, all that really made no differ-ence: the whisper would not merely be the supreme justification of football, it would also be the recognition of the dependence of human beings on one another, living and dead together. Yet he hesitated, unwilling to admit the true obstacle between him and Tinto's grave: there used to be a railing round the section owned by the parish for the burial of its paupers, and it had been removed through the agitation of Andrew's father.

Sharply he turned and hurried towards the low-lying obscure corner nearest to the pit bing. He thought he could hear faint sounds from the town: the spree was still on, and would continue after midnight. Tinto would have been foremost in it. All his life he had stood for the merry-making side of life. Many had disapproved of him, not really because they thought him wicked, but because, in spite of his coarseness, his drunkenness, and his lechery, he had represented a rebellion against the prevailing greyness, the sterile puritanism, and the inherited belief that exuberant joy was ungodly. True enough, the joy in the town tonight was exuberant; but Tinto had tried to make every day a day of Cup-winning: too much pleasure on earth weakened the promise of heaven and strengthened the threat of hell.

When he was amongst the paupers' graves, looking for the freshest one, he was smiling, as if he expected Tinto to be there to greet him, with a characteristic report on his new habitation and companions. When he found the grave therefore, and saw there was somebody sitting on the verge of grass round it, he stopped, shook his head hard, shivered, and laughed.

The apparition heard the laughter and turned, to reveal the face of Crutch Brodie streaming with tears and smiling. His cap was lying beside him, and his crutch: he looked like a war-victim begging by the side of a road; only the medals were missing.

Rutherford walked up to him. "Well, it's yourself, Crutch," he said.

Crutch touched his brow in a kind of salute; he was making to rise when Rutherford gently pushed him down.

"Sit where you are, Crutch," he said, "at Tinto's feet."

"I just came to tell him the news," said Crutch, with more cheerfulness than shame. "I promised."

"And do you think he's here to listen to you?"

"If what he believed himself is true, Mr. Rutherford, no, he's not here; but I was never so dogmatic myself."

"That's right, Crutch. It does no good to be dogmatic."

"One thing I'm sure of all the same, Mr. Rutherford: wherever he is, in whose hands, old Tinto's safe enough."

Gazing down at the fat, shy, simple, elderly cripple in the shabby clothes, Rutherford felt a warm cleansing affection for him. There was, of course, no way by which to show it. The cap on the grave waited not for money but for faith and love. Rutherford knew it would wait there for the rest of his life, surely not in vain: just as the pound note would lie on the restaurant table.

Crutch laid his hand where Tinto's feet would have been. "He said a lot he never meant. Nobody in Drumsagart should hae been offended. He loved the toon, Mr. Rutherford."

"I ken that, Crutch."

"The Thistle never had a mair faithful supporter."

"He was at every game, sun or rain."

Crutch smiled, with regret and no rancour. "When he was dying nobody came to see him."

"I should have gone, Crutch."

"He looked for you. He always had a good word to say for you, Mr. Rutherford."

"Yet I never went to see him."

"He kent you had your ain troubles."

For two or three minutes they were silent. Rutherford found himself shivering. The evening was turning chilly.

"One thing's often puzzled me, Crutch," he said. "How did he get the name Tinto? There's a hill called that, but what had it ever to do with him?"

Crutch smiled. "Did you think it was a nickname, Mr. Rutherford? No, it was his true name, just as William's mine. His mither was called Jessie Tinto before she married Charlie Brown. Tinto he was from the womb, you might say, to the grave here."

"I never knew that before," said Rutherford, genuinely astonished and, at the same time, strangely dismayed. How much else of the old man had he not known? How shallow had his interest been!

"A lot of folk thought it was a nickname," said Crutch reassuringly. "It sounds like one. They made a fool of him at school." Though he was smiling cheerfully, tears were again flowing. "Well," he went on, putting on his cap, "I can't sit here all night. Tinto would be the first to say I was daft. I did what I promised. I told him all aboot the game. I'd better get back now. It'll take me an hour almost. I'm getting terribly slow at the hopping." He made one or two slight efforts to rise, but failed. It was obvious that to rise up would require not only an exhausting but also an undignified struggle. He was reluctant to embarrass Rutherford.

"Give me your hand, Crutch," said Rutherford.

Crutch did so, after a moment's hesitation. As gently as possible Rutherford pulled him up.

"Thanks," said Crutch, "thanks, Mr. Rutherford." He settled the crutch under his arm. "I'm fine now. I'm slow but sure. You get on ahead. Don't have me making you miss your bus."

"I'm not in as big a hurry as that, Crutch," he said. "I'll walk with you."

"I take a wheen of rests, Mr. Rutherford. Six hops and a puff, that's me now."

"Then I'll take a puff along with you."

"No." Crutch, weeping, was agitated. "No. Let me be, Mr. Rutherford."

Rutherford saw, with anguish and yet with love, that he would be doing the crippled man a kinder service by leaving him to manage himself than by insisting on accompanying him. It was another dismissal, another exclusion, but this time without contempt or coldness or animosity: it had its cause rather in that ultimate, irremediable loneliness of every human being, which might bring regret and sorrow but which also ought to bring profoundest sympathy, as it did here.

"God bless you, Crutch," he said, and walked confidently away.